JOHNNIE WAS STA
Suddenly his eyes
away.

'I didn't, Jimmy, I didn't!' he said in a hoarse whisper. 'They didn't make me. They don't know. They don't know!'

'Who is it, Johnnie? Who is it speaking to you?'

Brinkmann reached for the boy's hand and grasped it. It was cold and clammy, like a piece of dead meat. Brinkmann tried not to confront the thought that had been hovering on the edge of his mind for days and now forced itself into full, inescapable view. *These children carried with them the stigma, like the odour of decay, of extreme old age.*

K. I. D. S.

Trevor Hoyle

SPHERE BOOKS LIMITED

First published in Great Britain by Sphere Books Ltd 1987
27 Wrights Lane, London W8 5TZ

TRADE
MARK

Set in 10/12 pt Compugraphic Plantin by
Colset Private Limited, Singapore

Printed and bound in Great Britain by
Cox & Wyman Ltd, Reading

To
Donald and Bernice

Acknowledgements

I should no longer be surprised at the extent to which people are willing to give their time, knowledge and expertise to a writer in the preparation and research for a book. People are very generous, and to the following, who accepted my intrusions and answered my questions, I offer my thanks and gratitude. Any errors of fact or discrepancies with regard to scientific matters, or to medical and psychological practice dealt with in this work of fiction are mine and not theirs.

Dr Laurence E. Burns, Dept of Clinical Psychology; Brian Kennell, Chief Medical Laboratory Scientific Officer, and Maureen Fidler, Microbiology Dept; Andrew Fidler, Haematology Dept; all of Birch Hill Hospital, Rochdale, Lancs.

My thanks also to Phil Davies for information on MIT; Glenda Ramsey, Terrell, North Carolina for background material on her home state; and my wife, Dorothy, for inspiration and encouragement.

Part one
Infection

1

Because he himself hated to be awakened roughly from slumber, Tom took Karel's hand and squeezed it gently. Her eyelids fluttered. For a moment she looked at him as if he were a stranger, her smoky blue-grey eyes confused and vacant, and then she smiled. Tom kissed her hand. As he did so his glasses slid down his nose, dislodging a warm bead of sweat.

'Where are we, Tom?' Karel blinked and levered herself up.

'We're just north of Richmond,' Tom said, massaging his temples. 'Let's eat and then you can drive. Okay?'

It was a few minutes after three p.m. and scorchingly hot. The dry landscape shimmered. The old metallic-blue Chevvy's air conditioning unit had never worked and Tom wasn't mechanically minded enough to fix it. Neither did he have the money to take it to a garage and get it done properly.

They were on Interstate 95, over three hundred miles from New York, with one hundred and forty miles still to go to Tom Margison's home town of Torrence, North Carolina.

The coffee shop was cool, shaded by venetian blinds and masses of greenery that sprouted from large earthenware tubs. The lunch hour rush had finished and there were perhaps a dozen customers, couples and families.

They ate in silence for a while. Tom couldn't shake off a faint sultry throb at the back of his head. The strain of the long drive perhaps, or was he worrying about his kid sister Danny, despite his parents' assurances on the phone last night? She was comfortable, they said. Given a transfusion. Don't get worked up, Tom. Accident. Knocked off her bike by a hit-and-run driver. Bastard. He'd like to get his hands on him for five minutes.

Karel took a delicate bite of club sandwich and dabbed her lips with a paper napkin. 'I hope they don't mind my staying. It's not really a very good time, is it?'

'Trix won't mind. She wants to meet you.'

'Your father doesn't?'

Tom forced a grin through the headache. That was quite revealing, he thought. Was she thinking more of her own father? Tom had never met Victor Lendrum, Professor of Microbiology at Columbia. From the way Karel spoke of him, though, he had constructed a pretty good mental picture. Urbane. Intellectually superior. Cold and remote. Like some damn robot. Her mother had died of cancer five years before when Karel was fifteen. Only to be expected that a father bringing up a female teenager alone through the 'difficult' years should set a strict moral tone. His own father had tried the heavy hand with him, Tom recalled, before he went away to college. Lecturing him about 'adult responsibility' (he meant sex and back-seat petting and getting someone into trouble – the usual guff).

There was a minor commotion in the corner. Tom glanced over his shoulder. A boy of four or five with a blond fringe had thrown some food on the floor in a tantrum and the distraught mother was fussing around trying to pacify or appease him.

'Kids,' said Tom, turning back.

'They're no different from the rest of us,' Karel said. 'Except they haven't yet learned to disguise their naked egos.'

'Is that what the behaviourists believe?'

Karel watched him carefully in case he might be teasing her.

'I'm not a behaviourist,' she said tartly.

'That's right. I forgot. You're a Jungian. Anima and animus and the collective unconscious. You know,' Tom said, 'when you come to write your thesis, that wouldn't be a half bad title. I can see it on the *Time* bestseller list now: *The Naked Ego*.'

'Too obvious. Been used before. So tell me, big-shot, what was your finals' paper entitled?' She shook back her corn-coloured hair and watched him with shrewd cat's eyes.

' "Quantum Theory and the Anthropic Principle".'

'Wow,' Karel said with a grin. Now she was teasing him.

'If you must know, DeVoss congratulated me personally on it,' said Tom loftily. Ward DeVoss was his head of department in the Centre of Theoretical Physics at MIT. 'He said some of my ideas on wave-particle properties relating to precognition deserved investigation.'

Karel shrugged. 'I wish I understood some of that stuff, but it's totally beyond me –'

She broke off as the blond-haired child went running by, arms extended, making the shrill noise of a jet engine. Evidently the mother had given up and the father couldn't care less; his booming laugh came from behind a hanging wall of greenery.

'You think psychology is hard to grasp, but quantum theory – my God! You're dealing with tiny bits of matter, waves and particles, pure energy, that don't even exist half the time. At least people are *real*. You can *see* them.'

'You can't see their emotions,' Tom pointed out. 'How do you measure happiness, for instance? How can you assess grief scientifically? It isn't possible. They're intangibles.'

It was an argument they had had before – usually late at night in Tom's room on campus, listening to Mahler's Fifth and drinking cocoa. And usually, as now, reaching no common accord.

Tom looked at the clock on the wall. 'Come on, let's move. It's ten to four and we've at least a two-hour drive.'

Tom swung his legs out just as the child came screeching down the aisle once again. He tripped over Tom's feet and went sprawling, and gave out a loud wail. He wasn't hurt, merely shaken.

Tom went down on one knee and helped him up. 'You all right, fella? Sorry, I didn't see you.'

The child had a chubby, snub-nosed face and ears that stuck out. His hair was brushed forward in a gleaming blond cap, and his round blue eyes were fringed by fair lashes. He gazed level-eyed at Tom through brimming tears, his chest shuddering. Then the small soft mouth tightened and twisted in a temper tantrum.

'You –' he yelled. 'You –!' and he swung his leg back and kicked Tom viciously on the shin.

Tom winced and straightened up. 'Just take it easy.'

The boy glared at Tom with wide mad blue eyes and deliberately took another running kick at Tom's ankle. Tom stepped briskly aside. He gripped the child by the shoulder and held him off. Under his breath he swore and made a threatening gesture as if to cuff him.

The child's eyes slid to the corner where his parents were sitting and he let off another deafening wail as if he really had been struck: he pressed his small fists into his eyes and tears squeezed through to dribble over his round cheeks. He cried at full volume, pausing only to suck in air. It was a superb performance. Tom looked at Karel, dumb-founded.

When he turned back the father was striding towards him. He was a big man wearing a check cowboy shirt with a gold crucifix glinting through the curly hairs at his throat. He came straight up and pushed Tom in the chest with the flat of his hand. A butterfly was tattooed on his thick wrist.

'Wayne! Wayne, are you okay, honey?' The mother followed close behind him. She wasn't an ounce under two hundred pounds. She gathered the sobbing child in her arms, cast a look that was pure venom in Tom's direction and marched off, holding the child's head on her shoulder.

The father stuck his finger under Tom's nose. He was pumping himself up. His neck pulsed.

'You four-eyed squinty son-of-a-bitch. Nobody hits my kid. Nobody.' His eyes were the same colour as the child's, only a dustier blue, with thick dark eyebrows.

Karel saw Tom give a sort of weak grin of disbelief and amazement, which wasn't the response the man wanted or expected; he squared up threateningly.

Tom raised his eyebrows. 'Now wait one second. You weren't here,' he said reasonably. 'How do you know what happened?'

'I can hear the kid, can't I? He doesn't cry like that for nothing.'

'He fell –' Tom said, pointing at the floor.

'You raised your goddam hand! My wife saw you!'

'I didn't hit your child. I didn't even touch him. But if you really want my opinion, he ought to be taken in hand and spanked –'

'Tom,' Karel urged him quietly. 'Let's go.'

The man flexed his shoulders. It was clear what he thought of Tom: a typical smart-ass college student, with his horn-rimmed glasses, clean-shaven features, and the long hair swept back from his forehead and gathered thickly on the nape of his neck.

He said softly, 'Are you advising *me*? About *my* kid?'

'If you exercised some control to stop him running around wild, this never would have happened,' Tom said. Not the wisest thing to say under the circumstances, Karel thought.

The man took a bunch of Tom's shirt in his fist and jerked him forward. He was the same height as Tom, slightly under six feet, though broader and hairier and three times as solid. Karel got out of her seat and tried to come between them. The man shouldered her out of the way. This angered Tom, and shamed him a little, and he pushed the man away. His shirt ripped and buttons pinged away and bounced on the floor.

'He never laid a finger on the child,' piped up a middle-aged woman sitting with her husband three tables away. Her husband was trying to shush her. 'But I saw it, Henry, he never –'

The lull gave Karel the opportunity to grab Tom firmly by the arm and pull him along the aisle. The man stood squarely, frowning and glowering after them. His glance flicked to the middle-aged woman and back at Tom. He held up his finger again and shook it. Karel dropped the bill and some cash on the cashier's desk and pushed Tom through the swing door into the hot sunshine. As the door swung shut it cut off the child's ragged whimpering cry.

Karel got behind the wheel and Tom sat beside her.

He was smiling to himself.

Karel started the engine and backed out. The Chevrolet shot forward, emitting blue smoke.

Tom laughed shortly, shaking his head. 'Are kids born that way or does it take practice?'

Karel was cursing and struggling with the wheel. He hadn't told her that the Chevvy pulled to the left. 'Ask me in two years when I've written my thesis. Did you have to say that to him? Christ, you're dumb, Tom. Even Adolf Hitler's parents must have thought the sun shone out of his ass.'

'What that vicious little monster needs –'

'We both know what he needs,' Karel said, 'but trying to tell his parents that is something else again, dumbo.'

Tom shook his head slowly and stared at the highway ahead.

Was something the matter with kids these days or was he getting older? They were given everything and wanted still more. Talk about naked egos. Where to put the blame? On TV? On materialism? On lack of parental control?

Enough of that, Tom decided. He was starting to sound like his father.

2

Afterwards, Danny couldn't remember whether she had seen the car or not. At any rate she couldn't describe the make or colour. There was a blank patch in her mind.

All she could remember was crossing the Old Post Road, a two-lane highway which bisected the town from the south, and cycling along Crescent Drive leading up to The Heights. The car must have shot out from one of the side roads without stopping. It accelerated away, leaving the rear wheel of the cycle twisted into the shape of a figure eight, and Danny bruised and concussed on the grey asphalt, with blood on her chin and splashed across her white blouse like a red sash.

In her left hand she still held the plastic handlebar grip. There were no eye-witnesses.

At Bennett Memorial Hospital she was wheeled into casualty and put on an emergency plasma drip while her blood group was cross-matched in the Haematology Lab. There didn't appear to be any bones broken but there was evidence of internal haemorrhaging. Not a great deal the duty intern and three nurses could do except make her comfortable in a side ward and stand by to await the lab's report.

The news from the lab wasn't good. AB rhesus negative. The young intern blanched and panicked a little. On the pink report sheet it said that the hospital had two packs of this relatively rare group in the cold store. The intern had already put out a call for the surgeon, Dr Ballard, who was on his way and would be ready to operate within thirty minutes. At the minimum, ten 450 ml. packs of blood would be required.

The senior staff nurse, Nurse Bryce, a hardened veteran, reminded him calmly, 'We do have a priority procedure for this situation, doctor.'

'Sure, yes, of course, I forgot. What is it exactly?'

'Check the stock in the blood banks at Charlotte and Winston-Salem. Have them send a batch by motorcycle courier or air, whichever is quicker. Do you want me to phone?'

The intern looked relieved and grateful.

The two packs of blood were brought down from the cold store and the staff were glad to be doing something at last. Hopefully, these should be enough to stabilise her condition until fresh supplies arrived and the operation could begin. The blood was fed into her. Danny's face looked ghostly pale against the beige plastic sheet her head was resting on. Drain tubes trailed from her mouth and nostrils. She had been cleaned up and now she appeared small and shrunken and very fragile. Every two minutes a nurse checked her pulse.

Her parents arrived just after six. They were ushered straight in to see Dr Ballard. He indicated two chairs and laid his pipe in the ashtray. He had thick white wavy hair and rather heavy pink jowls, an image that was avuncular and reassuring. He explained about Danny's condition and said that there was every reason to believe she would be all right.

Clinging to her husband's hand, her eyes taut with tension behind her clear-framed glasses, Trix Margison wanted to know why something wasn't happening.

'Unfortunately we don't carry sufficient stock of AB rhesus negative here in this hospital, so we've had to send for another batch.' Dr Ballard glanced at his watch. 'It's been promised to arrive by seven-thirty at the latest. All being well, we'll go into theatre at eight.'

Alarm came into her face. 'What do you mean, "all being well"? Could something go wrong?'

'No, that isn't what I meant, Mrs Margison. The blood has first to be tested to make sure there's no negative reaction with the antibodies in Danielle's blood serum. Perfectly straightforward, routine procedure. Then Danielle will go into pre-op and then we can proceed.' Dr Ballard smiled reassuringly.

Frank Margison said, 'How long will it take – the operation?' He was a tall, gangly man with a vee of thinning hair that sharply receded on either side, and to compensate he had let his sideburns grow long.

'That's difficult for me to say. I very much hope we should be through by midnight. Staff Nurse Bryce will keep you informed.'

The hard news came shortly after eleven-thirty. Dr Ballard came into the small side room where the Margisons were waiting, still wearing his green gown, a white line over the bridge of his fleshy nose and one across his forehead where his mask and cap had been. He went straight to Trix and took her hands in his.

'Your daughter is going to be all right. There's some

internal damage to the pancreas and the organs in the upper abdomen' – his hand indicated the general region on the green gown – 'but it isn't considerable. She lost a lot of blood and we had to carry out a complete transfusion. She's tough and she's healthy and I don't see any reason why she shouldn't make a full recovery.'

Trix Margison said, 'Oh God. Oh thank God.'

Tom was pleased that his mother and Karel seemed to hit it off. Frank was still in school, force-feeding chemistry into the fifth grade at Torrence High, so the three of them spent some time together. They browsed through the shops on Main Street, and in the afternoons sat drinking Trix's home-made wine on the patio at the back of the house, surrounded by the flowers, pot plants and trays of herbs on which Trix lavished such attention and loving care. She was the only one of the family with green fingers.

Then the weather broke, there were heavy showers, and Tom and Karel stayed in Tom's room reading and listening to Glenn Miller and Linda Ronstadt. It was very cosy and domestic, with the rain slanting down outside and pattering on the window, the overcast skies bringing a soft grey gloom into the room.

Seeing Karel stretched out on his bed, elbows propped either side of the book she was reading, hair draping her shoulders and catching a lambent sheen from the room's dusky light, also proved to be aphrodisiacal. *Her* body on *his* bed. A warm imprint where her breasts, stomach and thighs were resting. The mood was enhanced by the pure clear tones of Linda Ronstadt singing 'As Time Goes By'.

'Tom,' Karel said after a while. 'Do you think I ought to stay? Under the circumstances?'

'What do you mean?' Tom frowned at her over his glasses.

'This isn't the best of times to have a house-guest. With your sister in hospital. It must be a strain on your folks.'

'Have you heard them complaining?'

'Well, no . . .'

'Of course they don't mind having you here. In any case, Danny's going to be fine. The doctor told Dad she's going to be all right. Could even be out in under a week; I don't think he was just saying that.'

'Rotten for you, too, on your vacation.'

'We'll make up for it when Danny gets out,' Tom said. He reflected. 'She's a clever kid. Bright. I'm very proud of her. She won the art prize last year.' This reminded Tom of something. 'When I was in New York I got her a book on Van Gogh, one with large colour plates. Ever since she saw the movie on TV about his life – the one with Kirk Douglas – she's had a big thing about him. I bought her the Don Maclean record last Christmas.' He looked at her and smiled. 'Please stay. I want you to.'

Karel nodded slowly, and smiled back.

Tom studiously adjusted his glasses and dug back into Dashiell Hammett's *The Glass Key*, making his third start on chapter six. Trix was about the house somewhere. Any further thoughts about warm imprints on soft beds could lead to only one conclusion.

Tom took along a large tub of Danny's favourite ice-cream, blueberry chocolate chip, which the nurse said was permissible. Trix and Frank were going to see her that evening, and so Tom and Karel were the only ones during the afternoon visiting hour.

Apart from a faint bluish tinge underneath her eyes and a slightly pinched look around the mouth, she looked remarkably well, thought Tom. His old kid sister. Danny's hair was very dark and naturally curly; her brown eyes were widely spaced under strong dark eyebrows. She had the kind of colouring that tanned easily, and even now she was only a shade or two paler than was usual in the summer months. Tom thought – and had since she was six or seven – that Danny would be quite stunning when she got older.

He kissed her on the nose and produced the gift-wrapped

Van Gogh book from behind his back. 'Guess what, shrimp.'

Danny sank back into the pillows when she had unwrapped it, holding the large book in its shiny jacket at arm's length. She closed her eyes and a faraway smile came over her face. She opened her eyes and said, 'Tom, it's . . . it's . . . honestly, it's the best present I've ever had. Isn't it great?'

'Fantastic,' Karel said, smiling broadly.

Danny knew most of the paintings and drawings already. Her favourites were the portraits, *Girl Reading*, the jade-green-faced *Girl from Arles*, *The Schoolboy* in his smock and ragged cap, and especially *The Postman Roulin*, with his blue peaked cap lettered '*Postes*' in gold, his red lips and his luxuriant curly brown beard divided into two, reaching almost to the gold buttons on his tunic. The three of them chuckled over his pompous, self-satisfied expression.

It surprised Tom to find that Danny liked the sombre portraits done in pencil, black crayon, and pen and ink wash best of all. Surprising, when Van Gogh's use of slabs of fierce colour was what he was noted for, though Tom had no claim on art appreciation: he was of the school that knew what it liked and didn't know why.

Even Tom could appreciate the expert draughtsmanship and the artist's feeling for the subject of *Head of a Peasant*, though the young man's ear seemed a bit on the square side to him. Weren't hands and ears reckoned to be the most difficult things to draw?

The pictures painted in the last two years of Van Gogh's life, following his nervous breakdown, were powerful and unsettling. *Cypresses with Two Figures* was a livid writhing mass of dark green shapes, suggesting that the artist's fevered imagination had got out of control. To Tom, it seemed as if Van Gogh had attempted to reconstruct physically the trees and figures in thick coils of oil paint.

Karel shuddered and turned away, saying the picture was 'gloomy and doomy', yet Danny lingered over these later works with the same dreamy, faraway smile on her lips.

The nurse appeared at four to say that it was time for Danny to take a nap.

'Do I have to?'

'Sure you have to.'

'But I'm not tired!'

'You need all the sleep you can get if you're going to get better,' said the nurse, winding the bed down. 'And no watching TV on the sly. The night nurse said she had to come in and turn the set off at *ten o'clock* last night!'

'She told on me,' Danny said bitterly. 'I knew she would.'

'No, she did *not* tell on you, Danny,' said the nurse reprovingly. 'It was Nurse Chang's duty to report it, which she did. Not tittle-tattle. Anyhow, she said it was a programme about German politics or some such, which couldn't possibly have been of interest to you.'

'Why not?' Danny said, lying flat on the pillows and peering over the covers, her forehead knitting in a belligerent frown. 'Because I'm just a kid? She's a sneak. I hate her.'

'Hey now,' Tom said. 'Cut that out.'

The nurse sighed as she tucked in the covers at the side of the bed. She said, 'We used to have rules and regulations around here before your sister arrived. I'm beginning to wonder who's running this hospital.'

'Can I have blueberry ice-cream for supper? Please?'

'Yes, you can have blueberry ice-cream for supper – *if* you take a nap – starting now, this minute.'

Danny closed her eyes obediently, opened one of them, and winked it at Tom. He winked back.

The nurse reached across to pick up the book from the bed, and Danny whipped it inside the covers next to her.

Tom said, 'See you tomorrow, shrimp.'

As they followed her along the corridor, the nurse was shaking her head.

'I've never known a child like her. Incredible.'

Tom felt a glow of pride. 'She is pretty sharp for an eleven-year-old, I guess.'

'What?' The nurse stopped and faced him. 'I'm not talking about her IQ. After such a serious operation that young lady should be flat on her back for another week at least. Instead she's bright eyed and bushy tailed and raring to go. Must have the metabolism of an ox.'

'She's strong, all right,' agreed Tom.

'Strong?' the nurse echoed tartly. 'If you could bottle it you'd make a fortune.'

Standing motionless at the window in her red polka-dot pyjamas, Danny could feel the cool night air on her throat. She had been awakened by the sound of voices. Voices very faint and far-away. She shivered and listened intently as the voices rose and subsided, like waves of the ocean, coming from somewhere out there in the darkness. What were they saying? She couldn't make it out.

Her heart suddenly started to beat violently. The blood surged thickly through her body, pulsing in her head like a drumbeat.

The voices took up the same rhythm, chanting to the thud of a distant drum.

Danny turned away from the window and in the mirror above the washbasin glimpsed her shadowy self, the polka dots round and black like huge spots of blood. Blood. She looked at the pale blur of her face and saw that her eyes were glowing with a pale blue light.

And by her side, a shadowy figure. Hands grasped her roughly by the shoulders and spun her round.

'What are you doing out of bed? Do you know what time it is?' Nurse Chang hissed in a flat angry whisper.

She bundled Danny into bed and whipped the covers over her. She frowned and straightened up as her hand struck something.

'What's this doing here?'

'Don't take it, please,' Danny said as Nurse Chang reached for the Van Gogh book. There was a brief struggle, and Nurse Chang pulled it from her grasp.

'First TV and then getting out of bed, and now reading at this hour. I won't have it, young lady. Do you hear? Not on my ward. You can have this back in the morning – that's if you behave yourself. Do you understand that?'

Nurse Chang waited, framed in the rectangle of light from the door, one hand on her hip, but didn't receive an answer. She tucked the book under her arm and closed the door. Danny lay in bed listening for the voices. But no matter how hard she listened, they had gone, faded away.

3

The heat of summer settled over the town and Trix's earthenware troughs of plants and herbs in the patio garden responded with vibrant growth. The Margisons lived in The Heights, an oldish development of two-storey cedar-fronted houses built on the gentle slopes of the hills rising to the west of town. Most of the residents worked for the LeGrand Power Company, which after Fast Fleet Freight Carriers Inc was the largest employer in the area. The power company had a generating facility on the river feeding Lake LeGrand, which was roughly nine miles away.

A couple of times Tom took Karel walking amongst the lush green hills, as far as Holly Hill, and once they made love in a perfect idyllic grove, the sunlight speckling their bodies like a shower of gold coins.

Trix talked of decorating Danny's room, as a sort of homecoming surprise, but Frank said it wasn't necessary, as the room had been redecorated only last fall. Even so, Trix was determined to make it something of a special occasion. She became more nervous and more excited. Karel was drawn into a female conspiracy of preparation and the two of them drove down to Main Street one morning to do some shopping.

Left behind, Tom sat on the patio in the sunshine trying to read *The Eighth Night of Creation*, a weighty treatise on ecological doom by a French professor. A typically pretentious French academician's title, in Tom's opinion.

Trix and Karel raided the supermarket shelves, plotting and planning in whispers as if they might be overheard. There was something schoolgirlish about Trix, which Karel found rather endearing. Perhaps it was her physical appearance, Karel thought – the long, narrow, rather intense face at odds with the large round tortoiseshell spectacle frames through which her magnified eyes peered, round and blue and ingenuous. And her brown wavy hair, parted in the centre and hanging down over her ears, was probably the way she had worn it in high school. Karel found her easy to get on with and confide in. She was less sure about Frank; he was more guarded, defensive almost, and had never once looked her squarely in the eye.

Trix was leaning over and frowning at one of the lower shelves. 'Have you seen the price of roasted almonds! How they get their three per cent inflation I don't know.' She tossed the packet in the trolley with disgust, as if it might be contaminated.

'Rigged,' said Karel. 'It's three per cent if you earn seventy thousand dollars and above. Earn anything less and it's nearer eight.'

'That a fact?' said Trix abstractedly, hunting for something else.

At the delicatessen counter Trix ordered slices of garlic sausage, Danny's favourite, and a tub of Russian salad. The man behind the counter, middle aged and Italian looking, with a beer-drinker's paunch under his striped apron, asked after Danny. Trix's face lit up.

'She's coming home tomorrow, Tony! Dr Ballard is delighted with her. We're planning a little welcome home party.'

'Hey, that's really great, Mrs Margison,' said Tony, wrapping the garlic sausage. His moustache broadened above a beaming smile. 'Give her my best, will you? Tell her she's still my number one girl, okay?'

'Tony's son, Arthur, and Danny were in the school play together,' Trix explained as they wheeled the laden trolley to the checkout. She giggled and pushed her glasses on to her nose with her thumb, a mannerism that reminded Karel of Tom. 'They had to act this "love" scene together – Arthur was keen but Danny wasn't too happy about it.'

'Doesn't she like him?'

'Oh, she doesn't *mind* him,' Trix said. 'But at the time she was going through an anti-boy, anti-mush phase. You know what kids are. Whenever a love scene came on TV she used to run from the room with her hands over her ears, yelling at the top of her voice as if it were Dracula getting a stake through the heart. Annoyed the hell out of Frank.'

'I think I know how Danny feels,' Karel said, thinking of some of the 'love scenes' she had seen on TV.

The next day, which was Friday, Frank arranged to leave school early. He was due to pick Danny up from the hospital at three. Term finished the following Wednesday, and classes were winding down; in fact most of the students were eking out the last few days with sports and recreational activities.

As he was leaving he met Bernie Gooch, who taught ecological studies, in the second-storey corridor of the science block. Bernie was dressed as usual in his ethnic Indian cotton shirt and canvas trousers, his two big toes poking out lugubriously from cross-strapped brown leather sandals made in Sri Lanka. He had a full mountain-man beard. Strings of beads and coral shells swathed his hairy chest.

'When are you and Wanda Jane coming over for dinner?' Frank asked him. 'I've got some stuff on the computer I'd like you to see.'

'Whenever we get an invite. Say the word, man.'

'Let's make it after term's through. Next Friday okay?'

Bernie Gooch was distracted by a girl student walking by. He watched her swaying rump from the corner of his slitted eyes and growled in his throat like a bear. The girl didn't seem to mind. Everyone in the school knew of Bernie's reputation, though whether it was all bark and no bite Frank wasn't sure. Anyway, if Bernie was idiot enough to get entangled with the students, that was his look-out.

Frank went down the stairs. Bernie called out, wishing him well with Danny, and Frank waved a lanky arm and went out through a side door which led to the staff car park. He drove past the central circular flowerbed, *Torrence High* embroidered in pink and yellow flowers against the cool green turf. At the main gate Frank brought the car to a sudden halt, avoiding by what seemed inches a car that had suddenly appeared round the curve of the road. The car raced past, rocking from side to side.

It was a dark red Toyota with a scarred front wing and two teenage boys and a girl inside. It had North Carolina plates.

Frank stared at it hard, teeth set, his hands grasping the wheel. Only after it had vanished did he realise he hadn't noted the number. He nosed out cautiously and drove to the hospital.

By early evening they had eaten the food prepared by Trix and Karel, with Tom acting as gofer; Trix had had a little weep, and with them all sitting in the patio garden in the shade of the tasselled sun umbrella, Frank sprang a surprise of his own: he had made a reservation for them to take the lakeside lodge in the Green Mountain Forest in Vermont for three weeks, from late July.

The family had rented the place before, during one period for three consecutive summers when Tom was a teenager and Danny just a knock-kneed toddler. Tom had been seventeen on his last visit. The others had been twice since then.

Misty-eyed again, Trix leaned over to kiss Frank. 'That's wonderful, honey.' She smiled and glanced round brightly and topped up the glasses with home-made lemonade.

'You're coming too, aren't you, Tom?' Danny said eagerly. Despite the warmth of the evening Trix had insisted on wrapping a tartan blanket around her legs.

Tom said, 'Sure. If I'm asked.'

'Tom,' his mother frowned.

'Only kidding.'

'College humour,' said Frank with a lopsided smile on his lean face. He rubbed one of his sideburns. 'Forgotten what it was like since I stopped my subscription to *The New Yorker*. Sure we can fit in with your plans?' he said, lighting a cigarette.

Trix ignored him and said, 'Karel, please come too if you'd like. It's a sizeable place. There are two bedrooms downstairs and a smaller bedroom in the loft. We can put a cot up and you can share with Danny. Frank, tell her we've got acres of room.'

'We've got acres of room,' Frank said.

'I'd love to, but my father's due in from the Coast and I really ought to see him, it's been months. But thank you, anyway. It sounds really wonderful.'

'I thought he was at Columbia,' Frank said. 'Professor of Biochemistry or something.'

'Microbiology. He spends a lot of his time on the West Coast.' Karel shrugged. 'I'm not sure doing what exactly. Retained by a corporation out there as a scientific adviser.'

'High-flyer,' said Frank, his tone lightly sardonic. He took a drink of lemonade. 'That's where the action is, all right. Selling yourself to some high-tec outfit for the big bucks.'

'We go horse-riding too,' said Danny. 'There are stables near Middlebury. I rode a palomino pony last time called Whistler.'

Frank said, 'We're not completely dumb out here in the sticks. Not up to Columbia standards, of course.' He looked at Tom. 'And what about the superbrains at MIT? Up to your ears in charmed particles and mu-mesons as usual?'

Tom knew enough not to be drawn into this. Instead he said, 'I see you've extended your computer set-up since I was last home.' Frank's den was crammed with the computer buff's paraphernalia, over five grand's worth. 'What are you working on? Anything interesting?'

'I like to think so. Building up a database of chemical interactions to use in school. It's a big project, it'll take me the best part of a year. Classification of elements by structure and atomic weight. There are twenty or thirty variables to consider, which have to be converted into graphics scrolling and spreadsheets.'

Tom nodded, trying to suppress a yawn. At MIT he used a terminal nearly every day, and found the jargon of computer buffs deadly dull.

Trix looked worried. 'We'll have to see about the horse-riding, Danny,' she said. 'I'll ask Dr Helms what she thinks. We have to get you fit and well first, before you go galloping around Lake Dunmore.'

Tom was quietly amazed over how well she looked. The blue circles round her eyes had gone, and her body, if slightly thinner than he remembered, seemed sturdy enough. He said:

'How's your swimming these days, shrimp?' Tom had taught her to swim three years ago in the local municipal pool, shortly before he left for MIT.

'I've got my three lengths' certificate.'

Tom whistled. He pointed his finger. 'When we get to Lake Dunmore I'll give you ten yards' start over a hundred yards' distance.'

Danny's dark eyes sparkled. 'Bet?'

'Five bucks.'

'I'll take it. I've got fifteen dollars and twenty-three cents saved. You're on!'

'That stinks – twenty-five yards' start at least,' Karel objected. She gave Tom a withering look. 'You'd steal from the poor-box.'

'Your mother's right, Danny. Riding and swimming are out till you're back on your feet,' Frank said with the air of a final pronouncement on the subject. 'We don't want any more accidents, not in this family, thank you.'

'What *can* I do, Dad? That's why we go to the Green Mountain Forest, to have fun.'

'We'll have fun,' Frank said. Another final pronouncement.

While Trix was seeing Danny to bed, overriding her protests and pleadings, Tom and Karel went into the kitchen to make a pot of coffee. Frank had decided to open his five-star Courvoisier, which indeed marked it in Tom's book as a celebration.

'Why not come with us?' Tom said softly, sliding his arms round her waist. 'It's beautiful up there. Mountain air, clear skies.' She was wearing a fine-knit beige halter top that left her brown arms and shoulders bare. As he breathed in her perfume, the yearning became very strong. 'Great sex.'

Karel leaned away slightly, her hands pressed against his chest.

'Tom, I can't, you know that. *My* father's expecting me.' She glanced over her shoulder at the sound of Trix coming down the stairs and moved to the stove.

'What will you do in the summer in New York City, for God's sake?'

Karel unplugged the kettle and poured boiling water into the ceramic pot. 'I've got friends there. They won't all have gone away.'

'I hope you have a swell time,' said Tom dourly.

That night Tom had his *From Here to Eternity* dream in which Karel took Deborah Kerr's part and Burt Lancaster was transformed into a muscular bronzed Tom Margison, rolling about in the surf together. Danny was in the surf too, swimming for dear life. Tom tried desperately to reach her but a thousand tiny hands kept pulling him back. He saw her arm flailing frantically, and then disappear in the surf, boiling up red and thick and coiled as if painted by Van Gogh. He muttered and turned in his sleep.

4

Tom was rooting through the shed at the bottom of the garden, unearthing stuff he hadn't seen in years. Under a piece of sacking he came across his racing cycle, dusty, the chrome tarnished, the gears clogged with oil. Stacked in a cardboard box were his training weights, like fat red doughnuts in various sizes. My God, he must have been fit in those days. All this and swimming and track too. He doubted whether he could pedal up to Holly Hill now without gasping.

He was bent over a pile of mildewed magazines – old *National Geographics*, *Science Digests* and *Scientific Americans* – when Karel peered in, wafting cobwebs away. 'What's this, the Mummy's Tomb?' Her gleaming hair was pulled back from her face and drawn up into a pony-tail, revealing ears as white and delicate as porcelain.

She crouched down beside him and picked up a 1977 copy of *Scientific American*. 'These yours?'

Tom had acquired a dreamy-eyed look. 'I remember reading an article in one of those when I was about twelve, thirteen. It said that a solid table isn't really solid at all. There's more empty space there than actual solid matter. Or in a chair, or an automobile – in *anything* at all we think of as solid – including you and me. It blew my mind. Still does.'

He pushed his glasses on to his nose with his thumb and smiled at her with bared teeth. 'And they call me *mad*, the fools!'

Karel said placidly, 'I can't think why.'

They went out into the sunshine and Karel said, 'What were you looking for in there?'

'My past,' Tom said mysteriously.

'Barbells and *Scientific American*. The All American Boy. No dirty magazines?'

'With my imagination I didn't need them.'

'Black holes and pulsars,' said Karel reflectively. 'I wonder, could there be some symbolism there? The cosmic fuck.' The idea seemed to intrigue her. 'Comets with tails look a bit like sperm, don't they? And space the black womb of the cosmos.'

'Jeepers,' said Tom. 'Is that how psychologists' minds work? And I always thought you were a simple girl. No sexual hang-ups.'

Karel threw a punch at him. Her blue-grey eyes clouded for a moment and she said thoughtfully, 'That's just reminded me.'

'What?'

'You'll never guess what Danny asked me this morning.'

Tom waited.

'Whether parental repression can affect a child's sexual development.'

'Oh,' said Tom blankly. 'How did she phrase that?'

'In that way – in those words.'

'What did you say?'

'What *could* I say? How can you discuss complex psycho-sexual problems with an eleven-year-old? Where does she get stuff like that from?'

'I don't suppose they teach it in school,' Tom said vaguely.

'Damn right they don't! I won't be into child psychology myself for another two years.' Karel blinked and shook her head. 'That's some kid sister you've got there, Tom. The way she's going, the first female Nobel Laureate in Clinical Psychology.'

'Could be she read –'

Tom turned his head quickly. What sounded like a cry of pain or fear had come from the house. He ran along the narrow bricked path and across the lawn and leapt the three crazy-paved steps leading up to the patio. The sliding glass doors into the living-room were half open. Tom glanced inside and then ran past and through the screen door, propped open by a large smooth pebble, and into the kitchen.

His mother was kneeling on the green linoleum tiled floor next to an overturned straightbacked chair. Her brown wavy hair hung forward, hiding her face. A large pyrex baking dish was lying in front of her, broken into two jagged pieces. She was holding one hand tightly in the other, and blood was squeezing through her tightly pressing fingers. The words *wrist* and *artery* cut through Tom's mind like a knife. He noticed Danny standing on the other side of the kitchen, her brown eyes bright with alarm. She was wearing a pale yellow tee-shirt with Michael Jackson's head on it that clung to her bony chest, and faded blue jeans, her hands hanging limply at her sides. She turned her head mechanically as Tom came in and said, 'I didn't touch it, Tom. Honest.'

A look that was half scared, half bewildered flitted across her face.

Tom said automatically, 'Of course not,' and helped Trix to her feet. He led her to the sink. Karel appeared at the kitchen door, one hand on the jamb. Tom said, 'How bad is it?'

'I'm sure the damn thing moved,' Trix said absently to no one in particular. She was slightly in shock.

Tom ran cold water over the wound, which was on the outside fleshy part of her left hand. Not near anything vital, thank God. Reaching for the dish she must have fallen, and in putting out her hand to save herself gashed it on one of the broken pieces.

'Where's your first-aid?' Karel said briskly.

Tom jerked his head. 'Corner cupboard. Metal box with a rubber band around it. Or it used to be.' He turned Trix's hand from side to side under the flow of water and then gently pressed the edges of the wound together. When the blood had been washed away he lifted her hand for a closer inspection. 'I don't think it's serious, Mom. Not as bad as it looks, anyhow.'

His mother cleared her throat, as if she had been swallowing sawdust. 'My own stupid fault. Your dad said I'd fall off that chair one day, and now I have.'

Karel put some clear antiseptic salve on the wound and dressed it while Tom made some tea. Danny unhooked three beakers from under the kitchen unit and fetched the sugar basin.

'Where were you, shrimp? In here?' Tom said.

'I was – no, in the living-room. I heard a noise.'

Tom nodded. 'I see. Why did you say you hadn't touched it?'

'Because I hadn't. Didn't.'

Tom was silent.

'Honest.'

'I believe you,' Tom said. He gave her a smile and added, 'But no reason to say it if you weren't here.'

'Guess not,' Danny said in a small voice.

Tom proposed that he and Karel take Danny to Lake LeGrand that afternoon for a picnic. Trix was having several members of the wine-making circle over at three o'clock for a tasting, and when Danny's face lit up at the idea, Trix overcame her qualms and said yes – providing she didn't go swimming or get involved in any other strenuous activity.

'Promise me you'll keep a close watch on her, Tom,' Trix said anxiously. 'She's still recuperating, remember.'

'Why do you talk as if I wasn't here?' Danny said, rather heatedly. Her dark eyes sparkled with a dangerous light. 'I'm tired of you and Dad treating me like I was a little kid. I'm not any more. I wish you'd remember that.'

Trix gazed at her in shocked silence, and Tom stepped in quickly and said there was no need to worry, Lake LeGrand would be as calm as a millpond. They would hire a trimaran at Coble's Quay and laze around and not exert themselves even by casting a line. How was that?

Everyone got busy preparing and packing the food. Trix took a chicken out of the freezer, thawed it in the microwave, and cooked it in the oven. She made cold dips, cucumber and yoghurt, while Tom and Karel sliced vegetables, tomatoes and avocado for the salad. There was cooked ham, cheese, sweet and sour pickle, wholemeal bread rolls. Danny wrapped a melon in damp newspaper and packed fruit, ice-cream, a large plastic bottle of Coke, and two bottles of Californian rosé in the cold box. By one-fifteen they were ready to leave.

The lake was nine miles from Torrence, the other side of Holly Hill.

Tom had once kept a small sailing dinghy on the lake, and he and a few friends spent the endless blue days of summer fishing and scuba-diving. He had sold his diving gear, he now recalled regretfully, to raise the down-payment on his first car.

At the quay Tom picked out a twenty-two-foot trimaran called 'Tramp' and they loaded their provisions aboard. It was mid-week and out of season, so there were fewer than a dozen or so yachts and small craft in sight. The sunshine was clear and hot, but further out a haze obscured the opposite shore. As Tom had forecast, there was hardly a ripple on the surface of the green-blue water: they would have to use the motor and pick up whatever faint breeze there was away from the shore.

Tom sat in the stern, bare to the waist, wearing just a pair of old jeans with the legs sawn off and scuffed canvas shoes with the laces missing. Karel and Danny lounged on either side of the boat, trailing their fingers in the cool water. Karel's tan had deepened in recent weeks and she looked golden and radiant. She wore a floppy white hat, her hair trailing on to her shoulders and gleaming in the sunlight, and a loose cotton top that showed the shape of her breasts. Tom regarded her with an intense secret pleasure.

When they were some distance out, Karel said, 'Are there any fish in this lake? I don't see any.'

'Oh, sure, there are fish,' Tom said. 'Not as many as there used to be, though.'

'Why's that?'

'Haven't you heard of pollution?' Tom said.

'But it looks clear and pure.' Karel looked at him over her shoulder. 'Pollution from where?'

'People dump stuff in the lake, boats discharge sewage.'

'That's criminal.'

'It is criminal. You're right. But they keep on doing it.'

Karel looked back at the water and there was silence for a while.

'Eutrophication,' Danny said. 'Farmers use too much nitrous fertiliser and it runs off into the lake and feeds the algae, which blooms and exceeds the biological oxygen demand and the fish and other marine life are killed off.'

'Is that so?' said Tom, gazing at her. 'How do you know?'

'Must have read it somewhere.'

'Have you done it in class?'

'No,' Danny said matter-of-factly, after a moment's reflection.

Karel raised her eyebrows at Tom and he shrugged in eloquent dumb show. What the hell was she reading these days? More amazing was how she could retain such stuff. Photographic memory?

They were near the middle of the lake now, a vaporous heat haze making a diffused orange ball of the sun. Water slapped the glass-fibre hull as they drifted with the slight tug of undercurrent. There was hardly a whisper of breeze. It was very hot.

Tom's sense of elder brother responsibility began to trouble him and he rigged up an awning as shade while they ate. If Danny got a touch of sunstroke he would be in his parents' bad books for the rest of the vacation. Already he wasn't getting on great with Frank, and he couldn't figure out why. They'd hardly talked at all while Tom was home, and yet at one time, when Tom was a teenager, they had spent hour after absorbing hour in the den discussing every topic under the sun. It had been his dad who had encouraged Tom to try for the MIT scholarship, and fanned his interest in physics generally. And yet when Tom raised the subject of the CERN posting over dinner one evening, and how much it meant to him, Frank treated it casually, seemed almost indifferent.

'What does he get up to on the West Coast, your father?' Tom asked, pouring chilled wine into two cups.

'He's some sort of technical adviser. I'm not absolutely sure what he does. Companies employ him to advise them, that sort of thing.'

'On what?'

Karel tore off a chicken leg and handed it to Danny. 'Medical research projects. New drugs. He never talks about it.'

'Does it pay?'

'I imagine so. A professor's salary at Columbia wouldn't allow him to indulge his tastes,' Karel said with a crooked half-smile.

'What tastes would those be, exactly?' said Tom curiously.

'Paintings. Antiques. First editions. He's collected all the Hogarth Press editions of Virginia Woolf's novels. He goes to the theatre quite a lot. Opera.' Karel bit into a slice of cucumber with pointed white teeth, leaving a serrated edge. 'Victor was born in the wrong century. He'd have been happier in Renaissance Italy.'

'Yeah,' Tom said. 'Providing he was one of the Medicis and not one of the serfs.'

Karel laughed delightedly, rocking back on the wooden seat.

'Did I say something funny?' said Tom.

'Victor as a serf. Now that *is* funny – if you knew him.'

'I'm just waiting to be invited. Come on, shrimp, have some salad,' Tom said, dutifully offering the plastic container. Danny shook her head, her mouth full of chicken and yoghurt dip, a piece of ham in one hand and a bread roll in the other. Tom gave up.

Karel said, 'Why don't you stop off on your way back from Vermont?'

'Do you mean that?'

'Of course I mean it. I'm not in the habit of saying things I don't mean,' Karel said, giving him a severe look.

Tom beamed. 'I'd like very much to meet your father. He sounds an interesting guy,' he said.

'Yes,' Karel said. 'I suppose he is interesting.'

After they had eaten Danny complained that she was bored, so Tom opened up the motor to full throttle and the trimaran surged, not all that fast, through the placid water, forming a wake that was less than creamy. Danny went to the front of the boat and leaned over the prow, Karel staying close by with one hand raised in readiness lest she fall.

Eutrophication, Tom was thinking. He'd have to look that up and see if she was right. Hell of a thing when your eleven-year-old sister started confounding you with long words. Next she'd be discussing b-vector bosons and the characteristics of charmed quarks.

It was around five o'clock when they returned to the quay. Danny had enjoyed the trip on the lake and pulled a face when Tom said they ought to be heading back.

'I'll be in hot water with your mom if we're home later than six, little lady. She didn't like the idea in the first place.'

'She doesn't like me to have any fun,' said Danny sullenly.

'Don't talk stupid, kiddo. Mom worries about you. She's concerned, and quite natural too. You've been out of the hospital less than a week. Think how she feels.'

'I don't care how she feels.'

Tom felt a cold sourness in the pit of his stomach. What was the matter with kids these days? How had they become so hard, so ungrateful, so unfeeling? He recalled the obnoxious child in the drive-in with the blond fringe and wide mad blue staring eyes. A spasm of real anger came up inside him and he had to bite it back. He said, 'That's not very nice, Danny. Say you didn't mean it.'

'I thought you were on my side,' Danny said, staring him out.

'Not when you talk like a spoiled brat,' Tom said, unyielding.

Danny swallowed heavily and her chin quivered. She looked away and he could see her throat working. She said huskily, 'I thought you'd understand, the way that Dad treats you.'

'What's that supposed to mean?'

'Ask Karel.'

'Me?' Karel said cautiously, as if she didn't want to be asked any questions.

Tom was becoming exasperated with the conversation. 'Either say what you mean or shut up,' he said to Danny. 'It seems to me you're just trying to stir up trouble. What's the matter with you?'

Danny turned towards him, her lower lip jutting out defiantly. There was the same dangerous glint in her dark eyes Tom had noticed earlier that day in the kitchen. 'You think because we're kids we don't see anything,' she said. 'But we're not dumb. You can't fool us. We know what's going on in this rotten world.'

5

The two small local airports, at Statesville and Salisbury, didn't handle scheduled airlines, and so Tom had to drive Karel to the Smith Reynolds Airport in Winston-Salem, where she would pick up a connecting flight to Washington DC and thence to New York. The flight departed at nine-fifty on Friday evening, which meant that Tom would miss the Gooches, who were coming to dinner.

It was a seventy-mile drive, and to allow plenty of time they set off shortly before eight. Unknown to Tom, Karel had bought thank-you gifts for the family: a large illustrated book, *The Complete Herb Gardener*, for his mother, a bottle of Chivas Regal for Frank, and a beginner's set of oil paints, brushes, palette and instruction book for Danny – 'So you can start painting pictures yourself as well as look at them,' Karel said.

Trix hugged her and said to come again soon; Frank was jovial in an off-hand sort of way, making some tart witticism about 'the rotten core of the Big Apple', and on the doorstep

Karel and Danny had a whispered conversation from which everyone else was excluded. Girl talk, Tom supposed.

As they were leaving there was a light summer shower, which rapidly cleared, and the roads steamed like dry ice as Tom drove the Chevvy north and came on to Interstate 40 a few miles past Hickory. The countryside was green and gently rolling, with woods dotted in clumps here and there, and later the meandering silver thread of the Yadkin River to their left.

The landscape was familiar and unexciting to Tom, whose mind was on other things. At the moment New York held a glittering and seductive attraction for him. Because that's where Karel would be. Thinking of her there (alone?) his imagination played all kinds of dirty tricks.

Forget it. What was four weeks?

As if reading his thoughts, Karel reached out and put her hand on his thigh. Tom's breathing seemed to get stuck in his chest. His throat felt dry, and he had to resist the urge to swallow in case she read his reaction too accurately. Karel stroked the tight material of his trousers with her fingernails, which communicated itself like an electrical charge. And then he did have to swallow, and breathed out through his nose. His heart was thundering like mad.

'This isn't fair . . .'

'I won't if you don't want me to,' Karel said, not stopping.

'Jesus,' Tom said as her fingers delved softly, releasing him. He said, 'We're on the freeway, for Pete's sake. Truckers . . .'

'I don't see any truckers,' she said casually, bending her head. Her fingers were cool, her mouth was hot.

Tom eased back in his seat and tried to concentrate on driving.

At the airport he parked the car and walked with her to the departure lounge. It was after nine-thirty and the place was almost empty. Women in shapeless green overalls moved about pushing large vacuum cleaners. He liked this time of night in airport departure lounges; his only regret was that he wouldn't be sitting next to Karel on the plane, wouldn't be flying with her through the romantic darkness to New York City.

They stood near the wall, next to a phone booth, holding one another. Tom almost felt like thanking her, in gratitude for services rendered. Instead he smiled and looked into her eyes and kissed her on the mouth, his gratitude and thanks and all the other emotions contained in the kiss, feeling now incredibly strong and confident.

Tom stood at the angled window watching the plane taxi into the soft gathering dusk. The lighted oval windows looked pale and anaemic against the brilliant orange streak of sunset. He breathed out a long happy sigh and turned away.

Tom drove through the quiet streets up to The Heights and parked his car to one side of the driveway so that Frank would be able to get the Ford hatchback out of the garage in the morning. Tom thought he might sleep in late, it being Saturday tomorrow. They were leaving for Vermont the following Wednesday.

The house was silent and in darkness. The Gooches sometimes stayed till one, one-thirty, though evidently not tonight. He moved through the darkened living-room to the stairs and paused with one hand on the banister rail. There was a light under the door of Frank's den. Better let him know I'm home, Tom thought, as he walked the few paces along the short corridor and popped his head in. The monitor screen was aglow, and in the light of the desk lamp Tom saw Danny's dark curly head bent over the keyboard. She was obviously intent on whatever she was doing and didn't hear him.

Tom watched curiously as Danny tapped and a line of letters and numbers appeared on the screen. They looked to Tom like chemical formulae. Danny read them, consulted a typewritten page on the desk, and then tapped out several more rows, very rapidly, without stopping. Then she pressed a key and the computer whirred and clicked. At the top of the screen the word WAIT blinked on and off. Tom knew that the computer was either making a calculation or storing the data. What he didn't know, and couldn't conceive, was how on earth his sister could do this. He felt confused and slightly bewildered.

Tom opened the door fully and went in, adjusting the expression on his face. There was a sensible, logical explanation, naturally, though what it might be he couldn't think.

If Tom had expected Danny to be surprised or alarmed, he was mistaken. She barely glanced at him. Her face had a flat greenish light, reflected from the glow on the screen; her eyes were dark, liquid, shining. It crossed Tom's mind that perhaps she had a fever. He remembered Karel saying at the airport, 'Take good care of Danny,' and he wondered now, as then, what she had meant by it.

He cleared his throat and said, 'Working late, kiddo. I thought they'd abolished child labour.'

Tom sat on the corner of the desk and smiled down at her.

The flashing word WAIT disappeared from the screen and Danny started tapping again. Tom watched her in silence. He could feel his heart beating.

Nothing more was said for a minute or two as Danny worked at the machine. Her long slender fingers sped over the keys. Line upon line of mathematical equations and chemical symbols filled the screen. Once or twice she glanced at the typewritten sheet with barely an interruption to the steady flow of data being fed into the computer.

'There,' Danny said finally, punching a control key. 'That ought to do it.' She sat back in the swivel chair and folded her arms.

'Do what, exactly?' asked Tom in a voice that was edged with an uneasy reluctance, as if he dreaded the answer.

'Database for the chemical classification program. Simple. Why he took six months to get this far I can't figure, unless the guy's dumb.'

Tom found he was unable to speak. He could only stare at

the girl sitting in the chair, so calm and composed with her arms folded.

'How –' Tom began. 'How did you know how to do this?' He knew anyway that it was impossible. 'Who taught you?'

'Taught me?' Danny said, as if he'd insulted her. 'Any kid could do it.'

With an IQ of two hundred and twenty, thought Tom. And maybe not even then. Danny was bright but not *that* bright. 'How long have you been working on this?'

Danny looked at him levelly. 'Started tonight. Took about twenty minutes. I read through this stuff first, got the hang of it.' She smiled at him and her eyes, Tom now noticed, were duller, less luminous than before.

He looked at 'this stuff' on the desk: there must have been between two hundred and fifty and three hundred single-spaced typewritten pages. At a guess, about a hundred thousand words, and much of it numbers, symbols and other complex technical information.

As if answering his unspoken question, Danny said, 'It's all here, Tom. I haven't missed anything. Check it for yourself if you like.'

'That's okay. I'll take your word for it.' Tom gave her a quick smile. 'You're a little bundle of surprises, shrimp.'

'A long-tailed marine crustacean of the genus *Crangon*, closely related to the prawn and allied genera,' said Danny automatically.

She stood up and Tom almost flinched. She stood straight and very still and gazed at him with dark, vaguely clouded eyes. Then the cloud passed and she said brightly, 'I'm starved. Let's eat something.'

They went to the kitchen and together prepared sandwiches on wholemeal bread of cream cheese and pickle, and cut two wedges of the bacon and mushroom quiche made by Trix with herbs from her own garden. Tom had a Coke and Danny a Dr Pepper. They sat at the round wooden table under the basketwork lampshade with the fringe of purple tassels. Beyond the bright cone of light, the house itself seemed to be sleeping.

Tom wasn't hungry and had to chew every mouthful. Danny ate ravenously. She ate enough for two her size, finishing off the half sandwich Tom couldn't eat.

Tom was stuck for something to say, so he asked after the Gooches. Had Danny talked to them?

There was something impatient, almost scornful, in her shake of the head. 'I stayed in my room and looked at my Van Gogh book. *She* thinks she's Joni Mitchell and *he* thinks he's God's gift to women. Do you know who he's sleeping with now?'

'No,' Tom said.

'Stella Feinstein. They meet in a motel on the Old Post Road every Wednesday afternoon after school. Stella's supposed to be visiting her sister in Cherryville and Bernie is *supposed* to be running the High School camera club. Of course Wanda Jane doesn't know. But Bernie could be heading for real trouble.'

'Oh?'

Danny got up suddenly, opened a cupboard, broke off a handful of fruit cake and pushed it into her mouth. Her mouth bulging with cake, she said, 'Stella isn't on the pill and Bernie doesn't know it.' She laughed and choked at the same time. 'Is he in for a shock! Serve the bastard right.'

Tom was sitting with the palms of his hands pressed together, fingers tightly interlocked, as though he was praying. But he was too numb and shaken inside to pray.

Danny finished her cake and wiped the crumbs away. 'At least you're okay, Tom, you and Karel. I like her.' She lowered her voice to a throaty whisper. 'She has a coil fitted. So you're okay.'

Tom thought that if Danny wasn't mad, he must be.

'You should get some sleep. You're tired.' Danny walked round the table and went to the door. The cupboard door stood open. Danny smiled to herself and the cupboard door closed. Then she went out.

Tom moved through the darkened living-room to the stairs and paused with one hand on the banister rail. There was a light under the door of Frank's den. Better let him know I'm home, Tom thought, as he walked the few paces along the short corridor to his right and popped his head in.

But the room was empty.

Tom trudged upstairs to bed, deathly tired.

When Tom woke in the morning, having slept a dreamless sleep, he had a splitting headache.

6

'We'll leave your old heap in the garage,' Frank said. 'It's better out of sight, even if nobody in their right mind would want to steal it.'

Tom finished fastening the elasticated strapping which held his cycle on the roof-rack of the Ford, and gave it a twang to make sure it was secure. He did it twice more because he liked the sound.

'Is that everything?' Tom asked, stepping down. 'Has Mom packed the kitchen sink?'

Frank gave him a sour grin. 'Don't joke about things like that. Your mother would put wheels on the house if she could and take that along.'

Tom leaned against the car and held his face up to the sun, eyes shut.

'I've got a better idea. Let's move Vermont down here.'

It was a few minutes before nine on Wednesday morning and they were all set to go, practically. Trix was scurrying round the house like a demented mother hen, doing fifty things at once. She had been up since six. Tom and his father, long used to this, tried to keep in the still epicentre of the whirlwind. No matter how thorough the preparations over the preceding days, and sometimes weeks, Trix always managed to work herself into a flat spin on the morning of departure.

When Tom was a youngster he had scurried after her, anxious to help, but experience taught him that this only made matters worse – anything he did had to be done again his mother's way, which in the end meant it took twice as long.

Frank stood by the open hatchback smoking a small thin cheroot. He was wearing a light cotton short-sleeved shirt that outlined the bony points of his angular shoulders, slacks, and Nike training shoes. His cheeks were shiny where he had shaved closely with a safety razor, his long sideburns trimmed with such precision that they looked like strips of tarpaper pasted on.

The smell of Brut floated on the limpid, sun-warmed air.

While they were waiting the mail arrived. Frank had a word with the mailman and asked him to leave any packages next door with Mr and Mrs Keating. Tom wasn't expecting any mail, but there was a picture postcard of the New York skyline at sunset taken from the Statue of Liberty.

'Hi! Here am I, alive and well and living in Manhattan. The muggers have moved on to Park Av. Have a great time and see you in August. My fondest regards to your parents, a hug for Danny, XXX etc. to you.
K.

PS Victor would like to meet you.'

And why not, Tom thought tartly. I haven't got AIDS.

He tucked the postcard into the breast pocket of his sports shirt, wondering what was the matter with him. Several times over the past few days he'd noticed these flashes of irritation flaring up spontaneously and unpredictably. It was true that he hadn't been sleeping at all well; probably the heat was to blame. Or his dreams in vibrant Van Gogh technicolor.

Frank went round kicking the tyres. He kept glancing at his

watch and looking towards the house. There was still no sign of Trix. He waved to a neighbour mowing his lawn across the street and sneaked another look at his watch.

'I think we'll take seventy-seven,' he announced unnecessarily. They always took Interstate 77, then Interstate 81, which ran alongside the Shenandoah National Park, avoiding Washington DC.

'Take it easy, Dad. We'll get there.'

'I know. By midnight.'

'Do you want me to drive first?'

Frank shook his head. Already there was a sheen of perspiration on his high bony forehead divided by the vee of thinning hair. He threw down his cheroot and ground it underfoot on the driveway. 'Go and see what the hell's keeping your mother. Tell her we said nine o'clock and it's now twenty minutes after.'

Tom found Trix watering her herb garden. She said over her shoulder, 'Check the upstairs windows, Tom. Make sure the catches are down. Is Danny out front with you?'

'Nope.'

'She must be in her room. Have her come down right away, would you?'

All the window catches would be fastened, Tom felt certain, but he did as he was asked, and sure enough they were, including those in Danny's room, which was empty.

He peeked through the window of his parents' room, which overlooked the front lawn, but Frank was there alone, stamping up and down the driveway, swinging his arms. On his way along the landing Tom tried the door of the bathroom. It was locked. He said, 'Don't be too long, shrimp, we're all set to leave.'

Tom waited for a response, head tilted to one side, and when none came tapped on the door and called her name. He rapped again, harder this time, listening to the silence. He heard a sound like someone grunting or choking and hit the door with his fist. The grunting or choking sound continued.

Tom ran down the stairs and called to his father. He led the way back up the stairs and Frank went through the same procedure with the same result. Frank stood glaring at the door, breathing heavily, his forehead a maze of wrinkles. He raised his fist to hammer again and Tom said, 'We'll have to break it down.' Before his father could move or say anything he kicked the door next to the knob with his heel. Luckily he was wearing shoes with solid soles. But still the door held.

'What in heaven's name is going on?' said Trix, coming up the stairs.

Tom tried again and there was a splintering sound as the metal fitment was torn out of the door frame. Trix arm-wrestled Frank out of the way, pushed the door violently aside and went down on her knees, her glasses hanging from one ear. It seemed to Tom that she was trying to control all of Danny's jerking, shaking limbs at the same time.

There was foam on Danny's lips, the queer gurgling, choking noise bubbling through it. Her eyes were white and rolling. Her brown legs in white ankle socks and green plastic sandals were stuck out straight and quivering like divining rods. Trix was screaming at the top of her voice and trying to hold down the flailing limbs.

Danny lay rigid on the curly rug between the bath and the basin. Suddenly, she rose up from the waist, eyeballs white and gleaming, mouth bubbling foam, and beat at Trix's head with her fists.

Trix cried out and fell sideways, striking her head on the side of the bath with a hollow clunk.

Tom and his father stepped over her, manoeuvring awkwardly and trying to balance between the mother's slumped body and the child's pumping fists and rigid thrusting legs. They bumped against one another in a clumsy comic dance, and both nearly fell, grabbing out for support. Frank thrust out an arm and swept clean a glass shelf of shampoo bottles and conditioners and herbal rinses which fell with a clatter into the bath and skidded along the sides in a broken heap.

The air was dense and sickly with the mingled pungent odour of roses, lavender, sandalwood, wild mint and coriander.

Holding her arms flat by her sides, Tom sat next to Danny on the bed in his room, which was next door to the bathroom. He could feel the tremors and spasms in the thin wrists. Her eyelids were heavy and there was a sluggishness in the dying movements of her body. Every few moments she would tense and arch back, exposing the shiny corded ridges of her throat with the sweat running down.

Tom let go of her wrists experimentally. They were red and sore looking where he had held them. Danny twitched and trembled like a galvanic corpse, but the uncontrollable manic movements had subsided. The convulsions, or fit – whatever it was – had spent itself.

A door closed along the landing. Frank came into the room. His long face was ashen under his tan.

Tom said, 'Is Mom all right?'

'She has a slight concussion.' Frank went down on one knee by the side of the bed. 'I told her to lie still for a few minutes. She'll be all right. She wants me to call Dr Ballard.' He laid the backs of his fingers against Danny's forehead and she strained upwards and sank her teeth into his hand.

'*Jesus Christ Almighty!*'

Tom made a grab for Danny's wrists and held her down. Frank was staring at the tiny puncture marks as if they were stigmata that had suddenly appeared there. Drops of blood hung like ruby beads in the dark hairs of his hand.

'This is a hospital job, Dad. Not something we can handle ourselves.' Although he didn't say anything, it crossed Tom's mind that Danny had been bitten by a rabid dog. Was that possible? No, perhaps not. Such an injury would have required medical attention, and he could see no evidence of any wound.

Danny's eyes were fully closed now and her breathing rhythmic and steady. The twitching of her limbs had ceased altogether. She appeared to be asleep. Tom released her once again, more slowly this time, watching her closely for any sign of movement, hands poised to grab her.

'Call the hospital, Dad. I'll stay and keep an eye on her.'

When he looked at his father Tom was surprised to see tears standing in his eyes. His immediate reaction was shock at his own surprise. That and a kind of shame. Did he really think his father was bereft of all emotion?

Frank got slowly and awkwardly to his feet, a tall stooping man with the look of somebody who's just been kicked in the face. 'That damn hit-and-run bastard!' he said in a low trembling voice. 'The accident did something to her brain, damaged it.' He curled his hands, looking down at his daughter on Tom's bed.

'Danny'll get over this, Dad. It's a setback, that's all.' Tom tried not to sound as helpless as he felt. 'Call the doctor, please.'

Frank shambled to the door. He stopped there and wiped his eyes. As he did so he stared at the bite on his hand.

'I'll have to cancel the lodge,' he said vaguely, and went out sucking his hand.

Dr Mary Helms, the consultant neurologist at Bennett Memorial Hospital, was a small slim woman in her late thirties with short dark straight hair, no make-up, and a curt, capable manner that bordered on brusqueness. She wore a plain brown cardigan, a straight checked skirt, and sensible low-heeled shoes. There was no jewellery, not even a signet ring.

Tom and his parents followed Dr Helms along the pastel green corridor and through a series of doors into a short hallway with several rooms opening off it. All the doors had square glass panels set into them. A nurse was seated at a central table. In front of her a metal rack of monitor screens displayed rows of dancing green blips.

Dr Helms made a patting motion of the hand as the nurse was about to rise and marched with firm brisk steps to the third door on the left. She glanced through the glass panel and then stood aside, tugging the front of her brown cardigan down and folding her arms over her flat chest.

Tom hung back while his parents pressed their faces close to the glass. He could tell from the set of his mother's shoulders – like someone flinching from an anticipated blow – that she was trying her hardest not to cry. Trix had tied her hair back and applied a dab of lipstick. She hadn't slept without interruption for two nights and it showed in her drawn face and jerky, fretful movements.

While he waited Tom read the plastic sign above the glass panel, white letters on a red ground:

STRICT ISOLATION
Visitors must report to nurses' station before entering Isolation Room
1. Air-lock doors must be kept closed
2. Gowns and masks must be worn by all persons entering room
3. Hands must be washed on leaving room
4. Gloves must be worn by all persons entering room
5. Articles must be discarded, disinfected or wrapped and sent to C.S.S.D.

Tom frowned and was about to ask a question of Dr Helms, who met his gaze with her blank pale eyes, when there was a metallic crash and clatter as a porter, a thick-set, swarthy, balding man in brown overalls, used a trolley as a battering-ram to push open the double doors.

Dr Helms turned and called out acidly, 'Less noise, if you please! This is a hospital, not a funfair!'

The porter trod on tip toe, pushing the squealing trolley forward, and very gingerly began to load some oxygen cylinders and other equipment that was stacked against the wall.

'We've had to sedate the child quite heavily,' said Dr Helms at Tom's elbow. 'As you will note, there are marked signs of hyperkinesis.'

'What?' Tom said.

'Hyperactivity. Aggressive behaviour. Inability to control physical movement. The metabolism speeds up and overrides the normal inhibiting mechanism in the brain.'

Tom said, 'Is her condition contagious?'

'No,' said Dr Helms, casting him a sidelong glance that was wary to the point of suspicion.

'Then I don't understand.'

'I'm sorry?'

'Why you're keeping her in here.'

'Obviously so that she doesn't disturb other patients,' Dr Helms said coldly, as if Tom had impugned her professional judgement.

'But if she isn't contagious, why keep her in isolation?' Tom said.

'I have already explained that to you.'

'No,' Tom said, 'you've explained why she has to be kept away from other patients, so as not to disturb them. Not why she's in isolation.'

Dr Helms's nostrils were pinched and white. She held Tom's stare for a moment or two, and then her eyes flickered and slid away. She said icily, 'It is hospital policy to keep patients who are under observation in the Isolation Room. Merely a precaution, nothing more.'

Dr Helms turned aside with an abrupt swivelling movement and gestured to the nurse, who rose quickly, unlocked the outer door of the Isolation Room and held it open for Frank and Trix to step inside. She glanced towards Tom, who shook his head. The nurse closed the outer door behind her, unlocked the inner one and stood to one side.

'When you're through, leave your gowns, masks and gloves in here,' she said, meaning the narrow cubicle that acted as an air-lock. 'The patient's room is kept a few pounds below normal air pressure, as a containment precaution. When one of these doors is opened, the other must be shut. If both are open at the same time, an alarm goes off.'

As she turned the handle and tugged, there was a soft sucking sound, like the lid coming off a jar of pickles.

Tom moved up to the panel, not sure what to expect. Involuntarily he caught his breath. His teeth clamped down hard.

The small figure in the white shift lay flat on the smooth sheet. There was no pillow, to guard against accidental suffocation. Straps bound her at wrists and ankles, and a broad strap across her waist pinned her to the bed. The limbs shuddered. There was white foam on her mouth. But Tom's mind numbly refused to accept that this twisting, writhing body held by the restraining straps was that of his sister. No, it wasn't Danny. Even the face looked different.

For what seemed a long time he stood and stared at this stranger, his forehead pressed against the glass. He could feel the blood draining from his face and a tight hot dryness gripping him by the throat.

He watched his mother and father, gowned and masked, standing rigidly by the side of the bed, their arms interlocked.

And in that moment the dream – the same dream he had been dreaming now for several nights past – reared up in front of Tom's eyes in Van Gogh's garish colours and swirling brushstrokes.

Danny drowning in the blood-red surf.

Her arm waving.

Other arms waving too – a host of them, an underwater forest of waving arms. And in his mind's eye these arms joined together and became a chain. A chain of arms.

'There are more tests we intend to carry out,' said Dr Helms, pursing her small unpainted mouth. 'At this time, as you can see, she's in a restless coma. We are feeding her intravenously and monitoring her life processes. Actually, her condition is stable. I wouldn't want you to be alarmed unnecessarily by the child's appearance.'

The child, Tom thought. Hasn't she got a name?

He said, 'Can I ask you a question, Dr Helms?'

'Certainly.'

'Have you dealt with a case like this before, or a similar one?'

'Toxic shock coma, yes, several cases –'

'Not toxic shock coma,' Tom interrupted, his eyes fixed on her. 'That's something to do with diabetes, isn't it? I mean *this* kind of case – where a child has fits and then lapses into a coma for no apparent reason. With no family history of such a thing ever happening before. Have you?'

'It's rare,' she conceded after a pause.

'You mean no,' Tom said.

Dr Helms shook her head. 'Not personally, no.'

Whether she was a shade uneasy or simply reluctant to admit this, Tom couldn't tell. At any rate, something somewhere wasn't right.

'Do you have *any* idea as to the possible cause?' Tom said.

'I wouldn't venture an opinion, Mr Margison, until after the period of observation is completed. If you're worried about the child's welfare, you needn't be. She is receiving the best of medical care and attention.'

Tom got the distinct impression that Dr Helms was trying to head off any more questions. What was she more afraid of – the questions or the answers?

Frank led Trix through the outer door, cradling her head against his shoulder.

The porter had now loaded his trolley and was wheeling it to the double doors. Dr Helms glared at him, as if his very existence was a personal affront to her. The porter simply stared back at her, and pushed the trolley through the doors.

Tom knew how he felt. He too had had more than enough of Dr Helms for one day.

7

'I don't see what else you could expect,' said Bernie Gooch, topping up his glass with Trix's home-made elderberry wine. 'They're all quacks, every single one of 'em. Can't even cure the common cold. Remember me going to Doc Coburn for that ingrowing toenail?' he said to Wanda Jane. 'The guy was a positive sadist.' He drank half the glass and smacked his red lips, sucking the drops from the fringes of his thick curly brown beard. A red-spotted bandana encircled his tousled head – though he looked less the romantic guerilla leader and more the overweight tennis player, Tom thought.

Trix said anxiously, 'But Dr Helms is a specialist. She's a consultant to all the hospitals in LeGrand County.'

'Listen – they get their diplomas on parchment with the fancy gold lettering and it's a licence to print money. Ever see a poor quack? You bet. They all run Mercedeses and take their vacations in Japan or Kenya or some goddam place.'

'That doesn't mean they aren't any good, honey,' said Wanda Jane reasonably. 'You've got a diploma too.'

She was sitting on the carpet hugging her knees, which were swathed in a long skirt of some coarsely woven material with bright orange splotches on it. Her baby-fine ash-blonde hair hung down her back almost to her waist, like silvery gossamer. Her ankles were rather thick, swelling to bulbous calves, and she was solid right up to her breasts, which were large and heavy. As a teenager, Tom had fantasised over Wanda Jane's breasts – imagining the four of them (himself, Wanda Jane and her bosoms) in bed together.

Frank was sitting back morosely in his favourite armchair to the left of the fireplace. He was drinking the Chivas Regal Karel had brought him.

He had started drinking before the Gooches arrived at eight-thirty for drinks and a late supper. Trix kept glancing at the level in the bottle but so far had said nothing. Now she ventured tentatively, 'Maybe when Dr Helms has had the chance to observe Danny for a few days . . .'

'That wasn't what you said yesterday at the hospital,' Frank mumbled.

'I was upset.'

'*You* were upset?' Frank said. 'I was damn mad. I'm beginning to think Bernie's right about these people. Christ, she didn't even offer a prognosis –'

'I tell you, man,' said Bernie, sweeping his glass round, 'I'd trust those quacks about as far as I can throw a three-legged piano.' He hunched forward on the couch. 'Look what happened to the guys who were sprayed with Agent Orange in Nam. It took them ten years – ten *years* – to get compensation. The medical profession just wouldn't admit they'd been poisoned with dioxin.'

Trix frowned at Bernie and threw a sidelong glance at Tom. But Bernie was up and running now with a topic he'd aired many times before. He and Wanda Jane were big on environmental pollution, food additives, leaded petrol and the 'conservation of the biosphere'.

It struck Tom as odd when they polluted the biosphere just as much as anyone else with their two cars, motor boat and Bernie's 350cc trials bike. He sneaked a look at his watch.

Bernie poured himself some more wine and warmed to his theme. 'You've got to understand that the so-called medical profession has a vested interest in disease. Where would they be without it? Up shit creek without a paddle. You can bet they whooped and hollered when AIDS came along – it's fine to cure polio and diphtheria and TB so long as a whole raft of new diseases are there to take their place. It's a great system. We eliminate the old plagues and create some new ones of our own. Billions of dollars in research grants. Billions more in medical insurance. With all that at stake, it wouldn't surprise me if the bacteriological labs weren't cooking up some real goodies for the future on the positive feedback principle.'

Trix was aghast. 'I don't believe that,' she said faintly.

'They're doing all they can to find a cure for AIDS.'

'Sure they are,' Bernie agreed cheerfully. 'The drug companies have to eat. What I'm saying is that whenever we find a cure for one killer disease, nature obligingly comes up with another. If you believed in God or some kind of universal morality, whatever, you might be tempted to theorise that nature was trying to develop the ultimate disease to teach us a lesson.' He downed his wine in one long swallow and sucked at his beard. 'AIDS is the perfect example, where the body's built-in immune system is zapped. Beautiful! Now instead of dying of leukaemia we get wiped out by hives or dandruff or some goddam stupid thing. Don't you see? There's a kind of perfect universal symmetry to it.'

Wanda Jane added, 'Then there's all the shit in the air and water and in our food. It's everywhere. Don't you think so, Tom?'

She moved her eyes from her husband to Tom, next to him on the couch, and gazed at him steadily from under her fair eyelashes. Tom shrugged and gave a weak grin.

'Right on,' said Bernie, grabbing a fistful of roasted peanuts. 'We're creating more problems than we're solving. That's exactly what I'm saying.' He banged his hairy fist against his hairy mouth and chewed vigorously.

'I don't like to think about it,' said Trix, staring through her glasses at the empty fireplace. There was a husky quaver in her voice. Her lower lip was trembling. 'When I saw Danny yesterday I . . . I . . .'

'I guess you must be upset, honey,' said Wanda Jane with tremendous insight. 'I know how I'd feel if anything happened to Billie Jean or Sammy Ray. But maybe it's just a temporary thing, that kids get and grow out of, you know? Like asthma or eczema.'

Bernie cleared his throat and poured some more wine to fill the embarrassing silence broken only by Trix's stifled sobs. Frank was watching his wife blearily, his jaw resting in the palm of his hand. Tom closed his eyes.

'Come on now, honey, it's all right,' said Wanda Jane, going to Trix.

Frank and Bernie gazed at the wallpaper. Tom opened his eyes and looked at his watch and saw that it was a few minutes after ten o'clock.

Eventually Trix calmed herself sufficiently to go into the kitchen with Wanda Jane to get the supper, which she had prepared earlier. Bernie followed them and came back with another jug of wine.

He flopped down next to Tom, legs splayed out, his toes poking up through his sandals. He said, 'Believe you've got a steady girl now, Tom, so your mother tells me. Sorry to have missed her.'

'She had to go back to New York,' Tom said.

'Serious?'

Tom nodded. 'Sort of.' He glanced at his watch and said, 'I hate to do this, Bernie, but I've got somebody to see. Sorry we can't have a proper chat.'

Frank roused himself as Tom stood up. 'What the hell d'you mean, somebody to see? At this hour? Where are you going?' Strands of hair hung across his forehead and his eyes were slightly bloodshot.

Tom paused on his way to the kitchen.

'It isn't all that late. An old schoolfriend. He called earlier this evening and suggested we meet for a couple of drinks. Sorry about this,' Tom shrugged at Bernie, raising his eyebrows apologetically.

'You've got one helluva damn nerve!' Frank said, getting unsteadily to his feet. The tail of his shirt was hanging out. 'You *knew* we were having people round. Home-town friends not good enough any more, eh? Big college smart-ass, eh? We invite people round for a quiet evening and at the first opportunity you skedaddle. Can't wait to get out of the house, and your sister lying critically ill in hospital.'

Tom gazed at the carpet and tried to breathe evenly. Trix came into the room carrying a tray with plates of food on it, sandwiches, cold chicken and ham pie, and slices of quiche. She said wearily, 'Now what?'

Tom said, 'I'm sorry, Mom, I have to go out. I guess I should have told you before. See you later.'

He kissed his mother on the cheek and went round her to the door and stood aside for Wanda Jane to enter, who was bringing in a tray with the coffee things. Behind him Frank said, 'You've been a damn pain in the ass ever since you came home. I don't know why you bothered.' He jabbed the air with his finger. 'And I'll tell you, boy, I didn't like you sneaking round the house with that snooty girlfriend of yours. You must have thought we were prime suckers. Dumb hicks or something.'

'Oh please, Frank. Please,' said Trix. 'Don't start all that.' She looked utterly tired and worn out. 'Don't we have enough problems?'

Tom breathed out, turned on his heel and went upstairs. He used the bathroom with its broken door, and then went into his own room. He took all the cash he had, thirty-one dollars and some change, out of the desk drawer and put it in his pocket. He picked up his savings book and hesitated. There was a little less than two hundred dollars in his account. The guy – whoever he was – would want cash, not credit.

As he drove into town in his car, Tom kept hearing the man's low-pitched voice on the phone. He wouldn't reveal his identity over the phone, and Tom wasn't to say anything, not even to his parents; the man had insisted on that. The Chevvy bumped over the railroad tracks and Tom scanned the darkened side streets, looking for Wert Street. As he turned left into it and found a parking space a few doors along from the Blue Oyster Bar, Tom's head felt hot and his stomach chilled and shrunken, as if sucked dry by a vacuum pump.

It was no worse – and no better – a class of place than Tom had anticipated. A long dim hallway led from the front door, turned right-angles past a pay phone and a grimy wall hieroglyphed with felt-tip graffiti. It opened into a large smoky room with a central circular bar. There were three or four electronic games machines against the far wall and a pool table surrounded on three sides by wooden benches.

Tom stood at the bar, feeling conspicuous, and ordered a beer. The girl who brought it to him was about twenty, with uncombed mousy hair, her tee-shirt and jeans stretched tight and bulging in all the wrong places, and to add insult to injury she was cross eyed. Tom sat down on a stool and sipped his beer and tried not to stare at anyone. A man with red hair and a black guy were playing pool, and Tom would have laid good odds that at least three of the women at the bar were hookers. But he had no choice but to sit and wait. He didn't know the man's name, nor what he looked like. Over in the corner a very tall thin man with long straggling hair was leaning over and shouting obscenities into the face of a woman. No one paid any heed.

Five minutes went by, which seemed like thirty to Tom. He would have another beer, he decided, just one, and if nothing happened after that, leave. He wouldn't trust himself alone in this place later than eleven.

He was halfway through the second beer when a voice – the same rough, throaty voice, as if the vocal chords had been sandpapered – said in his ear, 'You on your own, Margison?' and when Tom turned sharply and nodded, the man jerked his head and said, 'Over here.'

Tom followed the man to a table on the opposite side of the bar. There was something vaguely familiar about the man, although Tom couldn't place him. He was wearing a dirty crumpled windcheater with a broken zip and a greasy baseball cap, the type with an elasticated band that left the top of the head bare. As he picked up his glass Tom saw that his fingernails were bitten to the quick.

The man grinned at Tom, at his frown of consternation, and sucked hard on a cigarette as if his life depended on it. He said, 'I was there yesterday at the hospital. You don't remember?

You was visiting your sister in Isolation. Your folks was there.' He was enjoying Tom's cloudy puzzled stare. 'You wasn't getting much out of that dried-up old witch, Dr Helms.'

'And neither were you,' said Tom, remembering the porter in the brown overalls.

The man seemed disappointed. 'You know who I am?'

Tom wasn't interested in massaging the man's ego. 'You said on the phone there was a cover-up in the hospital that had something to do with my sister. Are you going to tell me about it? Of course I'll pay you for any information – if it's genuine.'

'I go everywhere and I hear stuff,' the man said. 'Believe me.' He had a broad, Slavic face and a pug nose with hairs growing out of the nostrils. His skin was tanned and at the same time unhealthy looking, with large open pores. He breathed out cigarette smoke and said, 'I can get you in there.'

'In the hospital?' Tom said curiously. 'Why?'

'You want to see the records, don't you? I heard the old witch talking with one of the lab techs.' He jabbed the table with his bitten fingers, brown with nicotine stains. 'About the blood transfusion. They fucked up, man!'

'In what way?'

'Don't ask me, I don't understand all that technical mumbo-jumbo.' The man finished his drink and held up his glass. 'Mine's a bourbon on the rocks.'

Tom went to the bar and came back with a bourbon and a beer for himself. He now had less than thirty dollars on him. He said, 'Are you going to tell me your name?'

The man shrugged indifferently. 'Don't see why not. Ellis. I've worked at Bennett for three months. You can ask around.'

'I believe you,' Tom said. 'In any case it doesn't matter. How can you get me in? When?'

Ellis hunched forward and tugged at the peak of his cap. Tom noticed a tattoo of entwined hearts on his left forearm with the name 'Lizzie' in a scroll underneath. 'How much is it worth?' Ellis said gruffly.

Tom leaned back slightly and pushed his glasses on to his nose as he caught a whiff of the man's breath. 'You're selling, I'm buying,' he said. 'You say.'

'Fifty?'

Tom had feared several times that amount, but he merely nodded and said, 'All right. When?'

'Now.' Ellis grinned and jangled some keys in his pocket. 'Tonight.'

'Do you know where the records are kept? Can we get to them?'

'Fort Knox it ain't,' Ellis said, still grinning. 'I know all the ins and outs in that place.' His grin faded behind a pall of smoke. 'Money up front.'

Tom pretended to debate with himself and then said, 'Half now, half later.'

'Later when?'

'Later tonight when I've seen what I want to see.'

'Okay.' Ellis nodded slowly. 'Okay. We'll have another drink and then we'll go.'

'No,' Tom said. 'We'll go right now.'

They drove in Tom's car to Bennett Memorial, which was a short ride to the north of town, off Dellinger Drive, and parked about three hundred yards away, down an unlit and unpaved side road. Tom handed over the twenty-five dollars, thinking he would have to promise to mail Ellis the rest in a day or two. Too bad if Ellis kicked up a fuss; by then it would be too late.

They approached the hospital through the staff car park, which had fewer than a dozen cars parked in it. The two-storey building was mainly in darkness, with a light burning here and there. Tom followed Ellis down a short flight of concrete steps and heard a key grate in a lock. A metal door swung open and they were in the dimly lit basement, which had a low concrete ceiling and a maze of pipes, wrapped in wire and silver foil, along the walls. There was a subdued humming sound coming from somewhere. It was very humid. Ellis locked the door behind them.

Tom tried to remember the route they took but it was very confusing. In a tiny concrete cubby-hole Ellis opened a metal locker and threw a pair of brown overalls on to a chair.

'If anybody sees you and asks questions, just say you're maintenance,' Ellis said, sliding his legs into another pair of brown overalls.

'Do they work this late?' asked Tom, putting the overalls on.

'Somebody from maintenance is always on duty. But don't worry – we ain't going nowhere near the wards. The stuff you want is in the office next door to the Haematology lab.'

Ellis put his cigarette out and they went up to the next floor. Tom thought about Danny in the Isolation Room, alone, locked away. The beer had soured the emptiness in his stomach and he felt slightly nauseous. He hadn't given any thought as to what might happen if they were discovered and asked to explain their presence. It wouldn't look too good on his *curriculum vitae*, he supposed, whatever the explanation. In the next few minutes he forgot about that, and about Danny, as they walked through a series of open-plan offices, which were in total darkness. At last they came to a pair of double-doors, and Ellis fiddled with his bunch of keys before unlocking them. He leaned close to Tom's ear and said in his rasping whisper, 'The security guard checks these doors between twelve-thirty and one. That gives you an hour at least. Plenty of time.'

They passed through another large office, rows of desks with shrouded typewriters, and then into more identically confusing corridors. Tom was completely lost. He knew that without Ellis to guide him back, he'd just wander the hospital like a soul in purgatory.

Ellis again used his bunch of keys to gain access to the

Haematology Department (Tom could faintly read the sign in the darkness, and also the one underneath: 'No Entry to Unauthorised Persons') and led him past laboratory benches and dark glinting shapes of apparatus. 'In here,' Ellis said, speaking in his normal sandpaper voice, opening the middle one of three doors. He closed the door behind them, crossed to the window and lowered the venetian blind, and switched on the desk lamp.

The room was part office, part laboratory, benches scattered with equipment and a double sink underneath the window and three desks against one wall. There was a large green metal cabinet reaching almost to the ceiling with a heavy stainless steel handle and two calibrated gauges set in brass mountings. Ellis pointed a nicotined finger. Tom turned and saw a row of six filing cabinets.

In a movie, Tom thought, the file he was looking for would be missing, but this wasn't a movie and the file was where it should have been – in the 'M' section under 'Margison, Danielle Tracey.' Tom took the buff folder to the desk and opened it under the lamp. Ellis stood by the door, in shadow, smoking a cigarette.

The file contained three official-looking sheets, stapled together. The top one was pink, marked off into boxes, in which were typed the usual details of age, sex, blood group, and so on. There was also a 'Comments' box, which was disappointingly empty. The remaining two sheets were carbon copies of dockets registering the transfer of blood batch 'AB rhesus negative' from Winston-Salem to Bennett Memorial, and from the Haematology Department to the surgeon, Dr Ballard, both on the date when Danny had been admitted for the operation. Tom read through each sheet carefully and read them through a second time. If there was something fishy here, he couldn't spot it. These records seemed perfectly normal and above board. It crossed his mind that Ellis had invented the whole thing in order to make a fast easy fifty bucks. The asking price had struck Tom as suspiciously low.

Tom returned the file and shut the drawer. He stood looking round the room for a minute or two. Danny's blood group was one of the rarer ones, but that in itself didn't signify anything strange. He said, 'Are you sure you overheard Dr Helms talking about my sister's case? It wasn't somebody else? Another patient?'

Ellis leaned against the door, his arms folded, the cigarette hanging from the corner of his mouth. 'It was her. Why'd I call you otherwise?'

Tom had an idea why, but he said nothing.

He wandered round the room until he was standing in front of the large metal cabinet. The needle of one of the gauges registered -6°C. 'What's in here?' When Ellis shrugged Tom grasped the stainless steel handle and turned it. A fine puff of mist floated away as he pulled the heavy door open. The shelves were filled with plastic packs of blood. They were ranged in the various groups, O, A, B, and there, on the bottom shelf, two packs marked 'AB Rh Neg'.

The contents were a muddy brown in colour. Printed in white on the clear plastic it said: 'Whole Blood 450 ml'. And underneath:

COLLECTED AT: LA-7D
DATE BLED: JUNE 28

There was also a label stuck to the pack, on which was written in red block capitals: NOT TO BE USED – REFER DR HELMS.

Underneath someone had scrawled in black ballpoint, '*Suspected Contaminant*.'

Tom was frowning at this when Ellis said suddenly, 'Shit, what's that?'

A red light was winking on the side of the cabinet. Tom looked at the gauge and saw that the needle had risen to -2°C. Christ – an alarm device to warn if the temperature rose above a certain critical level. Tom slammed the door shut and locked the handle. At the same time Ellis had opened the outer door and was listening with his face screwed up against the cigarette smoke. Had the alarm sounded elsewhere?

Ellis's slitted eyes widened and became round and shiny with panic. Tom dived across the room and switched off the desk lamp and went after Ellis into the main laboratory. Through the dividing glass partitions he saw the lights in one of the distant offices go on.

Ellis dropped to his knees, below the level of the glass panels, and scurried on all fours between the lab benches. As Tom followed him he could hear doors being opened and closed. He said, 'For Christ's sake, put that cigarette out. They'll smell smoke.'

They reached the far side of the laboratory and Tom said, 'Now what? They'll have to come through here to get to the office.' He could hear footsteps marching closer.

Ellis was panting as if he'd scaled a cliff. 'We'll have to run for it,' he wheezed.

'Run?' Tom said. 'Run where?'

For an answer Ellis leapt up, jolted an iron rail with both arms stiffly outstretched, and crashed through a fire exit into the night. Tom didn't think twice. He dived after him.

8

'That isn't feasible,' said the red-headed receptionist. 'Not without an appointment. Dr Helms has a very busy schedule today.'

She gazed down her nose at the desk diary open in front of her. She tapped the page for emphasis with a silver ballpoint pen.

Tom shifted on to his other foot. 'Yes. I understand. But this is important. My sister –'

'Yes, I do know your sister is one of Dr Helms's patients,

Mr Margison. It's my job to know. However, there are rules and procedures. I would suggest that you call in and make an appointment to see Dr Helms.'

The receptionist regarded him with flat, professional eyes. The pen tapped out measured intervals of time, calmly, with great forbearance.

'Is Dr Helms in the building?'

'I can't really say whether she –'

'What *can* you say?' Tom interrupted rudely.

'I don't think we're going to achieve anything with that kind of attitude,' the receptionist reproved him, raising her pencilled eyebrows, 'are we now?'

'No,' Tom agreed. 'We're not.'

He turned away from the desk and started off along the corridor in the direction of Dr Helms's office.

'Mr Margison!' the receptionist shrilled behind him. '*Mr Margison*!'

All the corridors looked the same. It was confusing, having visited her office only once before. Tom walked along the pale green corridor, took a left, scanning the wooden signs sticking out at right-angles above the doors. Should he have turned left or right back there? Damn, he couldn't go back now . . . he brightened as he caught sight of the name he was looking for, halfway along.

Tom turned the knob without knocking and barged straight in.

Dr Helms, wearing the same drab cardigan, glanced up blankly from the file she was writing in. A frown creased her narrow forehead. She came erect in the chair and flipped the file shut. All the files, like the corridors, looked the same; Tom couldn't tell if it was Danny's file, and he couldn't read the name.

'This won't take five minutes of your time, Dr Helms,' Tom said, holding up one hand.

'It won't take *one* minute, young man.' A mottled pinky purple had erupted in her sallow cheeks. She stood up slowly and pointed with a firm, unwavering finger. 'Please leave this office at once!'

Tom shrugged. 'Sorry.'

'What?'

'No.'

'*No?*' said Dr Helms incredulously.

Tom half-turned at the thump of heavy masculine footsteps outside. They were sending in the heavy squad. Probably strap this dangerous maniac in a strait-jacket and toss him into a padded cell.

Tom said, 'We can discuss this quietly and reasonably, in private between ourselves, or I can go to the hospital authorities, the media, whatever it takes.'

'Discuss what, exactly?' inquired Dr Helms acidly.

Someone knocked on the door. A man's voice said, 'Dr Helms?'

'The blood you gave my sister.'

Dr Helms considered Tom with squinting eyes for a moment. 'It's all right,' she called out. 'I'll handle this. Thank you.'

Voices mumbled behind the door, and then footsteps withdrew.

Dr Helms seated herself and leaned back in the chair. She cleared her throat with a series of small coughs. 'Someone reported a disturbance in the Haematology lab last night. That was you, was it?'

'You wouldn't expect me to admit to it,' Tom said. He moved to a chair and sat down, facing her across the desk.

'I guess not. Do your parents know you're here?'

'I'm over twenty-one,' Tom said.

'So.' Dr Helms laced her thin hands together. 'What are you implying, Mr Margison? That this hospital has been in some way negligent in its treatment of your sister?'

'Has it?' asked Tom bluntly.

'You wouldn't expect me to admit to it, would you?' said Dr Helms, smiling faintly. Her smile faded. 'Let's get down to cases. I have a busy day ahead of me. You're concerned about the blood transfusion, is that it?'

Tom chose his words carefully. 'My information is that there may have been something wrong with the blood Danny was given, which is responsible for her condition.'

'What do you mean exactly, "wrong"?'

'Contaminated.'

'No. Absolutely not.'

'It wasn't contaminated?'

'I said no and I mean no.' Dr Helms met his stare full-on. 'The blood was subjected to the usual tests and found to be perfectly satisfactory.' Her small prim mouth tightened. 'We are professional medical people; what you are suggesting is improper behaviour or negligence of some kind on the part of the staff here. You do realise the seriousness of that?'

Tom didn't doubt for a moment that Dr Helms was a first-rate neurologist. What disturbed, what angered him, was the medical profession's inability to admit that occasionally it might be wrong: that it didn't have all the answers all of the time. No one expected them to be gods – they were human and fallible like everyone else – so why couldn't they let the mask slip once in a while?

'And yet, you don't seem to have any other explanation,' Tom said. He became aware that his fingers were digging into the upholstered arm of the chair. With an effort he relaxed them.

'I wouldn't go so far as to say that,' said Dr Helms coolly.

What would you go so far as to say? Tom thought. She hasn't a damn clue, he thought. All this is a smokescreen.

'Our investigation into the child's condition is still in progress. There doesn't appear to be any physiological damage as a result of the accident, so Dr Ballard informs me. But you must realise that coma brought about by shock to the nervous system is a difficult and delicate condition to treat. It isn't my job to make hasty judgements, nor in my nature, and I refuse to be bullied into making one.'

Tom stood up. This was the kind of empty, meaningless jargon he'd heard psychologists and sociologists use to explain something they didn't understand. And Jesus, people thought quantum physics an abstruse, imprecise subject! Compared to this it was a model of brevity and crystal-clear exposition.

'If you've no objection, I'd like to see Danny.'

'I do have an objection.'

'What does that mean?' Tom demanded.

'What I say. I don't wish you to see her at this present time.' Dr Helms smoothed the sleeves of her cardigan. 'We can't have people wandering in and out at all hours.' She pressed a button underneath the desk. 'I'll have someone show you out, Mr Margison.'

Tom took a pace or two towards the door and then stopped. Next time it would be the strait-jacket and the padded cell for sure.

He turned back. His face was pale and taut but under control.

'I'm not satisfied, Dr Helms. And I'm not going to let the matter rest here.'

Dr Helms had opened the file and bent her thin nose over it. She picked up her pen, and without looking up said, 'That's entirely your decision, of course. Though I'd be interested to know how you will be able to accuse this hospital of using contaminated blood without revealing how you came to that conclusion. Good day, Mr Margison.'

Someone tapped on the door. Tom opened it and went out.

Nurse Chang stood in the little hallway and pressed her snub nose to the glass panel. She couldn't understand where the light – a sort of dim luminescent glow – was coming from. That damn Margison kid again! Did she have a torch in bed with her? How had she come by it? In any case, the child was supposed to be under restraint – strict instructions from Dr Helms.

And if she wasn't, Nurse Chang would soon take care of that.

She found the right key on the bunch at her waist and unlocked the outer door of the Isolation Room. The only thing worse than night duty was night duty with a restless, troublesome patient. She had just settled into the Jackie Collins novel and was sipping her tea, the midnight hour slipping peacefully by, when she had been disturbed and made to get up. However, this wouldn't take long, she thought, closing the inner door behind her.

'What's happening in here?'

She leaned across to press the cord switch above the bed and all the strength went out of her fingers. The room remained in darkness and yet Nurse Chang could plainly see the Margison kid's eyes staring up at her. She withdrew her hand and stood quite still by the side of the bed, hearing a voice say, *Thank you for your help, nurse. You've been most kind and considerate.*

'That's okay,' said Nurse Chang mechanically. 'Think nothing of it,' and pulled the leather thong back to release the buckle. She could feel her own hands working at the other straps, even though she couldn't see them. All she could see were the Margison kid's eyes.

'You know where my clothes are kept,' Danny said, sitting up in one smooth slow movement. She swung her legs out of bed.

Nurse Chang nodded and backed away. She went to the closet and came back. Danny dressed herself and pulled on her sneakers, then went to the window and turned her head to one side, as if listening. Reflected in the pane of glass, Nurse Chang could see two darkly glowing liquid orbs, illuminated as if from within.

'There are more of us,' Danny said, turning from the window. 'At first there were only a few. Their voices were very faint. I could hardly hear what they were saying. Now they're so clear and loud – listen!'

Nurse Chang listened to a light stirring of breeze and a car going along Dellinger Drive.

'Can you hear them?'

'Why yes,' said Nurse Chang.

Danny smiled and pulled open the inner door. She went through the narrow cubicle and pushed open the outer door, Nurse Chang following behind.

'What's that?' Danny asked, pointing at a red light that was winking on a panel next to the desk.

'Both doors have been opened at once.'

'Hm. How come I didn't know about that?' Danny seemed rather vexed with herself. She frowned at the red light, screwing up her face, and it went out. 'Why don't you sit down, nurse?'

Nurse Chang sat down and looked across the desk at the Margison kid in a lightweight cotton windcheater, tee-shirt and jeans, standing there with a sweet smile on her lips. The kid's face was quite pale and wan, her dark curly hair ruffled, glossy ringlets hanging over her forehead. Her eyes were large and round and bright.

'What's that you're reading?'

Nurse Chang picked up the book to show the cover, and Danny nodded and hummed to herself for a moment or two.

Then she said abruptly, 'Where do you keep the medication?'

Nurse Chang opened a wide flat drawer by the side of her in which were several rows of shallow paper cups containing tablets and capsules, the early morning medication for the patients in Isolation.

'You haven't finished your tea,' Danny said.

Nurse Chang looked at the cooling liquid in the glass in its metal stand. Her hand went forward hesitantly to pick it up.

'Take your pills first, nurse.'

Nurse Chang emptied a paper cup into her mouth and reached for the glass, and Danny said, 'No, you must take your medication first,' and Nurse Chang emptied the second paper cup into her mouth.

'Go on,' Danny said, and waited and watched as the nurse picked up the paper cups one by one until the drawer was empty and her mouth was full.

'You can have your tea now,' Danny said, smiling.

Nurse Chang did as she was told and drank her tea.

Part two
Incubation

9

The driver paid at the cash desk, stuffed a dollar tip into the paper cup, and went out into the mild evening air, pungent with diesel fumes.

Neon signs on a fretwork of metal struts stood sharply outlined against a sky streaked with pink and magenta. Thirty or more rigs, black looming hulks with silvery exhaust pipes jutting upwards, were parked several rows deep on the pitted, oil-smeared concrete. Somewhere out of sight an engine grunted and set up a reverberating roar. Beyond the peeling ranch-style fence and strip of brownish grass that marked the perimeter of the truck stop, headlights formed a blurred river of light on the eastbound highway.

The reflections of those same headlights smeared themselves along the fifty foot length of the silvery tanker, with its gleaming stainless steel bumpers, fretted aluminium catwalk and ladder, and the triangular phosphorescent red sign at the rear warning of LPG – HIGHLY FLAMMABLE, with a tongue of orange flame to emphasise the point.

Approaching through the dark maze of silent trucks, the driver sucked in a last lungful of smoke and dropped the butt, grinding it under his toe. He took his job seriously and he took that red sign seriously too. He'd seen Jimmy Cagney in *White Heat* often enough not to become sloppy and indifferent.

The same went for his strict no-booze rule. One beer led to five and before he knew it he'd be leaning muzzily over the wheel, headlights splintering his eyes, and dragging forty-two tons of highly inflammable gas over the edge of a viaduct somewhere on the Ohio freeway.

His chest felt tight and his breath wheezed like an asthmatic's. He'd tried but couldn't kick the habit. It wasn't the nicotine so much, he reckoned, as the boredom. That strip of blacktop unwinding in front of you hour after hour like an endless conveyor belt was enough to make you smash your head through the windscreen. Smokes marked off the passing time, like ten-minute signposts through the day.

He was reaching up for the recessed handle, one foot on the studded plate, when he saw the small, bulky shape, in black silhouette, next to the huge boxlike wheelguard – inches smaller than the wheel itself, outlined in blue light from the neon signs above, a halo around the dark tousled head.

'What's up, kid? Are you lost?'

He couldn't make out whether it was a boy or girl until the shape moved forward a pace or two and a glancing sliver of light from a passing truck illuminated the round, chubby features of a boy, maybe nine or ten, with dark-brown curly hair hanging to his collar. He was wearing a blue or black windcheater over a check shirt, though the rest of him was in shadow.

'I need to hitch a ride. Will you take me?'

The driver smoothed his moustache thoughtfully. 'Where do you live?' he asked, squinting down at the pale round blob of the face.

'Oh, not too far from here,' the boy said quite openly. 'I have to get to Richmond. You'll take me, won't you, sir?'

'Richmond, Virginia?' the driver said. He shook his head. 'Sorry, that's about two hundred and fifty miles out of my way. I'm going to Pittsburgh. I –' He hesitated and then said, more sharply than he intended, 'What's your name, kid?'

'Jimmy Yerke.'

The boy watched him silently, outlined in blue neon.

'Why do you want to go to Richmond?'

'They want me to go.'

'They? Who's "they"?'

'Some friends. Shall I get in the truck?'

The driver was thinking hard. He was thinking that there might be money in this. If he turned the boy over to the police there could be a reward. The boy looked harmless enough, and besides, he could handle a kid this size, no sweat. Take him as far as Springfield and drive straight into the local police station – what could the boy do about it? Nothing. Not a thing. A grown man weighing over two hundred pounds and a fat little kid with pansy curly hair? His name in the papers. The guy who caught a runaway. He definitely smelled money in it somewhere.

'Sure,' he said. 'Climb up.'

When they were settled in the high cab, the boy at the far side of the long bench seat, legs dangling, the driver said, 'I can take you as far as Springfield. How's that? You'll have to hitch another ride from there, head for Charleston and then across country.' Play him along. Keep him sweet as pie till they made Springfield. 'That okay?'

'Yes,' Jimmy said. 'That's great. Thank you, sir.'

Polite little bastard, anyway.

The silver tanker pulled on to Interstate 70. As soon as it had picked up speed and was cruising at a steady sixty miles per hour, the driver lit a Marlboro and eased back into the padded seat, one hand on the wheel. He glanced across. The instrument panel threw a greenish wash of light upwards, forming dark green shadows in the boy's eye-sockets and along his protruding upper lip. He was looking straight ahead through the windscreen, without any expression, his chubby hands resting on his knees, where the blue denim had worn pale.

A few spits of rain hit the windscreen, and minutes later it was driving down hard into the headlights. The driver switched on the wipers, which swept horizontal swathes through the rain with rubbery squeals.

'What about your folks, Jimmy?' the driver asked, sucking smoke into his lungs. 'Won't they wonder where you are, be worried about you?'

'I guess not.' The boy smiled.

'Is that why you're running away? They mad at you about something?'

'I'm not running away.'

'So why are you leaving?'

'My friends are waiting for me.'

'Right. Sure. You said.' The driver nodded, head leant back, eyes on the slick-wet highway in the slanting rain. 'Who are these friends, you wanna tell me?'

Jimmy answered, but the words were lost under the roar and rumble of the engine.

'What?'

'I won't know until I get there. But I'll know them when I see them.'

What kind of dumb answer was that? 'You trying to say they're friends of yours and you ain't even met them?' The driver twisted his head round to look at him across the cab. Jimmy turned to look at him also. The green light made his face look waxy, masklike.

'I hear them and they hear me,' Jimmy said.

'What do you mean, hear them? On the phone, you mean?'

'I hear their voices all the time. I can hear them now. Every second they're getting nearer and louder. The more voices there are, the stronger we are. If you could hear them you'd know.'

Voices? Jesus, the driver thought.

If I could hear them I'd be as nutty as you.

He shook out a cigarette and lit it from the butt of the old one. The sign for the Ohio state line went by; they should make Springfield in a couple of hours, by eleven at the latest. As far as the driver was concerned, that wouldn't be a minute too soon.

Voices. Jesus.

The driver crumpled the empty cigarette pack and opened another, his fourth that day. Usually he didn't get through more than three. Maybe it was the kid making him jittery. Hard to say why, because Jimmy hadn't moved or spoken in the past hour. Whenever the driver glanced across at him he was simply sitting there with a slight frown on his face, as if thinking or concentrating all his attention on something. Or listening to those fucking voices, the driver thought with grim humour.

The rain had stopped and the traffic thinned out. There

hadn't been a sign for the past thirty or forty minutes. He couldn't recall driving along this narrow section of Interstate 70 before – it was more like a regular two-lane highway than a major freeway. Maybe there'd been a diversion sign back there he hadn't noticed. It was easy to fall into a kind of trance on these long hauls, when the automatic part of your brain took over the actual driving. Before now he'd taken the rig right through the centre of a city and afterwards couldn't remember a single thing about it – whether he'd driven through stop lights, up one-way streets, or what.

He felt a bit trance-like now. A bit distant, like when you had a bad cold. So he was startled when Jimmy said, 'There's the sign for Springfield. See it? You should take that route, it's quicker.'

Jimmy Yerke was looking at the driver's hands as he said this, and obediently the hands turned the wheel, swinging the tanker on to the lane marked 'Charleston'. The floodlit state marker for West Virginia swept by.

'You know what I'm gonna do, don't you, soon as we hit Springfield?' the driver said, lighting a cigarette.

'Tell me,' Jimmy said, watching the driver's hands.

'Turn you over to the cops.' The driver laughed wheezily. He started coughing, choked, hawked up phlegm and spat out of the window.

'We'll see what the cops have to say. What's the betting they're looking for you, huh?'

'You could be right,' Jimmy said.

'You bet I'm right. Knew the minute I laid eyes on you. Said to myself, "That's a runaway." Then when you told me that cock-and-bull story about visiting friends in Richmond, I knew for sure. I got kids of my own, see. Read 'em like a book.'

'Three boys,' Jimmy said.

'Right. Youngest about your age too.'

Thirty minutes later Jimmy said, 'Take the Interstate 77, that's the best way –'

'I know, I *know*,' the driver said. 'How long you think I've been doing this haul? Listen, don't get fresh with me, kid.' He lit a cigarette and sucked in a deep lungful of smoke. 'I can't wait to see the expression on the cops' faces when I hand you over in Springfield.' He laughed to himself and started coughing and choking. He couldn't get his breath. 'Jesus Christ,' he wheezed chestily. 'I gotta switch brands.'

Jimmy looked at the clock in the centre of the dashboard. It was three-fifteen a.m. Ahead of them the lanes began to diverge.

Left lane Interstate 77 north to Parkersburg.

Centre lane downtown Charleston.

Right lane Interstate 77 south for Bluefield and Roanoke.

He looked at the driver's hands on the wheel. The wheel began to turn and the tanker crossed into the right-hand lane. Jimmy sat back in his seat and seemed to relax.

At ten minutes past six, the sky ahead of them tinted in varying shades of pink and grey, they had passed through Roanoke and Lynchburg in the state of Virginia. The driver was desperately tired, having driven through the night without sleep, but he was determined to make Springfield or bust.

The kid was harmless enough, he supposed. Maybe he was running away from an unhappy home – parents who had mistreated him. Maybe he'd misjudged the kid after all, shouldn't turn him over . . .

But it was no good, he was too tired to think straight. And where the hell was Springfield?

He lit another cigarette.

Traffic was building up, mostly cars, as the early commuters joined the freeway from the suburbs. Soon both lanes were heavily congested and the driver had to slacken speed. Not far to go now, he thought, relieved, seeing a sign for the city limits. He was thinking dreamily of ham and eggs and coffee. He felt very tired. Damn near exhausted. Either he was getting old or the haul had been longer than he had reckoned on.

Jimmy was sitting up, paying attention. He'd spotted the sign saying 'Richmond City Limits' too. He was watching the road carefully as if looking for something. After a few minutes he said, 'You're out of cigarettes. Why not pull over and get some?'

He was right, the driver saw, shaking the pack – smoked his way through five packs. No wonder his mouth tasted like a grizzly's armpit. But he needed his smokes, couldn't concentrate without them.

'There's a place!' Jimmy called out, pointing.

It was a garage, with a small diner in a separate wooden building, set back behind bushes and a low redbrick wall. There were a few cars and pickups outside but no trucks; some of these smaller places didn't like heavy rigs pulling in, they took up too much parking space. This wouldn't take more than a couple of minutes – two packs of Marlboro and he'd be on his way.

In fact it was a tight squeeze getting the tanker in at all. Even with power-steering the driver had to work hard, hauling on the wheel with both hands and swinging the tanker round in a circle to avoid the parked vehicles.

The driver jumped down, his head swimming with fatigue. He ran, or rather staggered, into the diner, and came back almost immediately, stuffing a pack of Marlboro into his breast pocket and ripping open another pack with trembling fingers. He'd never wanted a cigarette so bad in his life. He jammed one between his lips and lit up before climbing back into the cab. The first deep drag made spots dance before his eyes.

Billowing blue smoke, the tanker pulled out into the flow of traffic, causing a bus to brake and several horns to blare. The driver cursed them, working up savagely through the gears and stepping on the gas, eyes screwed up against the writhing cigarette smoke. First thing, he thought, was to dump this kid at the nearest police station and then get something to eat. Or maybe he would sleep and then eat. Jesus, he felt totally wiped out. He'd done the run down from Chicago to Springfield a hundred times before without feeling like this. What the hell was the matter with him?

Two hundred yards farther on, the tanker laboured as it climbed the arched concrete bridge spanning the James River which widened a few miles downstream to become the bay area of Newport News, Hampton and Norfolk.

Leaning forward, both hands gripping the wheel, the driver blinked to clear the dark spots swirling across the pale streaked sky. Smoke dribbled from his nostrils and stung his eyes, bringing tears. He began to cough. His chest heaved as he fought for breath. But instead of air he sucked in more smoke from the cigarette stuck in the corner of his mouth. He choked and his vision blurred, the shimmering spots coagulating to form a dark red wall in front of his eyes.

Springfield, he thought. *Police ham and eggs sleep coffee cigarette runaway kid sleep*

Chest heaving, eyes stinging, mucus spitting from his nostrils, the driver clawed with both hands at his throat, trying to clear his air passages. His breath had seized up in a solid lump. He was drowning in phlegm.

Time to switch brands

Unguided and out of control, the tanker veered from the inside lane and scraped the concrete parapet of the bridge in a shower of red and blue sparks. Under the momentum of its full load of liquefied petroleum gas, it ploughed through the parapet and followed a graceful silvery trajectory in the direction of the James River two hundred feet below. Halfway down the gas ignited. A ball of white light tinged with purple erupted in mid-air. The shock wave lifted the nearside lane of traffic and tossed it across the highway. The sound of the explosion shattered the morning air like a gigantic door slamming, loud enough to hurt the eardrums.

From where he stood in the parking lot of the diner, Jimmy Yerke could see the plume of dark oily smoke rising up like a lazily drifting question mark. It obscured the broken parapet of the bridge, hid from view the chaos of mangled traffic on the bridge itself.

Jimmy stood listening for a moment, but not to the sound of tearing metal and breaking glass or the shriek of horns. The voices here were much louder and clearer. Very near in fact. Close.

Zipping up his windcheater, he walked steadily across the parking lot and dropped down into the gully at the rear of the diner. Soon he was lost to human sight among the brush and the thickly laden branches of the maple trees.

10

Tom mooched about the house, sat on the back patio for a while, then went into the kitchen with the notion of getting himself something to eat. He made a ham sandwich with mustard and chewed it slowly, mouthful by mouthful, as if swallowing cardboard. He couldn't figure out why, but sitting at the round pine table made him uneasy. In fact the kitchen itself, he realised, seemed to evoke unpleasant memories, though he was damned if he could think what they were. He'd always liked the house – liked it since the day they'd moved into it when he was thirteen; it was permeated with pleasant associations for him . . . and yet there was something about the kitchen that gave him goose bumps.

Oddly, even though it was broad daylight, the sunshine spilling in through the two windows, he kept picturing in his mind's eye how it looked at night, with the big tasselled shade throwing its cone of light over the table and picking out gleams and highlights on the smooth laminated surfaces and the wooden cupboard doors. It wasn't the mental switch from day to night that unsettled him, but the image of the kitchen itself at night, with the silent sleeping house all around. Was it Danny's absence, his grief at losing her, that was causing this strange creepy feeling, a slight hallucination perhaps? No, Tom thought, if anything, the reverse. Not Danny's absence. Her presence. In this ghostly night-time kitchen, which was like a photographic overlay on top of the daytime kitchen, Danny sat across the table from him eating hungrily. Her eyes held a peculiar vivid light, as if they were emitting a glow that was almost luminescent. She was smiling as she ate, a fixed, manic smile without humour, without warmth, without life.

A smile of cold malice and pitiless revenge.

Tom came back to himself, to the bright sunlit kitchen, his heart hammering in his chest. It was a dream, of course it was a dream, but a dream he had lived through before, sometime in the past.

He went to the sink and drank a glass of water straight down. There was cold sweat on the back of his neck and prickling his shoulderblades, making his shirt rasp uncomfortably against his skin. He stood at the sink, trying to order his thoughts. Part of his mind, that of the objective scientist, was attempting to observe and analyse the reactions of his other, human, emotional self. This other Tom Margison, he noted, was very frightened. Not at all used to daytime hallucinations and reliving past experiences he may never have had.

Tom threw the remains of the sandwich away, washed the plate and glass and put them on the plastic wire tray to drain. In the living-room he switched on the TV, just to hear the sound of human voices. The voices were fraught and high-pitched with emotion: the heroine's son was dying of cancer, her husband was having an affair with her best friend, and her mother had been critically injured in an automobile accident. Otherwise it was life as normal, the heroine battling bravely on through her tears and being comforted by a dishy doctor with dark quizzical eyebrows and a sculpted hairstyle.

After the drama came the early evening news.

The police were still looking and coming up with nothing.

The story had moved up to become the second item of home news after the power workers' threatened strike.

Tom sat watching it with the glazed fascination of a rabbit hypnotised by a snake. There were snapshot photographs of all the missing children, including one of Danny that Frank had given to the police. It had been taken at a beach barbecue last summer at Lake LeGrand. She was wearing a green tee-shirt and skimpy yellow shorts, a peaked cap advertising a local supermarket squashing her dark glossy curls. She was very brown, a glimmer of white teeth exposed in a shy grin.

Tom hadn't seen the photograph before. It had caught her at that moment of transition when the child, unknown to itself, is living through the terminal stages of childhood.

'The most baffling aspect of the whole affair,' the grey-haired newscaster was saying, 'is how nine of these children, all under the age of twelve, and from perfectly normal homes and families, can evade roadblocks and all-points alerts by state and highway police forces right across the country. All have vanished after acts of violence against parents, teachers and other adults. Connie Tyler reports.'

A serious-looking young woman was standing in front of a small courthouse building with fluted stone pillars. There was a statue of a confederate soldier on a plinth, casting a dusty black shadow across a wedge of green lawn.

'Laurel, Mississippi, is yet another small town, seemingly picked at random, where the mysterious disappearance of a young child is causing anguish, fear and suspicion. The fact that a child has disappeared is, of course, tragic for any community at any time. But when the circumstances of the disappearance are identical to a pattern emerging right across the country you can taste the hysteria in the air like nerve-gas. It's as though Laurel was quietly minding its own business when it was touched and tainted by the bubonic plague.'

The scene changed to a single-storey house with a red tile roof, the camera panning along the sun-dappled street to pick up Connie Tyler in the gravel driveway.

'Until just over a week ago, Karen Swanson lived here with her parents and six-year-old brother Tim. A bright, happy ten-year-old, popular with the other kids and liked by the neighbours, with above-average grades in school, Karen was somehow transformed in a matter of days from a sweet, lovable kid into a morose and destructive child, given to black moods and violent tantrums.'

The camera cut to a bedroom which had the appearance of being wrecked by a tornado. The bedcovers were torn to shreds, the dressing-table mirror smashed, broken toys scattered everywhere.

'This is the scene that greeted Barbara Swanson, Karen's mother, on her return home from a shopping trip. The minder, seventeen-year-old Debbie Marino from across the street, had fled, nursing cuts and bruises. Kid brother Tim was found cowering in the basement, while Karen herself was in a state that Mrs Swanson describes as "a zombie-like trance".

'Precisely what happened after that is uncertain,' Connie Tyler went on, speaking to the camera once more. 'All that Mrs Swanson can recall is picking up the phone to call the doctor, then waking up in hospital with concussion and a broken collar-bone. And Karen hasn't been seen from that day to this.'

There followed a couple of interviews with bemused neighbours and one with the local police chief, which was merely a repetition of what police chiefs all across the country had been saying for the past week: that despite house-to-house questioning, road blocks, public appeals, and a dragline search of ponds, rivers and reservoirs, there was no sign of Karen Swanson and not a single clue as to her whereabouts.

'Under normal circumstances we would suspect foul play,' the chief said, 'but with a rash of such disappearances, from North Carolina to California, and all with the same details, all bets are off. It's almost enough to make you start believing in the conspiracy theory.'

Connie Tyler's filmed report came to an end and the grey-haired presenter in the studio was interviewing a public health official on a monitor linked to Washington. As Tom expected, the responses amounted to nothing more than the usual bland reassurances that the Department of Health and Human Services was deeply concerned, that it had set up a special inquiry, and so on. When asked about the three children who had been apprehended, he said that they had been sent to 'a secure psychiatric unit', the identity of which he wasn't at liberty to divulge. There they would undergo clinical and psychological tests to determine the cause of their erratic anti-social behaviour.

These people really know how to stonewall, Tom thought bitterly. He switched off before the interview was concluded.

An hour or so later, about seven o'clock, Bernie Gooch came round, his long straggly hair bleached in streaks by sun and salt water: he and Wanda Jane and the kids had just got back from ten days on the Florida Keys. He wore his shirt open to the waist, showing off his bronzed chest and collection of beads and coral necklaces, though Tom felt that the effect was spoiled by the swelling gut tucked into his tight jeans.

They'd first heard of the disappearances on a bar-room TV in the last few days of their vacation. 'Man, we literally could not believe it! Wanda Jane freaked out – I mean, broke up completely. Danny and those other kids – just vanishing into thin air like that. Incredible!'

'It's up to twelve kids now,' Tom said. 'It was on the early evening news.'

Bernie shook his head and followed Tom through to the kitchen. Tom took a couple of beers from the fridge and handed one to Bernie.

'They've caught three of them. Got them before they could escape. They're in a clinic somewhere for observation and tests. Of course we're not told where.'

'How's your mother taking it? Wanda Jane tried to call her. Where are they, by the way?'

'She couldn't face it. Reporters and TV phoning day and night, hammering on the door. A pack of sharks closing in for the kill. Frank's taken her to stay with his mother for a few days. She was on the point of cracking up.'

'Where's that – Columbus?'

'A few miles north. Marysville.'

Bernie nodded and sucked at the fringes of his moustache. He said, 'There's a lone shark still cruising around out there.'

'What?'

'Some guy sitting in a car down the street.' Bernie jerked his head. 'He took a damn good look at me when I drove by.'

'The first two or three days the phone never stopped ringing. We had a television crew camped at the end of the driveway. Dad nearly waded in and assaulted them.'

They went outside and stood drinking their beer on the back porch. Tom leaned against the wall, looking at the shed in the far corner of the yard, remembering the morning when Karel had found him rooting through the mildewed stacks of science magazines and assorted juvenile junk. That seemed a lifetime ago. In fact not his, Tom Margison's, personal past at all, but somebody else's, a different person entirely.

'Did you see the item about those religious freaks down in Georgia?' Bernie asked him, scratching his armpit through the wide-open slit. 'The Beatifical Church of Christ's Holy Love, or some such. Naturally they're claiming this as retribution from the Almighty for following in the ways of the ungodly. "The sins of the fathers" type argument. We've been led astray and this is Divine Intervention to bring us back to the Chosen Path.' He patted his stomach and belched.

'So that's why the police can't spot them when they float through road blocks,' Tom said. 'They're spirited about by the Holy Ghost. How very convenient.'

'You have to admit, Tom, it is damn weird.'

'Yes,' Tom nodded. 'You could call it that, I suppose.' He sipped his beer.

'What do you suppose happened to them – you know, to make them act in that way?'

Tom looked at him silently for a moment. Bernie Gooch was having an affair with Stella Feinstein. The thought came to him, just hit him without warning. Tom knew it for a fact, yet didn't know how he knew it. He shrugged and said, 'I don't know, Bernie. I keep wondering whether . . . well, Danny was given a blood transfusion. Maybe that has something to do with it.'

'How do you mean?' Bernie said, staring at Tom. 'Some kind of bug?'

'You're the biologist, you tell me.'

Bernie scuffed his worn sneakers on the red-tile patio steps while he considered this. 'That might explain the violence, the aggressive behaviour,' he said eventually. 'If it affected the pituitary gland, which is a kind of regulatory mechanism, or even the hypothalamus in the brain. Without these controls – say they're malfunctioning, blown a fuse, whatever – the brain and nervous system just run amok. There's a medical term for it . . .' Bernie frowned through his tangle of sun-bleached hair. "Disinhibition", I think. The normal inhibiting control factors are absent and the entire system goes haywire.'

'Can that happen?'

'Oh yeah, sure. Happens to most life processes. In plants the metabolism speeds up, growth is unchecked. The plant literally grows itself to death.'

'That's in plants,' Tom said. 'What about humans?'

'You'd have to ask a quack about that, or a clinical psychologist. I guess – I'm not absolutely sure – something similar takes place.'

Bernie must have realised the stark implications of this, for he added quickly and with a glassy grin, 'Hey now, don't take my word for it – I'm kinda talking out of turn here. Not my field at all.' He drained the can to the last drop and, in a nervous reflex, crumpled it in his hairy fist.

Tom thought he knew how the can felt.

The long dragging evenings were the worst. Tom couldn't concentrate for more than a few minutes on a book, and if he put a record on he hardly heard a note. That only left the mindless drone of television to fill the blank hours.

Compulsively he found himself watching the late-night news. The fourth or fifth item concerned another family homicide, the Yerkes of Muncie, Indiana. Father and mother killed and their ten-year-old son Jimmy disappeared. Give or take a phrase or two, and the change of setting, the filmed report was identical to all the rest. Road blocks had been set up, bus and railroad stations watched, empty houses searched, and still no sign.

The story was now being run under the tag, 'Children of Violence', with a stark black-and-white drawing of a child with staring eyes and a tight-lipped grimace. This sickened Tom and made him mad. For a minute he thought seriously of ringing up the network and making a complaint, then realised that that in itself – as he was the brother of one of the missing children – would make a juicy item for tomorrow's papers and newscasts.

Tom went up to his room and put a tape into the machine. He put it in without looking and was glad when it turned out to be Billie Holiday singing 'Strange Fruit', one of his favourite tracks.

Tom undressed and got into bed and slid immediately into a heavy, drugged sleep. He started to dream. He was walking along a grey passage. He watched himself walk along it, his footsteps echoing and hollow. There were many doors with letters and numbers on them, which made him think he was in a military establishment of some kind. There was the loud, persistent hum of air conditioning. It seemed very real – so real that Tom could smell the mustiness of this subterranean concrete passage and feel the dampness on his skin.

He awoke and sat up in bed. The house was silent and still

all around him, a pressing silence that was almost palpable. His skin still felt cold and damp from the grey passage.

Strangely, although Danny hadn't appeared in his dream, she was somehow, in a way Tom couldn't fathom, connected with it. Her presence lay everywhere about him, not only in his dream but here in the silent, dark house. As near to him as his own heartbeat.

Tom threw back the covers and got out of bed. He was shivering. He put on his gown and went to the door and opened it slowly as if expecting to find someone on the other side. There was no one there. He started to breathe out, and then stopped.

Across the carpeted landing there was a light showing under the door of Danny's room.

For a minute Tom did nothing. She had returned in the middle of the night. Danny's come home, Tom thought.

He sniffed. There was a strong smell which after a few moments he identified as oil paint and linseed.

Tom stepped lightly forward, turned the knob and gently pushed the door open. The pool of light from the bedside lamp shone over the unruffled counterpane, the one that his mother had made, patterned with tiny blue forget-me-nots. The light cascaded softly over the matching blue carpet, faded and dimmed into the corners, making deeper, darker shadows. Tom saw now, almost with relief, that he'd been wrong. There was no one there: the room was empty.

Something gleamed and caught his eye. It was the shiny cover of the Van Gogh book, on the shelf next to a row of Roald Dahl paperbacks and other picture books. His father must have collected it, with Danny's other few possessions, from the hospital.

Tom sat on the bed and flipped through the pages. He felt that he ought to be looking for something but didn't know what. What had Danny seen in these paintings? They were brooding and rather morbid for an eleven-year-old. He looked at *The Road with Cypresses and Star*, painted towards the end of the artist's life when he was going quietly insane in the monastery near Saint-Remy. The moon and stars were made up of vague blotches with rippling haloes spreading out over a sombre countryside. Two figures, labourers, trudged home after working in the fields; behind them a horse and cart slid down a road as if swept along on a fast-flowing river.

Once again Tom smelled oil paint and linseed, even stronger than before. He laid the book aside and stood up. There was a small cupboard, fairly high up, above the built-in closet. In order to reach it Danny must have had to stand on a chair. Tom opened it and the smell poured over him, pungent, throat-catching.

There were three small paintings, about twenty inches square, propped at an angle. Tom took them down and laid them on the bed. He rubbed his fingers together. They were sticky with wet paint.

One was of blood-red surf bubbling up on to a beach, with a forest of thin pale arms reaching out above the spray – waving? drowning? Another showed a long grey tunnel with many doors, the light reflecting on damp concrete walls. The third was of a lake under a harsh sun that Van Gogh himself might have painted, its brassy waves of heat and light beating down on to the black surface of the water. And on the shore of the black lake stood a wooden house with a verandah, set against a backdrop of dense forest and distant mountains.

Two of these images were frighteningly familiar to Tom. They were of his own dreams – dreams he hadn't revealed to anyone. The brassy sun burning down on the black lake he was less sure of. Danny must have painted these in the few days after Karel's departure and before she had the attack in the bathroom.

Tom studied the paintings spread out on the bed and tried to think the thing through clearly and logically.

The trouble was, there was nothing either clear or logical about any of it. The inescapable fact was that here, freshly painted, were dreams he had had, which he had described to no one, depicted in pictures he had never seen before.

Danny had painted his dreams.

And no matter how hard Tom thought about it and tried to twist it round to fit the circumstances, it still didn't make any kind of rational sense.

How had he known the paintings were in the cupboard above the closet in the first place? Wouldn't Trix have discovered them before now, and if so, commented on the fact?

That was assuming the paintings were there to be discovered.

And how come the paint was still wet? How long did it take oils to dry? A week at the most? These might have been painted yesterday.

Tom went downstairs and got some newspapers from the living-room. He came back up, wrapped the paintings carefully and carried them into his room across the landing. He made space on the shelf behind his LP collection and stashed them there. He wasn't sure why he did this, but he was certain he didn't want his parents to see them.

11

It was called the Quiet Room. It contained a plain wooden table and a hard straight-backed chair. No need for bars on the windows because there were no windows. The walls were quilted with thick padding and the floor was covered from corner to corner with a gymnasium mat. Light came from a bulb in the middle of the ceiling enclosed in a toughened glass globe. A one-way observation panel allowed the medical staff to keep watch on the patient. The set-up was familiar to Jacob Brinkmann from those Hollywood movies which featured Gestapo interrogation techniques. All it lacked was a metal chair with straps and a device for administering electric shocks.

Brinkmann had arrived at the Golden Vale Psychiatric Unit in eastern Pennsylvania only hours before, and still hadn't got over his sense of stupefaction at the sight of the place. High concrete walls, tiny barred windows, electronically operated gates; it reminded him more of a blockhouse or a prison than a hospital facility.

Neither had the unit's director, the young, tall and tanned Dr Robert Fabius, inspired in Brinkmann much hope that the regime inside Golden Vale would be any different from its forbidding external appearance. Fabius wore an immaculate, tailored white coat (when Brinkmann wore one it looked crumpled the minute he put it on over his pear-shaped figure) with a fancy bleeper in the top pocket. His light brown moustache might have been trimmed by a laser beam.

'This is Donna,' Helen Murphy murmured in Brinkmann's ear as the nine-year-old child was led in by a female orderly, who then went out and locked the door which formed part of the padded wall. 'Here's her case sheet.'

There was a hooded lamp on a flexible metal stalk in front of Brinkmann. He bent forward into its cone of light, adjusted his heavy horn-rimmed spectacles, and held the paper at an angle to see better. He was aware of quiet breathing all around him. The cubicle accommodated six seats in two rows of three: Brinkmann sat in the middle seat, with Helen Murphy on his right and Dr Weiss on his left, while Fabius and the English psychologist, Dr Sampson, sat in the row behind.

'Good God,' said Brinkmann involuntarily.

It was hard, practically impossible, to believe.

At three a.m., Donna Perera of Jonesboro, Arkansas, had taken her father's large-bore hunting rifle down from the rack, loaded it, gone through to the bedroom and shot both her parents. She had reloaded the heavy weapon (what did those things weigh?) and shot her grandmother, who was asleep in another room. When neighbours arrived to investigate the horrendous noise, she despatched them too. She had spared her younger sister, Lucy, aged five, whom police found cowering under the kitchen table.

During the course of that warm and otherwise peaceful night, this demure, sweet-looking child had thus killed five people.

Donna herself was apprehended by a fluke – a police car happened to be patrolling the neighbourhood, arrived within minutes, and came across Donna changing out of her night-dress into her day clothes.

At first, the police assumed that an intruder had broken into the house and committed the atrocity. They were quite certain about that until an eye-witness showed up – the teen-age son of the neighbours, who had seen his parents murdered through the screen door and fled. Forensic evidence then proved that the only two sets of prints on the rifle belonged to Donna and the dead Mr Perera.

Brinkmann felt a cold hard lump, like something he'd eaten and hadn't digested, in the pit of his stomach. What did they have here? A new breed of monster?

Watching the girl, who was standing motionless in the middle of the Quiet Room, staring at nothing, Brinkmann said, 'I don't see any signs of behavioural abnormality. She doesn't appear restless or excitable. Did you try her with the Conners Rating Scale?'

This was the standard clinical test, measured on a rating of one to thirty, to determine the degree of loss of control exhibited by the child. The condition usually peaked between the ages of four and seven, after which, in most cases, the child gradually grew out of it.

'We haven't run any tests,' Fabius said. 'All we've done is to give amphetamines and keep them in a secure environment.'

Brinkmann turned his head in the narrow booth and stared at him.

'You've administered drugs? To all five of them?'

'We had to control them,' Fabius said, a shade defensively.

In the hooded lamplight his lean tanned face seemed carved out of mahogany. 'They're criminally dangerous. That's why they were sent here. You have the case sheets in front of you.'

'Couldn't you simply have restrained them?' Brinkmann asked. 'They have the strength of children, not sumo wrestlers. I'm sure you have enough secure environments at Golden Vale to contain five children.'

'In my opinion, Dr Fabius was acting in the best interests of all concerned,' said Helen Murphy, Dr Fabius's assistant. She was a thin, intense woman in her forties, with red hair, a strident manner and, Brinkmann suspected, an Irish temper to match.

'You are missing the point,' little Dr Weiss chipped in. He bounced up and down in his seat. 'If I may say so. If the children have been given medication of *any* kind it will obscure the true nature of the condition. Our observations are worthless. You see?' He threw out his hand towards the girl in the room. 'Her responses are dulled. She is a vegetable. What can we deduce from this? Nothing!'

'I gave instructions that the same procedure was to apply to these patients as to all our cases,' Fabius said tightly.

'You treat all the children with medication?' Brinkmann said.

'Yes we do.'

'What's the youngest patient you have here?'

'We take them from the age of two,' Fabius said.

Brinkmann turned back to the front. He said nothing.

His attention was caught by the expression on Donna Perera's face. Her eyes were large and round, shining, and they were looking straight at him, as if she could actually see him through the one-way panel. Of course she couldn't, he told himself; nevertheless, the illusion was extremely disturbing. Almost as if, Brinkmann was thinking, she was spying on them, instead of the other way round.

* * *

Afterwards, the team gathered in the conference room, which was in effect a full-scale lecture theatre, with closed-circuit TV, video screens and computer terminal. Golden Vale was better equipped than Brinkmann's own research facility back in Indianapolis, which made him wonder, rather sourly, where the money came from.

'I think you've met everyone,' Fabius said, looking round.

Brinkmann looked pointedly at a newcomer, a young man standing diffidently apart from the rest. Fabius beckoned him forward with a wave of his manicured hand. It transpired that Dr Peter Krill of Cornell Medical College was representing the Department of Health and Human Services.

Brinkmann shook hands, blinking through the thick lenses which gave him a heavy-lidded and misleadingly sleepy appearance. 'You'll know Professor Browne then?'

'He's my head of department,' Peter Krill nodded.

'Maurice and I are old friends. How is he? Is he well?'

'Well, yes, I guess so,' Krill grinned shyly. 'Professor Browne doesn't confide in junior members of the faculty,' he added disarmingly.

Brinkmann chuckled. He rather liked the look of Dr Krill. A pleasant young man, late twenties or early thirties, he guessed, with a relaxed manner and an easy grin.

Weiss plucked at his elbow.

'I have long admired your work,' he said eagerly, with a trace of a foreign accent. 'You gave the keynote speech to the International Psychiatric Conference in Belgrade two years ago. Excellent! It is a tremendous pleasure and honour to work with you, Dr Brinkmann!'

A somewhat premature sentiment, Brinkmann thought, who didn't believe in diagnosis by committee. If they weren't careful, with so many specialists around, they might come up with twenty causes and as many cures.

'What's your theory?' Helen Murphy asked him. She looked up at him with the frown which seemed to be a permanent fixture, her eyebrows knitted tightly above the thin ridge of her nose.

'Theory?'

'About what's been happening – to these children,' she said, as if Brinkmann was being deliberately obtuse. 'Fifteen up to now, and there could be others we don't know about.'

'No, no theory,' he said gently. 'I've always found it best to examine the patient first.'

'But there are hundreds of case studies of neurotic behaviour in children. From your experience in child psychology I thought you might have formulated a hypothesis to explain –'

'We are not dealing with case studies, but with children,' Brinkmann said firmly.

'Of course, this media attention hasn't helped,' Fabius said. 'Some parents won't have reported erratic behaviour in their offspring because they're scared. It'll have frightened them into keeping quiet and shielding children who ought to be reported.'

'That's understandable, surely. One would expect that,' Brinkmann said.

Helen Murphy's frown became doubtful.

'You don't agree?' Brinkmann asked her.

'I should have thought it the parents' duty to seek specialist help under the circumstances. Children who behave aggressively, anti-socially, should be dealt with in the proper way. That's why we're here. That's what we're trained to do.'

There wasn't a tremor of doubt. She was rock-solid in her belief. Whereas Brinkmann wasn't sure of anything where psychiatry was concerned.

He said, 'Perhaps, I don't know, some parents can treat their kids better than we can. A home environment, love, affection, caring. Respect for their individual needs. All those are in pretty short supply in most institutions.'

From the expression on her face it seemed that Brinkmann had committed the ultimate heresy.

Fabius caught Brinkmann's eye and politely indicated the large swivel-chair at the head of the long oval table, but Brinkmann smiled and shook his head, squeezing himself into the rather small chair nearest him. He was here to listen, not to pontificate.

'Dr Sampson,' Fabius said when they were all seated. 'Could I begin with you, now that we've seen the five patients?'

Sampson, dressed in English tweeds, was sending up clouds of blue smoke from a curly pipe. He tilted his bald head, revealing a scrawny neck inside a stiff white collar. He had a reedy, nasal squeak of a voice.

'My first concern is to establish a parental-offspring role model which might give us an indication of why these children behaved as they did. If we could isolate certain key traumas in early childhood, common to them all, I think we'd be making real progress.'

'What kind of traumatic event or events are we looking for?' asked Fabius intently. He clasped his lean brown hands and raised one quizzical eyebrow. Helen Murphy gazed at him with a dreamy, far-away look. 'Jealousy of the transsexual parent? Sibling rivalry? That the kind of thing you have in mind?'

'Frankly, I don't know,' Sampson admitted. 'My own casework has dealt with adults whose childhood traumas manifested themselves in problems in later life. They were, so to speak, on a long fuse. These children are on a very short fuse indeed – as if they'd short-circuited. That's fairly obvious, I should have thought.'

Weiss, whose field was biochemical genetics, was already getting excited.

'How can you say obvious?' he demanded, waving his hands. 'Not obvious to me. Not at all. What if there is brain damage? Or the child was subjected to toxic contamination during pregnancy? Or viral infection which doesn't show itself in physical symptoms? Or damage to the nervous system caused by some unknown biochemical agent – lead, for example?'

Fabius said plausibly, 'The medical records don't indicate

any of those conditions, Dr Weiss. We're looking for a *psychological* basis to this problem; that seems to be generally agreed.'

'Not by me,' Weiss objected. 'Of course the records don't show any of these things – there was no reason before to look for them or make a note of them.' He shook his head vigorously. 'Let us not leap to conclusions, especially the wrong ones.'

Sampson clamped his teeth on his pipe and puffed out more smoke. Brinkmann was doodling on the pad in front of him. He seemed bored. On the pad he had written:

Hereditary?
Social?
Environmental?
X –???

'You're a geneticist, aren't you, Dr Weiss?' Helen Murphy said.

Weiss nodded, somewhat guardedly, as if her question had contained a veiled slur on his professional standing.

'Might I suggest that you're not as familiar with psychological trauma and its effects as Dr Fabius? And indeed, our distinguished English colleague, Dr Sampson?'

'That is true,' said Weiss courteously, not at all ruffled. 'I am making a plea, a pitch, you might say, for open-mindedness. Certainly *I* don't know the cause of these horrific acts of violence perpetrated by such young children. It may be, as Dr Sampson proposes, that it has its basis in psychological trauma. But who can say? We must examine all possibilities.'

Brinkmann resisted the urge to applaud the little man. To his dismay, this was shaping up into a battle of the Behaviourists versus the Rest. There was a danger of the actual clinical truth getting lost somewhere in no-man's-land.

'I think that all of us here have open minds,' Helen Murphy said. She smiled brightly and nervously at everyone. 'The question is, which approach is most likely to bring results. And there's a time factor. Let's not forget that.'

In Brinkmann's ears this had the ring of a schoolmarm calling an unruly class to order. Stop talking. Sit up straight. Pay attention.

Fabius said, 'Dr Brinkmann?'

Brinkmann stirred himself, blinked and smiled. 'Yes?'

'As our foremost expert in child psychology, can you suggest an approach that might yield positive results?'

'Well,' Brinkmann said, rubbing the side of his stubbly cheek. Had he forgotten to shave? Again? 'It looks like we have quite a problem on our hands. Have the children been thoroughly examined? I mean, physically? Theories are all very well, of course, but a bit out of place until we know the full medical history.'

He saw Weiss's look of gratitude and relief: a comrade waving to him from another dugout on this side of the barbed-wire.

'Dr Krill is looking after that end of things,' Fabius said shortly. 'What about it, Peter?'

'I've done some preliminary tests on three of the children.' Krill shuffled some papers in front of him. 'Donna Perera, Craig Holley, and Stuart Brangham – the other two have only just arrived, so there hasn't been time. That's Johnnie Bromke and Clare Sachs.' He cleared his throat. 'So far there's nothing to indicate a common history of allergies or viral infections.'

Dr Sampson grunted and nodded to himself as he puffed on his pipe, looking rather smug.

'Neither – as far as we know – have any of the children suffered brain damage. Indeed, they're all pretty bright, with above-average IQs.'

Sampson glanced towards Fabius with a ghost of a smile.

'I see,' Brinkmann nodded slowly. 'No news is good news, I suppose. No conclusions then?'

'Well – nothing definite . . .' Krill seemed to hesitate.

Brinkmann looked at him with interest. 'You've found something?'

The young doctor scratched his ear. 'Two out of the first three files I looked at showed recent blood transfusions –'

Fabius said sharply, 'This hasn't been brought to my attention, Peter. A ratio that high could be significant.'

'Three cases is too small a sample, Dr Fabius,' said Krill. 'I need to examine the medical records of all the other reported cases. So if you don't mind, I prefer to keep my hunches to myself before then.'

'I'm sure we all look forward to that with great anticipation,' said Fabius, smoothing his tie. He glanced at Helen Murphy. 'The opinion of a medical doctor is always welcome, even in matters of psychiatry.'

Krill flushed slightly. Fabius might be a hot-shot behaviourist, Brinkmann thought, but he certainly wouldn't win any prizes at handling people. And why did he have the feeling, in his bones, that they were merely skating over the surface of the problem? This wasn't a matter of psychological disturbance pure and simple. There was something much deeper – much stranger – that had yet to come to the surface. He didn't know what it might be. But he knew he would recognise it the minute he saw it.

The long line of cars edged slowly forward into the funnel of black-and-yellow striped barriers. As each car reached the head of the line, two officers of the Highway Patrol stepped forward, one on either side, and scrutinised the occupants. When they were satisfied, they waved the car on and waited for the next, legs braced apart, thumbs hooked into their gunbelts. They had been engaged in this tedious occupation without a break for almost two hours, and they were good and bored.

The broad-shouldered, rather paunchy black man at the wheel of the Chevrolet wound the window down and stuck his head out. He asked to know what the trouble was.

'We're checking all vehicles on the Interstate. There's a search on for those kids.'

'Which kids?'

'Don't you watch TV? Those pint-size psychotic bastards who're killing their parents and going on the rampage. They're getting around somehow, though nobody can figure out how.'

'Oh, *them*,' the driver said, and glanced across at his wife. 'Sure, we've heard about them.'

The officer leaned forward to check out the car: typical family group, Dad and Mom in the front, cute little boy in the back. He said, 'Take care. Don't pick up any hitch-hikers – especially kids.' He banged on the roof and the car pulled away through the neck of the funnel on to the open road.

'They give me the creeps,' the woman said with a slight shudder.

'Who? The cops?' asked her husband.

'Those children. I don't know what the world's coming to, I'm sure. It said in the paper that their diet's to blame. Too much junk food. Too many chemicals. They don't get fed good wholesome food no more.'

Her husband grinned and glanced in the mirror at the boy in the back.

'She's got a bee in her bonnet about all them preservatives they put in food. You know, that monosodium stuff. Reads the label of every can before she'll buy it.' He chuckled in his throat. 'Still don't help her lose weight, though.'

The man was pretty big but his wife was bigger. Her face was round and shiny, the flesh sagging in folds from her jawline. She scowled across at her husband, as if he'd revealed a family secret to a stranger.

'You married?' the husband asked into the mirror.

The boy shook his head.

'I guess you're too young for that. Plenty of time. Don't rush it, boy. Sow your oats. Have a good time first, then you'll have something to look back on.'

His wife shot him another fierce look, but he just kept on grinning. He leaned forward to squint short-sightedly at the confusing array of signs overhead, directing traffic south on

Interstate 81 and east to Charlottesville, Richmond, and Norfolk.

'Take 64,' the boy said in a flat, neutral voice, and the man flicked the indicator and switched lanes.

'Hey,' the woman said, 'wait a second. That's east, ain't it?'

'Right,' the man nodded. 'East.'

'I thought –'

'Honey, the last time we followed your directions, remember where we ended up? Halfway to Orlando. We know the way, don't we, soldier?'

'Yes sir,' the boy said.

The woman frowned but said nothing.

'I did two years in Nam, did I tell you that?' the man said. 'Sixty-eight to seventy. Made sergeant. The jungle, you can keep it. Roll it up and take it away.'

'You told me,' the boy said. 'Second exit here. Keep left.'

'Phnom Penh, asshole of the universe. I was stationed there for six months. But what you couldn't buy there!' The man brushed his hand over his short wiry greying hair. He looked wistful for a moment. 'And it was all out on the street – I tell you, boy, grass, H, coke, angel dust – easier to buy than a pack of Marlboro.'

The woman sat silently, her face set and grim.

'Saw the evacuation of the embassy on TV. Saw a couple of guys I knew. When they pulled the plug, that was just one helluva mess. I cried.'

'It was bad,' the boy agreed, sitting with his arms folded in the middle of the back seat, watching the man's face in the mirror. The sun was directly behind them now, and the boy's face was dark, only the whites of his eyes showing.

'You're too young to remember,' said the driver. 'You'd be only a kid then. What unit you with?'

'The 23rd Armoured Corps.'

'You guys got it easy. I was with forward supplies. Infantry support. What they took, *we* took. What's your name?'

'Selwyn Porter Brown.'

'Where you from?'

'New Jersey.'

'Your unit based down here?'

'That's right.'

The man sucked reflectively at his lower lip. 'Don't recall the 23rd Armoured. Supplied most units, but not them.' He laughed suddenly. 'Armoured divisions had a tough time in Nam. Fifty yards off the road and they were up to their sumps in swamp. We lost more tanks there than in the whole of World War Two.'

'Can't you ever forget it?' his wife said irritably. 'It was fifteen years ago, John. This young man won't ever see a war like that again.'

'Don't bet on it. With this guy in the White House we'll be invading Central America first chance we get. Ain't that so, Selwyn?'

'I don't know,' the boy said. 'You're against that?'

'Yes I am,' the man said vehemently. 'It's their business what they do down there, not ours. We should get out and stay out. Nothing to do with us.'

'You're right, for a change,' said his wife. 'So let's drop it.' She glanced over her shoulder and looked quickly to the front again. Her fat round face had a worried, preoccupied look.

The woman had plenty to worry her, though what worried her most was that she found it hard to focus on any of it.

The signs bothered her. Richmond. Virginia Beach. Chesapeake. They were heading east, she was sure, when they should have been heading south into North Carolina. But John said it was okay, and he certainly seemed happy enough about it. Maybe she was mistaken.

Another thing that bothered her was the soldier. When and where had they picked him up? She couldn't remember. Had he been with them that morning when they left Washington DC? But she couldn't even remember leaving Washington DC, that was the damnedest part.

Something else, harder to pin down. Something so stupid

and ridiculous and – she had to admit it, crazy – that she tried not to think of it.

It was this. She kept hallucinating that the soldier wasn't a soldier at all, but a boy. About nine, ten years old. Wearing a blue-and-white check shirt and a dark green v-neck sweater. It struck her that for an hallucination it was amazingly, frighteningly precise.

This strange vision didn't happen all the time – just occasionally, like a second ago, when she glimpsed him from the corner of her eye, a little black kid sitting stiffly on the back seat. Then when she turned for a proper look, he was a soldier again, in a regular tan uniform and forage cap, the insignia on his collar winking in dull gleams. Even then she couldn't make out his face clearly. The sun was in her eyes and his face was a dark shadowy blur.

What she did notice was that the soldier's eyes never left the rear-view mirror. There was an air of tense concentration about him. He seemed to be watching her husband in the mirror with a purposeful fixed intensity that made the hairs on the back of her neck stand up.

John didn't appear to be aware of any of this. He drove with a vague, empty grin on his face, his belly lapping the wheel. Get him jawing about the army and reminiscing about the old days and he was happy. Just as the boy (soldier! of course he was a soldier, fool!) had got him to do.

The soldier had kept quiet most of the time, hadn't volunteered any information about himself, hadn't even spoken unless spoken to. Some young men were shy. They weren't all loudmouths.

He left them just inside the Richmond town limits, at the intersection of Interstates 64 and 95. He said, 'This'll do. Pull over,' and hopped out almost before the car had stopped rolling. He didn't offer to shake hands or even bother to wave.

This was taking shyness a mite too far, the woman thought.

As the door slammed, her husband accelerated away. He was still wearing his vague, happy grin.

'Nice kid,' he said, picking up speed.

'What?' his wife said, staring, as if he'd jabbed her with a pin.

'That young fella. Nice and polite. Shy I'd say. They're not all loudmouths.'

The woman nodded, and involuntarily half-turned to glance back, but then decided against it. Let's just say they'd given a lift to a shy, polite young soldier and leave it at that.

12

The bar was dimly lit, with pools of light and smoky shadowy corners, and about half full. The quiet murmur of conversation and clink of glass made a pleasant backdrop to a taped jazz piano that sounded to Tom like Oscar Peterson.

Tom sat on a stool at the bar and ordered Scotch and soda. After a moment or two he glanced round, but there was nobody he knew. Not surprising, really, considering he had not lived here for five years. He wondered idly what it must be like to remain in the small town you were born and grew up in. For some, he supposed, it must be cosy and reassuring, to be surrounded by the familiar sights, the same people, family, relations, friends. But in all honesty he couldn't say that he'd missed the town. His studies had more than filled any void there might have been – the satisfaction and excitement of being involved in an important field of scientific discovery. For Tom, particle physics was the most fascinating scientific endeavour of the twentieth century.

Was this where Frank had missed out? He must have nurtured lofty ambitions once – certainly above teaching fifth-grade chemistry to a bunch of indifferent stiffs. At some point – and quite recently too, Tom suspected – the realisation must have struck home that what he had was all he was going to get. And maybe seeing his son climbing the academic ladder had rubbed salt into the wound. His father had been dumped on: an average career in an average school in an average town, with nothing to look forward to except an inscribed gold watch and a retirement plan at the end of it.

His parents had returned the previous evening, bringing with them an atmosphere you could cut with a knife. Tom had sat with them watching the news bulletins, aware of Trix's white face and clenched hands on the arm of the chair. Frank had stalked around the house like a pale, gaunt ghost. One evening like that had been enough for Tom; he had to get out of that deathly atmosphere before something snapped, probably him.

'Things are pretty bad in Nicaragua?' said a voice to his right, a husky female voice. Tom didn't realise the question was addressed to him and looked over his shoulder along the bar before he turned back to the small slim woman with dark flowing shoulder-length hair. She wore a green dress of some shiny material, maybe even silk, and a collection of thin metal bracelets jangled on her bare brown arm as she raised her glass.

'I thought for the minute you were solving the Central America problem. You were concentrating hard enough,' the woman said in her husky voice, which sounded natural and uncontrived. She had green cat's eyes, and a cat's meditative lazy stare.

Tom had never been picked up in a bar before. He found the experience rather pleasant, indeed flattering.

He pushed his glasses more firmly on to his nose and gave her a quizzical smile.

The woman raised the flat palm of her free hand towards him. 'I'm Bernice. Hi.'

'Ah – hello,' said Tom. 'Tom.'

'Where are you from? Not Torrence.'

'My folks live here.'

'You on a visit?' When Tom nodded, she leaned her head

back and gazed at him shrewdly with slitted green eyes, as if pondering something. 'I wouldn't say you were a student because you don't have that college boy look. Am I right?'

'Kind of,' said Tom. 'I'm a post-graduate.'

'Uh-huh,' Bernice said, as if she'd been proved right about something. 'What do you do? I mean what are you studying?'

'Quantum Physics,' Tom said.

This immediately erased the lazy glint in Bernice's eyes. She blinked several times and said, 'Huh?' leaning closer on the bar.

'The study of particles and energy waves,' Tom said rather desperately. This wasn't the kind of chat that went very far with casual pick-ups, he realised. What ought they to be talking about? The weather? Movies? Game shows?

'Really?' said Bernice, catching his sober tone. Pressed against the wooden trim of the bar, her breasts welled up above the neckline of her dress. She was an attractive woman, a few years either side of thirty.

'I'm a singer,' she said.

Tom showed appropriate surprise.

'I got a recording contract with Index in Memphis. Blues. You like Blues?'

'Yes I do,' said Tom truthfully. 'Where are you working now?'

'Restaurant on North Styers,' Bernice said. 'Waitressing,' she added huskily and rather despondently. 'But I'm saving up to go to New Orleans, to try and get me a job. Singing, I mean.'

'Well, good luck,' said Tom, finishing his drink.

'No need to leave. It's early,' Bernice said.

Tom looked at his watch. It was nearly midnight. 'I have to go. It was nice meeting you.' He got down from the stool, glancing round the bar. At first he didn't know why he felt so edgy; then he noticed a man watching him from a booth near the back. All sorts of things went through Tom's mind. That this was a set-up, with Bernice as bait, and the man was waiting for Tom to bite. But the man was dressed neatly and conservatively in a business suit, and didn't look anything like Tom's idea of a pimp or con-man. Tom stared and the man turned away, quite casually, stroking a small prissy moustache.

'I have my own place,' Bernice said somewhat archly. 'Two-room apartment above a store on Dellview.'

'That's great,' Tom said feebly. 'Well, take care.' He discovered he was perspiring lightly. He backed away and waved his fingers at her. 'See you around.'

Bernice watched him leave, her green eyes resuming their lazy catlike stare.

Outside, Tom shivered in the warm night air. Bernie Gooch had remarked on a car parked down the street near the house and Tom had noticed it too. Yesterday, while talking to Professor Ward DeVoss at MIT, Tom kept hearing strange clicks on the line. Now this – a man in a bar taking an especial interest in him. Were these fragments as apparently unconnected as they seemed, or pieces of a larger puzzle?

When Tom arrived home he had a strange sense of *déjà vu*. The house was in darkness, just as it had been the night he returned from taking Karel to the airport.

Tom walked through the living-room and paused on the bottom step, his hand on the wooden banister. To his right was the short corridor leading to Frank's den. Consciously and deliberately, Tom hadn't looked to see if there was a light under the door. He didn't know why, but he felt frightened to look. Why should a light under the door of Frank's den frighten him? The other time when he had gone to look the den had been empty, hadn't it?

Tom took another step up the stairs and then, against his will, turned his head. There was a light under the door.

For a minute Tom did nothing. He could feel his heart beating very rapidly. What the hell was the matter with him? Probably Frank had forgotten to switch the light off, that was all. Tom walked the few steps to the door, and as he put his hand on the knob, the knob twisted by itself in his sweaty palm and the door opened. Tom swallowed and stepped back involuntarily.

'Well look here now. Look who it is. Come on in. What have you been up to?'

Dressed in his blue robe, slippers on his bare feet, Frank stood holding the edge of the door, swaying slightly.

His father beckoned him in and shut the door. The room smelled strongly of cigar smoke. The bottle of Chivas Regal, less than a quarter full, had made a pattern of interconnecting circles on the paper-strewn desk. A glass was on top of the silent blank monitor.

'Thought I heard somebody sneaking around,' Frank said.

'I wasn't sneaking,' Tom said. 'I was on my way to bed.'

'Not sneaking,' Frank said in a slurred voice, speaking to an unseen third party. He made a loud noise, halfway between a hiccup and a sharp implosion of breath. 'Just tom-catting round town in the middle of the night, huh?'

'I went out for a drink,' Tom said.

'Did you? Did you really now?' Again he addressed the invisible third presence. 'Says he had to go out for a drink. Hear that?'

'Is Mom all right?'

'Sure she's all right! Five Mogadon and she's out for the count. Sleeping like a baby. Her daughter's disappeared and her son's sneaking around town in the middle of the night. But otherwise couldn't be better. Fine.'

Tom said, 'I think I'll go to bed.' He was still standing by the door, and as he turned to leave Frank said, 'Have you been fooling with this fucking computer?'

It was the snarl rather than the oath that shocked Tom. He stood there, rooted to the spot, his heart beating heavily in his chest. He could see Danny sitting in the swivel chair, her dangling feet not touching the floor. He struggled to remember where the memory came from, when he had seen her in the den, but he couldn't. It remained elusively on the blurry edge of his mind.

Tom said, 'No, I haven't been near it.' He watched his father pick up the glass in his long fingers and clunk the neck of the bottle against the rim. Frank set the bottle down with a thump and recovered his balance like a man teetering on a tightrope. He drank.

'What's the matter with the computer?' asked Tom.

'Crashed. Fucked. I dunno,' Frank said, wiping his mouth with the back of his hand. 'Must've crashed. Keeps telling me "File Full, File Full", when I know it isn't. How can it be full when I haven't put the stuff in there?' he demanded.

'I don't know,' Tom said.

'You don't know,' Frank mimicked unpleasantly, sneering at him. 'Jesus, get this. The big noise from MIT doesn't know something! Don't tell Professor DeVoss that or he'll have you fired. Oh! – I was forgetting – Professor DeVoss thinks the sun shines out of your asshole. You're his brightest star pupil, isn't that right?'

Tom felt very tired and suddenly he hated his father. He wanted out. What was Frank blaming him for? For what had happened to Danny? For his own frustrations, balked opportunities? Something hit Tom out of the blue, dropped on him like a bombshell. He said, 'Did you say anything to Karel while she was here?'

Frank unwound himself and attempted to look Tom straight in the eye. He pulled his robe across his narrow chest as if asserting a parental right. 'I told her I didn't like her screwing under my roof.' He waved the glass about. 'You and her sneaking around in the middle of the night. You didn't fool me. I heard you. I heard the bed springs creaking.' He sucked at the empty glass. 'I heard you,' he repeated lamely.

'Did you now,' Tom said, in a quiet, seething fury. He had never been so angry with anyone before. He wanted to smash his father in his drunken maudlin face. 'Bully for you, Dad. What a pal.' He opened his mouth to say more, but didn't, or couldn't, and instead wrenched the door open and went out.

* * *

His stomach was knotted so tightly that Tom found it impossible to sleep. He lay in the darkness, his eyes closed, his mind adrift in a swirling grey fog.

For a while he drifted in the grey blankness, and it seemed that his body weighed nothing, was free of earthly restraints and capable of moving at will anywhere he desired. The feeling was so real, and so authentic, that he wasn't surprised, on opening his eyes, to find himself looking down on his body sleeping peacefully on the bed . . . while he was somewhere above, hovering high up in the corner of the room.

Tom didn't feel frightened, because he knew that he must be dreaming. In fact it was exhilarating to leave his sleeping body where it lay and have the freedom to go anywhere he liked. He rose higher – through the ceiling, above the shingles, watching the house get smaller and smaller, surrounded by all the other houses up on The Heights, the lights of the town spread below him until they too grew faint and misty with distance and vanished.

The fog closed in. It enveloped him. He could smell its dampness and feel its coolness on his skin.

A door opened in the grey fog. A small slender figure beckoned to him. Tom followed it. It had short dark glossy hair. It had dark liquid eyes in a pale, oval face. The face looked up at him. It was smiling.

It was Danny.

She took his hand and led him through the doorway into a grey corridor. The damp concrete walls were painted with symbols and numerals and arrows in faded yellow; the doors were covered with strange markings. There was a loud hum of air conditioning.

Danny put her finger to her lips. Tom looked round but there was no one there.

I knew it, Danny said. *I knew I could reach you.* She was smiling. *Did you like my pictures? I painted them for you.*

'I hid them,' Tom said. 'I thought they might upset Mom.'

I know. I think you're right. She wouldn't understand.

'*I* don't understand.'

Danny looked sad. *I hoped you might, Tom. We need someone we can trust.*

'You trust me, don't you?'

It's the others. She glanced round fearfully. *If they knew I was speaking to you . . .*

'Are you a prisoner here? Can't you leave?'

None of us can leave the group. We're strong together. We must stay together always.

'There must be another way, Danny,' Tom said. There was an icy spear of sweat sliding down his back. He was shivering and sweating with fear.

Danny's face was wavering in front of him. It swelled up like a bloated balloon and then shrank away. He was losing it.

'Let me help you!' he shouted desperately, the words thick and muffled in his mouth.

Her face came close, inches away from his, though when she spoke her voice was a distant, hollow whisper.

The others will hear. I must leave.

'Tell me what to do – tell me how I can help you!'

You'll know where to find us, Tom.

'Where?' he cried. 'Where are you?'

You'll know . . .

The small slender silhouette was framed in the doorway; the door began to close.

'DANNY!'

Then the door shut completely on the figure and the small bleak rooms and damp gloomy corridors and Tom was once again alone in the swirling grey mist. But he had seen Danny – he had spoken to her.

She was alive!

13

The child made a sucking noise with his lower lip and gazed vacantly at the ceiling. He had a round, cherubic face, wide blue eyes, and sun-bleached hair parted in the centre and falling in long strands over his ears.

'Miss Teale's okay,' he said at last, indifferently. 'She lets us read *Return of the Jedi* in class.'

'You like Miss Teale then?'

'Sure.'

'If you like Miss T-Teale, why did you do what you d-did to her?' Brinkmann said, feeling his stammer return as it tended to when he was under stress. He glanced down at the tape cassette deck to make sure the green light was on. How much left? Ten minutes?

'What was that?'

'You know very well what you did, Craig. You t-told me you remembered it very clearly,' Brinkmann said patiently. He leaned forward, elbows on knees, so that his face was level with that of the nine-year-old child, who was sitting in the armchair across the low table, legs dangling halfway to the floor. 'What I want to know is, why. We don't hurt people we like.'

'Can I go to the bathroom?'

'You went to the bathroom before we started. Are you going to tell me why you did it?'

Craig made a popping noise with his lips, like water gurgling out of a bottle. He twisted his head and looked out of the window. The bars divided the sky into long blue stripes. Brinkmann waited.

'Somebody told me to, I guess,' Craig said, swinging his legs.

'Who t-told you to?'

'I forget.'

He met Brinkmann's steady gaze, blue eyes unsmiling,

then twisted his head towards the window. It seemed to Brinkmann that he was listening to something. No, not *to* something – *for* something. But no sound could get in or out of the soundproofed room.

Brinkmann wondered if his colleagues were finding it as difficult to make progress with the other children as he was with Craig Holley. In the adjacent interviewing rooms five private sessions were being carried out: Weiss with Stuart Brangham, Fabius with Donna Perera, Sampson with Johnnie Bromke and Helen Murphy with Clare Sachs. They were to compare notes later and discuss further treatment – though the little Brinkmann had gleaned from this morning's session would make a pretty threadbare contribution, he felt. Craig Holley was a master of the art of evasion, as slippery as an eel.

Brinkmann sighed gently and tried again.

'Will you answer my question?'

Craig looked at him, his head on one side. 'Do you wear false teeth?'

'No.'

'Why do you say t-t-told then?'

'Craig,' Brinkmann said quietly. 'Answer my question, please.'

'Which one?'

'Who told you to hurt Miss T-T-Teale?' Damn it.

Craig shrugged and said, 'What's so special about her? People get hurt on TV all the time. They get wasted, shot, blown up . . .' He mimed a vast explosion with his hands and mimicked the gritty sound in the back of his throat, complete with echoing reverberations and falling debris. He smiled glassily at Brinkmann.

'You stabbed Miss Teale in the chest because you saw it on TV. Is that what you're t-telling me?'

'Yeah.'

'You expect me to believe that?'

Craig swung his legs and yawned.

'Do you imitate everything you see on TV?'

'Some stuff. Depends. Ralph brought home these video tapes. Horny stuff.'

'Who is Ralph?'

'My brother. He's fourteen. He's got magazines too. Under his bed. Wrapped up in a sleeping-bag. Swedish.'

'Do your parents know you watch these tapes and look at these magazines?'

Craig swung his legs idly to and fro. His knees were brown, with small pale scars where he'd fallen or bumped himself. 'Hell, no,' he said. 'They'd have a blue fit. Mom especially. She doesn't even know about Dad's.'

'Dad's what?' Brinkmann asked.

'My Dad has a load of that stuff in the basement. It's his workshop. He makes shelves and things for the house. He goes down there nights and plays with himself.'

Brinkmann said, 'Your mother doesn't know about it and yet you do. How come?'

'Well,' Craig said, moving his fingers like a spider's legs along the arm of the chair, 'adults are pretty stupid, aren't they? They're always saying one thing and doing another. I'm hungry,' he suddenly announced. 'Can I have some pie?'

'Go on with what you were saying.'

'What about?' Craig bent forward until his eyes were level with his running fingers.

'Why you think adults are stupid.'

'They're so dumb. Dumb. Dumb-dumb-dumb.' Craig drummed his fingers on the chair-arm. 'Like my Dad. He goes to church every Sunday, you know? We have to say grace at mealtimes. He's always preaching to us about God and stuff. Be kind to others, keep your mind clean and pure, don't think evil thoughts, remember how Jesus suffered for our sins. That's what he tells *us* to do. What *he* does is cheat on his income tax, screw his customers at the garage, and play with himself in the basement.'

He gave a harsh bark of a laugh that sounded oddly like an old man's. A scathing, bitter laugh, without humour or pity.

Brinkmann took out his handkerchief and wiped his forehead. A low-pitched beeping made him glance down at the tape deck. A red light winked on. He switched the machine off.

Craig bounced up out of the chair, a grin transforming his face. Since coming off the methylphenidate the children were much more lively and responsive. Fabius had been against it, and so had Dr Sampson, but Brinkmann had more or less insisted. It had taken three days for the drug to work itself out of their systems.

'Can I go and play now with Donna and Stu? We play this great guessing game. I'm getting to be real good at it.'

Brinkmann caught him by the wrists, gently but firmly, and held him still.

He said, 'You do know why you've been sent here, don't you, Craig? Do you know the reason?'

Craig blinked his round blue eyes and nodded. 'People are scared of us, I guess. We know too much.'

'Is that all, Craig?'

'What else, Dr Brinkmann?'

Brinkmann released him and Craig just stood there, arms by his sides. The corners of his mouth curled up, he smiled, and then he started to laugh as if somebody had whispered a terrifically funny joke in his ear.

'Wow! Attaboy, Johnnie!' Craig said, his face convulsed with laughter.

'What's happening? What can you hear?' Brinkmann said, knowing perfectly well that Craig couldn't hear *anything* from outside. Knowing it and yet somehow not believing it.

He got up and unlocked the door and opened it. There was one hell of a commotion in the corridor. Three orderlies in white smocks ran past. Somebody was yelling. A red light was flashing above the door of the room where Sampson was locked in with Johnnie Bromke.

Brinkmann closed the door behind him and snapped the security lock. Two of the orderlies were breaking down

Sampson's door. It splintered and flew open and they charged in, emerging moments later with Johnnie Bromke clamped between them, struggling and spitting, eyes rolling wildly, head jerking like a mechanical doll's. Behind them, the other orderly was supporting Dr Sampson, who had a gash on the side of his face and a purple swelling on his shiny, domelike head.

'What happened?' Fabius demanded, striding past Brinkmann.

Weiss and Helen Murphy appeared.

'That child – that monster – attacked me,' Sampson said through pale lips. 'Went berserk. Flew at me. Look!' He touched the raw gash and held up his bloody fingertips for them to see.

'Next time I'll kill you!' Johnnie Bromke screamed, and almost broke free. The orderlies swung him round and slammed him with considerable force against the wall. One of them twisted the child's arm up his back.

'Stop that! Stop it!' Brinkmann cried out. He pushed forward and grabbed the orderly's shoulder. 'You're supposed to restrain him, not break his arm!'

'They're doing what they're paid to do,' Fabius said sharply, glaring at Brinkmann. 'I will not allow attacks on members of staff. Take the child to the Isolation Room,' he instructed. 'I'll be along in a few minutes.'

The orderlies dragged the struggling child away. Fabius turned on Brinkmann. 'It isn't your place to tell my staff how to behave. They have to deal with problems like this every day. In future please do not interfere in the running of this facility and in the procedures laid down to maintain correct institutional care. That is my responsibility, Dr Brinkmann, not yours.'

'It was my impression that this was a clinic, not Gestapo headquarters,' Brinkmann said.

'*You* weren't assaulted,' Helen Murphy remarked tartly.

'These are young children. Are we supposed to demonstrate our superiority by battering them into submission?'

Fabius said, 'We're getting nowhere fast with this approach. In view of the urgency, I recommend that we try electro-therapy. At this moment in time it's a matter of control rather than cure.'

Weiss goggled at him. 'You are seriously suggesting that we subject these children to electro-therapy?'

'There's a time factor involved here,' Helen Murphy said. 'We've been asked to produce results. We'd better start producing.'

Brinkmann said, 'You can't mean electrical stimulation of the hypothalamus? An experimental technique that so far has been used only on rats?'

'With excellent results,' Fabius said calmly. 'As the brain's control centre, the hypothalamus is the obvious candidate to regulate hyperactive behaviour. Read Firmin on the subject. His clinical studies –'

'Damn Firmin and his clinical studies,' Brinkmann said. 'Stimulating the hypothalamus of rats generates uncontrollable rage and manic behaviour. I don't call that a cure.'

'We already use stimulants, such as amphetamines, to control hyperactivity. We don't know how or why that works either, but the fact remains that it does. Stimulation is an accepted medical procedure.'

'This is cure by experimental torture,' Brinkmann said. 'It's less a treatment than a desperate last resort.' He shook his head slowly, his eyes fixed on Fabius. 'I refuse to countenance it. I will not sanction it.'

Weiss blinked, and looked relieved. Helen Murphy tightened her lips.

Sampson held a handkerchief to his face and said bitterly, 'So we do nothing? Is that what you're suggesting, Dr Brinkmann? We just sit back and – and allow these attacks to continue? No medication? No treatment whatsoever?'

'We cannot t-treat what we don't understand,' Brinkmann

said. There was a tremor in his voice, and his throat ached with the effort of trying to constrain his boiling anger.

'How can we d-discover the actual cause, the real cause, if we're masking the symptoms by drugs and electro-therapy?' he went on. 'These are children, human beings, not laboratory animals to be experimented upon.'

'And I must remind you, Dr Brinkmann,' Helen Murphy said, 'that we're here to get answers and results quickly. This isn't a long-term research project. We don't even have weeks, much less months and years. We have a duty to give the public results. If this isn't going to reach the proportions of an epidemic we need action *now*.'

'Yes,' Brinkmann nodded. 'I'm aware of that. But it must be the right kind of action. Humane. Caring. Not the nightmare of the concentration camp.'

'Three more cases have been reported,' Helen Murphy informed them over lunch. 'Which brings the total to twenty-eight. The same pattern – violent and indiscriminate attacks resulting in five deaths. The three children have disappeared without trace, like the others.'

'What ages are they?' Brinkmann asked.

'Eleven, ten and eight.'

'Eight!' Weiss exclaimed. 'Good God. They're getting younger.'

'Is this what you might have expected?' Fabius asked Brinkmann, his tanned, handsome face carefully composed, his voice evenly modulated.

'I didn't know what to expect,' Brinkmann replied frankly. 'I haven't dealt with too many cases of eight-year-old multiple murderers. But you've treated very young children, Dr Fabius. What's your opinion?'

'They show all the signs of disinhibited activity to a high degree, approaching the paranoid state. Total loss of control leading to acts of violence.' Fabius inclined his groomed head to Dr Sampson. 'That child this morning lost control and went berserk.'

There was a long strip of adhesive plaster on Sampson's cheek and a purple swelling on the side of his head.

'What happened exactly?' Brinkmann asked him.

'I was testing for attention span and loss of control using the "threat-and-reward" method. Sit still for thirty seconds and you will receive a piece of candy. Don't sit still and you will be put in the Quiet Room for half an hour until you regain control.'

'That approach does work sometimes,' Brinkmann nodded. 'I've used it myself.'

Weiss blew out a gust of air and threw up his hands.

'But these aren't *normal* cases of hyperactivity! My God, if only it were that simple! As if you could solve the problem with a piece of candy!'

Brinkmann smiled. He looked across the table at Sampson, who was regarding Weiss with piercing watery blue eyes. 'When did this happen?'

The English psychiatrist switched his watery blue stare to Brinkmann, as if this might be a trick question. 'This morning.'

'Yes, of course. I meant at what time?'

'Towards the end of the session. Twelve-fifteen, twelve-twenty, or thereabouts. Why, is it important?'

'Interesting, yes. Important, I don't know. The interviewing rooms are completely soundproofed, aren't they?' he said, turning to Fabius, who nodded. 'The interesting thing is that I was with Craig Holley this morning. He *knew* the attack had taken place – or was about to – while I didn't hear a thing till I went out into the corridor.'

'That isn't possible,' Helen Murphy said. She glanced rapidly at Fabius.

'I wouldn't say impossible,' Brinkmann said. 'We are dealing with a very strange form of hyperkinetic behaviour.'

Weiss nodded his agreement. 'Hardly one of the classic forms; certainly none with which I myself am familiar.'

'And which are they?' said Helen Murphy icily.

Weiss reddened a little but remained silent.

'One factor seems to me highly significant,' said Fabius thoughtfully. 'Many of these children are continually being fed images of violence and arbitrary killings. TV, videos –'

'The Bromke boy mentioned that too,' said Sampson. 'He said that television is his major leisure activity. The minute he gets home from school he switches the set on – that seems to be his only interest.'

'If that's so,' Brinkmann said mildly, 'can we expect the other nineteen million children between the ages of eight and twelve to go out and start slaughtering the general population? And what do we advise the Department of Health and Human Services to do? Ban *The A-Team*?'

Weiss coughed to hide a smile. Sampson said angrily, 'You can have your little joke, Dr Brinkmann, but these children – these little monsters – have actually killed people. Not accidentally or in states of emotion, but coldly and clinically, with cunning and premeditation.' He took out his handkerchief and dabbed the swelling on his bruised head. 'That boy Bromke would have killed me too if he'd had the chance.'

Brinkmann said, 'I wonder why they don't kill each other.'

'What?' Fabius said, frowning. Everyone was looking at Brinkmann.

'Their aggression is always directed at parents or teachers or other adults. They never attack other children.'

'Authority figures, quite obviously,' said Helen Murphy.

'Obviously?' Brinkmann said. 'Hyperactive children don't limit or regulate their behaviour to fit in with other people, be they adults or children. It's a total loss of control. They're just as likely to behave aggressively towards their playmates as adults.'

Sampson said, 'What then? Have you a theory, Dr Brinkmann?'

Brinkmann shrugged. 'Perhaps when Dr Krill sends in his report we'll know where to start looking.'

'You really believe there's a simple physiological basis for this behaviour?' Fabius said with thinly disguised scepticism. 'A virus? A disease? Or a contaminated blood batch that has affected nearly thirty children from practically every part of the country?' He shook his head slowly, doubtfully.

'Something similar happened in Australia,' Weiss reminded him. 'A dozen babies and small children died or became seriously ill due to blood contaminated with AIDs. What happened there could happen here.'

'All this is mere conjecture,' Helen Murphy said brusquely, throwing down her napkin. 'What's more, it's damned dangerous. If the media got hold of a story like this, there'd be wholesale panic. We're supposed to calm people, not plant hysterical fears in their heads.' Her eyes glittered with a hard light. 'After what happened this morning I'm inclined to agree with Dr Fabius that what we need is a more positive approach. We can't allow these attacks on the staff to continue, and we don't have time to luxuriate in precious theories and half-baked notions. This is a medical institution, not an academic ivory tower.'

Weiss looked at her, his eyes clouded and watchful.

'I have not heard of this positive approach of Dr Fabius's,' he said quietly. 'But I hope it isn't anything as "positive" as electro-shock therapy.'

With new cases being reported practically every day, Dr Peter Krill was constantly on the phone making long-distance calls to family doctors and group practices right across the country. The long hours spent working late in the office had been worth it, Krill felt. He now had the medical records of twenty-six children, including the five at Golden Vale.

These showed that within the past three months, every child had been given a blood transfusion.

The next step had been to contact the hospitals that had given the transfusions in order to learn the serial numbers of the individual blood batches. Now he was ready to visit the central records office of the American Association of Blood

Banks in Washington DC, for what he hoped would be the final clinching evidence.

Warned of his arrival, the director sent someone to meet him at Washington National Airport, and Krill was taken directly to the computer processing facility in the annexe at the rear of the Blood Banks building. The director, Darryl Traine, a small neat man with rimless glasses and a spotted bow-tie, was waiting to greet him.

Krill showed the paperwork which accredited him to be on special assignment for the Department of Health and Human Services, working to an urgent and confidential brief for the Chief Secretary, Meg Willson. It was important, indeed vital, he explained, that none of the staff knew the purpose of his visit.

'That's no problem. I'll handle the processing myself,' Darryl Traine said. He looked at Krill steadily for a moment. 'Do I get to know, or am I a security risk too?'

Krill relaxed a little. Up till now he had confided in no one. He hadn't even called Brinkmann at the Clinic to tell him how the investigation was proceeding. But sooner or later he had to tell someone. Besides, he needed Darryl Traine's cooperation in shutting off the supply of contaminated blood at its source.

Krill opened his attaché case and took out the medical records and the list of twenty-six blood batch serial numbers. 'I want to know where these were given, and the name or names of the donor or donors. Can you do that?'

'If they're on file, which they ought to be, the answer is yes.' Darryl Traine frowned. 'What's going on? An epidemic?'

'It might turn into one. These batches were all given to children. The ones who are going around killing adults and then doing a disappearing act.'

'Christ.' The director went three shades paler and led Krill through into the starkly lit data-processing centre where fifteen operators, mostly women, were seated at consoles. The silence and calm and rapt concentration reminded Krill of a ritual of some kind – adepts in the temple of an implacable god, worshipping mutely at the hooded green screens.

Darryl Traine chose a terminal away from the others and wheeled another chair forward. Krill sat down. In spite of the air conditioning he was perspiring lightly. He laid the sheet of serial numbers in front of Darryl Traine, who glanced at it and started tapping.

Krill watched in silence as the list was punched into the machine. Lights blinked on the panel while the main-frame ruminated. There was a series of clicks and a name appeared on the screen. Krill leaned forward, his mouth dry. Then he subsided, angry and bitterly disappointed. His home-grown theory that one person was responsible for contaminating the blood batches was blown to smithereens as name after name flashed up on the screen. Five. Six. Seven. Eight. Nine names altogether.

He unclipped his pen, and Darryl Traine said, 'That's okay. I'll get you a hard copy.'

A few moments later Krill had the printout in his hand.

'Is that what you were after?' Darryl Traine turned a key and the screen faded to grey.

Krill nodded. 'What are these?' he asked, pointing to the numbers and letters in front of each name: LA-D7, LA-N3, LA-E4, and so on.

'Those are the collecting stations where the blood was taken. "LA" is Los Angeles, and the rest refers to the particular location.' Darryl Traine reached for a plastic ring-binder and flipped to the appropriate page. He took a pen and wrote down the districts. There were six of these: Vernon, Maywood, South Gate, Lynwood, Bell, and Alhambra, all in or around the central Los Angeles area.

'What about addresses of the donors?' Krill asked.

'The collecting stations keep those. That shouldn't be a problem.'

Something of Krill's previous excitement began to creep back. He had the names of the donors and he knew where the blood had been given. There was more tracking down to be done, more than he had anticipated. But at least he was one step nearer – a gigantic leap nearer in fact.

Over coffee in Darryl Traine's office, Krill asked him about the blood already in stock from the nine donors. It was of course vital that no further contaminated batches were passed along to hospitals.

'If it's whole blood I can place an embargo on those serial numbers right away. But with plasma . . .' The director shook his head.

'What do you mean – you can't trace that?'

'With whole blood it's simple. The donor gives the blood, it's refrigerated, then fed to the patient within twenty-one days. There's a direct link between the two that can be traced. But if the blood is used for its plasma content, the plasma is extracted, spun down and mixed with batches collected from other people. Thirty, forty – who knows how many? There's no way to trace it from donor to recipient.'

Krill stared at the list of names. These nine people, all male, he noted, were responsible for the spread of contaminated blood. So far, nearly thirty children had been affected. But if some of the blood had been used for plasma extraction, as Darryl Traine suggested, stocks of the contaminated strain could be sitting in hospital refrigerators at this very moment, waiting to be used.

A hundred bottles of clear plasma swam before his eyes. They multiplied into a thousand, then into ten thousand.

He grinned weakly with the nausea of fear. He had assumed that the contaminant could be stopped, the epidemic contained. It had been a false assumption. Thirty kids might be only the beginning.

'Have you run blood tests on the five cases under observation?' the director asked him. 'Maybe you can isolate the contaminated strain from that end.'

Krill nodded, blinking to clear his thoughts. 'I ran some

preliminary tests and found nothing. That is, nothing significant. I also sent samples to the Centre for Disease Control in Atlanta.'

'Response?'

'Nothing so far.'

'Okay,' Darryl Traine said, in the manner of someone coming to a decision. 'I'll put an immediate embargo on all blood supplies with those serial numbers. Let's hope and pray there aren't any more in the pipeline.'

'Any more?' Krill said stupidly.

'Sure! Come on now! We've traced nine suspect donors, but who's to know if there aren't more contaminated donors whose blood hasn't been used yet – and who are still giving it? There's no way of telling.'

Krill got up, slid the files into his attaché case and fastened the double clasps. He felt that he ought to be running, with a helicopter waiting outside, and Concorde on the runway.

He said, 'As soon as I come up with anything I'll be in touch.'

'Where next?'

'Back to the Clinic tonight, report to Dr Brinkmann, get my stuff together,' Krill said. 'Tomorrow, Los Angeles, first available flight.'

14

With one eye on his mirror, Tom drove down South Mountain Street, turned left on to Church Street, and drove up the ramp into the parking lot of the new shopping mall. This was Torrence's pride and joy: three levels of glass, stainless steel, bronze sculpture, and cascading fountains and waterfalls gently plashing under a rainbow hue of concealed lighting.

It was a few minutes after three o'clock in the afternoon. It was easy to mingle and quickly get lost amongst the crowds.

Tom wandered about for a bit, looking at window displays while watching the reflections of passers-by and keeping a sharp look-out for anyone who appeared to be loitering. He went into a couple of stores, browsed through the merchandise, and came out by a different door. On the top level, set at right-angles in a recess, were three pay-phones. Tom slipped into the furthest booth so that he was partially hidden by the glass panels of the other two but still had a view of the main shopping plaza on which a constant stream of people flowed and eddied. Nobody dawdled or glanced in his direction.

The phone rang endlessly, and he was on the point of giving up when Karel came on the line, her voice almost drowned by a solid disco throb and a hoarse tormented female who sounded like Tina Turner. Tina Turner went away and Karel came back, a little breathless.

'You caught me practising my aerobics. Where are you, Tom?' Karel said, sounding puzzled.

'Torrence.'

'I mean where are you calling from? You haven't installed a pay-phone in the kitchen, have you?'

Tom explained where he was, and then said, 'I don't know who or why, but somebody is listening in to my phone conversations. Unmarked cars with out-of-town plates drive up and down The Heights day and night. Men in sunglasses wearing belted raincoats with upturned collars follow me to the pizza parlour. But apart from that I'm having a swell vacation.'

'You're reading too much Raymond Chandler,' Karel said, though her voice sounded guarded and hesitant. 'What's happening down there? Are you all right?'

Tom laughed without much humour. 'I can't swear to the guys in sunglasses and raincoats but it wouldn't surprise me. I must know something they want to find out. I just wish I knew what it was.'

'Who, for God's sake? Is it because of Danny and those other kids?'

Tom fed more money into the slot and said, 'I've spoken to her – to Danny. She tried to warn me about something.'

'You have? But – when? Where?'

'In my dreams.'

'Tom –' Karel said impatiently.

'No, really, I'm serious.' Tom laughed shakily. 'I've got a regular hotline. She's in some kind of military installation. Underground, I think, though I'm not too sure. With all the other kids.'

'What do you mean – you actually *saw* them?'

Tom's attention was distracted by a man at the top of the escalator who was looking left and right as if searching for something or someone. He was wearing a plaid jacket and open-necked shirt and carrying a small brown-paper package. Tom instinctively shrank back and moved the receiver to hide his face. With a frown, the man moved on and out of sight.

Tom said suddenly, 'Can I come and visit for a few days?'

'Of course you can. When?'

'Tomorrow? Or maybe the day after. I'll call you before I leave. Is that okay?'

'Sure.'

Tom hesitated and said, 'I want to see Ward DeVoss but first I need to talk to somebody. I mean talk to you,' he amended. 'I need to get a few things straightened out first. You don't mind?'

'You know without asking,' Karel said.

'Is your father home?'

'Yes, but that's okay. He'd like to meet you. You're welcome to stay as long as you like. Why do you want to see Professor DeVoss?' she asked curiously.

'I think he might be able to help me.'

'How?' Karel sounded more mystified than ever.

'That's pretty difficult to explain over the phone. Damn near impossible to explain anyway,' Tom said. 'We've been working on a Quantum Field experiment, trying to establish a connection between quantum theory and parapsychology –

precognition, psychokinesis, all that stuff. It has something to do with sub-atomic particles that don't obey the normal laws of cause and effect –'

The operator came on the line. 'Hello, caller? If you wish to continue with this call, deposit one dollar twenty-five cents please.'

Tom sorted through his change, found he was fifty cents short.

'Listen, Karel, I'll call you tomorrow.'

'Ask her to make it collect,' Karel said.

'No, let's leave it. I can't explain. I'll call you tomorrow.'

'Tom, please don't –'

'I'm sorry, caller, I'll have to disconnect you unless you deposit one dollar twenty-five –'

Tom put the phone down. He closed his eyes and massaged his temples, breathing in and out slowly. Just as well he hadn't said any more. It would have made him sound crazier than he did already. What the hell, Karel might have inquired sweetly, had sub-atomic particles to do with unmarked cars with out-of-town plates and the suspicion that he was being followed by men in sunglasses and belted raincoats?

Not the easiest of questions to handle, because he didn't know the answer. The plain fact was, he couldn't think of anyone except Ward DeVoss to turn to. He'd never exhibited any psychic powers before, never seen a ghost, didn't believe in contact with the spirit world beyond the pale, or wherever it was supposed to be.

Having said that, there were some pretty weird and way-out theories being tossed around in quantum theory at the present moment.

Time-reversal particles that travelled faster than the speed of light (an Einsteinian impossibility) and could therefore transmit knowledge of future events into the past. Particles that disobeyed all the everyday rules of cause and effect by experiencing an effect that preceded its own cause. Particles that could communicate instantaneously with one another across light-years of space, influencing each other's behaviour and making a horse's ass of the accepted wisdom that light-speed was the fastest means of communication in the universe.

Perhaps DeVoss and the parapsychologists could make some sort of sense of it all, Tom thought – his creepy awareness of Danny's presence, the dank concrete passageways, the oil paintings . . .

Tom stepped on to the escalator. Halfway down he got the prickly feeling on the back of his neck that he was being watched. When he turned and looked upwards there was no one there. So much for his sixth sense, Tom thought, and chuckled out loud so that two or three people glanced sharply at him and veered out of his path.

Krill drove the rented Ford along Beverly Boulevard until he was in sight of the concrete bulwark of the Hollywood Freeway, which lay across the maze of streets below like an asphalt snake. The blast of traffic and the gentle bloom of carbon monoxide fumes filled the still, sultry air of late afternoon.

He glanced down at the typed list of names and addresses lying on the seat next to him, and then at the street map.

Arthur Lyle, 2125 Oakwood Avenue.

Four of the nine names already had ticks against them, giving the misleading impression that Krill had done a good day's work. In fact the ticks represented six hours of wasted time and God knew how much mileage navigating the seedier environs of downtown LA. Neither was this area much of an improvement, despite the proximity of the Wilshire Country Club a dozen or so blocks to the west.

The hourly news bulletin came over the radio and Krill turned up the volume.

'Schools in several states have been closed due to civil unrest and disturbances thought to be caused by the backlash against the wave of attacks by school-age children on teachers and other staff.

'In Modesto, California, a group of thirty to forty adults

stoned children at a community play-centre, causing serious injury. Playgroup leaders had to barricade themselves and children inside the building and await a police escort before leaving. There were fourteen arrests.

'A school in Plainfield, New Jersey, was gutted by fire in the early hours of this morning, following threats by phone and through the mail. According to a police spokesman, the suspected arson was incited by the deaths a week ago of a middle-aged black couple, whose stomachs were found to contain rat poison. Subsequently, their nephew, Selwyn Porter Brown, aged nine years, disappeared. No connection has been established between the suspected double homicide and the child's disappearance.

'Ernest Lee Nord, aged forty-one, of Colorado Springs, Colorado, today admitted keeping his twin daughters, Lisa and Debi, age ten, chained together and locked in the basement without food and water for five days because, quote, "I thought they were out to get me, like all those other monsters. I don't trust any kids any more." After medical examination both children were taken into community care. Mr Nord is undergoing psychiatric tests –'

Krill snapped the radio off.

The frontages of baked red earth on Oakwood Avenue, separated by leaning picket fences, were largely given over to dismembered cars and pickups, rusting fenders, dented door panels and piles of worn tyres. Either the neighbourhood had gone in for automobile renovation or – more likely – was following the good old American tradition of leaving mechanical junk to rot and rust where it lay.

Krill counted off the numbers until he came to 2125. As he stepped out of the car the air wrapped itself around him like a sticky, suffocating blanket.

The garden gate, held by only one hinge, was wedged against the brick path, so he had to kick it several times to get in. A piece of rotten timber fell out. Krill sighed and pushed it aside with his foot. One thing for sure; this wasn't his day.

Behind the twisted screen door Krill could see that there was a wad of yellowing circulars and advertising free sheets stuffed into the letterbox. A For Sale card was stuck in the corner of the front room window, with the name and telephone number of the realtor underneath.

Krill had nothing better to do, so he knocked on the front door. The echo told him what he had guessed already. He wandered along the side of the house. The yard at the back was even more of a desolate wilderness than the front.

He went out of the gate and dragged it shut. As an afterthought he kicked out a couple more of the palings, but it didn't make him feel any better.

Two barefoot young men in grubby sweatshirts and patched jeans were working on an old green Buick next door. The car was resting on piles of bricks instead of wheels, so obviously they weren't going anywhere in a hurry. They looked up from underneath the hood as Krill called to them. They were small and swarthy, with straight jet-black hair. Krill took them to be Mexican.

'I'm looking for Mr Arthur Lyle. Do either of you have any idea when he left or where he went?'

The men stared back at him with dark, impassive eyes. Krill hoped that they wouldn't get the notion that he was a repossession man or from a credit company. Then one of them gave a quick shake of the head. The other just went on staring.

'I see. Well, can you tell me –' He glanced up and down the quiet street. This really was a pretty unsavoury district. 'How long has the place next door been empty? Weeks? Months?'

'Don' know,' said the head-shaker in a strong Spanish accent. He made an abrupt, dismissive gesture with an oil-smeared hand. 'Nothin'. Don' know.'

They went back to their tinkering. Krill returned to the car. He sat there for a few minutes, cooling off, and then took out his pen and made another tick against the list. Strike one Arthur Lyle. Five down, four to go. He was getting a slight headache, a miserable combination of heat, frustration, and bafflement. He was plain pissed-off, in fact.

He debated whether to call Brinkmann at the Clinic but on further reflection decided against it. There was nothing to report, except that he'd wasted a day and worn himself to a frazzle chasing after five mythical blood donors. No point in worrying Brinkmann with his problems.

There was a lump of something on the narrow wooden stairs that looked like human excreta. Krill carefully stepped over it on his way to the second floor. The hallway was gloomy, made darker still by the dark-green paint smeared on the walls, and by worn linoleum the colour of used engine oil, patched with brighter squares of an incongruous sky-blue.

Krill swallowed the sour taste rising in his throat and knocked on the door of 27. He'd seen some dumps and dives in downtown LA but this one took the prize. He wasn't even sure that this was the right address, and was beginning to hope it wasn't. Joe Stalito was an elusive character. Krill had followed his trail from a rooming house in Boyle Heights to a flophouse off Olympic Boulevard, and finally here, via the Salvation Army, to this piece of condemned property three blocks south of the Hollywood Freeway near the Shriners Hospital.

The man who answered the door was short and wiry, with hard, shiny eyes like brown pebbles in a pale, ravaged face. He wore a stained sweatshirt hanging loose over crumpled cord jeans. His bare feet were grimy between the toes. He looked at Krill suspiciously, not caring much for the neat suit and button-down shirt and polished shoes.

Krill had his medical ID card ready.

'Do you mind if I come in for a few minutes? It's a routine matter. Some checks we're carrying out in the Los Angeles area.'

'You're not selling health insurance? Collecting for charity?'

Krill smiled and shook his head. 'It won't cost you a cent.'

A large grey cat took advantage of the open door to brush between his legs and disappear behind the furniture.

The apartment consisted of just the one room, with a divan bed over in the corner. Behind a sagging curtain a single tap stuck crookedly out of the bare plaster over a square pot sink. Next to it was a two-burner gas stove with a million spent matches embedded in the grease, and a food locker patched up with metal foil to deter the roaches. There were dirty plates, cups and pans everywhere, and open packages and empty tins with flies buzzing over them. A saucer of milk and a plate with some reddish meat were on the table next to an unwrapped loaf of sliced bread.

Krill watched where he stepped and tried to breathe shallowly.

The man shifted a pile of discarded underclothes and some yellowing newspapers from a chair and dumped them on the floor. As he straightened up, Krill got a foul blast of the man's breath, a blend of bad teeth and last night's whisky fumes. He clenched his jaw to stop himself shying away.

'To tell the truth, I bin feeling pretty lousy myself,' the man volunteered, inspired by having a doctor on the premises. 'Stomach,' he grimaced, rubbing the hollow pit beneath his ribcage. He offered the chair to Krill. 'Can't keep nothin' down.' He fetched up a belch as if to prove his claim.

Krill nodded sympathetically and turned his head away, swallowing. He laid his attaché case on his knees and opened it. His hands left damp patches on the mottled leather. There was no air conditioning and the windows were shut tight.

'Can I get you something? Coffee? Something stronger, maybe?'

'No – no thanks.'

The man lit a cigarette and sucked in a lungful. He hitched up his shapeless cord jeans and straddled the arm of the sofa. His scrawny veined arms were hieroglyphs of purple and green tattoos.

Krill said, 'According to our records, you've given two

donations of blood in the past ten months. Both at the donating station at Washington and La Salle. Is that correct?'

The man stared at him, then blinked rapidly. 'Who told you that? Not me.' He shook his head. 'I never gave no blood to nobody.'

'It's down here in the file. September the fourteenth last year and July the ninth.' Krill held up two pink slips. 'We have your signature both times. Here, see?'

The man craned forward and squinted at them through the cigarette smoke. His eyes flickered, and then he smiled.

'You got the wrong fella. That ain't me.'

'You're not Joseph Stalito? But this was the address I was given by the Salvation Army –'

'He's gone. Left the place.' The man jerked his head. 'Couple of months ago.'

'Do you know where?'

'Not sure. San Francisco maybe.'

'Are you a friend of his?'

'Friend? Naw. Wouldn't say that. Met him once or twice.'

'So you are . . .?'

'What?' the man said, screwing up his face so that it became a maze of cracks and fissures, like cracked icing on a cake.

'Your name?'

'Oh, yeah, sure.' The man grinned, showing brown stumps. 'Stevens. Nick Stevens. This guy, Joe Stalito. Why d' you want him?'

'Just a routine matter, Mr Stevens. We're trying to trace a number of blood donors in the Los Angeles area.' Krill caught a movement in the corner of his eye and saw the large grey cat leap on to the table and start lapping milk from the saucer. It was a mangy-looking animal with a stumpy tail and tufts of fur missing, as if it had been in a fight. Krill was thankful he hadn't accepted the offer of refreshment. The cat had probably licked every piece of crockery in the place and left its hair everywhere else.

Stevens got up and shuffled over to the stove. He lit the gas and set the kettle to boil. 'I'm making coffee – want some?'

'That's kind of you. No thanks.'

Krill closed his attaché case. He sat with it on his knees, frowning at the wall opposite. Picture postcards and snapshots were taped to the grimy wallpaper. 'Do you happen to know anyone who might know of Mr Stalito's present whereabouts? Friends, relatives, employer?'

'Sorry, can't help you, doc. I never really knew the guy.' He shrugged his narrow shoulders, which stuck up like points through his sweatshirt, the cigarette dangling from the side of his mouth. 'This ain't Pacific Palisades, as you might've noticed. We don't keep track. Don't ask too many questions neither.'

'I understand.' Krill stood up, feeling the shirt scraping on his back. He stood looking at the little gallery of cards and muddy photographs, a queasiness rising in his throat. If he didn't get out of this stinking oven to the fresh air he was going to pass out or throw up.

Stevens was saying something but Krill wasn't listening. Instead he was gazing at a photograph of a man and a woman leaning against the hood of a car in a Bonnie and Clyde pose. The woman was red-haired, in her forties, wearing too much make-up, bulging out of tight pink trousers; the man was small and runty with a sharp beaked nose and close-set brown eyes, hard and shiny, like those of a crafty sewer rat. His arms were covered with tattoos.

Written in a looping schoolgirlish hand, in green ink, across the bottom corner, it said, '*Thanks for a terrific weekend. To Joe – love always and forever, Marie. XXX.*'

'What's the idea, Joe?'

The man looked sharply round. His face twitched.

'My name ain't Joe. I already told you once. It's – uh –'

Krill watched him struggling to remember what name he had given.

'You told me it was Nick Stevens,' Krill said.

'Yeah. Right,' the man said slowly, his eyes shifting round

the room as if seeking a weapon or a means of escape. The grey cat had finished the milk and was eating the meat. 'Listen,' the man said. 'Are you a cop, or what?'

'You need to have a good memory to be a good liar, Joe.'

The man turned off the gas. 'Okay. What is it you want? I ain't done nothin'. Are you really a doctor?'

'Yes,' Krill said. An immense surge of elation and relief swept over him. Goddammit, he'd got one at last! With seven down and two to go. Not before time. He unfastened the clasps on his attaché case. 'Sit down, Joe. I'd like to ask you a few questions.'

15

Otto Weiss bounced into the room without knocking and swung a chair round, straddling it with his short legs to sit facing Brinkmann, elbows propped on the chair back, hairy knuckles clasped under his chin.

'The results from the Centre for Disease Control have just come in, and the first tests are positive. Would you care to lay a little bet, Jacob?'

Brinkmann looked up from the desk where he was writing up his notes. He took off his thick-framed glasses and peered at Weiss from under shaggy brows.

'Let me see,' he mused. He leaned back and gazed at the ceiling, twiddling his thumbs. 'They've identified antibodies in the blood samples. Preliminary tests suggest either retroviruses or toxoplasmosis, but they're not sure which.'

Weiss looked cheated. He frowned. 'Have you seen the report?' he inquired suspiciously.

'No, I haven't,' Brinkmann said mildly. 'But it isn't too fantastic a deduction, Otto, when you think about it. According to Peter Krill, all the children have received a blood or plasma transfusion within the past three months. It was almost certain that some contamination or foreign organism had been transferred into their bloodstreams. An easily identifiable microbe or viral infection would have been found and screened out by the transfusion service before the blood was given. As it wasn't, it must have been a rare or unknown strain they hadn't come across before. Such types usually fall into two categories: retroviruses, such as the AIDs virus, or *Toxoplasma gondii*, the parasite which attacks patients with immunosuppressive diseases. A simple process of elimination.'

'Oh yes, I see,' said Weiss sarcastically. 'Very simple. Do you always work by the empirical method, Jacob? I mean, why bother with laboratories at all? It seems you can work the whole thing out in your head!'

Brinkmann smiled. 'The reason you're annoyed, Otto, has nothing to do with my methods but because I didn't confide in you.' He poured himself a glass of water and sipped at it, watching the little man with amused eyes.

'I don't mind in the least,' Weiss said airily, 'providing you didn't confide in Dr Fabius instead.'

He glanced curiously at the evidence of Brinkmann's industry, piled high on the desk. Several fat textbooks lay open, their pages bristling with markers and reference slips. Files, charts and assorted papers were strewn over the leather-bound blotter. Evidently Brinkmann did more work here than down in the interviewing and observation rooms.

'I've been trying to figure something out,' Brinkmann said, sucking at his pen. His fingers were ink stained, Weiss noticed, and there was a smear of ink on his chin. 'What are the factors we expect to find in hyperkinetic behaviour?'

Weiss ticked them off. 'Excitable, impulsive, overactive. Brief attention span, easily distracted. Outbursts of temper and quick changes of mood. Generally unpredictable behaviour. Will that do?'

'And these are the result of . . .?'

'Loss of control. Lack of inhibition on the part of the patient.'

'In other words, disinhibition.'

Weiss nodded.

Brinkmann wrote something down. 'And this usually occurs in children of above-average intelligence, does it not?'

Weiss nodded.

'So this type of behaviour would seem to be related to a high degree of intelligence, an above-average IQ. Do the children we have here conform to this pattern, would you say?'

'Absolutely.' Weiss's nod of the head was emphatic. 'As soon as they came off the methylphenidate they exhibited quite phenomenal intelligence, well above the norm. I found that with Stuart Brangham – that he was counselling *me*, his mind was so quick. Cynical too, sharp, and sexually precocious.'

Brinkmann made another notation. He pondered what he had written for a moment or two, and then held out the paper to Weiss. Weiss took it and stared at it, blinking rapidly.

He glanced up at Brinkmann, his mouth pursed slightly.

'Hyperactive Intelligence Disinhibition Syndrome,' Weiss said softly. His face cleared and he became more animated. 'Yes, yes of course. I see what you're getting at now. An excessive amount of neurological activity within the brain which is not inhibited by any of the usual checks and controls. Instead of regulating itself, as in normal social behaviour, the brain runs away with itself like a – a nuclear power plant when the lead rods are withdrawn.'

'And the more intelligent the child, the greater the brain activity.'

'Leading to breakdown of control and excessively violent behaviour.'

The two men looked at one another.

Weiss looked down at the paper in his hand. 'May I propose a small change? In place of "Hyperactive", I suggest the more clinical term, "Kinetic." He gave Brinkmann a narrow stare. 'Kinetic Intelligence Disinhibition Syndrome. K.I.D.S.'

'You have a wicked sense of humour, Otto. A little too close for comfort, wouldn't you say?'

Weiss shrugged and grinned.

Brinkmann got up and went to the window, absently tucking his shirt inside the bulging waistline of his trousers. He chewed his lower lip and gazed beyond the high walls and electronic gates to the idyllic setting of trees nestling in the folds of green hills. 'But giving the condition a name doesn't solve it,' he said broodingly.

Weiss said, 'At least we now know – we have a strong indication – that a virus or parasite transmitted during blood transfusion is to blame. That's a definite advance, Jacob. We can now approach it from the standpoint of clinical psychology and have done with all this behaviourist nonsense.'

'I wonder if Fabius will see it in the same way?'

'But he must!' said Weiss heatedly. 'You know what he's planning, what he's itching to do, with the help of that Murphy woman. Now they'll have to stop and think for five minutes.'

'I hope you're right.'

'You don't sound very confident.'

'You learn very quickly not to be too confident about anything in clinical psychology,' Brinkmann said.

Weiss suddenly banged the back of the chair with his fist. 'We *have* to convince Fabius and the others that this is the correct approach, Jacob! They must be made to see that drugs and electro-therapy and sensory deprivation won't get us anywhere – worse than that, they could do positive harm. These people are trying to treat a condition they don't understand – aren't even attempting to understand, which is worse.'

Brinkmann turned from the window and looked at Weiss. Without his glasses his heavily lidded eyes seemed very large and pale and naked.

'Have you heard anything from Peter Krill?'

'Not since he went out to the West Coast.'

'Ah, well, we must wait and hope,' Brinkmann sighed. 'Let's get some coffee.' He slipped into his jacket.

As they were going out into the corridor, Weiss said, 'About this K.I.D.S. theory of yours, Jacob. What we need is a method of testing it. Some form of proof that will convince Fabius and the rest.' Weiss held up both fists and punched the air. 'Hit them hard with evidence even they can't possibly refute or ignore. There must be a way . . .'

Brinkmann said, 'I'd feel a lot happier if I knew why it affects only children. We must assume that the blood has been given to adults also, as part of regular transfusions, but it doesn't appear to have caused the same reactions. Why not? Why only children? And why is their aggression directed only at adults and not at other children?' He glanced at Weiss with a grave expression. 'We are only at the beginning of this, Otto. Only the beginning.'

A male orderly sat at a table in the corridor outside the dormitory, which for reasons of security was sealed off from the rest of the Clinic. There were bars on all the windows and the glass panels in the doors were strengthened with steel mesh. He could keep an eye on the children by looking through the panel in the door, and, if necessary, operate the dormitory lights from the corridor outside.

His instructions were to check the sleeping children every hour, on the hour. There was a red button on his table, which he could press in an emergency.

At two a.m. everything was peaceful. The children were huddled forms beneath the blankets; three beds down one side of the dormitory, underneath the windows, two beds facing them on the opposite wall. The orderly went back to his desk and picked up the Commodore software book he had been studying. He was trying to write his own games programs, and finding it difficult and perplexing.

```
480 REM ENTER CRYPT
490 LET CHS = 1 TO 5
500 PRINT 'GAOLER ON GUARD'
```

The salesman had told him – as of course he would – that *The Ghoul in the Crypt* was one of the easier games to start with. Thank God he hadn't started with a hard one! He sighed and tried to screw up his concentration for another attempt.

In the dormitory, Craig Holley threw back the blankets and swung his legs out to sit on the edge of the bed. The other huddled forms moved, threw back the blankets, swung their legs out and sat up.

In unison all five heads turned towards the door. The light from the corridor made a pale rectangle of the glass panel. No sound came from outside. As one, without sign or speech, the children rose and came together in the middle of the room.

Craig Holley touched Donna Perera's hand. Donna Perera touched Stuart Brangham's hand. Stuart Brangham touched Johnnie Bromke's hand. Johnnie Bromke touched Clare Sachs's hand. Clare Sachs reached out and touched Craig's hand. The circle was complete. Then, closing their eyes, they stood facing inwards in a silent blind circle, faint shapes in the pale light from the corridor, like diminutive Druids praying to a pagan god.

Beyond the tiny barred windows the enormous night rolled over America.

Out there somewhere were scattered voices, distant and discordant, rising in chorus. Each child in the circle heard the voices, and in their heads they added their own voices to the wailing chorus.

The dormitory remained silent and dim.

The circle remained motionless.

The night rolled overhead.

Their voices mingled and became one voice, as of many small streams joining together to form a deep, fast-flowing river. And in this river they lost themselves, lost their individual selves, and became one strong solid being. They thought as one, knew what they must do and how it was to be done. It was very simple. Very clear and precise. Very easy, in fact. If they did it together.

The orderly was having great trouble concentrating. The words and symbols on the page kept going fuzzy, and this stuff was damned difficult to understand as it was, without eyesight problems. Maybe he was trying too hard. He shook his head irritably and bent over the page.

```
510 PRINTSPC F [E]
520 PRINT 'ENTER HORIZONTAL COORDINATES'
530 NEXT X
540 PRINT 'GAOLER RELEASES GHOUL FROM CRYPT'
550 INPUT HC
560 PRINT 'TAKE KEY'
570 PRINT 'UNLOCK DOOR'
580 PRINT 'ACT NOW'
```

Hey, wait a minute; he was beginning to get it now. Yes, he could understand that. It was odd how it all came to him in a flash. Like learning to ride a bike as a kid. One minute you couldn't, it was impossible, the next you could. It was very simple. Very clear and precise. Very easy, in fact.

```
590 GOTO 540
600 PRINT 'URGENT – ACT NOW!'
```

He pushed his chair back and stood up. The crypt was long and dark, vanishing to a point in the narrow gloomy distance. The hewn stone walls gleamed, dripping with moisture.

```
610 GOTO 560
```

What was 560? He checked back. Ah yes, 'TAKE KEY'.

He saw his hand go down to the bunch of keys hanging from his belt. The keys were enormous. He saw his hands sorting through the keys, which in the light of the flickering torches were shiny and dazzlingly bright, so that he had to squint against the glare. Holding the appropriate key, he walked to the door with the glass panel reinforced with steel mesh. The light from the burning torches threw a mesh of squares over five small faces clustered just inside the door, gazing up at him.

620 GOTO 570

It was getting easier. He knew that one without looking – 'UNLOCK DOOR'.

The key slipped smoothly into the lock. His fingers gripped the key and started to turn it. The faces watched him blandly through the mesh, five pairs of dark liquid eyes.

As the key turned, moving the tumblers, a voice said angrily, 'What the hell do you think you're doing? Lock that door at once!'

The orderly said, 'GOTO 600.'

'What?' Fabius said.

'URGENT – ACT NOW!'

'Give me that key, goddammit!'

'REM GAME INTERRUPT,' the orderly said, struggling against the pressure of Fabius's hand. He tried again to turn the key and Fabius turned it back, both hands clamped over his. The two men swayed back and forth, grunting and panting. Fabius swore and gripped the orderly's wrists. The orderly was jerked to one side as the key, chained to his belt, was wrenched from the lock with all Fabius's strength.

'REM GAME LOST,' the orderly babbled in a rage. 'GOTO 570,' he kept repeating. 'GOTO 570 . . .'

Fabius hit him with his fist and the orderly staggered back and fell against the wall and slid down sideways. Fabius pressed the red button. He turned back quickly in case the orderly should try anything, but he was lying on his side, propped on one elbow, mumbling something about 'Endproc, endproc, endproc.'

Fabius went to the glass panel. The small pale faces were upturned, expressionless, the light from the corridor imprisoning them inside the spidery shadow of fine steel mesh.

16

Tom left very early on Sunday morning, just after six-thirty, and arrived in New York late in the afternoon. He hadn't exchanged a word with Frank all day Saturday, and Trix seemed oddly complaisant about his leaving; he assumed she must have guessed that something had taken place between them.

Tom had been to New York several times, but never before had he seen the streets awash. A thick grey humid blanket lay over the city, a few hundred feet off the ground, shrouding the upper storeys of the buildings in a dense, warm mist, and the rain teemed steadily and unceasingly down in a semi-opaque liquid curtain.

The Lendrums' apartment was in a large old building on West 114th Street, between Broadway and Amsterdam Avenue, just two blocks from Columbia University. He ran from the car with his raincoat over his head, and by the time he reached the entrance it was sodden right through to the lining.

Two flights up, Karel threw open the door and Tom squelched into the hallway, leaving a damp trail on the glossy parquet floor, and dumped his travelling bag on the umbrella stand. When he turned to her Karel saw that there were bluish circles under his eyes; she was immediately concerned as usually he looked so healthy. She brushed the damp strands of hair out of his eyes and kissed him on the lips, and smiled.

'You look awful.'

'You look terrific.'

She wore a baggy dark-blue turtleneck sweater and loose cord pants tucked into soft leather boots. Her hair was pinned up in a shining coil on top of her head and her features touched in with the lightest of make-up. Somehow the combination was girlish and innocent, and at the same time earthy and provocative.

The rain battered down outside the long narrow windows, filling the elegant apartment with a soft grey gloom.

The living-room had a bare polished wooden floor, and was actually two separate rooms divided by heavy mahogany shutters, now folded away against the pastel blue walls. Three pairs of French windows opened on to a small balcony crowded with plants in tubs and troughs. Everywhere throughout the apartment there was evidence of Lendrum's passion for works of art and fine antiques. In two ceiling-high glass-fronted bookcases, in alcoves on either side of the fireplace, his prized first editions gleamed dully in dark rich bindings and faded gold-leaf lettering.

Karel made a large Scotch with ice and brought it to the sofa where Tom was slumped in a heap.

'Anybody follow you?' she said, raising an eyebrow as she handed him his drink. 'Peter Lorre? Sydney Greenstreet?'

Tom drank and rested his head, eyes closed. 'There's a big red cross on the Pentagon war board,' he said. 'Smack over this building. Any second now the marines are going to come swinging in through those windows, throwing grenades and yelling like banshees.'

'Somebody must think you know something.'

'Perhaps I do.'

Karel sat astride the arm of a chair, swinging her leg. 'Do you?' she asked quietly.

Tom rubbed his eyes and covered up a yawn.

'What was all that stuff on the phone about?' Karel asked with a frown. 'About seeing Danny and those other kids? There must be quite a clan of them now, thirty or more. Do you know where they're hiding out?'

'All I know is that I don't know what the hell's happening. Something screwy. I keep dreaming about Danny, feeling her presence everywhere. She's trying to tell me or warn me about something – I keep getting these same images.'

'What is it she's trying to communicate?'

Tom opened his eyes wearily. He shrugged. 'Must have been a bad connection.'

'Maybe you didn't interpret it properly.'

'How? Why? Tell me.'

Karel leaned one elbow on her knee and looked at him. Tiny arrow-shaped wrinkles furrowed her brow.

'What if these images you keep seeing are symbolic? You know how it is with dreams, everything is supposed to stand for something else. A woman dreaming of riding a horse is a symbolic image for frustrated sexual desire –'

'You've been at the Freud again.'

'If you don't want my help, just tell me to shut up,' Karel said, flushing. 'I don't like being patronised.'

'Okay,' Tom said, finishing his drink and putting the glass down. 'Shut up.'

'Thanks.'

'You're welcome.'

The dinner that evening was a much more formal affair than supper at home with his parents. Tom had put on a clean shirt and grey slacks but he still felt casually underdressed to the point of slovenliness, as if he'd stumbled by accident into the wrong party and been asked to stay. Karel had changed into a dark plum-coloured dress with a neckline cut square across her breasts, very severe and classical in style, which looked terrific against her tanned skin and silvery-blonde hair. Victor Lendrum appeared in a cream linen suit, a hand-stitched cream shirt edged with the faintest pink piping, and a deep cerise necktie marked off in diagonal stripes. His eyes were deep set and his nose and brows hawkish, the effect heightened by the lines etched and splayed backwards from his gaunt cheeks. He was of medium height, with sloping shoulders, and rather slender. Tom reckoned him to be in his early fifties.

Lendrum sat at the head of the rectangular table, Tom and Karel on either side facing each other. They were served by a silent middle-aged Portuguese woman.

Lendrum inquired about his studies at MIT and Tom felt relieved to be able to speak on a subject he knew something about; antiques and first editions were not in his line.

'Did you see the article by Salaman in *Nature*?' Lendrum asked him.

Tom shook his head and swallowed his food before answering. 'No – no, I didn't. I haven't done much reading recently.'

'Quite an interesting piece on time independent theory and zero-point energies. Though some of his ideas on matrix mechanics are pretty shaky.'

'Really?' Tom said. 'I guess so.'

'You've read Villars's book on matrix mechanics, I take it?'

Karel giggled at the expression on Tom's face. 'Can't say I have, sir,' he said, glaring at her.

'No? Pity,' said Lendrum coolly.

Tom felt himself going red. Karel pressed her fingers over her nose. Tom ignored her and said, 'Professor DeVoss – he's my head of department – has been working on a Quantum Field experiment with some people in the Department of Parapsychology. He's been trying for some time to formulate a scientific basis for ESP and precognition.'

'Is that so?' Lendrum said, without much interest. 'Worth doing, I suppose, if you believe in that sort of thing.'

Tom didn't pursue it. The safe and familiar subject of quantum physics suddenly seemed a minefield. It occurred to him that Victor Lendrum probably knew as much about quantum physics as he did about his own field of microbiology. Was there anything at all, Tom wondered, the man didn't know something about?

This thought stayed with him while they were drinking

coffee at the other end of the living-room, sitting beneath a large modern abstract canvas that consisted, to Tom's inexpert eye, of a fried egg on top of a block of grey concrete sticking up out of a desert. Karel put a Mahler symphony on the stereo while her father poured brandy into three glasses the size of small vases.

'Have the police been in touch with you about your sister?' Lendrum asked. 'Do they know what's happened to her?'

It was the first time Danny had been mentioned, though Tom had assumed that Karel had told her father about the missing child.

'No,' Tom said. 'We don't know anything more than what's been on TV and in the papers.' Not strictly true, he thought. But he wasn't going to start telling Lendrum about his weird dreams. If Karel was merely sceptical, Lendrum would probably laugh him out of the house.

'I think it was something to do with the blood transfusion Danny – my sister – was given,' Tom said bluntly. 'Contaminated blood that wasn't detected by the screening process. Do you think that's possible?'

Lendrum considered this for a moment and nodded slowly. 'Yes, it's possible. The screening process is fairly basic, as I understand it, and the checks at the donating station rather crude, mainly to determine whether the donor is diabetic.' He frowned and said, 'What kind of contamination are you talking about? Bacteria? Virus? Radiation?'

'Well – I'm not sure,' Tom said. 'You see, my sister was involved in a road accident –'

'Yes, Karel told me about that. But didn't she recover?'

Tom nodded. 'It seemed so at first. Then she started having fits and went into some kind of highly restive coma. The specialist at the hospital wouldn't commit herself as to the cause. In fact I think she was pretty baffled by the whole thing. Anyway, I heard a rumour that the blood Danny was given might be at fault. I can't think of any other explanation.'

'You say she went into a coma,' Lendrum said. He was

leaning back in the chair, one leg crossed elegantly over the other, the brandy glass dangling negligently in his left hand.

'Yes.'

'Did the specialist offer a diagnosis?'

'She called it hyperkinesis,' Tom said. 'The metabolism of the body speeds up –'

'Yes, I know what hyperkinesis is,' said Lendrum. He brooded for a while, stroking the tip of his nose with his index finger. 'I think you're mistaken,' he said eventually. 'As I understand it, hyperkinesis is usually the result of brain damage. I think it much more likely that the accident itself is to blame.'

Tom said, 'Then why didn't Dr Helms, the nerve specialist, say so? Surely she would have told us? And what about all the other children? Have they suffered brain damage too?'

Lendrum looked at him steadily. 'So you're convinced it was the blood transfusion that caused it?'

'I don't know what to think, sir,' Tom said wretchedly. It was on the tip of his tongue to tell Lendrum about his dreams. About the grey corridors and the square concrete rooms, about Danny standing in the open doorway beckoning to him. But he didn't.

'Well now,' said Lendrum. 'Perhaps you're right. I was merely hypothesising from what you've told me.' He smiled briefly, which sharpened his profile and made it almost predatory. 'After all, I'm not a doctor of medicine.'

'Bernie Gooch, a friend of ours, thought it might be socially or environmentally related. Something to do with food additives or pollution in the air or in the water.' The Mahler came to an end and the needle clicked in the groove. Karel got up to turn the record over. Tom went on, 'He said that as we conquer certain diseases we create others to take their place – "new plagues for old" idea.'

'Really?' said Lendrum. 'Interesting notion, but nonsense of course. What is your friend, an encyclopedia salesman? More brandy?'

He took Tom's glass and went over to the drinks cabinet.

'No,' Tom said, 'as a matter of fact he teaches biology in the local high school.'

'Ah!' Lendrum smiled indulgently. 'That would explain it. Every high school in the country is bulging with would-be Nobel laureates, each with his own pet crackpot theory.' He gave Tom a penetrating glance. 'Was he the one who put this blood transfusion idea into your head?'

'No,' Tom said stolidly. For some reason he felt a prickle of annoyance, as if Lendrum had insulted his intelligence.

Maybe his father had been right all along. These damn superior city people really took the cake. Did they imagine that the rest of the country was populated by illiterate peasants?

17

Captain Chas Dignum listened over the headset to the squawk coming from Nashville. Those air traffic boys were always complaining about something. Yap-yap-yap. He couldn't be bothered to pay attention to it. And anyway, he didn't need them; his instrumentation told him everything he needed to know.

He gestured to his first officer to cut them off, but Greg was too preoccupied listening to them, a deep frown on his face, to obey the request. Captain Dignum shook his head, more in sorrow than in anger, and eased the control column forward. Through the sloping forward windscreen he could see the lights of O'Hare Airport. He'd landed there so many times he could do it blindfolded.

The aircraft tilted as he applied slight left rudder, while with his right hand he adjusted the trim. The runway lights stretched before him in an inverted vee-shape, almost meeting on the dark horizon. He nudged the pedals the slightest touch to align the 737, and the aircraft shuddered as it encountered the wind currents at lower altitude. More turbulence than he'd expected. Automatically his hand went out to the trim wheel.

His first officer said something – shouted something – but Captain Dignum was concentrating all his attention on landing the big bird. Then the flight engineer started jabbering. Both men were yanking levers and punching buttons. What the hell was happening? Had they gone insane? He yelled at them to lay off. He was five hundred feet over O'Hare, coming in at one hundred and seventy knots on a westerly approach, for Christ's sake, and they'd chosen the trickiest moment of the flight to go berserk.

He felt the column move under his hands as the first officer grabbed the twin control column, and with all his strength Captain Dignum fought back. The two men wrestled for supremacy.

Captain Dignum was the stronger, easing the aircraft down into the black wedge of night between the sparkling runway lights, closing his eyes and breathing a silent prayer as a solid thump told him they were safely down.

'Be sure and check those temperature and pressure medians on tanks one and four,' the supervisor said. 'The printout showed abnormal readings on last night's shift.'

'Yeah, yeah. Don't I always?'

'So you say. Keep an eye on them.'

'Uh-huh.' Win Metcalf cradled the handset of the phone, hitched up the sagging seat of his grey overalls, and with the clipboard under one arm plodded along the gloomy concrete tunnel lined with pipes, electrical conduits and huge control valves painted in different colours.

Small and round as a barrel, with pouchy eyes and hanging jowls, he emerged from the tunnel into a vast cavern a hundred feet high, which housed eight holding vessels, each containing thirty thousand gallons of naphtha derived from shale oil. The heavy aroma of petroleum fumes hung in the humid air. Signs cautioned NO NAKED LIGHTS and HIGHLY FLAMMABLE. Plastic discs with a symbolic orange flame in a black circle were plastered everywhere.

The gauge of Tank 1 was a mite high, but nothing out of the ordinary. He tapped it with his knuckles and the needle jerked up a degree or two. He noted the reading on the clipboard, then checked the pressure gauge. Slightly higher too, but it was a balmy Virginian night outside, which would explain it.

He went along the row of tanks, entering the readings on the clipboard. Once an hour on the hour. It really wasn't necessary, he told himself. The readings were continually monitored anyway, up there in the AD/11 control room, by three guys with white coats and degrees and fat paycheques, who played gin rummy and drank enough coffee to float the *Titanic*.

Mind you, they probably never even glanced at the gauges up there in that carpeted, softly lit, air-conditioned lounge. They had the double fail-safe system. They had their fancy computer. And of course they had *him*. The crabby little guy who lived like a mole, clad in baggy overalls, whose chest wheezed with all the fumes he'd sucked in over the years. Win Metcalf laughed his dry rasping laugh. What he'd like, really like, would be to sit back on his butt and watch them handle an emergency. Find out what those degrees and white coats were really worth. And whether they could earn those paychecks when it came to the crunch. Yessir, he'd like to see that.

Win Metcalf unbolted the metal cover of the master fuse panel and swung it open. He shone his flashlight on the circuit diagram. It was the work of a few seconds to remove the fuses of the alarm system and the fail-safe backup, which automatically vented the tanks when temperature and pressure levels went too high.

He'd give them up there in AD/11 fifteen minutes to realise that something was wrong: circuit failures were registered on the control room board. After fifteen minutes he'd put the fuses back in. But Win Metcalf had a private bet with himself that they wouldn't notice a thing. Wouldn't even miss a hand of gin rummy.

Leaning back in his padded chair, Ted Shanks watched the red tail-light of the three-five curve away and finally vanish on the down-line to Shreveport. On the large illuminated panel in front of him, the signalman saw the green marker click into its slot, telling him that the freight train had cleared the points junction, opening up the branch line to Bastrop. He punched up his marshalling schedule on the monitor. There was a thirty-two-wagon train due at three-fifteen, joining the main line here for Jackson, where it would be rerouted to New Orleans.

Ted hummed a few bars of the old blues classic, 'Mystery Train'. That would be the regular night-run from the chemical plant at Bastrop, lit up like a Christmas tree with the yellow lights warning of a hazardous load. It trundled through the peacefully sleeping town of Monroe three nights every week. Ted wasn't sure what it carried, though he could have asked his brother-in-law, who worked as a despatcher at the plant.

He poured himself a black coffee from the thermos, and sipped the steaming liquid as he gazed out across the criss-cross of tracks, gleaming like silvery slug-trails under the gantry lights suspended fifty feet above the control box. He liked being alone and peaceful at this time of the night. Some guys couldn't take it, couldn't stand being alone, with time to think. After five years in the job Ted still relished and appreciated the solitude, a million miles away from all the mad daytime hustling and bustling.

A buzzer sounded on the panel. Ted glanced up at the clock: three-ten. The Bastrop train tripping the electronic relay, warning him of its approach. Now he had to switch the points junction to bring it on to the Shreveport–Jackson main line.

Ted reached out for the control lever in its grooved slot, and it struck him – odd thing, never had before – that it was just like the slide control on his stereo system back home in Sterlington. He was a big blues fan, had over six hundred albums, and could sit for hours listening to Muddy Waters, John Lee Hooker, Sonny Boy Williamson and Blind Lemon Jefferson. He smiled as he pushed the lever forward and heard John Lee coming over the speakers. Great stuff! He adjusted the volume, moving the lever back mid-way, and tweaked the balance to get it perfect. One of his all-time favourite tracks too – 'Union Station Blues'.

With a happy, contented smile, Ted closed his eyes and leaned back in the padded chair, mug of coffee in one hand, the other beating time on the arm of the chair.

A red light flared on the panel, blinking on and off, accompanied by a low yet persistent beeping, which Ted couldn't hear over the raw grating guitar and thudding bass.

Through the wide-angled window a glimmer of distant lights appeared in the darkness as the diesel locomotive hauled its ponderous load round the curve, building up speed as it approached the mainline junction.

'I was at the Union Station this mornin'
When my baby got on board.
Lord, I was done there tryin'
When my baby said way down inside . . .'

Part three
Eruption

18

The Secretary of State was awakened by Fred Holbeck, one of his senior aides, at a few minutes before five-thirty. It had taken twenty minutes for the cipher experts and intelligence staff in the communications room of the State Department to check back and verify with Reuters that the information was genuine and not some colossal, incredible hoax. They monitored all the major news-gathering agencies and had a tape of the night's bulletins set up and ready to run when the Secretary of State appeared, unshaven and heavy-lidded, still tasting the bean sprouts he had eaten the previous evening.

He watched the run-through with expressionless flat grey eyes, drinking hot sweet tea from a mug. He hadn't been in the job long, less than six months, and his staff watched from the corners of their eyes to see how he would react to his first real test 'under fire'.

Characteristically, he bared his teeth in a slow snarl of a smile (he had been the mid-west collegiate welterweight boxing champion of '63) which some interpreted as hawkish pugnacity, others as a badly disguised nervous spasm.

Item by item, the Reuters' bulletin rolled up the bank of green screens.

00.06: United Airlines Tristar, Flight 023, on the red-eye run from LAX to JFK hit a power cable on its descent over Paterson, New Jersey, and ploughed through an old people's home, killing all 155 passengers and crew and 22 residents.

01.15: PanAm 737 en route from Miami to Chicago lost power in both engines and crashed with the loss of 119 lives in the Great Smoky Mountains, Tennessee, 14 miles south of Gatlinburg. It was several magnetic degrees and more than 50 miles off course for no apparent reason.

01.39: A propane tanker on the Pennyrile Parkway turnpike,

Kentucky, exploded at a truck stop near to Hopkinsville, killing 16 people and injuring 30 others. Sitting on the toilet reading *Hustler*, the driver escaped with mild concussion and abrasions when the ceiling fell in on him.

02.25: Cox River petrochemical plant, West Virginia, exceeded pressure and temperature maximums, two fail-safe valves failed to operate, and a chain-reaction ripped through the complex, killing over 100 people in the local community, injuring many hundreds more, and causing wide-spread devastation.

03.18: 14 wagons carrying hazardous PCBs toxic waste were derailed on the outskirts of Monroe, Louisiana, sending a dense cloud of poisonous gas over an area of 90 square miles. Death toll difficult to estimate, though unconfirmed hospital sources place it in excess of 200. (Update 4.30: 272).

03.40: Main grid power failure on the eastern seaboard of South Carolina brought emergency standby generating capacity into operation in hospitals, factories, army installations and coastguard stations from Wilmington to Charleston. Cause unknown.

04.28: Iranian supertanker of 250,000 tons lost all navigational aids whilst negotiating the thin chain of islands along Raleigh Bay, North Carolina, and went aground on Cape Hatteras. No loss of life reported, but spillage of low-grade crude effectively blockaded all fishing ports on the Albemarle Sound and Pamlico Sound.

The Secretary of State called forward his senior aide. 'Status report, Fred.'

Holbeck was six-feet-three, a broad-shouldered, loose-limbed Texan with a tanned, fleshy face and a full set of perfect teeth. He looked like a Madison Avenue executive in his tailored business suit and striped shirt with button-down collar.

'There's been no overt threat to national security, sir. These appear to be random occurrences.'

'*Random?*' The Secretary of State shot him a glance. 'Seven major disasters within the space of five hours? What are you telling me?'

'Well, sir –' Holbeck hesitated. He looked round at the circle of faces, distinctly uncomfortable. 'There *may* be a connection. These kids who've disappeared could be the cause.' The Secretary of State was staring at him. 'We've received a report from the director of Golden Vale Clinic, Dr Fabius, that the five children in his charge have been able to exert some kind of psychic influence. In fact,' he cleared his throat, 'they almost broke free. They put one of the orderlies in some kind of – uh – trance. He was about to release them when Fabius stopped him.'

'You mean those kids at the Clinic are responsible for all this?'

'No – no, Mr Secretary. They've been separated and put under sedation. But there are more than thirty children who've disappeared and are still unaccounted for. Possibly they might – I mean, it could be that, uh –'

'Spit it out, Fred.' The Secretary of State was crouched forward, almost in a pugilistic stance. 'They could be *ganging up* on us? Is that what you're saying?'

'Yes.'

'That's great. That's just terrific.' He brushed a hand through his tousled white hair. He glared round. A pale, dark-haired man with rimless glasses was standing quietly at the rear, his arms folded, his face expressionless. Jerry Derker of the National Security Agency. Dammit, he hadn't wasted any time – here already, spying for the NSA. There was no love lost between the California-based agency and the State Department.

'Any more screwball notions, Fred?' growled the Secretary of State. 'Why not bug-eyed monsters from outer space? We haven't used that for a couple of weeks.'

Holbeck said, 'There is some evidence to support this theory, sir. The tower at Nashville monitored the last voice communication with the PanAm 737, a few minutes before it crashed. The flight captain was asking for landing instructions, yet he was fifty miles off course over the Great Smoky Mountains.'

'He was trying to land in the mountains?' The Secretary of State's gruff voice was squeaky with disbelief.

'Well, no – he didn't think so. He thought he was approaching O'Hare.'

'I think I need something stronger than tea,' the Secretary of State said, putting the beaker down. 'Jesus Christ Almighty.' He was dying for a cigarette and was resisting the temptation mightily. He turned to his media attaché, Hal Curtis, a dapper, meek-looking man with fidgety hands. 'Have Reuters put this out on the wire?'

'I assume they have, Mr Secretary.'

'You *assume* they have?'

'Well – yes. I haven't specifically checked.'

'Can we embargo it?'

'I wouldn't think – no, sir.' Hal Curtis shrugged his sloping shoulders. 'It'll have been picked up worldwide. With a single event we'd have a chance, but not with so many on such a scale.' He gave a weak, apologetic smile which irritated the Secretary of State to the point of white fury. First chance, he'd get rid of the man.

The Secretary of State leaned his clenched fists on the communications console and gave his slow snarl to the flickering green screens. No one uttered a sound. He stood hunched there for several long moments and then said, 'Fred. Who's ultimately responsible for Golden Vale Clinic?'

'In the Administration, sir? Meg Willson.'

'Get her.'

Holbeck pointed a finger at one of his assistants.

'Who's the duty officer for Delta Force?'

Delta Force was the crack squad of hand-picked marines,

every one a specialist, trained in anti-insurgency operations and threats to national security, under the direct and personal jurisdiction of the Secretary of State.

'Lieutenant-Colonel Lennox.'

'Request his presence.'

Holbeck signalled to another assistant, who picked up a red phone.

The Secretary of State muttered something. Holbeck leaned forward.

'Sir?'

'What can they want, Fred? What the hell do they *want*?'

Holbeck had no answer. He said quietly, 'Anything else, sir?'

'No. Yes.'

Holbeck waited.

'For crying out loud, somebody get me a cigarette.'

This was serious. Critical, Meg Willson reckoned. In her three-year tenure as Secretary of Health and Human Services she'd never known such a scare. Being summoned to the State Department in the early hours of the morning was proof enough. Something very big was going on. They were getting panicky, demanding action and initiatives and – she could smell it in the air – heads on a platter.

Meg Willson was rather fond of her head. It contained a first-rate brain, and in outward appearance a cool assurance that wasn't faked. She was good with people. She got along with both sexes, avoiding the stereotype of the armour-plated female career politician. Her staff liked her, almost idolised her, because she was dedicated to her job and loyal to them.

Under normal circumstances she and the Secretary of State had an amicable working relationship based on mutual respect. On this occasion he tossed a newspaper at her, sat back and beat time on the desk with his silver pen. It was the early edition of the *Washington Post*, the ink still damp on the front page banner headline.

Fred Holbeck, along with a dozen or so scientific and military advisers, hovered in the background. It still wasn't seven a.m., and the large office's lamps still burned.

Meg Willson read the first two columns and felt herself turning pale.

'I hope you took a course in crisis management, Meg. You're going to need it,' said the Secretary of State grimly.

'Has this been confirmed? All of it?'

'Every word is true.'

Meg Willson put the newspaper down and wiped the ink off her fingers with a tissue. The ominous silence in the room was unsettling. All eyes seemed to be focused on her.

'I'll do everything I can to help, of course, Donald. What is it you need? Name it.'

'Results, Meg. You've had those kids for weeks at Golden Vale. What have you come up with?'

'I don't understand. What are you saying?' Her expression was half smiling and half frowning, utterly confused. 'You think those children are responsible for *this*?'

'We don't know – that's the truth of it. But we've just had seven straight disasters in a row. That's not coincidence.' He tapped the newspaper with his hairy knuckles. 'Airplanes crashing, power systems failing, chemical plants exploding, tankers running aground – none of this happens for no reason. If those kids can kill people and then just vanish into thin air, get around the country without being spotted, who knows what they're capable of?'

'You're looking to me for an answer?'

'That's the consensus.'

'Not from where I'm sitting.'

'I'll tell you where you're sitting,' said the Secretary of State, leaning forward and clasping his hands. 'In the hotseat.'

Meg Willson plucked a thread from the sleeve of her tailored grey jacket. Even at this ungodly hour she'd taken pains with her appearance, unlike the bleary-eyed, unshaven man opposite her. It was necessary and very important to maintain the cool, calm, professional image.

When she glanced up her eyes were hard and ice-blue.

She said tightly, 'We have a bigger problem on our hands than you realise. Haven't you read about it? Innocent children are being chained and beaten and locked up in basements. Schools are being closed by vigilante mobs. The incidence of child-abuse has gone up over a thousand per cent. We're running scared of our offspring, Donald –'

The Secretary of State waved her to silence. 'That doesn't concern me. *They* don't concern me. *This* concerns me.' He jabbed the paper. 'If those telepathic monsters are responsible for this, I want them found. And the only way to find them is through those kids you've got locked away at Golden Vale. Do you get it? Am I making myself clear?'

'Telepathic monsters? What are they, some kind of alien invasion? For God's sake, Donald, these are our children!'

'That's right.' The Secretary of State nodded. 'And they've declared war.'

He'd said it before he realised he meant it. And it scared him to think that it was true. He had two little daughters of his own, Jeannine and Hayley, aged seven and five. Like all parents he had asked himself the same endless circle of questions. What was the cause of this sudden hatred and aggression against the adult world? Some form of collective paranoia? Or was there a reason – a reason so simple and obvious that everyone was blind to it? Young people had always resented the older generation, had wanted to sweep away the old and replace it with the new; that was accepted, a natural part of growing up.

But this wasn't like that. Nothing like it. This was naked violent confrontation. Meg Willson had introduced the word 'alien', and that, he now realised, was what they were faced with – the adult world at war with an alien species.

He spelt it out to her. 'Golden Vale is your direct responsibility and so far you've come up with nothing. The time for pussy-footing around is over. Either you break those kids or we'll get somebody who can.'

'Which method do you prefer? The rack and thumb-screws or the boiling oil?'

'Don't get cute, Meg. I've got a press conference to face in three hours' time. This guy you've appointed –' he glanced at a pink briefing note in front of him '– Brinkmann. He's a personal friend of yours, isn't he?'

Meg Willson nodded cautiously. 'That isn't the reason he was appointed, if that's what you're hinting at. Dr Brinkmann is one of the best child psychologists in the country. And he's the best man for the job. In point of fact, Donald,' she went on with some vigour, 'he's come up with a theory which might help to explain –'

'I don't want theories, I want results.' The Secretary of State swept his arm dismissively and picked up the note. He snarled a smile. 'K.I.D.S. I like it. It's catchy. But where exactly does it get us?'

'You've been in touch with him?' Meg Willson said coldly.

'The State Department has its sources, too. They help us find out what the fuck's going on. Not a lot, it would seem, judging from this.' He pointed his finger like the barrel of a gun. 'This one's for the record. We don't care how you do it. Just see that it's done.'

Meg Willson got up and stood stiffly by the chair. This time all the eyes in the room seemed to be avoiding hers. 'You'd have made a swell Gestapo officer, Donald.'

The Secretary of State chose not to reply to that.

Jack Werneth didn't dawdle after the meeting; he disliked gossip and wasn't a great mixer. He was striding along the glass-walled corridor towards the Microbiology Laboratory when he heard Sally Schroeder call his name. She gave him a hesitant, nervous smile, her pale blue eyes under fair brows giving the impression of myopia even though he knew she wore contact lenses. Her blonde hair was drawn tightly back into a neurotically neat bun.

Sally was in charge of all the experimental animals used at Biotech, of which there were several hundred, mainly mice, rats and guinea pigs, but also a few domestic cats and dogs.

'Can you spare a minute, Jack?' she asked a trifle breathlessly.

Werneth shrugged and nodded, and folded his arms, waiting with an impatience he didn't try to hide. Poor plain little Sally. He could snap his fingers and she'd come running, but she wasn't his type. Now if it had been that new young Jap kid recently arrived from Columbia, working in cellular biology – Yuki something-or-other – well, he wouldn't have minded a piece of that. He approved of the way Jap women treated their men. Trained from birth to please, he'd read somewhere.

'What is it? I'm busy, Sally,' Werneth said, when she just stood there blinking up at him.

'Can we talk in your office?'

'Is it important?'

'I – I don't know. I need your advice.'

Sally Schroeder gazed up at him imploringly. Werneth scratched his beard and finally nodded, jerking his thumb. He loped off ahead of her and pushed open the door, leaving it to swing to behind him. Sally came in and closed the door carefully, making sure it was shut.

Glass panels from the ceiling to halfway down the walls gave a view of the lab, row upon row of benches and equipment, with white-coated technicians, analysts and assistants bent to their tasks. Beyond the smoke-blue windows the hard Californian sunshine streamed relentlessly down on trim sprinklered lawns and neat gravel paths.

It had been one man, Louis Herne, now president and chief executive, who had founded Biotech a mere twelve years before; it was said to be currently worth half a billion dollars. Werneth didn't doubt it. Not when a single contract with the Defence Department had a bottom line of thirty million. That was one of the research projects presently going through the lab – finding a way to alter genetically the yellow virus fever to make it more effective. Transmitted by mosquito, yellow fever had caused millions of deaths over the centuries, and as the body had no natural immunity it was considered a biological warfare agent of great potency and potential.

Louis Herne was a smart operator all right. Werneth detested the preening pompous prick. Attended daily by his personal masseur, cosmetician and manicurist. And with that ridiculous hair, tinted and blow-waved as if he had the starring role in a glossy soap opera.

Werneth poured two cups of coffee and handed one to Sally. She took it and the liquid almost spilt. She raised the cup with both hands to her unpainted mouth and slowly sipped, her eyes above the rim wide, unseeing, scared.

'Now then,' said Werneth patiently, with something of an effort. 'What is it? One of your rats bit you?'

Sally smiled weakly and shook her head. Fucking dumb broad. No sense of humour.

'Jack – do you remember that Sporozoa strain we tried out on domestic animals about six months ago? We were testing for cell damage and cysts formed in the eye. We injected about a dozen cats and dogs.'

'Sure, I remember that. We're still working on it.' He gestured vaguely towards the lab. '*T. gondii*, right?'

Toxoplasma gondii was a parasite belonging to the generic class Sporozoa. It was widely distributed throughout the animal kingdom. As Werneth recalled, the idea had been to boost the resilience of *T. gondii*, with the object of making it more virulent to humans. Once in the bloodstream, infection persisted for long periods in a latent phase. Eventually it formed a huge cyst in the brain or the tissue of the eye, which, when it burst, spread thousands of tiny spores, or zoites, throughout the system. Usually the effects on human beings weren't all that severe – skin rashes, sore throats, glandular fever – though in pregnant women it caused abortions, or if the woman happened to go the full term, the child was born with cerebral calcification which resulted in mental deficiency and early death.

Jack Werneth had never really figured out what biological warfare application the geneticists and microbiologists had in mind. Except maybe that *T. gondii* was present in all races and was easily cultured in the lab. But then that wasn't his problem. They came up with the theories and devised the test programmes, he put them through the lab. End of story.

Sally set her cup down and leaned on the edge of the desk. She said slowly, 'I've been reading up on the epidemiology of *T. gondii*. Infection is most common in children. It seems the worst cases occur with immunosuppressed patients whose natural defences are inoperative, causing progressive lesions in the eye and the brain.'

Werneth was frowning down at her, vee-shaped wrinkles appearing beneath his receding, swept-back hair. He wasn't getting her drift. 'So what?'

'Those kids, Jack.'

'Which kids?'

'Don't you watch TV or read the papers?'

She couldn't be serious. But his heart gave a painful thump inside his chest. He had received a sudden and very ugly premonition.

'It wasn't a regular strain of *T. gondii* we used for the injections, was it?' Sally said.

'Well, no . . .' Werneth admitted. 'The genetics people played around with a few variations. They speeded up the breeding cycle for one thing, so that when the cyst ruptured it . . .'

He paused, his deep-set eyes sliding away evasively. The connection that Sally Schroeder was making was plainly ridiculous. He wouldn't accept it for a minute. A super breed of parasite, developed in the lab, which most commonly attacked children. Hysterical fantasy.

He said shortly, 'It couldn't happen. You think we've accidentally developed a new strain of toxoplasmosis that sends kids crazy? Not possible.'

'Why not?'

'Okay,' said Werneth, exasperated. 'You tell me how.'

'I don't know. But bacteria don't read textbooks.'

This was an old saying in the lab: it meant that the behaviour of organisms didn't always follow what accepted pathological practice said it should. There were exceptions to nearly every rule.

'Christ, where do you get these ideas?' Werneth said, tugging at his beard. He was getting angry now. 'Dime novelettes? Where's your evidence – or is it "female intuition"?' he sneered at her.

Sally gazed up at him with her myopic blue pitiful stare. She shook her head.

'Then what? There's something else?'

Sally continued to look at him. Her lips trembled.

'What, for Christ's sake? One of the animals die on you, go berserk, or what?'

'No. Escaped.'

'What escaped, exactly?'

'One of the infected cats.'

'When was this?' Werneth's mouth was suddenly dry and sour.

'Five – nearly six months ago. Within a week of being injected.' A nervous spasm flickered across her face. 'I didn't log it.'

Werneth was staring at her. 'Holy shit,' he said under his breath. 'That was pretty dumb. Why the hell not?'

Sally shook her head jerkily, like a bird. 'I – I was afraid to, I guess.'

'You were *afraid* to?' Werneth ran a hand through his receding hair. 'Jesus Christ, woman. If a whisper of this gets out they'll go through your records with a fine toothcomb. Mine too. They'll want to know what happened to every damn specimen, alive and dead.'

'What are we going to do, Jack?'

'We?'

'You'll help me, won't you?'

Werneth looked at her pale, frightened, upturned face for several seconds. That's all it took to calculate the odds. Sally had let the animal escape – that was her tough shit, not his. He was in the clear. But just supposing the *T. gondii* parasite was, even indirectly, somehow responsible for the children's erratic and aggressive behaviour. A special breed of parasite developed right here in the Microbiology lab. Then the crap would really start to fly, and Werneth knew he'd get his share, right in the kisser. So. The first thing was to check it out. Run a few tests. In secret, of course. If the worst came to the worst he'd have some quick thinking to do. Slide out from under. After all, if Sally hadn't let that fucking cat escape in the first place . . .

He put his arm round her shoulders and smiled down at her. 'Sure, honey. Leave it to me.'

19

It was an oddly unsatisfactory day for Tom. The city was refreshed after the rain, a warm balmy breeze blowing and clear blue skies above. They'd spent an hour or so wandering through Central Park, then looked at the collection of Greek sculpture in the Metropolitan Museum of Art, caught a cab downtown and browsed through Scribner's bookshop. But the sights of Manhattan, and even Karel's company, failed to distract him. The city seemed all pointless frenetic activity. He tried to lose himself in it, to have fun, to let go, but it was as though everything he did and saw was infected and poisoned by his own bad humour.

He made an effort to be chatty and cheerful, though Karel could tell it was rather a stiff, unnatural pose, like a cardboard mask Tom carried round with him on a stick.

They lunched on hot pastrami sandwiches on rye and ice-cold beer in a delicatessen overshadowed by the Empire State building, and Karel pointed up at the antennae winking in the sunshine atop the famous landmark.

Tom shrugged and nodded. Why not?

The express elevator took them to the enclosed observation deck on the 102nd floor where they leaned against the rail and gazed out at the East River, with the grey sprawl of Queens and Brooklyn beyond. On a good day it was said you could see for sixty miles.

It started at first as a faint throbbing headache. Tom closed his eyes. He shouldn't have had the beer; drinking in the middle of the day didn't agree with him. Karel was saying something. Tom saw her lips moving, but the words had no meaning. He closed his eyes again and found that he had left his body. He could see himself, next to Karel, both of them leaning against the rail, while the conscious part of him hovered several feet above. The feeling wasn't unpleasant, not even frightening, just rather strange.

The two figures receded and became foreshortened as he rose higher. Now he was looking at the tops of two heads, one blonde, one dark, through the intervening sheet of glass above the observation deck. The smooth close-slabbed side of the building slid by him, followed by the lead flashing and ornate stone moulding at the very peak of the tower, and then the crow's nest of television and short wave antennae dropped swiftly away until he was suspended in mid-air fifty feet above the Empire State building.

New York in brilliant piercing sunlight lay spread out beneath him.

He could see the traffic moving through the grid-iron pattern of streets, the people on the sidewalks tiny insignificant dots, hardly visible except for their shadows. He continued to rise until the buildings themselves merged into a jumble of shapes, and the entire island of Manhattan – a long sliver of land with the green square of Central Park at its centre – lay far beneath him.

A door opened in the sky. Framed in the opening stood a small, slender, familiar figure. He moved nearer, simply by expressing the desire to do so. The face was obscured by a shadow, and this disturbed him. Something had happened, but he couldn't think what.

Warm living flesh touched his. A pale, slender hand crept into his hand and Danny said, *Come with me. I have something to show you.*

'What is it?' Tom said. 'Where?'

Trust me. I won't hurt you.

Tom looked into her eyes and recoiled. They weren't Danny's eyes any more. They were milky and opaque, like clouded glass, and he thought desperately, She's going blind!

That's one of the side-effects, Danny said. *It's happened to some of the others too. Jimmy and Karen and the twins. Bad blood.* Danny's mouth split in a grin. *But just you watch!*

It appeared to Tom like a series of fast, almost subliminal cuts in a movie, jumping from shot to shot before the eye had time to take it in properly. A bearded man with receding hair in a white coat. Curved glass containers filled with bubbling liquids. Wire cages. Hidden eyes behind mesh. Shaded lamps. Polished wooden counters. Metal trays and plastic tubing. A tap dripping into a stainless steel sink.

Silence. Night.

'Where are we? What –?'

Shhhhhh.

A single blue flame. The blue flame spread, feeding others. The flames leapt and blossomed into yellow flowers with crimson edges. The glass containers cracked and exploded. The metal trays buckled, the plastic tubing melted and dripped. Everything was swallowed up in a shimmering white wall of intense heat.

Somebody screamed.

It was the fat woman standing behind Karel who had glimpsed the look on Tom's face, the vacant look of a catatonic. He blinked and grinned at her stupidly, and she screamed again.

'For God's sake don't do that again!' Karel said, herself ashen. 'What happened to you? Couldn't you hear me?'

'Why, were you saying anything?'

She was stunned and speechless for a moment.

'I've been yelling at you for five minutes, goddammit!'

'Have you?'

'Yes!'

'Oh,' Tom said. 'Sorry. I've been on a trip.'

The fat woman fainted.

A door closed quietly in the apartment and footsteps sounded on the parquet floor. Tom sat up as Victor Lendrum came into the room. Why did he always feel he had to be on his best behaviour with Karel's father? Tom didn't know how to take Lendrum, on what level their relationship functioned, if at all.

'How are you feeling now?'

Lendrum's face was grave and attentive.

'I'm fine, thank you.'

'Often get these attacks, do you?'

'No,' Tom said, trying to keep the annoyance out of his voice. Attacks? That made it sound as if he suffered from fits.

'You scared the hell out of me,' Karel said, pulling a face at him.

'A most distressing experience,' Lendrum observed quietly. He sat down in a curved walnut chair with an embroidered back and crossed his legs, adjusting the crease in his trousers the tiniest fraction. With that superior patrician face he would make a good poker player, Tom felt.

'Where was the fire? Do you know?'

'Well, not exactly . . . a laboratory, I guess,' Tom said vaguely. 'It was late at night, dark outside. There was plenty of equipment, specimen trays, and – cages, I think. Lab animals?'

'I *hate* all that,' Karel said.

Lendrum sat composedly, hands clasped on his knee. 'And

what do you suppose your sister is trying to tell you, Tom? You really believe you're in touch with her?'

'I believe she's in touch with me.'

'With what purpose?'

Tom shook his head ruefully. 'If I knew that, there wouldn't be any need to involve Professor DeVoss and the people in the Theoretical Physics Department.'

'Oh, yeah – particles travelling backwards in time and arriving before they started out,' Karel said, tossing her hair back. 'And you have the nerve to criticise psychology for not being a proper scientific discipline. Just explain to me, Tom, in words of one syllable, how something can take place before it happens.'

Tom said mildly to Lendrum, 'I think your daughter has what you might call a vehement scepticism about the whole project. But if it'll help Danny in any way, I'm prepared to try it.'

'You haven't answered my question,' Karel said. She sounded almost angry. 'Just tell me – explain to me – how this Quantum Field experiment works. I'd like to know.'

To Tom's surprise, Lendrum came to his rescue.

'You can't compare psychology and theoretical physics, Karel. Sub-atomic particles are in fact tiny packets of energy with extraordinary properties. They exist as finite forces, affecting space and time and everything in the universe. It's possible to track them, to study their behaviour under laboratory conditions. From that one can construct an hypothesis and test it by repeatable experiments.' He turned to Tom. 'What interests me is how Professor DeVoss intends to set about the Quantum Field experiment. Do you know, Tom? Does *he* know?'

It wasn't just a big question, it was *the* big question: how to tune in to the wave impulses reaching Tom from an outside source, focus them, and interpret them in meaningful terms. If thought waves were capable of travelling through space (and how else to explain the images placed in Tom's mind by his sister?) there was, theoretically, no reason why these same waves couldn't be detected by the incredibly sensitive equipment used to track sub-atomic particles with a life-span measured in trillionths of a second.

Tom had discussed it with Ward DeVoss on the phone, and DeVoss had tentatively agreed to give it a try. There were dangers, of course. You didn't lightly fool around with 750 MeV (million electron-volts) of particle beam energy, which was the operating capacity of the Bates Linear Accelerator.

The real crunch would come in trying to marry the 'hard' science of quantum physics, with its immense energies, cyclotrons and enough equipment to fill several office blocks, and the barely respectable fringe study of parapsychology, which dealt with such nebulous concepts as ESP, precognition, Jungian synchronicity and blind faith.

True, there was a middle-ground where these two disciplines met and overlapped, sharing, perhaps, a common metaphysical or philosophical frame of reference. But it was precisely this territory that was unknown, unexplored, and rife with ambiguity: about as easy to quantify as pinning a soap bubble to the wall with a six-inch nail.

Lendrum smiled at Tom's obvious perplexity. He wasn't smiling when he said, 'You know, Tom, using quantum physics to probe into a person's mind isn't exactly your everyday lab-bench experiment. I hope DeVoss knows what he's doing – and doesn't plan to bombard your brain with neutrinos or mu-mesons, or anything quite so foolish.'

Karel had gone very still and was gazing at her father with a deep frown.

'How dangerous is this?' she asked suspiciously.

'I wouldn't know, my dear. I doubt if anyone does. I'm sure that Tom and Professor DeVoss will take all the necessary precautions. Do the authorities at MIT know about this?' he asked Tom.

'No. We haven't told anyone.'

'That's very wise. The last thing you want is for the State

Department or some Government agency to come along poking their beaks in. After all, you never know what use they might make of such information.'

'Are you seriously trying to tell me that this could *work*?' Karel said, glancing from her father to Tom and back again.

Lendrum regarded Tom thoughtfully. 'We must wait and see,' he said.

Joe Stalito winced and pulled a face like a gargoyle as Peter Krill removed the syringe from his scrawny tattooed arm. The nurse took the syringe and injected the 75ccs of blood into a sealed plastic bag. She wrote on a label and stuck it on to the bag. Krill watched all this anxiously, but the nurse, a buxom woman in her fifties, was experienced and capable, her movements deft and unfussy.

'Giving blood isn't a federal offence, Joe,' Krill said, swabbing the needle mark with a cotton wool pad soaked in alcohol. There were several old puncture marks dotted along the blue artery, Krill noted, but for the moment he said nothing. 'Why didn't you admit it when I asked you?'

'Yeah, well –' Joe Stalito shrugged. 'I don't like to be hassled, you know? Nothing against you, doc,' he assured Krill earnestly. 'You were straight down the line. No complaints.'

He warily eyed the nurse as she placed the plastic bag in the refrigerator.

'What happens now? You run tests on that or what?'

'We'll send it to a lab in Atlanta.'

'*Atlanta?* Why? What the hell for?'

'No need to get panicky, Joe. They have special facilities there, that's all. They'll run some tests and send us the results.'

Joe Stalito lit a cigarette, in contravention of the notice on the wall, and sucked in a deep lungful. He smiled nervously, his brown teeth wreathed in smoke.

'Guess I'm kinda special, huh?'

'You could be.'

'Is it rare, my blood?'

'Pretty rare.'

'That why you need it so bad?'

Krill glanced at the nurse, who was tidying away the syringe, plastic tube and metal bowl. He was reluctant to say too much in her presence; in fact he didn't want to say anything to anyone until he had the results from the Centre for Disease Control in Atlanta. He said, 'You happen to be one of nine people who according to the records donated a particular type of blood in the Los Angeles area. There could be a constituent factor – that is, something in your blood we have to trace and identify.'

Krill smiled reassuringly and forced himself to pat Joe's shoulder, in spite of the stained, reeking sweatshirt that hung on his narrow frame like a mouldy sack.

'Don't let it worry you. You've been feeling okay, haven't you?'

'I get these stomach cramps I told you about. Like somebody twisting a knife in my gut.'

'How long have you had them?'

'Six months, maybe longer.'

'Do you take medication?'

'I got some stuff from the druggist. Brown stuff in a bottle. Tastes like tree bark.'

Krill said, 'Thank you, nurse. Is it all right if I use this room to talk to Mr Stalito? Five, ten minutes?'

When she had gone and closed the door Krill pulled up a chair and took the list of names from his pocket and read through them aloud. 'Any of these names familiar to you? Are you personally acquainted with any of these people?'

Joe Stalito dragged on his cigarette, shaking his head. 'Nope. Never heard of them.'

'You're absolutely sure?'

'Don't know any of them, doc, honest.'

Krill put the paper away. 'I have to ask you some personal questions, Joe. I want to emphasise that this is a medical matter, nothing to do with the police. Do you understand that? But it's important you tell me the truth.'

Joe Stalito shrugged. 'Go ahead.' He was using the cigarette to demonstrate his casual indifference and yet his body was tense, a tiny muscle jumping in his upper arm.

'Have you had any homosexual contacts?' Krill said, trying to keep his voice as neutral as possible. Even so, Joe Stalito was offended.

'Do I look like a faggot? I got a girlfriend – you saw her picture! Ask anybody! I like women and they like me.'

Krill let that one pass. 'Is there any history in your family of mental problems – chronic depression, schizophrenia, any kind of psychosis? Your parents, grandparents, close relatives?'

Joe Stalito gave the appearance of thinking about this while he tapped out a cigarette and lit it from the butt of the old one. He shook his head.

'You're certain about this – none of your family has been treated for a psychological condition?'

'No. Nobody.'

'Okay. Last question. Are you on drugs?'

'You mean hooked?' Joe Stalito laughed and Krill eased back slightly to avoid the gust of breath. 'Sure, I smoke grass, who doesn't? But I never touch the real shit. Not me. I seen 'em with a habit. No thank-*yew*. Include me out, as they say.'

'What about your arm?'

'What about it?'

Krill took the sticklike wrist and extended the arm to show the tiny puckered scars in the crook of the elbow. Joe Stalito jerked his arm back and glared suspiciously at Krill, his eyes red rimmed in his drab white face.

'What the fuck are you trying to lay on me? I come here of my own free will, I take your goddam test, I don't make no trouble, and what do I get for it? Some goddam smartass quack tryin' to set me up on a narcotics rap.' He pointed his nicotine-stained finger at Krill. 'I got rights, just like anybody.

I could sue for – for – for slander, for deforming my character or somethin'.'

'You couldn't because I haven't accused you of anything,' Krill said patiently. 'Just tell me how you come to have those needle marks on your arm. You're not diabetic.'

Krill waited.

'You'll have to tell me sooner or later.'

'Don't have to,' Joe Stalito said sullenly.

'I'm sorry, but you do.'

'You're not the cops.'

'That's true. But I can – and will – involve the police if I have to. I don't want to have to do that, Joe. It's up to you.'

'Thanks a lot, doc.' The sarcasm was laid on with a shovel. He spoke to the pastel green wall. 'You trust a guy, you try your best to help, so what happens? You get dumped on.'

Krill said, 'Listen to me, Joe. This is important. I'm not asking these questions in order to incriminate you, but I have to know the truth. You and eight other people in this area gave blood for . . . wait a minute. Did you donate your blood or sell it?'

'I got a few dollars,' Joe Stalito said with a shrug.

Krill cursed himself. It had been staring him in the face and he hadn't seen it. For many people, especially those on the shadier fringes of society, selling blood was one way to eke out their security benefits and the few dollars they made by hustling and dealing in stolen goods. It was highly likely that, as a group, such people would be host to sexually transmitted and drug-related diseases – a whole damn raft of them. Screening identified the worst of these and the blood was not used; though you couldn't screen for something you had no prior knowledge of.

What had fooled him, he realised, was that some of the addresses had been in respectable, well-off districts and not just confined to the poorer areas of the city. Of course he hadn't been able to track down any of these so-called respectable, well-off people that the Blood Bank's central computer had thrown up, so it was impossible to draw any conclusions about their actual status.

He said, 'Wait here a minute, I have to check something out,' and went to the door.

Joe Stalito was on his feet in his laceless sneakers, his skinny throat working with anger or fear, Krill wasn't sure which.

'You're going to call the cops.'

Krill shook his head curtly. 'I keep telling you – this isn't a police matter unless you choose to make it one. Sit down and have another cigarette. Do you want some coffee? I'll have the nurse fetch you some.'

The nurse was in the next room, looking through a card index with a preoccupied frown on her face. 'Do you think you could find the man in there a cup of coffee?' It was several years since Krill had worked in a hospital but he knew that certain members of the nursing staff, particularly the older ones, had to be handled with kid gloves. Smile when you ask for anything. Only octogenarian surgeons could risk being crusty and get away with it.

His eyes flicked down to the plastic tab above the row of pens on her formidable starched bosom.

'Nurse Allison, do you happen to keep a record of payments made to people who've given blood?'

'Those who've attended this hospital, yes we do, doctor. Is that what you want?'

Krill unfolded his list of names. 'It'll do for a start.'

She took down two large ring binders and laid them on the desk. They were indexed alphabetically, Krill saw, which made things easier.

'The man in there's a donor, isn't he?' Nurse Allison said.

Krill nodded.

'I thought so.' She was still frowning. 'But didn't you say his name was Stalito?'

'That's right,' Krill said, leafing through the pages.

'I *knew* I'd seen him before – actually it's those tattoos on his arms I remember.' She indicated the card index file. 'In fact I was looking for the name . . .'

Krill raised his eyes to gaze at her.

'Joe Stalito didn't give his blood here,' he said hollowly.

'The man in there certainly did.'

'Are you certain?'

'Absolutely.'

'Under what name?'

'That's just it, doctor, I can't remember.'

Krill showed her the list and Nurse Allison pounced on it at once.

'There – Saler. Gary Saler. I was right. Let's have a look.' She delved into the card index. 'Yes, here we are. Gary Saler. Last attended on June the eleventh.' She handed the card to Krill.

'There are a lot of guys around with tattoos.'

Nurse Allison drew herself up a little. 'Doctor, I remember him quite distinctly. Saler or Stalito, or whatever his name is, it's the same man.'

'Did he produce his ID and social security number?'

'Of course,' Nurse Allison said in an offended tone. 'No one is allowed to give blood without the proper documentation. We stick to the rules here, doctor.'

'Yes, of course, I wasn't trying to imply –'

Krill stared at the list and then at the card, held in either hand. Something flashed in his head. His heart started to thump violently. Eight of the people on the list weren't donors at all, which was why he'd drawn a blank on them. Only one person was. The cunning little weasel next door had got hold of stolen IDs and social security papers and gone around selling blood at different hospitals and donor stations.

It was so simple and yet it explained everything.

Why Joe Stalito had at first pretended to be someone else. Why he was so pale and washed out. And why he couldn't explain the puncture marks on his arm.

My God, thought Krill – it meant that one person was the

source of the contaminated blood. One man was solely responsible for the spread of the disease affecting children the length and breadth of the country. One man had done all this. The man in there.

Krill opened the door and his breath seized up in his chest at the sight of the empty chair. Then a wheedling, complaining voice said, 'What about that fucking cup of coffee you promised me, doc? I don't like being treated this way. I got my rights, for chrissakes!'

20

Johnnie Bromke lay on the couch, sweating. His eyes were shut and he was breathing through his nostrils. The sound was very loud in the shadowed room. It reminded Brinkmann not of a young boy but of an old man near the end of his life. The narrow chest rose and fell with a spasmodic motion, the fists curled at the boy's side twitching and white to the knuckles.

'And when do you hear the voices? All the time or just when you're sleeping?'

Johnnie's lips trembled. 'Mostly at night. They wake me up.'

'What do they say?' asked Brinkmann quietly. 'Can you tell me what they say to you?'

A long shuddering breath. 'They want me to go with them.'

'Do they say where?' Brinkmann rested his elbows on his knees and waited a moment or two. 'Johnnie, do the voices in your head say where you have to go?'

Johnnie twisted on the couch as if in pain.

'To go with them,' he repeated. And then, 'We belong together, all of us. When we are all together we are strong. We can do nothing alone . . .'

'But do they say where?' Brinkmann persisted gently. 'Where is this place you have to go to? Tell me its name.'

Johnnie's hand raised itself and pointed to the corner of the room. His face had a drawn, waxy pallor, again like that of an old man.

'There –'

'Yes?'

'Under the ground.'

The hand fell back and tightened into a rigid fist. The boy's lips stretched across his face in a ghastly grimace as if he were enduring the most terrible torture.

Brinkmann straightened up and laced his fingers together. He had been pushing hard, perhaps too hard. He was balancing a tightrope between delicately probing the boy's unconscious to release what was locked away there, and a complete breakdown and possible disintegration of personality.

At least they were making progress, he felt. Yes, most definitely. The hours of quiet conversation had paid off. And Weiss had reported a breakthrough with Donna Perera, who had actually talked about that horrendous night when she had taken a shotgun and wiped out five members of her family. She saw the series of incidents, Weiss said, as if she were watching a movie on TV and she was one of the actors. It had been at the same time real and make-believe, a confused mixture of reality and fantasy, the two inextricably interwoven.

'She feels no guilt or remorse,' Weiss had told Brinkmann. 'For the simple reason that these are not real people, not flesh and blood. You see somebody get killed on TV in one show and up he pops in another, good as new. People die and are effortlessly resurrected.'

Brinkmann wasn't satisfied. 'But why kill them in the first place? You haven't given me a motivation, Otto.'

Weiss had mulled this over in silence. 'No. Except the disinhibition of their psyche releases the impulses lurking in us all. Why does man have the urge to kill? We kill animals and one another, often for no valid or discernible reason. In most of us this desire is controlled, repressed, but here the normal inhibiting mechanism is absent.'

It couldn't be that simple. There was, for instance, the extraordinary degree of empathy that existed between the children. How to explain that? Some form of collective will-power? Together, it seemed, they were able to pool their mindpower and use it to influence others – to influence the thoughts and behaviour of people *at a distance.*

Ever since the night when Fabius had come across the orderly in the act of unlocking the door to the dormitory, care had been taken to keep the children separated. As a group they presented a threat. On their own they lost this mysterious 'power' – or at any rate it was greatly diluted – and reverted to silent, sullen withdrawal.

The next step, Brinkmann had convinced himself, was to try to understand the significance of the 'voices' that Johnnie and some of the others had spoken of. And under his patient questioning, a few answers were slowly beginning to emerge. He just needed time and perseverance, and to be left alone to get on with it.

Johnnie Bromke had relaxed and was breathing steadily and evenly. The dead waxy pallor in his cheeks had been replaced by a faint tinge of colour. His hands were open, moist, palms uppermost.

The effect of the sodium pentothal was wearing off. It was rather an old-fashioned drug to use, though Brinkmann favoured it because it could be precisely controlled and the side-effects were minimal. It did no more than put the patient into a light sleep, allowing the deeper, murkier stuff to bypass the censor of the conscious brain.

'Can you hear me, Johnnie?'

The boy mumbled something and opened his eyes. Brinkmann drew in a breath. The irises were cloudy; he had noticed the same with Clare Sachs the day before.

He passed his hand across Johnnie's face and the boy blinked.

'How do you feel?'

Johnnie was staring into the corner of the room. Suddenly

his eyes rounded in terror and he cowered away. 'I didn't, Jimmy, I didn't!' he said in a hoarse whisper. 'They didn't make me. They don't know. They don't know!'

'Who is it, Johnnie? Who is it speaking to you?'

'I wouldn't do that. They can't make me!'

Brinkmann reached for the boy's hand and grasped it. It was cold and clammy, like a piece of dead meat. Brinkmann tried not to confront the thought that had been hovering on the edge of his mind for days and now forced itself into full, inescapable view. *These children carried with them the stigma, like the odour of decay, of extreme old age.*

'Where's the voice coming from, Johnnie? Can you see him? Can you see Jimmy?'

Johnnie nodded, still staring into the darkened corner of the room.

'He says I mustn't – can't – mustn't say –'

'But you can say, Johnnie. It's all right. You can tell me.'

'No, I can't – he won't let me –'

'Yes you can. You're safe. You're here with me.'

There was a single peremptory knock on the door and Robert Fabius strode into the room. In the corridor outside were two men in green camouflage uniforms and forage caps with the peaks pulled down over their eyes. They were armed.

'Dr Brinkmann, I've been ordered to take charge of this clinical investigation. This facility is now under the jurisdiction of the State Department.'

Brinkmann stood up. He had gone white. He advanced on Fabius, who retreated a step or two.

'You – imbecile! You –' Brinkmann was shaking. He pointed to the red light above the door. The words were thick in his throat. 'Do you know what that means? Do you? Under no circumstances is the doctor to be disturbed with his patient.'

'Yes. Except that this child is no longer your patient, Dr Brinkmann,' said Fabius stiffly. 'You have no authority here, no medical standing. This matter is now out of your hands.'

Brinkmann took out his handkerchief and wiped his forehead. His hand was trembling. He looked at the boy lying on the couch, gazing vacantly into space. Too late now. Wherever he was, he was out of Brinkmann's reach.

He turned back slowly to Fabius. 'Do you know what you've done? Do you know what you're d-d-doing?'

'Yes, perfectly,' Fabius replied. He made a gesture to the men in the corridor. 'Please see that Dr Brinkmann returns to his quarters and stays there.'

Visible evidence of the new regime at Golden Vale became apparent the next day. Guards were posted at the gate and patrolled the grounds. Sensitive areas of the Clinic were off-limits to anyone without security clearance. Strangers started arriving, who despite their civilian dress bore the unmistakable stamp of military intelligence. A distraught Weiss sought out Brinkmann and they walked together in the grounds, away from human and electronic eavesdroppers. Weiss was in a quandary. What ought he to do?

'Do you want to quit?' Brinkmann asked him.

'What else can I do, Jacob? How can we stand by and allow this to happen?' Weiss' pudgy hands circled the air emptily. 'Apart from the purely moral and humanitarian point of view we have our duty as doctors, the ethics of our profession to consider.'

'Leaving won't prevent it happening,' Brinkmann said soberly. He had considered the options open to him very carefully, and had decided to stay, whatever restrictions Fabius decided to impose.

'We can make a formal protest to the Medical Association.'

'And what good do you think that would do?'

'They have a duty – a responsibility – as do we –'

'So have the State Department – and they'll make sure that their duty and responsibility override all others.' Brinkmann looked back at the low white building with the tiny barred windows. There was something fundamentally sick about a society that treated its errant young like the inmates of a psychiatric concentration camp. Especially when they had been nurtured and warped by that very same society that locked them away and pumped them full of drugs.

'Meg Willson is a personal friend of yours, isn't she?' Weiss said hopefully. 'The Clinic is ultimately her responsibility. Speak to her, tell her –'

'I already have. I called her this morning.' Brinkmann wearily shrugged his heavy shoulders under his shapeless suit. 'She can do nothing. She's over the same barrel. The hawks have taken over the dovecote, my friend.'

Weiss looked as if he was going to cry.

'This man Fabius – he astounds me. We have the results of the blood tests from Atlanta, we have Peter Krill's report on the donor he traced, we have proof that the K.I.D.S. hypothesis is probably correct – we have all this and it doesn't shake him one iota. He still insists that his barbaric "modern methods" are the only way to achieve results. Drug and shock and beat them! That's the answer!'

'You missed out sensory deprivation,' Brinkmann said. 'He's planning to use the SD Chamber.'

'*No!*'

'Oh yes.'

'He told you this?'

'Not Fabius, Helen Murphy. They've been given a deadline by the State Department. The children have to be found and stopped before any further disasters happen. Fabius knows how – or so he thinks.'

'But Jacob, we were so *close*,' Weiss said despairingly. 'Donna was starting to trust me a little, to open up. It was like – like fine-tuning a radio signal and listening in to a communications channel with information continually flooding in.' He waved his hands in circles. 'It's here in the air all around us, everywhere . . .'

Brinkmann nodded, recalling Johnnie Bromke's hand pointing to the corner of the room. 'Only we no longer have a receiver.'

They turned and walked back along the gravel path.

'You've noticed the physical changes of course,' Brinkmann said. 'The eyes, the skin tone, the hair.' Weiss nodded silently, eyes downcast. 'The hyperkinesis has affected their metabolism, speeded up the body's natural processes. They're living at fifty times the normal rate. Burning themselves out.'

'Yes!' Weiss stopped and drew himself up to his full five-feet-four. 'You are absolutely right. We have to stay. Fabius wants results at any cost. We must do all we can – whatever we can – to protect them.'

'You're speaking of the children.'

'Why – yes,' said Weiss, blinking behind his glasses. 'Who else?'

'Well,' said Brinkmann softly. 'It occurs to me that Fabius and the others could be the ones who need protecting.'

A hush fell as Louis Herne entered the room. A young fresh-faced executive sprang forward, found a chair for the company president, and all but bowed as he ushered him towards it.

Herne's mane of silvery white hair gleamed like the bow wave of an ocean liner at full speed. His tanned face was crazed with a mosaic of fine lines, like carefully preserved parchment. Probably the rest of his ageing body was just as well preserved, thought Jack Werneth uncharitably.

Werneth glanced round at the dozen or so department heads assembled here. Something was up. There was an atmosphere as potent as nerve gas. The president of Biotech wasn't in the habit of flying down from San Francisco to the research and development division in San Diego to exchange pleasantries with his senior personnel.

Lynch, Herne's right-hand man, had followed him in, and behind Lynch came two other men. One was small, pale, dark haired, with rimless glasses and a bland, closed face. He was a new one to Werneth, but he had government or secret service stamped all over him. The other guy – Werneth frowned, a corrugation of wrinkles appearing on his high forehead – was somebody he knew very well indeed. Victor Lendrum.

In fact Lendrum was looking straight at him as he took his seat. Werneth nodded. Lendrum's expression didn't alter.

'Gentlemen,' Lynch said, shuffling some papers. 'As a company working on classified government defence contracts we have to be – and seen to be – scrupulously careful about matters of security. There have been certain rumours circulating about which Mr Herne is naturally concerned. Over the next ten days we intend to carry out, with your cooperation, a systematic review of procedures department by department. This meeting is notice of that review.'

He blinked rapidly and passed a gaunt hand over his domed head.

'We have to tighten up, keep a close watch on our sterile areas, ensure that all records are accurate and updated. We have called in Professor Lendrum, whom most of you know and have worked with, in his capacity as one of Biotech's senior scientific advisers over the years. He will require complete access to all records, facilities and experimental work in progress. If there are any questions either myself or Professor Lendrum will try to answer them.'

Werneth tugged at his beard. There was a hollow feeling in the pit of his stomach. Something here didn't add up, but he was damned if he could figure out what. Sally Schroeder wasn't dumb enough to have talked; he himself hadn't said a word. What rumours was Lynch referring to? He hadn't heard any rumours.

Lynch hadn't introduced the small, bland, faceless guy, Werneth noted. Who was he? State Department? CIA? They wouldn't have involved a security agency – and dragged Lendrum all the way from New York – unless there was cause for concern. Damn it all, they *knew* something. But how?

Questions were being asked but Werneth was only half listening.

The meeting broke up. Werneth was in line, filing through

the door, when somebody touched his sleeve. It was Lendrum, his finely etched features and sharp prominent nose giving him the appearance of a shrewd, vigilant hawk. They shook hands.

'Anything interesting in the pipeline, Jack?' asked Lendrum in his quiet, evenly modulated voice.

Werneth gave a shrug that was more of a nervous twitch. He was three or four inches taller than Lendrum but he always felt intimidated by the other's coolness and gravity. He exuded a kind of effortless God-given superiority that Werneth resented.

'Not much. We're having some luck with African swine fever. A new strain with double the normal toxicity.'

'That sounds promising. I might come down and have a look.'

'Do that. Any time.' Werneth grinned and gestured vaguely. 'What's all this about, anyway? I haven't heard any rumours about slack security.'

'No? Well, perhaps it's a fuss about nothing. But as Lynch said, we can't be too careful.' Lendrum glanced over his shoulder at the small pale man in the rimless glasses. 'We don't want to upset the NSA, do we?' he said, lowering his voice.

Werneth had guessed right – or nearly right. The innocuous-looking guy was with the National Security Agency, possibly the most secretive and subversive arm of government. They got up to tricks that even the President himself didn't know about.

Then Lendrum said out of the blue, 'Are you still working on the toxoplasmosis project? I haven't seen it mentioned in any reports recently.'

'I'm not sure. I'd have to check. I think so.' The words came out in a rush, spitting like machine-gun bullets. Werneth tugged at his beard. 'It's difficult to keep track of everything going through the lab,' he said apologetically. 'Any reason for your asking?'

Lendrum looked into Werneth's eyes and actually smiled, a pretty rare occurrence. But it was a smile without much warmth. 'No reason. Just curious. Keep up the good work, Jack.'

'Yeah. Sure,' Werneth said mechanically, and got out quickly, before Lendrum's curiosity threw up any more questions that scared him half to death.

Twenty minutes later, in Louis Herne's office, Lendrum, Lynch, and Jerry Derker of the NSA sat in white moquette armchairs watching the company president having a quiet nervous breakdown. He was fumbling with a tumbler of neat whisky, trying to get as much of it as he could into his mouth. He was sweating heavily, his silvery ocean wave of hair wilting over his eyes.

'I'd appreciate some evidence, some *hard* evidence, Victor,' Lynch said, studiously ignoring the pathetic wreck opposite him. 'As far as we know there hasn't been a viral or toxic leak here for over seven years. Apart from which, I for one don't see any link between toxoplasmosis and the aggressive behaviour of these young children. The particular strain we're developing has been tested on all kinds of lab animals without apparent effect. I've examined the records myself. No erratic or hyperactive behaviour. No side-effects. Nothing.'

'Records can be falsified,' Lendrum said.

'We don't know that. How can you be so sure?'

'I wasn't, until half an hour ago when I spoke with Jack Werneth. He almost jumped out of his skin when I mentioned toxoplasmosis. He's covering up.'

'What – that there *has* been a leak?' Lynch was out of his depth.

'Possibly. We believe –' Lendrum's curt nod included Jerry Derker in this '– that Werneth suspects that *T. gondii* strain to be the culprit. They were working with a particularly virulent mutant type.'

'You're familiar with this line of research?' Lynch asked, giving Lendrum a fish-eyed stare.

'I ought to be. I instigated it.'

There was a chasm of silence. Lynch passed a hand over his shiny head of skin. Jerry Derker was gazing out of the window at the unclouded pale blue sky. There was a clink and a gurgle as Louis Herne tipped the crystal decanter.

'But why should he want to cover up?' Lynch persisted. 'We're all involved – the company – everyone.'

'For that very reason,' Lendrum said, 'that we're all involved, Werneth included. It was developed in the Microbiology lab under his supervision. He doesn't care what happens to the company, or you or me or anyone. But he cares very much what happens to Jack Werneth.'

'What do you propose we do about it?'

Lendrum tapped his fingers on the arm of the chair and studied the carpet. Jerry Derker's glasses flashed as he casually turned from his contemplation of the sky and said, 'Nothing.'

Lynch's long bony face was a picture of total mystification.

'Are you serious? We don't take any action whatsoever?'

'That's correct,' Derker said gently. 'We do nothing.'

The tiny mouse brain had been sliced into transparently thin segments and placed on slides. Slides had been placed on top of those, enclosing the specimens in a sterile glass sandwich. The animal had been injected and killed six days before. This lapse of time was necessary before the Romanowsky stain test could be applied and the slices of brain examined for parasitic organisms.

Encased in skin-tight surgeon's gloves, Werneth's hands felt as clammy as shrink-wrapped liverwurst.

He pushed the hooded cowl of the lamp away to prevent extraneous light spilling in, selected a slide at random, and switched on the microscope. After a couple of fingertip adjustments, Werneth pressed his eyes to the moulded rubber eye-pieces and brought the cross-hairs into fine alignment.

Marked by the purple dye, thousands of crescent-shaped organisms formed a huge pseudocyst in the tissues of the mouse brain. They had invaded the cell-structure, multiplied, and the cells had ruptured, releasing them to attack other cells and invade the central nervous system. The brain was packed with them. Tens of thousands of the parasite *Toxoplasma gondii.*

Not the regular common-or-garden variety to be sure. These babies were a special breed, a master race. And they'd been bred right here in the lab: another technological triumph for Biotech, another ace up the sleeve for the U.S. Defence Department, another milestone in bacteriological warfare.

Werneth straightened up and squeezed his eyes shut to adjust them to the darkened laboratory. The dim white face of the clock on the wall said one-forty. His lips felt dry, his throat parched.

He had to think this through, and it had better be good.

It had been Lendrum's idea to conduct research into this more virulent strain of *T. gondii*, while he himself, merely following orders, had put the programme into operation and overseen its progress through the lab. Sally Schroeder had been responsible for injecting the test animals and observing the results – and for maintaining security, Werneth reminded himself.

So, considered in that light, Lendrum and that stupid bitch Schroeder – who had let the cat escape and then damn well not logged it – were the ones to blame. He'd only been doing his job. Done it well too. Why the hell should he, of all people, be sitting here sweating in the middle of the fucking night, trying to save their skins? Give me one good reason, he thought, why I should take the rap for somebody else's crazy schemes and gross incompetence.

Unfortunately, that wasn't how others would see it. The finer points of blame and responsibility – who had done what and why – would get pushed aside when the shit hit the fan. They wouldn't appreciate the technical subtleties and qualifications. To them it would be stark black and white. Jack

Werneth was head of Microbiology, and his department had played a central role. Get out of that one, Jack.

He tried another tack. Supposing it was possible to isolate the antibody in the infected blood, then maybe they could produce a serum to combat and overcome the virus. This was entirely feasible. They had developed the new strain of *T. gondii* here, they had the lab animals, they had the equipment and expertise. In fact, as Werneth now realised, it *had* to be done here at Biotech and nowhere else because they alone possessed both the new strain of *T. gondii* and the knowledge of its probable, or potential, effects.

Werneth considered this, thinking it through, staring with unseeing eyes at the glass slides glinting in the light of the lamp. He was no miracle worker, no medical saviour. It was purely and simply a question of practical expediency. His career. His reputation. His neck.

Werneth took the slide from the microscope and placed it with the others in a sterile plastic container. He put what remained of the mouse brain in a glass jar half filled with saline solution and screwed the lid on tight. He then took the container and the jar to the refrigerator chest. He was about to lock them away when something occurred to him. In a day or so, certainly by the end of the week, a team of investigators would come snooping round the lab. They would demand a detailed accounting of every specimen in store. They would want to know what was on the slides, who had prepared them, the reason why, and what the results were.

That would force his hand, Werneth thought with a sick jolt to the stomach. Isolating the antibody and preparing the serum – assuming it was practicable – would take several months of sustained and intensive work. The only evidence that a rogue parasite had been developed in the lab, and allowed to escape, was on these slides and in this jar. Sally Schroeder might suspect, but even she wouldn't know for sure – unless he chose to tell her.

Werneth dropped the container and the jar into a black

plastic bag, sealed the neck, and carried it to the electric incinerator in the corner. He set the dial, switched it on, and waited for the temperature to build up. In a few minutes he could feel the heat pulsating from the galvanised steel casing. Opening the lid, Werneth tossed the bag into the glowing red mouth of the chute.

Immediately there came the explosive crack of breaking glass, followed by sizzling and hissing sounds. Werneth stroked his beard and smiled. Those vicious little bastards were now frying in hell. And he was badly in need of a drink.

He reached to switch the incinerator off and screamed. The fingertips of his plastic glove melted as he touched the dial. Werneth jerked his hand away, leaving behind shrivelled pieces of skin. Bent double, he yelled and cursed, holding his burnt raw fingers close to his chest.

The incinerator was clicking and rumbling. The red needle was hard up against the stop marker. This shouldn't happen – couldn't happen – Werneth told himself. There was an automatic cut-out when the temperature reached 400°C. There was just no way the machine could have gone out of control. No fucking way.

Werneth was still telling himself this when the toughened glass of the temperature gauge cracked across the middle and the metal dials and switches started to drip. He spun around, clutching his hand, and ran. He had got halfway to the door when everything turned red. The blast lifted and hurled him on a wave of furnace heat. At once the lab turned into a giant incinerator, pulverising everything in the fiery heart of its inferno to so much dead grey ash.

21

Fred Holbeck waited for the message to sink in, then stepped forward with the rest of the bad news. He was holding several sheets of yellow flimsy in his large tanned hand.

'Mr Secretary, we've also received a number of classified reports from internal sources –' He held out the sheets.

'Read them.'

Holbeck cleared his throat. The assembled staff in the State Department Crisis Centre and the operators crouched over their VDUs made a silent, receptive audience.

'Timed at three-thirty hours. Item: Main grid power failure in South Carolina brought emergency generating systems into operation at the Charleston naval weapons station in order to maintain nuclear warheads at a critical sixty degrees and thirty per cent humidity.'

'I'm still listening,' the Secretary of State said when Holbeck paused.

'Timed at four-fourteen hours. Item: Strategic Air Command listening post on Seal Island, Georgia, responsible for monitoring Soviet bombers over the western Atlantic, lost all radar cover for nineteen minutes. Power was maintained during this period but the screens remained blank. Cause yet to be established.'

Holbeck read on in his Texan drawl, detailing instances of loss of national defence capability at two further missile bases, a radar installation, and a Category A underground data processing nerve centre, which indicated that it was a prime target in the event of nuclear war.

When he had finished, the Secretary of State refilled his mug from the large thermos on the desk. He spooned in brown sugar while the room waited, the screens buzzing, a distant electronic relay chattering to itself.

'What's our present status, Fred?' he asked, looking directly at Holbeck for the first time.

'Everything back on-stream, Mr Secretary. No permanent damage or impairment of facilities reported.'

'Then it was just a warning.'

'Looks that way, sir.'

The Secretary of State sipped his tea. He was trying not to think of nicotine. He said, 'Haven't we any idea yet where these little bastards are hiding out? No electronic or radio interference that would indicate their location?'

Holbeck raised his eyebrows at one of the scientific advisers, a tall stooping man with mournful eyes, who shook his head.

'Not a beep, sir. Whatever this force is they're using, we can't trace it. We've tried every frequency on the scale, including short-wave and infra-red. Nothing registers.'

The ultimatum was still on the screen and the Secretary of State read it again, his lips moving silently.

THE EVENTS OF THE PAST SEVEN DAYS ARE A DEMONSTRATION AND A WARNING. UNLESS ALL RESEARCH, DEVELOPMENT AND MANUFACTURE OF BIOLOGICAL AND CHEMICAL WEAPONS IS HALTED IMMEDIATELY, TO TAKE EFFECT WITHIN FORTY-EIGHT HOURS, FROM MIDNIGHT EASTERN TIME, WE SHALL PROCEED WITH A SINGLE ACT OF SUCH SCALE THAT NO PERSON LIVING IN THE UNITED STATES WILL ESCAPE ITS CONSEQUENCES. THE GOVERNMENT MUST ACCEDE TO THIS DEMAND OVER ALL MAJOR TV AND RADIO NETWORKS. IT MUST ALSO SET UP AN INDEPENDENT BODY TO REGULATE AND ENFORCE THE COMPLETE BAN ON ALL FORMS OF BACTERIOLOGICAL WARFARE.

THE CHILDREN OF AMERICA

'Was this picked up by the news agencies and wire services?'

'No, sir,' Holbeck said. 'It came through on one of the Pentagon security channels.'

'I thought you needed the code to gain access to them?'

'That's right,' Holbeck confirmed. 'You do.'

The Secretary of State glanced round with his hard flat stare. 'Some security channel. Some code.'

'They must have infiltrated our computer database,' said one of the military liaison officers. 'I guess,' he subsided lamely.

'Thank you, Lieutenant, for that imaginative and reassuring deduction.' The Secretary of State jerked his thumb at the screen. 'Fred, what the hell is this biological and chemical stuff all about? Why pick on that? Do they know something we don't?'

Holbeck shrugged. 'That's hard to figure, sir. We're spending about a billion dollars a year on biological weapons research, but that's a fleabite out of the entire defence budget. Frankly, I don't know why.'

'All right. Next question. What's this "single act" supposed to mean? What are they talking about?'

'They have any number of options,' Fred Holbeck said. He snapped his fingers and one of his staff placed an open file in his hands.

'Detonating a missile in its silo. Blacking out total radar cover over the U.S. Causing a nuclear reactor to go critical and leave us with a China Syndrome on our hands. And that's not taking into account the millions of tons of nuclear and chemical waste on the move around the country at any given time.' He wagged his head stonily. 'They have so many options, sir, we can't even begin to consider a fraction of them.'

'Are you serious? This is just a bunch of crazy kids.'

'That's right, sir,' Holbeck agreed. 'Last time they killed several hundred people. Now they're threatening the entire country. Next time we could be counting the dead in millions. That's how crazy they are.'

'Can they do that or is it just a bluff?'

No one seemed to want to meet the Secretary of State's eye.

No one had an answer. Delta Force was on full alert, kitted up and ready to go – but go where? You couldn't fight what you couldn't find. Now they'd been given forty-eight hours. If they failed, the question of whether or not this was a bluff would be answered by the history books.

The Secretary of State snarled to himself. He knew that everyone was watching to see how long his nerve would hold out before he had to turn tail and call the President. Maybe that time was close, but not yet. Not just yet. He said, 'What's happening at this damn Clinic? You're not telling me we can't squeeze the truth out of five snot-nosed kids.'

'We are making progress there,' Holbeck informed him. 'Brinkmann has been replaced and Fabius believes he'd found a way to break them. He's pretty confident that one of the kids is ready to crack . . .'

'What do you mean, "ready"? *When?*'

'Fabius didn't commit himself to a precise time, sir.'

'He didn't? Too bad. We've been given an ultimatum of forty-eight hours, so I don't see why he should be left out of the fun. He's got twenty-four hours. Tell him that.'

When Holbeck remained standing there like a block of sandstone rock, the Secretary of State barked, 'What are you waiting for?'

Holbeck was plainly in the grip of an internal struggle.

'Do you want me to brief the President, Mr Secretary?'

'Do you think it slipped my mind?'

'Well, sir, I just thought –'

'It didn't. I'm handling this. That's all.'

Tom was on a high. Two things had contributed to this. First, Ward DeVoss had called and told him that they were all set with the Quantum Field experiment. Tom was to leave for MIT in the morning. The second thing was a small item tucked away in the late-afternoon edition of the New York *Daily News*. Tom rarely bought a newspaper – usually magazines and science journals – and the fact that he *had* bought one, and today of all days, struck him as too amazing to be mere coincidence.

It was six p.m. He walked briskly along Central Park West and turned east past the few blocks near the university to the apartment.

Karel let him in, wearing an apron. Her nose was shiny and her cheeks were flushed. It was the housekeeper's evening off and she was in the middle of preparing dinner. Lendrum was in his study, having returned from a trip earlier in the day. Tom leaned against a worktop in the long, narrow kitchen, watching her slice vegetables. He folded the paper and propped it before her. She chopped and diced until he started jabbing his finger.

Finally she stopped and looked at the short item at the bottom of page nine headed: *Mystery Fire Destroys Lab*.

In half a dozen lines it said that fire department investigators were sifting through what was left of the research laboratory of a San Diego pharmaceuticals company.

'How do you know that's the same one?' Karel said when she'd read it.

Tom wouldn't be put down. 'A man was killed in the fire, just as I saw it. What more do you want?'

'It doesn't say he had a beard.'

'My God, you're a hard woman to convince.'

'Healthy scientific scepticism. Isn't that what you're always preaching, professor?'

Tom bit her on the nape of the neck. He felt light headed, balanced on a knife-edge, as if he were living on his nerves. He knew that when he came down it would be with a thump.

They ate at the polished walnut table at one end of the elegant living-room, Victor Lendrum wearing a plum-coloured velvet smoking jacket that Tom thought didn't exist outside of Charles Boyer movies. Lendrum was as ever reserved and polite. Trying his damnedest, Tom couldn't visualise anything remotely like a normal, happy father–daughter relationship between these two.

But then, the father–son relationship in his own case wasn't exactly the perfect role-model; to the outsider it too must have seemed barely tenable.

'Tell me something, Tom.' Lendrum toyed with his crystal wine glass. Diamonds of reflected light moved across his tightly drawn features. 'You say you saw your sister, Danny, in this underground . . . place. But you've no idea where it was – or is, should I say.'

'No. It was dark and damp, with corridors and lots of small windowless rooms. I got the impression that it was underground and hadn't been used much. Danny was scared that we might be overheard or discovered.'

'By the other children?' Lendrum seemed genuinely interested.

'I guess so.'

'But you – didn't see any of the others?'

Tom shook his head. He was puzzling over the change in his sister the last time he had seen her. When she had shown him the burning lab. What was it exactly? He said, 'The other day there was something different about her. She looked young and yet old at the same time, like a – a –' He swallowed. 'An old woman inside the body of a young girl.' Now he remembered. 'There was something wrong with her eyes too.'

'Her eyes?'

'They were blank – glazed looking. The irises were very pale, almost colourless. As if there was a layer of skin over them.'

'Milky?'

'Yes,' Tom said, 'Milky.'

Lendrum drank some wine and dabbed his lips with his napkin. 'The cause of that could be any number of things; perhaps a secondary symptom of another complaint.'

'Cysts in the eye formed by progressive lesions leading to focal chorioretinitis,' Tom said. 'And eventually blindness.'

Lendrum glanced at him sharply, his lips tightly compressed.

'Have you been reading up on this?' Karel asked Tom.

Tom was frowning down at the table. He shook his head slowly. 'No, I haven't.'

'How come you know so much about it?'

'Acquired or congenital toxoplasmosis,' Tom said, looking at a whorl of grain on the table. 'It's related to the same class as the malaria parasite. Carried in the gut of animals.'

'The pure science curriculum at MIT has certainly broadened in scope,' Lendrum said, pouring wine from a decanter into the three glasses with a nerveless hand. 'You're very well informed for a quantum physicist. Do you know what the cure is?'

'There is no cure. No drug affects cysts. And because the disease is found in immunosuppressed patients it's difficult to treat.'

'Yes, well, of course, this is very interesting, I suppose, but it doesn't mean very much, does it?' Lendrum said.

'Doesn't it?' Tom said.

'You sound very positive about this, Tom,' Karel said. 'How can you be so sure?'

'I don't know. I just am.'

Lendrum gave a faint, scornful smile. 'A quite remarkable method of diagnosis, Tom, through the medium of a dream –'

'It wasn't a dream,' Tom said stubbornly. 'I saw her. I was there, with her, with Danny, in the shelter.'

'While your body remained somewhere else,' Lendrum said, raising his eyebrows in mock amazement. 'What do they call it? "Astral projection"? The spiritual body roaming at will through the universe.' He was smiling broadly now. 'Even more remarkable.'

'I thought scientists were supposed to keep an open mind, to question rather than reject all assumptions and possibilities,' Tom said coldly. 'If it was any different Einstein would have remained a patent clerk all his life and we'd still think of the atom as a solar system in miniature.'

'Okay now,' Karel butted in. 'Let's call it a tie, shall we? I always thought quantum physics and microbiology shared some common ground, but there we go, silly me, wrong again.' She pulled a face at Tom, wrinkling her nose, but he didn't respond. She didn't like his fixed, intense expression; in fact it scared her. 'What's wrong? Are you all right?'

Tom had seen once again the bearded man working late at night in the laboratory. The explosion, the fire, the wrecked equipment, the broken glass. But before that – something before that. Go back, go back. He rewound the spool of memory in his head to what the man was doing at the bench, a scalpel glinting in his rubbery fingers. Doing what exactly? Tom struggled hard to remember. Why was the laboratory so important? Why couldn't he make the connection, find the missing pieces to complete the pattern?

He got up, or rather staggered up, from the table, and stood swaying slightly. A door had opened in the fog. Maybe it was Danny who had done it – leading him by the hand through the gloomy grey labyrinth to this blinding, shocking revelation.

'That man in the lab, Wer – Wern – *Werneth*. Werneth. He was trying to find out if it had caused the aggressive behaviour in children. He was scared to death that it was the virus they were developing for the Government. He had to destroy the evidence before you found out. It was your research,' Tom said. 'You developed it, didn't you?'

Lendrum was shaking his head sadly and wearily. He raised his hands and pressed them gently towards the table. 'Tom, calm yourself. This is all nonsense and you know it. All this must have been very difficult for you, upsetting, we appreciate that. We understand.'

'Are you seriously accusing my father?'

Karel had risen to her feet, fists clenched by her sides, confronting Tom.

'You have no right to say such things, just because you've got some crazy notion that Danny is communicating with you. For God's sake, don't you see how crazy this is? Don't you?'

Tom swept his arm out to the paintings on the walls, the

antique *objets d'art* arranged tastefully on tiny carved tables, the rare first editions and leather-bound folios behind glass. 'Stuff like this doesn't come cheap, I bet. A professor's salary wouldn't pay for the frames, never mind the pictures, but a quarter-million-dollar consultancy retainer would, sure enough.'

'This is preposterous,' Lendrum said, throwing down his napkin. 'You don't know how or why these children have been affected in this way any more than I do. You have no evidence at all that a virus in the bloodstream is responsible. Nobody knows.'

'The children know.'

'By divine inspiration, I suppose,' murmured Lendrum sarcastically.

'No – that *is* the crazy thing.' Tom laughed. 'But whatever this virus was you developed. It didn't only make them hyperactive, it expanded their consciousness and speeded up their mental processes. It brought out latent powers we probably all possess but have forgotten how to use. That's a neat, sweet irony, isn't it? You gave them the power and they use it against you.'

'Utter nonsense,' Lendrum snapped. 'There isn't a shred of –'

Tom went through into the hallway, grabbed his coat and went out of the apartment. Karel shouted after him but he didn't answer.

22

The sensory deprivation room was eight feet by eight feet by eight feet. It was actually a room within a room, a solid wooden framework lined with one-foot-thick polystyrene padding on walls, ceiling and floor. The only light came from a small blue fluorescent tube protected by steel mesh. When this was turned off and the door panel sealed, the occupant existed in total silence and darkness; even his own voice and the sound of his breathing were sucked in and swallowed by the thick padded cocoon. Two hidden speakers, in the floor and ceiling, were used to introduce what was technically known as 'white noise' into the environment: a deafening sustained hiss, like a radio channel between stations, which never varied in pitch, timbre or intensity.

Many of the techniques had been borrowed from the treatment of American flyers shot down in the Korean war and further refined by the Chinese in Vietnam. Isolation from the outside world, combined with sensory deprivation, led to disorientation of the subject and a complete breakdown of personality. It was then possible to undertake a thorough reconditioning of the subject's psychological profile and to instil new behaviour patterns by the threat-and-reward system.

Volunteers from U.S. prisons and the armed forces had lasted an average of fifty-two minutes in the SD Room before beating soundlessly at the walls and pressing the panic button. When released they were grey-faced and wild-eyed, some of them babbling and giggling like imbeciles.

Sampson proposed an initial two-hour period, as a 'softening-up session': one hour of silence and darkness, one hour of white noise. This was to be followed immediately by interrogation. If results were not forthcoming or were inconclusive, increase to three hours, then four, and so on, until the breaking point was achieved.

Helen Murphy pointed out the dangers. 'If we succeed in disintegrating their personalities completely – wiping the slate clean – maybe we'll lose the information we're after. After all, we don't want to end up with mindless shells.'

Fabius sided with Sampson. 'Their minds are far too strong for that, Helen. They've shown themselves resistant to everything – drugs, behavioural therapy, conceptual modification, psychoanalysis. We must press ahead with an intensive course of SD on the lines that Sampson proposes. We have a deadline. And God knows, we've wasted enough time with Brinkmann and his namby-pamby methods.'

The first subject was Craig Holley. His heartbeat, blood pressure and respiratory system were checked and he was sealed inside the SD Room.

One hour of silence and darkness and one hour of white noise later he was released, his functions checked again and found to be within a percentage point of normal. Under close questioning he showed no signs of deterioration, nor any inclination to cooperate. The only discernible difference in him was that his hair had started to turn white.

Donna Perera was put in next. There was no panic button installed in the SD Room and so no way of knowing how the subject was behaving or reacting. The subject might have gone mad in there, tearing at the walls, listening first to the deafening hush of silence and the blood pounding behind the eardrums and then to the steady unvarying inescapable hiss of white noise. There was no way of telling until the panel was opened and the subject taken out by the white-coated orderlies.

One after the other the children were put through the ordeal. Afterwards the medical examination and the interrogation. They had been inside for over twice the length of time a sane adult could stand and yet, except for a couple of minor physical characteristics, appeared unchanged, their minds locked tight, untouched by trauma, unassailable.

The children were returned to their separate, guarded quarters and a discussion went on late into the night.

'One of them has to break,' Fabius said. 'That's all we need – just *one* of them to show the first faint crack.' He paced restlessly up and down the office adjoining the SD Room. A chair under a cone of spotlights stood in the corner, where the post-session interrogations took place. 'It doesn't matter which one – they must all have the same information.'

Helen Murphy was looking through the medical records,

horn-rimmed glasses magnifying the bags under her eyes.

'There's nothing here to even hint that their metabolism has been affected. Blood pressure, pulse, respiratory function, everything is normal. You wouldn't think they'd just been through a traumatic experience that would send most people insane. It's as if they pulled the mental shutters down.'

Fabius halted. 'Is there any possibility that they could have helped each other?' he asked suspiciously.

'I don't see how,' Sampson said. 'They've been kept apart.'

'Maybe distance isn't important. If some kind of collective willpower is operating they could focus their concentration on the subject undergoing sensory deprivation. Damn it, they could be in constant communication with one another and we wouldn't know it!'

Helen Murphy said, 'You mean they're not actually alone in there at all, psychologically speaking?'

'I don't like this kind of talk,' Sampson said irritably. 'Brinkmann was trying to peddle the same kind of nonsense. I thought we'd got rid of all that. I suggest we increase the SD period to four hours. They'll crack, I promise you.'

'All right,' Fabius agreed. 'Who's the best candidate?'

They all thought for a moment, and Helen Murphy said, 'Brinkmann got the Bromke child to talk. Maybe he's the weak link . . .'

Sampson nodded brusquely. 'You're right – he could be the chink in the armour,' he said, blinking his watery blue eyes in growing excitement. 'We must press home our advantage while the boy is disorientated. Forget the others for the time being.'

Johnnie Bromke was brought in. He had a pugnacious, street urchin's face and straight dark hair cut in a ragged fringe. There was something about him that made Helen Murphy shudder. At first she couldn't figure out what; and then she could. It occurred to her that there was an old man squatting inside the boy's skin.

Fabius said, 'Right, let's get on. Take him through.'

An orderly touched the boy's shoulder. The boy looked up at him, his face devoid of expression, and obediently followed the pointing finger.

The silent, black emptiness was like a beating heart. Contracting and expanding in vast rhythmic surges so that Johnnie Bromke was crushed and smothered and then falling freely with dreamlike slowness through starless night. One minute the soft walls were closing in to form a suffocating narrow airless cubicle, the next they had receded to the outer bounds of the universe, leaving him floating in nothingness.

He listened.

Sometimes the girl's voice was very near, a whispering echo inside his head. Then it would fade and he was alone again. He tried speaking to the girl, calling to her through the inky black silence:

Here I am. Please help me. Here I am. Please help me.

But she was gone and he was lost and alone.

Until she came back, her voice swelling sweet and strong in his mind:

We're here. We can help you. We're here. We can help you.

Johnnie felt happy then, and smiled. He could see her dark shining hair curling around her head. She was smiling too, a pretty girl with warm brown eyes. She was his friend. She would help him – and help Donna, Craig, Stuart and Clare too. He tried to find the others, casting out the net of his thoughts, but it came back empty. That sometimes happened, and it wasn't too bad, he didn't really mind, not as long as his new friend stayed with him. He said:

Can you feel where I am?

There was no answer, no whispering echo, and Johnnie felt terror clawing at him, tearing his mind into shreds that fluttered in the claustrophobic void.

Yes, we feel it. (The voice was back!) *You're not alone. Where are the others?*

I can't feel them, Johnnie said. *You search for them.*

Why won't they help you?

They can't.

Why?

We're not strong enough. We need your help. I feel others there with you. You're much stronger than we are. Help us!

The pretty, dark-haired girl held out her hands to him. Johnnie reached out to her. *Danny* –

Come to us.

He floated nearer to her in the inky starless void, arms outstretched, but try as he might he couldn't touch her. She began to fade.

Don't leave me!

No answer.

Please!

Then her voice was very close, whispering right inside his mind:

You're not alone, Johnnie. We won't leave you. Wait.

'Did everyone get that?'

Danny opened her eyes and looked round the circle of joined hands in the centre of the bare concrete room. The physical contact helped to concentrate and focus the energy of the group.

One or two, slow in surfacing, opened their eyes.

Karen Swanson said, 'I think somebody should stay with him. He feels scared to me.'

'He is scared,' Morey Lang said. 'But it needs all of us to reach him and hold on to him. We've got other things to do, Karen. We can't afford the time and effort.'

'I got a picture of a tall guy in a white coat,' Selwyn Brown said. 'I saw it plain as anything in Johnnie's head.' His round black face, like a polished bowling ball, shone in the room's dim light.

Jodie looked at her blond twin brother, Paul, and they said together, 'Fabius.'

Scott Nassar held out a hand behind him, found a chair,

and sat down. The action reminded Danny of an old man, deaf and partially blind, she used to see in the park. The old man must have been over seventy, and it chilled her to think that Scott was not yet ten.

It wasn't only their minds that were accelerating – their bodies too, their entire metabolism, was running out of kilter.

Jimmy Yerke turned his milky stare upon her and Danny quailed. He mustn't read her mind, he mustn't! The thought that Jimmy was probing into her brain with his grubby feelers made her ill with a repugnant loathing.

She clamped her mind shut against him, closing down each stray unguarded thought one by one.

'Let's wipe out this Fabius creep,' Jimmy Yerke said. His tangle of curly hair, almost to his shoulders, framed a pale, taut, intense face, the milky eyeballs like two cloudy spheres. 'We fixed that bastard in the lab. Incinerated his ass.' He chuckled in his throat. 'There's nothing we can't do if we put our minds to it.'

'Killing Fabius won't get them out,' Danny said quietly. 'They're under guard there. There must be another way.'

She looked round at them huddled together in the damp, claustrophobic bunker. With the arrival of the twins, Jodie and Paul, a week ago, that made twenty-seven. There could be more on their way. At night, in her dreams, Danny heard the thin, plaintive cries of others seeking them out.

Morey Lang, tall for his age, with a ginger crewcut and drenched in freckles, said, 'It isn't only Johnnie and the others in the clinic we have to think about. They could break him. He'd tell them about us – where we are. They'll find us!'

'They're going to find out anyway,' Karen Swanson said. Her party dress was rather grubby and one of the puffed sleeves was half torn off. Her calm icy-blue eyes regarded them flatly, rather like a society hostess fallen amongst disreputable company. She said, 'We ought to get out while we can. Sooner or later somebody's going to check out this place, make sure the power's on, the water supply's working –'

'We can handle *anybody* who comes,' said Jimmy Yerke smugly. He stared at a spot on the wall and a black, smoking circle appeared, spreading outwards. 'Zap!'

'Jimmy, quit that!' Danny said sharply. 'You know what we agreed. None of that down here. It could be dangerous.'

'How they gonna get in for a start?' Jimmy Yerke said, squinting sideways as if his view was impeded by an invisible obstacle. 'Tell me that. This place was built to withstand a hundred-megaton direct hit. It's sixty feet underground, with two-inch solid steel doors –'

'You're missing the *point*,' Karen said. She was used to having her own way; it was tiresome having to explain the simplest thing. 'This place was perfect – it had food and water and was stocked with supplies – as long as nobody knew about it. Once they know where we are – forget it.'

It was true, Danny thought. Time was running out for them here.

Morey was looking at her – not just *at* her but *inside* her. She could feel on the back of her neck the cold prickling of flesh she experienced whenever one of the others had entered her mind and read her thoughts. *Yes*, she heard him say inside her. *I agree.*

Aloud he said, 'We have to think about the ultimatum, don't we? Keep them away – or keep *out* of their way – until they agree.'

Danny had a fleeting impression of gleaming rails converging to a distant vanishing point across a vast empty landscape. She heard a low shuddering rumble, the protesting shriek of metal wheels, felt the earth reverberate under an immense weight.

'Can we really do it?' Selwyn Brown asked.

'The threat is what matters,' Danny said.

'Send in the A-Team,' Jimmy said gleefully. 'Boom! Wipeout!'

'You've watched too much television,' Danny said.

Jimmy grinned. 'I don't only watch it,' he said cryptically.

Danny had tried to see into Jimmy Yerke's mind and failed. Either it was a murky, impenetrable trash heap of TV gore and romantic violence and casual blood-letting, or perhaps he had just become very clever at blocking his thoughts to outside scrutiny.

'What the hell, let's go ahead and do it,' Jimmy said. 'They'll believe it then, all right.'

Morey shook his head. 'That wouldn't achieve anything. As Danny says, it's the threat, not the act itself, which is important. We have to convince them that we really mean it, that we can carry it out.'

Jodie glanced up suddenly at the ceiling, her eyes locked in a rigid, glazed stare. 'Yes, Paul?' she whispered.

Morey Lang raised his hand for silence. Everyone watched Jodie as she communed with her twin brother sixty feet above. She listened and nodded and said, 'Paul says there's somebody moving around near the entrance.'

'Police? Army?'

Jodie's gaze went back to the ceiling, and then she shook her head. 'No, just somebody prowling around.'

Danny looked at Morey and could read his thoughts plainly enough.

Time is running out . . . if we're going to move it had better be soon.

Joe Stalito was one of those people who begin to believe a lie if they live with it long enough. Distorting the truth was second nature with him, so that very soon the truth became lies and lies became the truth, and he was unable to differentiate between the two.

It didn't seem to make any difference that Krill had the nine medical records in front of him; that the blood types matched Joe's; that he had been positively identified by medical personnel at all but two of the hospitals and donor stations. Despite all this Joe Stalito was still insisting on his innocence.

Showered and scrubbed, deloused and dressed in a pale blue

antiseptic shift that reached to his spindly white ankles, Joe sat on the bed in the barrier ward of the hospital annexe. A plastic name tape – *Stalito J.* – dangled like a cheap bracelet on his thin wrist with its knotted blue tangle of veins.

'You went back on your word, doc.' He scowled at Krill. 'You told me I wouldn't be kept here. That was your promise. Just routine you said. This ain't routine, for chrissakes. Look at me!'

'Would you prefer a police cell, Joe?'

'There you go again, threatening me! I got my *rights*. And what about Tiger?' Joe whined. 'Who's gonna look after him?'

'Who?'

'My goddam cat. Who's gonna feed him?'

'He seems to do a pretty good job on his own.'

'I feel responsible for him. He's a live creature,' Joe said, displaying a new-found sense of Christian duty.

Krill sighed heavily. He was running short on tight patient smiles and bland reassuring words, was clean out of nice liberal sentiment altogether.

This pathetic creature on the bed was a walking biochemical lab with a tenacious and virulent parasite seething and multiplying in his bloodstream. The man himself might be innocent, an unsuspecting carrier, but the fact remained that he was host to a highly dangerous, perhaps deadly disease.

'You might not realise it, Joe, but I happen to be the best friend you're ever likely to have,' Krill told him, tight lipped. 'Until you do realise it, we're going to sit here, you and me, going round and round in circles and getting nowhere. You've lied to me from the start – about every damn thing you could possibly lie about. This could be a police matter, I could easily make it one, but I'm giving you a break.' He took hold of the lean tattooed arm beneath the flapping sleeve and shook it roughly. 'Am I getting through? Do we understand one another?'

Joe Stalito mumbled something.

'What?' Krill almost shouted.

'I didn't do nothin'. What'd I do?' Joe Stalito whined.

'You mean apart from sell contaminated blood under nine different names, eight of them false? Listen to me, Joe. I want you to think about this and think hard. Somewhere, somehow, you became infected with a bug. I need – I *have* to know when and where and how it happened. You're the only one who can help me. These stomach cramps of yours, when did they start? Can you remember?'

Joe reached for his Camels, lit one, and sucked hungrily on the smoke.

'Before this place.'

Krill craned forward. 'Which place?'

'This place where I'm living now. It was at the last place – couple of blocks off Sunset.'

'The pains started then?'

'Yeah.'

'When was this?'

'Well, um, let me think. I left there in – yeah, in May. I been bad for a while before that. Yeah, I remember now, just after Marie and me got back from our trip. We spent a few days in San Francisco. A couple of weeks after that I got sick.' He grimaced, his Adam's apple jerking in the stringy neck. 'Real motherfucker of a pain, like acid burning my gut. Couldn't eat anything. Puked up this green stuff.'

Krill was silent for a moment, trying to work out the chronology. He said, 'When did you take the trip – March, April?'

'Second week in March. It was damn cold, I remember. That's when Marie got the chill, riding the ferry across the bay to Sausalito.'

So by April, Krill calculated, Joe was back in Los Angeles and doing the rounds of the hospitals and donor stations using the IDs and other documentation he'd stolen or paid a few dollars to obtain from his underworld pals. Most blood, except that spun down and mixed with other batches to form plasma, was used within twenty-one days. In Joe's case, having one of the rarer blood types, AB Rhesus negative, the batches might be despatched all over the country in response to emergency appeals.

Allowing for an incubation period of, say, three to four weeks, the timing was spot on. Initial symptoms of the disease had first exhibited themselves during May, building to a peak in June and July. That would be when the infected plasma was starting to be used, Krill reckoned.

And now the sixty-four-thousand-dollar question: what had happened to Joe Stalito in that vital period dating from the trip to San Francisco in March to the beginning of April when he was back in LA?

Had he contracted the disease in San Francisco or on his return?

And, most important of all, from what source?

Animal, vegetable, chemical or mineral?

'Tell me, Joe, did you seek any medical attention for your stomach complaint? See a doctor?'

Joe laughed. It was a disagreeable sound, like the whinny of a bronchial old nag, made more unwholesome by the sight of his brown stumps of teeth.

'I keep away from hospitals, doc,' he wheezed, which struck Krill as rather ironic under the circumstances. 'Marie told me – never trust the quacks, they invent diseases you ain't got to screw you for every last cent, and she was right.'

'Sounds like she spoke from bitter personal experience,' Krill said.

'Yeah.' Joe seemed suddenly despondent, cast down.

'She's not a very healthy person then?'

'Healthy?' Joe said, and stared at Krill with red-rimmed eyes.

'She suffers from ill-health.'

'Not any more she don't,' Joe said huskily. 'She's dead.'

'What?' Krill said, staring at him. 'Marie? Your girlfriend? When?'

'May ninth.'

'How?'

Joe shrugged his spindly shoulders under the baggy white shift. 'Woke up one morning and she was dead.' He cleared his throat noisily. 'They said it was pneumonia. I told you – she got this chill on the ferry. Never got over it. She was bad for weeks.'

'Was there a post mortem?'

Joe looked confused. 'Naw, that's what the police doctor said. He just kinda . . . well, I guess, looked at her for a couple of minutes and stuck that thing on her chest and said it was pneumonia. Then they took her away.'

'You were living together at the time?'

'I moved in with her after we got back from 'Frisco,' Joe confirmed. 'Not straight away. Two, three weeks maybe.'

'About the time you started getting the stomach pains,' Krill said.

'Yeah.'

'So the apartment you're in now was Marie's originally?'

'She didn't have no folks, no other relatives,' he said defensively. 'So I just took over – kept it on, paid the rent, looked after Tiger.' He gave a weak guilty smile, as if seeking Krill's approval.

Krill gazed down at his tan soft leather shoes with the cream stitching. One of his socks, he noticed, was inside-out. Without looking up he said quietly, 'Tell me about the cat, Joe.'

'Huh?'

'Where did Marie get the cat?' Krill said, enunciating every word.

There was a long pause, and when Krill raised his eyes Joe was scratching his neck ruminatively with a nicotine-stained finger, his eyes roaming vaguely across the ceiling. 'Can't remember,' he said at last.

Krill patted Joe's hand. Very gently. He said, 'If I have the slightest doubt you're not telling me the truth I can get you twenty years to life, just like that.' He raised his hand in front of Joe's face and snapped his fingers. 'We're talking big league stuff now. Not county, not state. Federal. Want to stick to that?'

Telling the truth for Joe Stalito was like walking on hot coals. His emaciated face went through a dozen tortured expressions.

Finally he said in a voice that was barely audible, 'Marie worked in the kitchen of this place in San Diego and one day she happened to see this cat – Tiger, that was the name we gave it – hunting for scraps in the trash can. She put it in a cardboard box and brought it home. It didn't belong to anybody. Just any ordinary cat. Jesus, a cat is a cat, doc. Since when was picking up a stray a federal offence?'

'It isn't,' Krill said. 'I lied. What was the name of the place where Marie worked?'

This time Joe was genuinely struggling to remember. 'Hell, they got hundreds of those big research labs down there and they all sound alike to me. One of them –' His face lit up. 'They had a fire there! A few days ago. You must have seen it, doc – it was in the papers and on TV.'

Krill straightened up, nodding very slightly. 'You're right, Joe. I believe I did at that.'

After he had instructed the Los Angeles Health Department to pick up the infected cat from Joe Stalito's apartment and hold it in strict quarantine pending tests, Krill rang the Golden Vale Clinic and asked to speak to Dr Brinkmann. But Dr Brinkmann, the switchboard operator informed him, was not able to accept the call.

'Isn't he there?'

'Yes, he's here. He's not permitted to accept any calls. May I connect you with Dr Fabius?'

Krill was about to say yes, but didn't. He put the phone down and sat staring at it, frowning, for some time. Not *permitted*? What in hell's name did that mean? What was going on?

He looked out of the window for a minute or two more,

then reached for the fat yellow San Diego phone directory. Biotech Pharmaceuticals Inc had several listings, including the address of its research and development division.

He returned to the barrier ward and explained to Joe that he had to stay there until they could find an effective drug that would kill the parasite in his bloodstream. Joe didn't take the news well; he whined and cursed, and this despite being probably the luckiest man alive.

23

Lit from below by the instrument panel, the face of Ward DeVoss was a rugged terrain of crags and gullies. The scar which ran at thirty degrees from his left temple to just above his bushy right eyebrow (the result of a motorcycle accident when he was eighteen) appeared as deep as the Rift Valley. Through the observation window, Tom was a dim, insubstantial figure seated in a high-backed chair, connected to a maze of multicoloured wires leading to an array of sensitive brain-scan equipment.

'Shields in place,' a technician reported, standing before the main control bank.

DeVoss relayed this to Tom over the intercom. The thirty-ton, fourteen-inch-thick shields of carbon fibre-impregnated lead soaked up stray radiation which might interfere with the experiment.

But the zero-mass, neutrally charged particles they were seeking would pass through them as if they were so much featherlight gossamer – and in passing through Tom, it was hoped, would interact with cells in his brain, producing electrical activity which would then be processed, digitally enhanced and projected on to a screen in the form of a computer-simulated image.

By DeVoss's side, Professor Marion Keyes of the Health Sciences and Technology Division, MIT's leading expert in biomedical electronics, watched over the instrumentation recording Tom's EEG trace and alpha and beta brain rhythms. If the Quantum Field experiment succeeded, and Tom Margison proved to be a good subject, they might be the very first to detect and display meaningful shapes and patterns directly from the human brain. What those images might turn out to be, no one could tell. DeVoss was prepared to be amazed if they got anything at all – fuzzy triangles, shimmering circles, even an out-of-focus blob.

'If this works, Marion, I hope you realise what we'll have here,' said DeVoss in his gravelly bark of a voice. 'The ultimate lie-detector.'

'I'm more interested in this as a diagnostic tool. An objective visual depiction of the workings of the unconscious mind.'

'Come on, Marion, where's your imagination? We could have a machine for looking into the future! A twentieth-century crystal ball!'

It disconcerted her when he said things like this with a straight face. Was he making fun of her?

'That's assuming these particles of yours exist to begin with,' she retorted tartly.

'Sure they do. No question about it. The question is, can we find 'em? Don't forget that we'll be dealing with a probable, not an actual reality. Quantum theory proposes any number of alternative futures based on the random behaviour of sub-atomic particles. To turn Einstein on his head, it's like God playing dice with the universe and human destiny.'

Although not herself a physicist, Keyes was familiar with this argument. In the mysterious and paradoxical world of quantum theory, the fundamental 'packets of energy' which made up all matter, animate and inanimate, were said to inhabit 'states of probability'. In simple terms this meant that an infinite number of futures, lying side by side, existed simultaneously and thus were all equally plausible. Far from being cut and dried, deterministic, the future of the universe and all its creatures depended on chance, on the random, 'probable' behaviour of the fundamental constituents of matter – on God playing dice.

DeVoss was mumbling to himself. Marion Keyes leant nearer.

'DeVoss–Keyes . . . Keyes–DeVoss . . .'

'What are you up to, Ward?'

'Just wondering which will sound best on the Nobel Prize citation.'

Keyes shook her head disapprovingly; Professor DeVoss's sense of humour sometimes struck her as positively juvenile.

For the next hour the twentieth-century crystal ball remained resolutely and disappointingly cloudy. Nothing – not even a fuzzy triangle or an out-of-focus blob. The dials, gauges and meters monitoring electrical stimuli and the marker pens scribbling the peaks and troughs of Tom's brain activity showed perfectly normal readings.

DeVoss conferred with his colleagues; this wasn't working. 'Anybody got a bright idea?'

Professor Stark of the Psychology Department suggested a nerve relaxant, to help increase Tom's receptivity, but DeVoss wouldn't hear of it.

'When something comes through – if it comes through – it has to be caused by external stimulation, not drug-induced fantasy. We wouldn't be able to distinguish between them. Let's keep the drugs cabinet locked.'

Greg Smith, like Tom a physics graduate reading for his master's, had a couple of thoughts.

'Okay, let's hear them,' said DeVoss gruffly.

'You recall when we were attempting to excite K-meson activity in the Bates Linear Accelerator? We set up a strong electromagnetic field which acted as a kind of funnel –' his hands caressed the air in exquisite gestures '– which focused the stream on a given point. Isn't that what we're seeking to do here – concentrate the energy field?'

'Within reason,' DeVoss said. 'Tom happens to be a live human being, not a component in a linear accelerator.' His mind was working fast as he spoke, sniffing out the possibilities like a bloodhound given an exciting new scent.

Greg Smith took a silver pencil from the breast pocket of his neat dark-green jacket and reached across the chart table for a block of graph paper.

'There's no reason why Tom should be in range of the field.' He was sketching fluently. 'The electromagnetic flux could be *outside* the shields – here, here, and here – directing the particles to a target point, say, here . . .'

When Greg Smith had finished DeVoss knew at once, without the slightest doubt, that the idea held promise. It had the elegant simplicity that was the hallmark of theoretical physics at the highest intellectual level. His admiration for Smith's incisive thinking was tinged with envious regret that younger, sharper minds were forging ahead, plucking ideas and concepts out of the air, leaving him to trail behind like a lumbering dinosaur. But no complaints. It was the collective achievement that was important, not vainglorious personal prestige. He was sufficiently the man of science to accord intellectual brilliance its proper and rightful due, whether his own in the past or someone else's in the present.

DeVoss spoke with Tom over the intercom while technicians made ready the 750-megavolt beam energy generator. He explained Greg Smith's idea and could tell, from his tone of voice, that Tom grasped its implications as quickly as he had himself.

'You happy about this, Tom? It's you that's in there, not us. Your ass, your decision.'

'I'm happy,' said Tom cheerfully. 'Just so long as somebody doesn't press the wrong button and raise the lead shields by mistake. Fire away.'

The hum and throb of the generator filled the lab.

Seated on a high swivel chair, Greg Smith kept watch over the power readings on the main board. DeVoss had one eye on

Tom through the angled window, the other on the hooded screen. Marion Keyes was standing over the EEG machine, frowning at the jittering marker pens.

After twenty minutes of silent, rapt, intense concentration, Ward DeVoss said faintly, 'Oh my sweet Jesus.'

They had an image.

It was made up of tiny squares, garishly coloured like a child's clumsy attempt at crayoning in blocks and shapes and smudging over the lines. Even so, the computer-simulated picture on the screen was unmistakably that of a girl, ten or eleven years old, with dark glossy curly hair and large laughing eyes, lounging back in a rowing boat and trailing her hand in the water. A brilliant summer sun flecked the waves of the lake with glittering highlights.

DeVoss said tersely, 'Tom's sister, Danielle.'

Marion Keyes glanced over her shoulder. She said in a low excited voice, 'Professor Stark, can we talk to Tom or will it interfere with his concentration?'

'No, no – it may actually help him. Increase his receptivity through positive feedback.'

Keyes looked at DeVoss, who nodded. She pressed the tab.

'Tom, we have an image of your sister. She's in a rowing boat on a lake. Do you see that too?'

Tom sounded pleasantly drowsy, drifting and far-away.

'We spent a day on Lake LeGrand earlier this year . . . just before she disappeared. I was thinking about it, trying to focus on Danny.'

Keyes covered the mike and said to DeVoss, 'This isn't coming from outside, Ward. We're picking up Tom's memories.'

'Let's walk before we run, Marion.' He called across to Greg Smith, 'Any fluctuations in the field?'

'Steady as a rock. The beam's tight.'

The image on the screen disintegrated. Keyes became aware of a dull pain in her lower back, caused by sitting tensely in one position. She jumped as if stung as the screen came to blurred life again. Mountain peaks and steep, thickly wooded slopes falling to the mirror surface of a lake. Timber houses with red shingled roofs and porches dotted amongst the trees.

She described the scene and Tom said dreamily, 'That's where we used to spend our vacations in Vermont. I guess it's thinking of Danny, trying to bring her to mind.'

'Just let your mind drift. If something comes through we'll pick it up. You're doing fine.'

'I'm not getting anything like I did before,' Tom said. 'I was seeing all kinds of –'

He broke off with a kind of choking gasp. The screen went dead.

DeVoss was on his feet, staring through the observation panel. 'Tom, are you all right? Can you hear me? Damn!' He bent over the mike. 'Tom!'

Sitting quite comfortably, eyes closed, face calm and in repose, Tom was bathed in a faint blue light. DeVoss remained half standing, the upthrown glow making a moon landscape of his craggy features.

Marion Keyes dragged at his arm. 'Ward, look at the screen . . .'

'Fuck the screen. Turn off the power!' he shouted to Greg Smith.

'He's okay,' Keyes said. She looked rapidly to Stark at the EEG machine for confirmation, and turned back. 'It's coming through, Ward, look at the screen, man!'

DeVoss did so and sank back into the chair.

At first sight it appeared to be a long white mechanical snake moving across baked reddish earth. It was only after several moments that he realised it was a train – a white train comprising massive missile trucks bristling with gun-turrets – trundling over a rocky, treeless landscape.

DeVoss recognised it at once from newspaper photographs and TV reports.

It was the 'Armageddon Express', which transported

nuclear warheads by secret routes from the armaments plant in Texas to military bases all over the country.

Marion Keyes said in a puzzled voice, 'Where's he getting this from? I don't understand, do you?'

She turned to DeVoss, but he wasn't looking at the screen. He was gazing with deeply furrowed brow at a small pale man wearing rimless glasses who was leaning, arms folded, against the chart table. Just inside the door were two others, both well over six feet, in dark suits and buttoned waistcoats. One carried a pocket transceiver cradled against his huge chest, the antenna extended. The other took off his mirrored sunglasses and tucked them into his breast pocket.

'Hi. We're the 6th Cavalry,' said Jerry Derker conversationally.

'You've got what you came for,' DeVoss said harshly. 'What more do you want?'

'Quite a bit more, actually,' Jerry Derker said. He turned away from the observation panel and smiled his joyless smile. He waved his hand. 'Please – carry on. Don't let me interrupt.'

'This is a scientific facility, not a goddam interrogation chamber for the NSA. We're bringing him out.'

Jerry Derker shook his head.

'I said that's it, the end, *finito*,' DeVoss said. Anger had drained his face; the scar on his forehead was like a white brand.

'Not so, Professor.'

'You have no authority –'

'I have the authority. Right from the top. Now. We continue with or without you. It's up to you.'

DeVoss goggled at him. 'How do you propose to carry on without me? Or without any of us? What do you think this is – an amusement arcade? There's a man in there surrounded by seven hundred and fifty megavolts of power, for Christ's sake.'

Derker glanced down at the bank of instrumentation. He

reached out and touched a lever, stroking it with his fingertips. 'This raises the lead shielding, so the label says.' He shrugged. 'I can press a lever as good as the next guy. See?'

'*Don't* –' DeVoss yelled, and lunged forward. One of the men standing with idle menace behind him grabbed both his shoulders and held him back with ease.

'All we're asking for is a little friendly cooperation,' Derker said mildly, tapping the lever. 'But if you won't help us, we'll have to do it ourselves. What do you say?'

Marion Keyes looked swiftly at DeVoss. 'We have to, Ward. We can't possibly leave these people in charge here.'

'They've no goddam right to be here,' DeVoss said. 'It's Tom I'm worried about, not national security –'

'Professor DeVoss,' Greg Smith said urgently. 'What else is there? They only have to touch the wrong button or press the wrong lever and there'll be no need to worry about Tom any more. There's enough high-voltage energy in there to vaporise him.'

'I think he has a point,' Jerry Derker said. 'To be perfectly honest with you, I haven't a clue about any of this. You two?' he appealed to his colleagues, who didn't move a muscle. 'I don't think they have either. No, I'm pretty sure that between us we'd make a terrible botch of it.' He sounded almost apologetic.

DeVoss went to his chair and sat down. Derker moved aside. He looked at his two colleagues and signalled something. The one with the transceiver clicked a switch and murmured into the instrument behind his cupped hand. Derker waited for Marion Keyes and Greg Smith to take up their positions, and then said, 'We're getting along fine. Now, we already know about the White Train. That's on tape. You've got that on tape, right?'

DeVoss nodded, staring straight ahead.

'Great. I've got some questions. I want you –' he pointed to Marion '– to ask him. Just ask what I tell you. Nothing more, nothing less, nothing else.' He folded his arms. 'Shoot.'

* * *

Time didn't mean anything in his semi-dreaming state. Tom might have been sitting in the chamber surrounded by the lambent blue light for hours, days, weeks, he didn't know. Above and to his left he could see the yellow rectangle framing DeVoss and Marion Keyes. Now and then Marion's voice murmured in his ear, encouraging him, telling him of the images they were seeing on the screen. It was easier, and the results were better, Tom had found, if he just let his mind drift without trying to control it, or even to concentrate. Like being pulled, gently, this way and that by the tide, the current tugging at him, sweeping him out, drawing him back.

It was very restful.

At first the images of Danny at the lake and on vacation in Vermont had confused him. Then when he realised that they were memories and past associations he cleared them away, making room for random thoughts to come crowding in: pictures of the armoured white train in the harsh brown landscape . . .

What did that mean? He had the vague feeling of a threat of some kind, but couldn't pin it down.

He cast his mind free again and a crowd of faces swam into view.

Faces of children.

A boy with long curly hair and a fixed, hateful stare. A girl in a soiled party dress with a blue ribbon in her tangled ringlets. A thin, serious, freckled kid with a red crewcut. The round, shining, puzzled face of a little black boy. Twins with silvery blond hair and the same cloudy, myopic gaze.

More faces – all young and yet at the same time old, age and cynicism and a kind of sour despair imprinted on the smooth firm flesh of youth.

These, Tom supposed, were the other children, the ones who had disappeared. Was he seeing them through Danny's eyes? Were these her thoughts, her visions, beamed to him through time and space by the stream of mysterious particles and focused by the electromagnetic field to excite the molecules of his brain cells?

A voice was speaking softly to him; he strained to listen. Then he relaxed. It was Marion.

'Yes, I hear you, Marion.'

'We're getting kids' faces – you see them?'

'Yes.'

She was silent for a moment, and then said, 'The background is dim. We can see the faces clearly but that's all.'

'That's right,' Tom said dreamily. 'I see them too.'

'Where are they?'

'Where?'

She paused and said, 'We need to know where they are. Where are the children, Tom? Can you see? Can you show us?'

Tom concentrated but at once the image broke up in his head and he was left with nothing. Fragments. He spoke into the button mike clipped to his shirt. 'It's no good, I'm losing it. I've got to wait for it to come to me. I can't force it.'

Marion said, 'You're doing okay. Take your time.'

Tom closed his eyes. His mind moved in a grey fog. Everything was grey, formless. He became aware that his hands were curled into hard fists and consciously released them, flexing his fingers and letting them hang loosely.

A door opened the slightest crack and he found that merely by wishing, he could move towards it. He pushed the door open and entered. He was back in the gloomy concrete corridors, symbols and numerals and arrows painted in faded yellow on the walls, doors with strange markings, tiny bleak rooms with metal tables and chairs and tubular frame beds.

A hand touched his. It was Danny.

He said, 'Come back to us. We can help you – there are people who want to help you.'

She laughed. It was an old woman's laugh, harsh, discordant, ugly on the ear. Tom recoiled. His flesh felt cold and clammy.

Like they're helping those poor kids at Golden Vale, you mean? Her face suddenly swelled nearer, the eyes milky, opaque. *Do you know what they do to them? Shut them away in black padded rooms. Inject them with chemicals. Is that how you want to help me?*

'Killing people isn't the answer.'

Neither is poisoning their blood.

'What do you mean?'

The virus they were developing at Biotech. How do you think we came to be like this? They injected a cat and it escaped.

'Was that why you started the fire?'

Danny looked at him with her solemn white stare. *That was Jimmy's idea. Wipeout.*

The door began to close.

'*Danny!*'

Then she was gone and he was once again alone, lost and drifting in the fathomless grey mist.

Ward DeVoss handed Tom a mug of sweet black coffee and said, 'Like a spot of brandy with that? I've got some somewhere.' He looked round his office and went over to the desk.

'No, this is fine. Thanks.'

Greg Smith said, 'We've got it all on tape if you want to see it. Bloody amazing stuff, Tom.'

Tom nodded absently and winced as he burnt his lip on the hot coffee. He seemed remote, his mind elsewhere. DeVoss exchanged glances with Greg Smith and then looked at Tom, sitting hunched over in the chair.

'Feeling okay?'

'Yeah. I'm just cold, that's all.'

DeVoss glanced again at Smith. It was a beautiful late summer's day, the temperature outside around seventy degrees. Here in the office it was only slightly cooler.

'At least you know she's alive,' DeVoss said.

'I knew that before. I've known it all along.'

There was a long, uncomfortable silence. Tom was hunched forward, holding the mug of coffee in both hands, staring at his feet. DeVoss got up and stood gazing rather moodily out of the window. There were guards posted all over East Campus, from the Theoretical Physics lab to the Guggenheim Centre for Space Research. Derker hadn't been kidding. This came right from the top.

'I still can't figure out what that train was all about,' Greg Smith said.

'It doesn't take too much figuring,' said DeVoss calmly, not turning. 'The airplane crashes, the chemical plant explosions, the power failures. It's just the next stage in an escalating sequence of disasters. They're gonna blow the White Train.'

'Are you serious?' Greg Smith said in a hushed, shocked voice.

'Five'll get you ten.'

'Jesus wept. What do they want?'

'Revenge,' said DeVoss simply, turning back into the room. 'We've screwed up the world, we've screwed up our kids, so what the hell do you expect? Gratitude? It's their way of saying, "Screw up". Can you blame them?'

'But – wiping out thousands, maybe millions of innocent people – is that the answer? What kind of solution is that?'

'Who said anything about solutions? Perhaps the only solution is to clear the board and start all over again with a new game-plan.' DeVoss smiled bleakly and snorted. 'Or better still, a new fucking game.'

The door opened and Jerry Derker came in. Tom raised his head and stared at him, his eyes dark and hollow in his pale haggard face. He said in a flat, neutral voice, 'Find it, did you?' When he didn't answer, Tom went on, 'Come on, Derker, you could read the markings on the walls. What was it? Nuclear fallout shelter?'

Jerry Derker nodded.

'Where?'

'Near Richmond, Virginia.'

'That should make you very happy,' Tom said. 'Why aren't you smiling?'

'Because I don't think it's funny.'

'Are you the spook who's been following me, bugging my phone?' Tom said. He nodded to himself. 'It must have been you or some other devious little turd like you.'

'That's not very funny either,' Derker said, his eyes glittering, 'and it's definitely not very smart.'

Tom stood up. He was a head taller than Derker.

'Take it easy, Tom,' DeVoss cautioned him. 'You've had a tough day. You look beat.'

'Don't worry about me, I'm fine,' Tom said. He looked down on Jerry Derker. 'The bottom line on all this is Biotech, isn't it? Millions of dollars spent on biological and chemical weapons research. But something went wrong. Instead of being used against the Reds or the peasants in Nicaragua, your prize virus got loose and infected American children.' He laughed harshly. 'That must have raised a sweat, Derker – taxpayers' dollars funding a project that poisoned their own kids.'

Derker was gazing at Tom with pale hooded eyes.

'You're naïve, Margison. You're also a fool. What do you suppose this is, pat-a-cake? You think a bunch of psychic superbrats can hold the U.S. Government to ransom and get away with it? They've already killed several hundred innocent people, now they're threatening to explode a thermonuclear device somewhere in this country, putting millions more at risk. What do you say, we sit back and take it?'

Tom picked up his jacket from the back of the chair and put it on.

'You're not going anywhere,' Derker said softly, shaking his head.

'Tom – wait. Listen,' said DeVoss quickly as Tom went to the door.

'You heard me,' Derker said.

'Screw you, and the NSA, and the U.S. Government,' Tom said in a voice that was ragged and hoarse. His face had gone taut, under pressure of tremendous mental strain. 'I'm through. I'm leaving.'

Jerry Derker shrugged and turned away with a weary grin.

Tom leapt forward in fury, grabbing Derker's shoulder and spinning him around. His lips were drawn back into a thin, bloodless line.

'You've got what you came for! What else? *What else?*'

Derker pushed Tom away and held him at arm's length, his other hand slipping casually inside his jacket.

'Don't fuss so. I'll keep you informed, Mr Margison.'

24

'I absolutely agree, Edward,' said the Secretary of State into the telephone. 'That's what I'm working for – that's what we're *all* working for – to keep this ultimatum out of the media.' He listened and nodded. 'Yes, of course, that too. But I can't send Delta Force anywhere if I've no place to send them.'

There was an edge of asperity in his voice. He tightened his lips.

'Yes, sure. Of course. We have an open line to Golden Vale. We're doing everything we possibly can –'

He swivelled round as Fred Holbeck came into the room and waved him to sit down. Listening and nodding, he rolled his eyes at the ceiling.

He said, 'The minute I hear, you'll hear. In the meantime I'll stall the media as best I can.'

The Secretary of State put the phone down and slumped back. He worked his fingertips into his eye-sockets and then blinked blearily at Fred Holbeck, who was still standing, his broad tanned face empty of expression.

'The President finally has the jitters. He's afraid he'll get dumped on. As if *he's* the only one with a vested interest.' He noticed Holbeck's face and said, 'What's up, Fred?'

'There's been a development, sir.' Holbeck was gripping the back of the chair, his knuckles white.

'Yes, yes. Good or bad?'

'Jerry Derker –'

'Oh Christ, not that creep.'

'The NSA have been keeping tabs on a guy called Tom Margison, the brother of one of the missing kids. He's a physics student at MIT, and they've been running some tests on him. Derker thinks he may have come up with the "single event" ultimatum . . .'

'And?'

'The White Train.'

'*What?*' The Secretary of State stared blankly in front of him. 'Oh my God.' He glanced up at Holbeck, his eyes hard and bright. 'How reliable is this? Is Derker sure about it?'

The big man squirmed. 'Well, sir, Margison is hooked up to some kind of machine or device in the physics lab. It's supposed to – I mean, it reads or processes –'

'Fred,' the Secretary of State said very calmly. 'With Doomsday less than thirty-six hours away this is no time to get tongue-tied. Is this information reliable or isn't it?'

Holbeck swallowed. 'I guess we have to go with it. Margison picks up thoughts or images in his mind from his kid sister. One of those images was of the White Train. That's the only explanation anybody can come up with.'

The Secretary of State released a pent-up gust of air. 'You know something? That is One Big Beautiful Target. That train runs twenty-four hours day and night over thousands of miles of track.'

He swivelled round to his computer terminal and tapped out a sequence of letters and digits. A map of the United States appeared on the screen, the White Train's routes flashing as red dotted lines, spreading out from Texas into virtually every part of the country.

'Oh brother. Look what we have here.' The Secretary of State lit a cigarette and calmly blew smoke at the screen.

'There is just no way in hell we can cover this. They have their pick, from Bangor to Charleston.'

'Stop the train running?'

'This isn't the Chattanooga choo-choo, Fred. This is the main transportation link for our entire nuclear missile programme. Without it we might just as well pull down the shades and call it a day.' He reached for the phone, then had second thoughts. 'Who do we have at MIT?'

'Nobody in the Physics Department.'

'That's just great. So we just sit here and twiddle our thumbs and wait patiently for the information to come courtesy of the National Security Agency.'

Holbeck nodded unhappily.

'Son of a bitch!' The Secretary of State squashed his half-smoked cigarette into a large glass ashtray and sprang up. He paced back and forth in front of the walnut bookcases, smashing his fist into his palm. 'If anybody knows where these kids are hiding out it's got to be Margison. He's our only lead. Why don't we haul him in, apply a little gentle persuasion?'

'I don't think that would work. Margison doesn't know what he knows until it's processed through this machine.' Holbeck plainly wasn't enjoying this. 'We have to go with it, sir. He's still there, in the lab. I'm receiving updates from Derker's people.'

'Okay. Okay.' The Secretary of State swung round, balancing on his toes like a boxer limbering up for the ninth. 'Tell Derker I want –'

One of Holbeck's assistants, Sondra Teague, had slipped into the room and was standing by the door, holding up a yellow communications flimsy. Holbeck beckoned her forward. He took the flimsy and read it through. He read it through again and straightened up to his full height, as if a crippling burden had been removed from his shoulders.

'They've got the location.'

'Let's have it.'

'South-East Reserve Command Centre, Richmond, Virginia. The nuclear shelter for state government command, police and medical services in the event of thermonuclear attack.'

The Secretary of State rubbed his hands. 'Couldn't be better.' The Delta Force headquarters were in North Carolina. 'Brief Lennox yourself, Fred. Use my phone. I want Delta Force on the move one hour from now.' He danced forward and, taking Sondra Teague firmly by the shoulders, planted a kiss on her forehead.

The orderly raised the two locking handles and swung the thickly padded hatch open. The pale blob of a face and two staring eyes could be seen inside the black depths of the chamber.

'Move it along,' said Fabius over the intercom. The orderly reached inside and grasped the boy by his upper arm, almost lifting him out. Johnnie Bromke found his feet and stumbled down the three wooden steps, white to the lips, mute, his hands shaking in tremor like an old man's hands.

Standing at the window of the observation room, Brinkmann could feel the sweat gathering on his neck. He clenched his hands and took a deep, steadying breath. He had been invited by Fabius to witness the 'progress' they had made in just a few days. 'At last we're getting results,' Fabius boasted. 'Come and see for yourself!'

So this was progress. This silent, shaking, gibbering wreck.

He turned as the boy was brought into the room and led to the seat under the focused glare of lights. Johnnie's spiky hair stuck up around his square, street urchin's face. His eyes were dull, glazed, blank.

'Name?' Helen Murphy barked, standing outside the fierce cone of light.

'Johnnie Bromke, ma'am,' he answered at once, jerking out of his trance. A nervous spasm flickered across his cheek. He gazed up at her from under fixed lowered brows.

'You know what you did, Johnnie?'

'Yes, ma'am.'

'And that it was wrong?'

'Yes, ma'am.'

'What made you do it?'

'The voices in my head, ma'am.'

'Which voices?'

'The other kids, ma'am.'

'Which other kids?'

His arm shot up as if galvanised and pointed to the far corner of the room. 'They're out there somewhere, ma'am, out there somewhere.' He spoke rapidly in a quavering voice, almost gabbling. 'I hear them coming to me, from way out there – but I don't know just where, out there somewhere – there – out there –'

'These voices tell you to do evil things, is that right?' Helen Murphy said, leaning over him, thrusting her face near his.

Johnnie Bromke licked his lips and nodded.

'What?'

'Yes.'

'I can't hear you.'

'Yes, ma'am,' he said more loudly.

'And do you still hear the voices?'

'No, ma'am.'

'What'll happen if you do?'

'You'll put – put – put me back in there.'

'In where?'

'In that place. Dark. Noise –'

'So you'll never do anything wrong again, will you?'

Johnnie shook his head. 'No, ma'am. No, no.'

'Because if you do . . .'

'No, never, I won't, ma'am, no!'

Helen Murphy straightened up and looked at Brinkmann, her eyes bulging triumphantly. 'You see, Dr Brinkmann, it is possible, it can be done. Using the proper corrective methods and behavioural control.'

'Yes, I do see,' Brinkmann said at last.

'Johnnie is our first success,' she said proudly. 'He no longer hears the voices. He is beyond their power.'

'Then you've failed.'

Helen Murphy looked at him sharply. 'Failed? How?'

'If Johnnie can no longer hear the voices, then he no longer knows where the missing children are. His link with them has been broken. Isn't that what you were told to do? To find out where they are?'

'But Dr Brinkmann, this is only the first stage,' Helen Murphy said brightly, as if explaining a technicality to a layman. 'The first step. Next we start on the others.'

Brinkmann saw the light. They were using Johnnie Bromke as an example. They were breaking him down, piece by piece, degree by degree. Disintegrating his personality, so that what was left could be used as a threat and a warning. *This is what will happen to you if you refuse to cooperate.*

He had underestimated them, or rather, failed fully to understand the depth of their callous and ruthless disregard for those in their charge. This realisation shocked and chilled him, as did the fear that now rose up inside him, turning his stomach to water. They were embarked, Fabius and his staff, on a most dangerous, perhaps deadly, game. Dealing with a power that was beyond their comprehension and imagination. And – perhaps the most frightening thing of all – they didn't even know it.

'You do realise, don't you, that what you're doing goes against all recognised medical ethics?' He was speaking to Fabius, doctor to doctor. 'Don't you understand? Their blood is infected – poisoned – by a virus that Peter Krill has traced to a single donor in Los Angeles. The Centre for Disease Control in Atlanta has isolated a variant strain of the parasite *Toxoplasma gondii*. My God, man, you're trying to cure a physiological complaint by behavioural methods.'

'Interesting,' Fabius said, with a singular lack of interest. His tanned face remained imperturbably handsome and unconcerned.

'We are dealing here with a blood contaminant,' Brinkmann said, blinking rapidly behind his thick-lensed spectacles. He couldn't believe that Fabius had failed to grasp this simple fact.

Fabius shrugged. 'That may be so, doctor. But knowing it didn't get us very far. Now, as you see, Johnnie is responding to treatment.'

'Treatment?' Brinkmann said, almost choking on the word. 'You call what you're subjecting this child to, t-t-treatment?' He shook his head in impotent outrage. 'Breaking his mind into little pieces is going to cure him of a parasite in his bloodstream?'

'Perhaps not cure,' Fabius admitted with a faint smile, 'but our task is not to cure; it's to discover how they are able to exert this psychic influence over others and how to prevent it.' He lounged back in his chair, long legs elegantly crossed. 'You seem to forget, Dr Brinkmann, that these children are murderers. They have killed parents, relatives, attacked teachers and others in the community. Are you blaming all that on a *virus*? On a *parasite* in the blood?'

He crinkled his eyebrows in pained disbelief.

'You haven't followed or supported Robert's – Dr Fabius's approach to this problem,' said Helen Murphy loyally. 'In fact, you've been openly hostile to it. Just because your methods failed, Dr Brinkmann, doesn't give you any kind of right to criticise the work of others. Quite the reverse. One thing's for sure –' Her colour was high under the thick pasty layer of powder, her magnified eyes bulging fiercely through the green horn-rimmed frames. 'We've already achieved far more than you and that Viennese quack, Weiss, ever did!'

Brinkmann said, 'You've admitted that you have no interest whatsoever in trying to cure these children or help them in any way.'

'That isn't the purpose –' Fabius began, but Brinkmann ignored his interruption.

'But even before these children arrived here, this place was nothing more than a business enterprise designed to con parents who were worried about their children. Ordinary kids with the problems that everyone faces when they are growing up, treated like criminal psychopaths – pumped full of drugs, locked away in padded rooms, made to undergo psychiatric torture so that you could charge fat fees. Any child that wet its bed would have "a severe personality disorder" or be found to be suffering from "pubertal maladjustment trauma" or some other fictitious complaint dressed up in meaningless jargon. A kid who stole fifty cents' worth of junk would be put through an intensive, and exorbitantly expensive, six-month course in cognitive self-instructional therapy. And at the end of it, what would you have? A child who was more confused and disoriented than on the day he arrived. But of course that doesn't matter, does it? That the child may be ruined and shattered for the rest of his life. The money's in the bank. Send out another five hundred glossy brochures and wait for the suckers to roll in with their offspring. Golden Vale is a shameful blot on the practice of psychiatry in this country, and you, Dr Fabius, are a d-disgrace to your profession.'

Fabius raised his hands and clapped loudly and very slowly. Helen Murphy snorted.

'Go back to your ivory tower, Dr Brinkmann,' Fabius said wearily. 'You shouldn't be allowed out into the real world. Not with such fine, delicate sensibilities and that bleeding-heart conscience of yours.'

'I wish I felt able to leave,' said Brinkmann quietly.

'I was forgetting – of course. You have to protect these innocent little murderers, haven't you?' said Fabius with a thin contemptuous smile.

'It isn't the children who need protecting,' Brinkmann said.

Fabius's smile slipped to one side. He got up and stuck his hands in the pockets of his immaculately tailored white coat. 'You don't look too good. Take my advice. Go lie down.'

'What next?' Brinkmann said thickly. He did indeed feel sick.

'What do you mean – with our little friend Johnnie here?' Fabius glanced towards the dazed cowering wretch in the corner. 'We're almost through with him. One more session I think. Helen?'

'Oh yes, I think so, Dr Fabius,' the woman answered, gazing up at him devotedly through her spectacles.

'You actually think you're winning,' Brinkmann said wearily.

'Of course we are,' Fabius said curtly. 'There's your proof.'

Brinkmann looked at the boy. He stiffened slightly and frowned. He'd caught a glimpse of . . . a strange expression lurking there.

'In any case, I hardly think your opinion matters, Dr Brinkmann,' Fabius said. 'You're here on sufferance. Please remember that.'

Halfway down the stairs Brinkmann paused, his heart beating fast. He might have been mistaken – he hoped to God he was – but he could swear he'd seen a smile on Johnnie Bromke's face.

Lt.-Col. Elmore S. Lennox of Delta Force was the first man to enter the South-East Reserve Command nuclear defence shelter. It had taken just two hours and forty-seven minutes to plan, mount and execute the operation, from the time the order was received from the State Department to the moment Lennox burst through the door, machine-pistol in hand.

Three cordons of troops ringed the site, which was situated in a secluded woodland on government property nine miles south of Richmond, adjacent to the Pocahontas State Park. All roads in the vicinity were sealed-off by Delta Force supported by national guards and state police.

Overhead, helicopter gunships equipped with infra-red and heat-sensitive detectors patrolled strips of the park, swooping in low to investigate the movements of suspicious-looking deer, rabbits and squirrels.

Behind Lt.-Col. Lennox came a squad of twenty hand-picked men, including two army psychologists who had given instructions that on no account were the men to pay heed to stray, inconsequential inner thoughts, or 'voices'; all orders had to come directly from the lips of their commanders, and if possible those lips should be seen to move as the orders were given.

Tall, loose limbed, a hardened vet with a row of ribbons from Vietnam (including a Purple Heart), Lennox didn't relish the job he had been given to do. He had two kids of his own. The thought of killing children – even 'cold-blooded, psychotic mass murderers', as these had been labelled by the top brass – turned his stomach.

He flattened himself against the sweating concrete wall, weapon cradled in the crook of his arm. The dank gloomy corridor was empty. Two men darted through the doorway carrying powerful halogen lamps which illuminated the place with daylight brightness. Shielding his eyes, Lennox moved stealthily on, men crowding in behind him.

He pointed to a door and two men kicked it open. A square metal table, a few twisted tubular chairs, metal cabinets with rust stains. A pile of cardboard litter in the corner. Nothing else. Nothing human. No children.

Already his senses were telling Lennox that the shelter was empty. It had an abandoned, deserted feel to it. Even the air smelt stale and unused.

Room by room they moved on, corridor after corridor, their alertness and keyed-up expectation waning as more rooms and corridors revealed their empty secrets.

There were signs that somebody had been here, all right, and recently too. Food lockers had been broken into. Brown paper packages and cardboard boxes bearing the state crest of Virginia, with its Latin motto "*Sic Semper Tyrannis*" ("Ever thus to tyrants") enclosed within a laurel wreath, had been ripped apart. There were plastic bags in the kitchen bulging with empty tins, and a row of upturned mugs on the draining board washed clean and without a speck of dust.

Lennox breathed out a long sigh of relief, which he hoped wasn't subversive or disloyal to his oath of allegiance. They had been here – lived here for some time, judging by the evidence – but had moved on, gone away, disappeared.

Outside in the fresh air he called forward his signals officer and asked to be connected via Fort Bragg to the State Department. He felt light hearted, almost happy. He had been spared the butchery, at least for the time being.

The ringing of the telephone awakened Victor Lendrum at two-twenty a.m. He put on his robe, slipped his feet into soft leather moccasins, and took the call in his book-lined study. The light from the parchment-shaded lamp dazzled his eyes for a moment, reflecting a blank white glare from the papers and open books scattered on the red leather surface of the desk.

It was three hours earlier in California, eleven-twenty p.m., Pacific Time.

Lynch sounded his usual phlegmatic self, though Lendrum knew that the head of Biotech's research and development division wouldn't have called him at this hour unless it was important. It was.

Lendrum listened, sitting back in the winged leather chair, eyes closed. The dazzle of white papers formed a green shimmering after-image on his retinae.

'Who is he?' Lendrum asked. 'A doctor you say?'

'He's with the Department of Health and Human Services. He said something about the Golden Vale Clinic. I've never heard of it.'

'It's the psychiatric unit in Pennsylvania where the children are being deprogrammed.'

There was a buzzing stillness on the line while Lynch digested this information.

'What exactly does he want?' asked Lendrum. 'Did he make any demands? Threats? Is he planning to talk to the media?'

'I didn't get that impression,' Lynch said slowly, as if trying to recall the phone conversation in fine detail. 'He said he had information relating to a possible hazardous leak of a biochemical substance from one of our labs. I asked him to be more precise, and he seemed reluctant. I pressed him and he said *Toxoplasma gondii*. I then asked him how he came by this information but he refused to say.'

'He spoke to you personally and no one else?'

'Yes.'

Lendrum opened his eyes and found that he was looking directly at a studio portrait of Karel on his desk. He shifted his gaze and said, 'So what did you arrange? Have you planned to see him?'

'No. I said I'd call him in the morning to fix a meeting. I wasn't going to arrange anything until I'd spoken to you.'

'You didn't tell him that?' Lendrum said sharply.

'Victor, of course not.' Lynch sounded pained. 'Just because he has my name doesn't mean he has to have yours as well.'

The words were gently barbed. Lendrum smiled to himself.

'He insisted on meeting me here, though,' Lynch said.

'That seems best,' Lendrum said.

'What?'

'Why yes. It's more convenient that way. Where's he staying?'

'Holiday Inn in LA. La Cienega Boulevard.' Lynch cleared his throat noisily. 'You mean you want me to fix up a meeting? Here at the lab?'

'That's right,' Lendrum said easily. 'Make it for –' he glanced at the green numerals on the digital clock '– two p.m. your time. That gives me a few hours to sort something out.'

Suddenly, Lendrum leapt out of the chair, gripping the phone tightly. He pressed it to his ear, his face a tight maze of furious concentration.

'Are you taping this?'

'Taping it?' Lynch said in a bewildered tone. 'No –'

Lendrum slammed the phone down and ran from the room. As he came out Karel emerged from the darkened doorway of the living-room. She was wearing jeans and a light sweater. She didn't look sleepy, her eyes were wide open and her hair wasn't tousled. She went past him and into her room along the hallway and came out with one arm inside a nylon windcheater. She pulled it on as she went past him again, flipping out her blonde ponytail.

Lendrum wet his lips.

'Karel, you are not to leave. If you're prepared to listen I can explain. Do you hear me? You're to stay right – Karel!'

The door slammed. Lendrum stood in the hallway for ten seconds. He went into the living-room, switched on a lamp, poured himself a brandy and drank it straight down while looking at the telephone receiver lying on the Chinese gilt table. He poured another and went over to the phone. After a moment's pause he pressed the cradle to get a tone, and started dialling.

25

Ward DeVoss stormed into his office, practically kicking the door off its hinges. Tom looked up. He had never seen him so angry. The scar was like a jagged fissure dissecting his head. Greg Smith shot up out of his seat, nervously rubbing his fingertips together.

DeVoss slammed a file down on the desk. 'This fucking country', he bellowed, 'is rapidly turning into a fucking police state!' He clenched and opened his fists several times, staring at the floor.

'What do they want now?' Tom said wearily.

'Can you believe this? They want us to continue with the Quantum Field experiment.' He threw himself down in his chair and stared moodily across the room. 'The National

Security Agency. Ye Gods! Faceless, nameless, and brainless.'

Tom looked at him blankly. 'But they know the location. Derker saw the tapes. I don't –'

'They'd gone. Flown the coop. Derker's spitting blood. He's gonna get his ass kicked from here to Timbuktu, which will give me a great deal of personal satisfaction. However –' he swung round in his chair to face Tom '– the fact remains that you're the only one who might have a clue in hell where they've flown to. Do you know?'

'No. If I did, would you expect me to tell them?'

DeVoss bit his lip. 'These boys play rough. They can't live with an ultimatum from a bunch of ten-year-old kids. Loss of face. They'll find a way, Tom.'

'By putting me back in the chamber?' Tom got up and went to the window. 'Screw them,' he said softly to the glass.

The door swung open and the frame was almost filled by the NSA man with the black moustache. He peered inquisitively into the room for a moment, then moved aside, and Karel pushed past him.

She turned to look at him, and then quite deliberately closed the door in his face.

'That's a pretty neat trick. How did you manage it?' DeVoss asked out of interest. 'I'm not even allowed to call my wife and you just stroll in here. What are you, a member of the magicians' circle?'

Tom was curious too. He was watching her face closely.

'It was easy,' Karel said, shrugging. 'I told them who I was. Professor Lendrum's daughter. Open sesame.' She grinned, but it came out strained and tired. She looked pale, with dark circles under her eyes.

'Hello, Tom.'

Tom nodded.

There was a silence during which DeVoss looked at Tom, then at Karel, then raised his eyebrows at Greg Smith. All this was beyond him.

'What changed your mind?' Tom said stonily.

'I didn't change it,' Karel said. 'It wasn't made up.' She pressed her hand to her forehead. 'Do you mind if I sit before I fall down?'

Greg Smith took her arm and led her to a chair. Tom hadn't moved. He wanted to but couldn't. One half of his mind was saying, *This is Karel.* The other half was saying, *This is Lendrum's daughter, dummy.*

He turned away and said softly, almost under his breath, 'I've got to get out of here.'

DeVoss said wearily, 'Tom, what the hell are you talking about? They've got the entire East Campus sealed tighter than a drum. They've got three gooks in the lab, four men on the door, and twenty guys in wrap-around sunglasses on the steps outside itching for the chance to blast somebody. You still don't seem to understand these people. Once they've got hold of you they stick like shit to a blanket.'

'I've got to help Danny,' Tom said in the same low voice.

'Are you listening to me? You won't even make it to the parking lot.' A vein was pumping in DeVoss's neck. 'Don't you realise what this is? It's a national emergency. Those plane crashes and radar blackouts and all that other stuff have got them running around like headless chickens. They've been trying to locate those kids for weeks. Now they've got the White Train to worry about. Think about that – a nuclear explosion that could happen way out somewhere in the desert or in the middle of Pittsburgh. You're the first one – the *only* one – to have made contact. You're their only hope. Let you go? Are you serious? They'd sooner release Charlie Manson.'

'Couldn't I do something?' Karel said.

'Not unless you pack a magic wand in your magician's kit.'

Greg Smith frowned at Tom, rubbing the side of his face. 'If they want to put you back in the chamber, why not let them?'

'What?' Tom said. 'Me help *them*?'

'I didn't say anything about helping them. No, I was just thinking. That's the one place – inside the Quantum Field chamber – where they can't get at you. Even the NSA isn't dumb enough to fool around with seven hundred and fifty thousand volts.'

They were all looking at him.

'Go on,' DeVoss said.

'Well . . . there are two other exits from the chamber. And there's also a power conduit tunnel under Vassar Street linking the lab with the Cyclotron. And right next to the Cyclotron –'

'The Albany Street parking garage,' DeVoss said. He looked round at Tom. A slow smile was crinkling the corners of his mouth. 'This could be interesting, not to say entertaining.'

'Karel could park there and be ready and waiting,' Greg Smith said. He looked eagerly at Tom. 'And while you're heading north up Main Street the NSA will be sitting here, minding the store.'

'Wait a minute,' DeVoss said. 'They can still see him through the observation panel.'

'Not if we lowered the radiation shields.' Greg Smith shrugged. 'As far as they know, he's still in there, taking part in the experiment.'

'There'd be nothing on the screen,' DeVoss pointed out. 'No images – and no EEG trace or alpha rhythms. Nothing.'

'We've already got them on tape. Nearly six hours' worth.' He grinned. 'We just play them back. They'll never know the difference.'

DeVoss stood up, flexing his meaty fists as if bursting for action.

'What do you say, Tom?'

'You're not going to be popular with the NSA,' Tom said.

'To hell with that,' DeVoss snarled hoarsely. 'They think they can just walk in here and take over a place of learning, a free and independent university department? Hah! This isn't a police state yet – though by God it's getting to be that way.' He said to Greg Smith, 'Just one minor point, mastermind. About the volts. The minute Tom steps outside the shields he's going to end up a piece of burnt toast.'

'Oh no,' Greg Smith said. 'It won't be turned on, will it? And how are they to know? They're brainless gooks.'

'He thinks of everything,' said DeVoss with a touch of chagrin.

'There's one possible foul-up none of us have thought of,' Tom said. 'How long is Derker going to sit happily staring at fake images and readings? He's after results, remember.'

'I guess we could give you two, three hours' head start, Tom,' Greg Smith said. 'Say with the odd technical hitch here and there. And let's face it, the particle beam accelerator is rather fickle. It could always break down, with a bit of help.'

'All right,' Tom said. 'Let's do it.'

The engine sounded as though somebody had dumped ten pounds of ball-bearings in the oil sump, a horrible mangled rattling and grinding. Twenty miles out of Los Angeles, on Interstate 5, it finally became too much for Krill. He pulled off the freeway at Capistrano and stopped at the first gas station with a repair bay he came to. The engine coughed and choked and died, blue smoke leaking ominously from underneath the bonnet.

After the smoke had wafted away a mechanic with a beaked nose and oil-stained baseball cap leaned inside to take a look. He poked, prodded and twiddled for five infuriating minutes while Krill shuffled his feet and looked at his watch. It was twelve forty-two. He'd calculated two hours for the journey and he wasn't even a quarter of the way there. The Ford wasn't going to make it, not without major surgery.

'Can I hire a car here? I've got to be in San Diego for two o'clock.'

'We don't hire out,' the mechanic said, still under the bonnet. His voice was flat, uninterested. 'This is hired, ain't it?'

'Yes. It's hired,' Krill said. 'It's also not moving.'

The mechanic backed out and propped himself on the wing with two outspread grimy hands. 'It ain't the sparks.'

'Sparks?' Krill said impatiently.

'Electrics. Distributor seems okay. Driven far?'

'This morning, just from LA. There was no problem when I started out.' Krill looked at his watch. 'I have an important business meeting. I *have* to find some transport. Where's the nearest rental place?'

'None around here.'

'Oh come on. How far's the centre of town?'

The mechanic pointed his beaked nose down the road. 'Three, four miles. They got a Budget, and a Hertz,' he offered, 'and I think they got a –'

'Any will do. The nearest one. Can you give me a ride?'

The mechanic thought about this and then shook his head. 'I can't leave the station.'

'But there's somebody in there,' Krill said, nodding to a young boy, about sixteen, sitting in the office reading a magazine. 'How long will it take? Fifteen minutes at the outside.'

'Sorry. Can't leave Conrad in charge.'

'Let *him* drive me.'

'He's under-age.'

Krill turned a complete circle in frustration. He looked at his watch. He took out a fold of money in a clip, extracted a twenty and three tens and held them out. 'Look, close the place down for fifteen minutes. You won't sell fifty dollars' worth of gas in that time, you'll actually make on the deal. This is extremely important to me. *I need a car.*'

'Don't you want me to fix this?'

'Yes. *Yes*. But I haven't time to wait. You fix the Ford and I'll pick it up later. I need a car now, this minute.'

'Guess I could manage that,' the mechanic said after further deliberation.

'Thank you,' Krill said, with a rush of relief. He gestured towards the building. 'Can I use your phone?'

'Long-distance?' the mechanic said suspiciously.

'San Diego. Don't worry – I'll pay for that too.'

Jesus, what was the matter with people these days? Krill

thought, striding across the forecourt and into the tiny office. Nobody wanted to help any more. He nodded at Conrad, whose eyes slid from the magazine page and back again without a flicker, and picked up the phone. He had Biotech's number in his address book and dialled it direct, asking to speak to Dr Lynch. He was connected to Dr Lynch's secretary, who said Lynch was unavailable at that moment and asked who was calling.

'Dr Peter Krill. I have an appointment to see Dr Lynch at two. Would you tell him that I've been delayed. Please apologise for me and say I hope to be there about two-thirty.'

'I'll convey the message, Dr Krill.'

Krill thanked her and hung up. Conrad had at last been forced to move: there was a dark blue Chrysler with twin aerials waiting for gas.

As Krill stepped out of the office the mechanic came up.

'These two fellas –' his nose and the peak of his baseball cap swivelled round '– say they'll give you a ride into town. They'll drop you at Budget.'

'Well – thanks,' Krill said, surprised and glad. 'That's going to save a lot of trouble. How much do I owe you for the phone?'

'Forget it. Glad to help out.'

News to me, Krill thought. He said, 'I'll call you later today about the Ford. If it isn't ready I may have to have it picked up.'

The mechanic nodded and trudged off into the service bay.

Krill got his attaché case from the Ford and climbed into the back of the Chrysler. The driver, who wore mirror sunglasses, glanced over his shoulder and smiled. 'They always break down when you need them most.'

He slid the automatic shift into Drive and the car pulled away.

Two miles along the road the car turned left at an intersection. Though Krill's geography was hazy he had the impression they were heading towards the beach. 'Is this the quickest way into town?'

The driver shook his head without turning round. 'Didn't you want the Budget rental place?'

'I didn't mean for you to go out of your way.'

'No trouble,' the driver said. 'Small detour.'

Windblown sand was heaped against the kerbsides. Stiff wiry stalks of grass leaned back under the steady sea-breeze. They went past a few lonely whitewashed wooden houses, little more than shacks, and bumped over runnels of sand snaking across the cracked concrete. Krill put his hand out for the reassuring feel of the door-handle and found that there wasn't one. His back was rigid and aching.

'Here we go,' the driver said. The car swung sharply to the right, bounced over the kerb, and stopped on a small sandy plateau a few feet from the cliff-edge. Another car was parked there, a grey Ford, the exact same model as the one Krill had been driving. It too had a yellow Hertz sticker. He looked at the plate. It was the same car.

Krill clutched the attaché case tight under his arm. Only that morning he had mailed copies of the documents it contained to Meg Willson at the Department of Health and Human Services. He wondered now whether that had been a premonition on his part. But he hoped to God that it wasn't, and that he was wrong.

Ten minutes later the man in the mirrored sunglasses was using a piece of brushwood to dust over the tracks of the Chrysler, moving backwards to where the car was parked on the road. The other man was sitting in the passenger seat looking through the contents of the attaché case. The tracks of the Ford remained, etched deep into the sand right to the edge, but the car had gone, and so had Krill.

Part four
Termination

26

Tom discovered he was voraciously hungry. No wonder; he couldn't remember his last meal. He felt as if he'd lived through several lifetimes sitting in that chair at MIT, clamped with sensor pads and swathed in wires, the eerie half-light surrounding him like a soft blue husk.

Time had played a few cute tricks on him so that he was no longer sure what was real and what he'd dreamt or imagined he'd dreamt. For hours – so it seemed – he had watched an armoured white train lumbering across a plain of desert scrub and baked red rock. He had wandered through a timeless, endless mist to find Danny standing in a doorway, beckoning to him. There had been grey corridors and chill bleak rooms, and, somewhere beyond that, watching eyes and whispering voices.

What else?

A smear of images and impressions he hadn't been able to sort out yet.

All that stuff from years ago . . . Danny as a small child, family vacations at the lodge, boating trips on the lake, himself at high school and afterwards MIT. Was that just his straining and overtaxed brain churning up the sludge of his unconscious? Even now, lying back and being lulled by the luxuriously smooth ride of the Pontiac, images sombre, bleak and frightening invaded Tom's mind . . .

. . . A child shut away in a padded inky-black tomb, a noise like Niagara Falls screeching in his ears. Hour after hour after hour. Who? Where? Why were they subjecting this poor kid to such horrendous torture? What had Johnnie done to deserve –

Christ.

He even knew the kid's name.

Johnnie – Johnnie – Johnnie –?

Bromke.

As if the floodgates had been opened, the lead shielding raised to allow myriads of memory particles to bombard his mind, Tom received the blinding light of revelation.

Johnnie Bromke was undergoing his ordeal at the Golden Vale Clinic, Arcadia, Pennsylvania. Danny and the others had left the fallout shelter near Richmond. An ultimatum had been given that unless the Government abandoned its biological warfare programme the children would derail the White Train which carried nuclear warheads to missile bases the length and breadth of the country.

How much of this had been recorded on tape in the lab? The White Train certainly – DeVoss had mentioned that to him. And of course Derker, the NSA and the State Department would know about it too.

But what about the ultimatum? Had that been on the tape? DeVoss and Greg Smith had said nothing about it. Did this mean, Tom wondered, that outside of the Government and the security agencies he was the only one who knew?

The only person to know that an ultimatum had been issued?

Such knowledge, were it to leak out, would cause widespread panic on a scale unprecedented in the history of the United States. The American people under threat from their own hydrogen bombs – and to compound the irony, the fingers on the nuclear trigger those of their own children.

The sins of the fathers, this time around, it seemed, were to be visited upon everyone.

Instead of taking the main route north, Interstate 93, Tom chose to head due west on highway 2, through Leominster, Fitchburg and Gardner, stopping to fill up the tank at a small garage off the highway. They had been driving for almost two hours, Karel at the wheel, Tom dozing on the broad bench seat, and he was expecting their luck to run out any minute. Their head start wouldn't amount to much once Derker rumbled what was happening – or to be precise, not happening.

They crossed the state line into Vermont and a few miles

further on, just outside Brattleboro, pulled over at a truck stop. Tom ordered the all-day breakfast of orange juice, hot bacon rolls and coffee for himself and a sandwich and iced tea for Karel. She hadn't a lot to say for herself; she didn't even feign a smile at his feeble jokes. Tom knew what the matter was, but avoided the subject of Victor Lendrum. It was something she would have to come to terms with by herself, and in her own time. He'd said his piece the other evening in the apartment.

He was drinking his second cup of coffee when a blue and cream Ford with the crest of the Highway Patrol went past, travelling south. A few minutes later it came back, did a U-turn on the parking lot, and stopped.

They watched a patrolman climb out, his gunbelt and bulging holster supporting a paunch shaped like a pear drop. As he ambled across to the diner, Karel looked at Tom and reached out for his hand. He held her hand and stared back, shaking his head almost imperceptibly. There was nothing to be done, nowhere they could run to; they just had to sit it out and wait.

Tom took off his glasses, folded them, and put them in his jacket pocket.

The patrolman waddled in and called to someone in the back named Fred that he wanted two coffees to go, one black, no sugar, one with cream and sugar. When the coffee came he opened a little hatch on the plastic cake-stand, took out a jam doughnut and held it up before taking a bite. He threw some money on the counter and went out with the cartons of coffee, munching the doughnut.

He hadn't once looked round the diner, not even spared a glance in their direction. They watched him get into the car and kept watching as it lurched on its springs back on to the highway and sped off south.

Karel took out her handkerchief and wiped the palms of both hands. Tom said in a low voice, 'They're probably looking for me by now. Everything depends on whether they know which car to look for.'

'DeVoss would never tell them,' Karel said.

'No. DeVoss wouldn't,' Tom said, putting his glasses back on without looking at her.

Now they took the fastest route straight up Interstate 91, then on to 89, coming off it just south of Barre. The sun was high and bright over the mountains. Directly ahead of them were the ski resorts of Sugarbush Valley and Mad River Glen. It was pre-season and the roads leading into the Green Mountain National Forest were quiet with local traffic.

'I was fascinated by those names when I was a kid,' Tom said. 'Every year when we were driving up I must have asked a million times if we were on our way to Sugarbush and Mad River Glen. You know how kids think about names. They become magical. You build up whole fantasies about them in your imagination – Sugarbush was a mountain of solid striped candy dotted with liquorice sticks instead of trees.'

'What was Mad River Glen?' Karel asked. 'A funny farm?'

Tom screwed up his face at her. 'Wrong again, smart-ass. Come to think of it, it was a fierce black torrent at the bottom of a steep shaded valley, rushing into this huge black lake . . .'

Tom's cheeks began to tingle. The black lake of his dreams. The same black lake that Danny had painted. Had she planned the move, or known about it, even then? Or were they back in the murkily ambiguous world of precognition and inexplicable glimpses of the future?

'Is that why you think she'll come back here?' Karel said. She turned her head to look at him. 'You still haven't told me *why* we're here. How you happen to know.'

'I don't – for a fact,' Tom said. 'But it suddenly dawned on me that I was fighting, resisting these same images which kept on recurring. I thought they were interfering with the thing I was trying to find out, obscuring it, you know? But now I don't think so. I was being told something and couldn't see the wood for the trees. So instead of resisting the impulse I gave in and let it sweep me along. Followed my instinct, intuition, whatever you care to call it.'

'Except that you believe intuition has a scientific basis. Your mu-mesons and quarks and packets of energy up to their little tricks, pushing us where we think we don't want to go. Only they know better.'

'They run the universe,' Tom said lightly, not to be drawn by her gentle mockery.

'What if you're wrong?' Karel said, turning the wheel to follow the narrow road which wound steeply upwards through the outer fringes of the forest. The slopes above them were thickly wooded with spruce and larch and fir, the trees standing so close together that they seemed to form a solid barrier. 'Supposing Danny and her friends aren't here and we've made the trip for nothing?'

'You'll have the satisfaction of telling me I was wrong.'

Beams of sunlight filtered through the branches to make a slanting gold bead curtain which the car brushed through. They were now quite deep into the forest, still climbing, though not as steeply as before.

Ten minutes later Tom said, 'Not far now.' There were drops of sweat beneath his eyes and along his upper lip. 'We're almost on top of the western rise. In a couple of miles you'll be able to see Lake Dunmore.'

'Are there many lodges along the lake?'

'Not many on this side. Five or six maybe. But they're hidden from each other in the trees. It's what the brochures call "a secluded wilderness".' He grinned with an effort. 'As distinct from an unsecluded one.'

They pulled over on to a patch of gravel at a point where the road curved and started to drop. They got out and stood looking down over the descending and regimented banks of tree-tops to the pocket-sized valley tucked in the folds of mountains. At the bottom a scimitar of sunlight was reflected on the flat, calm surface of the lake.

Sam Wells belched softly on the hot dog and wiped his lips with the mustard-smeared tissue while he listened to the controller's voice over the radio.

'Pontiac ID confirmed. Heading north on Interstate 91. How many passengers, did you see?'

'Sam reckons there were two,' his partner reported. 'Young guy, mid-twenties, dark hair, fitted suspect's description. Also young woman, about the same age, blonde. Sam went inside the diner but he didn't get too good a look. We were warned not to approach or alert.'

'Right. You didn't follow?'

'No. Who are they?'

'Who knows? But they merit an all-points over seventeen states.'

Sam and his partner exchanged looks.

'We still in on this or what?'

'Stay in the vicinity of Brattleboro. We may need road-blocks along the state line. We tracked them on to 89 and then lost them. But they're somewhere around there. That part of the state is humming, from Burlington to Barre.'

'Funny, they don't look like they robbed Wells Fargo of fifty million dollars,' Sam's partner said.

'Since when were the State Department interested in a measly fifty million dollars?' the controller scoffed. 'Use your imagination. And keep Sam off the hot dogs. They give him dyspepsia and make him fart. Out.'

Helen Murphy popped her head into the observation room, but it was empty. Robert had been working on the Perera child all morning and the cone of lights were still focused on the vacant chair. His notes were there but he wasn't. She glanced through the panel at the SD chamber, its crude wooden structure resting on fat pneumatic rings to reduce vibration. The red light was off, indicating that it wasn't in use.

He must have gone back to his office in the main block, she concluded. The past twenty-four hours had been frantic, ever since Holbeck had called from the State Department. Apparently they had discovered the children's location, somewhere near Richmond, Virginia, only to find the place deserted, the children fled. Fabius had been promising them information for days now – what the hell was the delay? Was he going to crack those kids or wasn't he?

Poor Robert. She had been in the office and seen him whiten. She had wanted to take him in her arms and comfort him.

Helen Murphy closed the door and went in search of him. She had a new idea she thought might work.

Inside the SD chamber, Dr Fabius screamed and shouted and battered the eighteen-inch-thick spongy yielding wall with head, fists and feet. He continued to shout and scream for several hours, running back and forth on deadened feet in total blackness and silence, driving himself into a frenzy and finally into total madness.

Almost vertically below them, masked by branches of trees further down the slope, the red shingled roof of the lodge with its square stone chimney was laid out in plan view as in a blueprint. No smoke came from the chimney, but it was early afternoon, the sun was hot, and there would be no need of a fire till evening.

Beyond the shingles, the wooden roof of the boathouse sloped down to the lake, whose smooth shimmering surface could be glimpsed through the close-packed trees.

Tom paused in his descent, took Karel by the hand and led her a few yards off the path into the screen of bushes. There they crouched, their breathing sounding unnaturally loud in the stillness of the forest.

'Why don't you stay here?' Tom said. 'Let me go down and find Danny, see that everything's okay.'

Karel was shaking her head.

'Karel, listen to me. It's safer this way. Then if for any reason I don't come back you can –'

'I can get killed by one of those homicidal kids or eaten by a bear.' She wafted a buzzing fly away from her hot face. 'Forget it. All for one and one for all. Catch this native New Yorker sitting on her lonesome in creepy undergrowth. No thank you.'

Tom shook his head and sighed. 'I'm not trying to play the hero. I just don't want both of us to get caught.'

'I would've thought with your amazing psychic powers you'd know already who was down there. Are you *now* telling me you can't see through timber walls and shingles after all?'

'It's Danny who has the amazing psychic powers, not me.'

'Then she should know we're here.'

'Perhaps she does,' Tom said, looking round.

Keeping off the path and using the trees and bushes as cover, they started down the steep slope. After several minutes, when they had sight of the back porch and the shuttered rear windows, Tom began to have real doubts. There wasn't a soul moving down there. He was going to look pretty foolish in Karel's eyes if after all his impressive talk about the mysterious powers of intuition they came upon an innocently empty lodge on the edge of a placid lake.

Right at this moment, he had never felt less intuitive in his life; only sweaty and sticky and vaguely uneasy.

Something small and furtive darted away from under his feet, making Tom halt, body rigid with tension, heart beating violently. He glimpsed a grey furry back vanishing in the undergrowth. A quiet rustling of leaves and twigs. Then silence.

Tom let go a long shallow breath through his nostrils. He took off his glasses and wiped the misted lenses on his shirt. Before he had time to put them back on, Karel whispered, 'Tom?'

'What is it?'

'I think –' her breath fluttered in his ear '– there's somebody behind us.'

He put his glasses on. Karel was staring at him, her entire body frozen, her head held stiffly. Tom could see the fine silvery hairs standing up on the nape of her neck. Very slowly he turned to look, and said, foolishly and unnecessarily, 'Keep still. It'll be all right.'

Two wizened aged dwarfs with blond hair were watching them from between the slender trunks of the trees. Behind Karel's shoulder Tom spotted another diminutive bent figure, this one dark haired, a little distance away; then, slowly turning his head, he saw three more figures, dotted farther up the hill-side above them.

Something made a rustling sound nearby, practically at his feet.

He glanced down quickly to confront a face like dirty cracked parchment, smiling blindly up at him from the depths of a bush.

'I knew you'd find us. Hello, Tom.'

Danny led them unerringly down the path to the porch and into the house.

She stepped over a bundle of clothes just inside the kitchen door and went down the two stone steps into the L-shaped living-room. The wide sliding windows gave a picture-postcard panorama of the lake, the forested slopes beyond, and the low range of peaks to the east, topped in the far distance by Pinnacle Mountain.

Blankets were scattered about and plates with remnants of a meal were stacked on the rough stone hearth. In the corner Tom noticed a head-high pile of cardboard boxes stencilled "*Property of U.S. Govt: National Defence Supplies*", and underneath the state crest of Virginia.

A door, which Tom knew gave on to a short passageway leading to the two main bedrooms, opened and a dozen or more children filed silently in. Those who had been in the forest came through the kitchen door and the room quickly filled up.

Not all the children showed signs of ageing or blindness, Tom noted.

Some were ruddy cheeked and clear eyed, in fact perfectly

normal at first glance. And yet there was a solemn and forbidding intensity about the gaze of these children too that made him look away. It gave him the unpleasant, goosepimply feeling that a score of tiny sharp scalpels were probing into his brain and stripping it bare.

Tom could hardly bear to look at Danny at all. It was hard for him to know what he truly felt about her, she was so physically altered. He had to bite back a shuddery loathing for this blind, aged mockery of a young girl that was his own flesh and blood.

A total, stony silence settled over the room. Tom reached for Karel's hand, which was cold and limp and boneless. He looked round, and the roomful of eyes, some glazed and white, others hard and bright and piercingly sharp, stared back at him.

'What have you told them?' asked one of the ancient children in a throaty, cracked voice.

Karel flinched at the sound. Her hand came to life in Tom's, seeking comfort like a small frightened animal.

'Nothing,' Tom said thickly. He was shaking all over. His insides had turned to water.

'We know why you're here,' Jimmy Yerke said, his opaque, blank eyes fixed on Tom. 'You're too late. We're going ahead. Midnight. *Wipeout*.'

'We're going ahead if they don't agree to our conditions,' Karen Swanson corrected him. Somewhere along the way she had changed her party dress for an adult-sized sweater. The sleeves were rolled up, bunched above her bony elbows, and the rest of the garment hung down voluminously to just above her knees. Her once snow-white ankle socks were grimy, her bare legs dirty and scratched.

Jimmy Yerke snorted. 'Don't be a dumb asshole. They won't agree. They'll never agree. We should have done it right off – like I said in the first place!'

'That won't help. That won't cure you,' Karel said. 'Don't you want to be made well again?'

Morey Lang's freckled face split in a mad grin. 'You think we believe in *doctors*? After what they did to Johnnie Bromke?'

'I see,' Tom said. 'You don't make any exceptions. You hold us all responsible.'

'You're one of them. A scientist,' someone said in a peculiar nasal whine.

'You let it happen.'

'All of you let it happen,' someone added.

'You're all responsible.'

They were closing in, crowding in on all sides, their upturned faces pale and ghostlike. Jimmy Yerke was smiling, his blind eyes on the exact centre of Tom's forehead. A thin sharp searing pain shot through Tom's head as if someone had inserted a white-hot needle into the depths of his brain. His consciousness dimmed like a faulty light bulb, then flared up into an excruciating arc of brightness.

Tom gasped and grimaced with the pain. He opened his eyes to find himself leaning, half collapsed, against Karel, her arm around his waist, his head humming like a dynamo. The room swayed and swam, the rank of faces merging and overlapping. He felt shivery and sick.

'Let's finish him,' Jimmy said gleefully. '*Wipeout*.'

'You can't do it,' Tom said.

'Watch us,' Jimmy said.

'You can't do it,' Tom repeated, 'because none of you wants to die.'

'You got it twisted,' Jimmy said. 'It's *you* that's gonna die!'

'The virus in your bloodstream is eating you alive,' Tom said, 'and there's not a thing you can do to stop it. You're slowly going blind, your minds and bodies are decaying, you're getting old sixty years ahead of time and you haven't even lived your lives yet. But none of you wants to die. I don't know if there is a cure or whether one can be found, but I do know that we're the only hope you've got.'

Morey Lang said scathingly, 'You think we should trust you, just because you're Danny's brother?'

'No,' Tom said. 'You can trust me because you know I'm telling you the truth.'

'Maybe,' Morey Lang said doubtfully.

27

'This is hardly going to make ours the most popular administration in history,' said the Secretary of State. He glanced up at the civilian advisors and military brass grouped round the large table on which was laid out a one inch to the mile map of the state of Vermont.

'They've perpetrated homicide on a large scale,' someone pointed out. 'We're simply protecting our people. What's the alternative?'

'And who's to know?' Hal Curtis said. 'The media embargo is holding up – there's not been a single mention of the threat to the White Train. If we can keep that under wraps, why not this too? It's a military operation, sir. The Pentagon won't leak.'

The Secretary of State grunted. 'I know for one. Wiping out a bunch of kids isn't your regular act of counter-insurgency – even a bunch of kids who've done what these have done.'

There were no takers for that one.

'Is there no other way we can handle this?' he asked, studying the map. Red tape marked off the boundaries of the Green Mountain National Forest. Within this, coloured plastic tabs, like roulette chips, showed the deployment of various military units. Command HQ was at Lebanon, about twenty-five miles south-east of the forest, where Interstates 89 and 91 dissected.

Two hours before, Fred Holbeck had left by army chopper to act as liaison between the commander of ground forces,

General Walter 'Mike' Todd, and the State Department in Washington.

'I don't think we have time to consider any alternatives,' said one of the generals. His gold signet ring winked as he gestured to the large segmented clock face above the banks of monitor screens. 'The deadline expires in eight hours. What other way is there except by means of a military solution?'

'What about the cause, the reason why they committed those acts?' said the Secretary of State, chin sunk on his chest. 'They just go crazy, or what? Are we breeding a new generation of psychopathic killers?'

Everyone wisely took this to be a rhetorical question.

He raised a shaggy eyebrow. 'Nobody got anything to say? We're all agreed then. Swell. A neat and tidy "military solution".' Beneath his gentle tone was a cutting edge of sarcasm. He didn't expect a response from his inner circle and he didn't get one.

The thin red hand swept another minute away.

16.04.

There was a flurry of activity at the central console, where controllers and monitoring staff maintained a twenty-four-hour vigil, receiving and despatching communications traffic.

'Mr Holbeck on the line for you from Lebanon, sir.'

For a second the Secretary of State thought he was fighting a different war. He would have preferred it. He nodded to the controller who patched Holbeck through to the PA speakers.

Somebody handed the Secretary of State a cordless mike.

'General Todd informs me that the designated area is now totally secure, sir,' Holbeck reported. 'Nothing moving in or out.'

'Thank you, Fred. I have a map in front of me. Can you give me their exact location yet?'

'No, I'm afraid not, sir.'

'Not?'

'No, sir. The Green Mountain Forest is more than two hundred thousand acres. Our latest information has them somewhere between Middlebury to the north and Pittsfield to the south. Do you have those?'

'Yes.' The Secretary of State spread his outstretched fingers on the map. 'That's over twenty miles, Fred. Over four hundred square miles of mountains, lakes and forest.'

'We couldn't risk keeping too close a surveillance on Margison and Lendrum without alerting them, in which event they would have been warned off. Their last actual sighting was on route 7 – do you have that? – about five miles north of Brandon.'

The Secretary of State leant over the map. 'Near Lake Dunmore.' He straightened up, and in a reflex action glanced up at the clock. 'Just tell me one thing, Fred. How does General Todd propose to conduct a search-and-destroy operation over four hundred square miles in under eight hours? What has he got there, the bloodhound battalion?'

'That isn't, as the General sees it, the prime problem,' Holbeck explained. 'It's a fairly safe assumption that the children – we reckon there are upwards of twenty of them – have had to seek some form of shelter. They're not out in the wild. That being so, we can concentrate the search on the habitable buildings in the area. We've got the park rangers and the forestry wardens here with us, sir, and they tell us there are no more than fifty buildings of reasonable size – holiday lodges, boathouses, hikers' overnight shelters, that sort of thing. These have been marked out and individually targeted. General Todd estimates that his men could reach and isolate any of these inside four hours. Personally I think that's a little optimistic, but, well, he assures me he can do it.'

The Secretary of State felt a few drops of tension drain away. It was partly Fred Holbeck's calm Texan drawl that did it. But probably more to do with the fact that he had been granted a tiny margin, breathing space, a few precious extra hours for considered judgement.

It was also true, and he didn't fool himself about this, that he shrank from issuing the order to move in. He could see it writ large in the history books: 'Child-Killer'. 'The Man Who Massacred Children'.

He needed those few hours all right. As many as God and General 'Mike' Todd could give him.

'That's understood, Fred. Tell the General "Well done" and to hold the situation as is. I'll get back to you –'

Fred Holbeck cut in. 'Mr Secretary . . . sir, I said that locating the children wasn't the prime problem, as General Todd sees it.'

'Go on,' the Secretary of State said heavily. 'I'm listening.'

'He's concerned that when we do locate them there won't be enough time to prevent them carrying out the threat. If they can turn this power on at will and direct it at the target . . . well, sir, as the General points out, there's nothing he can do to stop it. Do we know – does anyone know – how much time it takes? A few seconds? Minutes? Hours?'

The Secretary of State looked round the circle.

There were experts in practically every field here – intelligence, communications, counter-insurgency, nuclear detonations, strategic defence, psychological warfare. The assembled brainpower and repository of knowledge were impressive. And not a single damn one of them could answer that question.

'You've caught us with our pants down, Fred. Whatever we advised would be a blind guess.' He passed a hand over his eyes. 'Does General Todd have an option?'

'Yes sir, he does. First-strike.'

'Without precondition.'

'Yes.'

'How?'

'Short-range missile homing in on a radio beacon.'

The tiny margin the Secretary of State had promised himself, the breathing space he had luxuriated in a moment ago, evaporated into thin air. It was a simple Go-NoGo situation. Take it or leave it. Either do the job with ruthless military efficiency or don't do it at all.

So what else had he expected? the Secretary of State asked himself wearily. That the military would tiptoe in like a fairy godmother, take the children by the hand, feed them cookies, lead them gently away?

'Mr Secretary – you still there?'

'Yes, Fred, I'm still here.'

'What do I say to General Todd, sir?'

'Tell the General . . . tell General Todd to deploy his forces inside the designated area and to pinpoint the location of the – the target.'

There was an awesome silence filled by a faint buzz on the line. Everyone in the room had become very still.

'Is that all – sir?'

'No further action to be taken except on my express word of command,' the Secretary of State snapped. '*That's* all.'

He made an abrupt throat-cutting motion for the controller to terminate the audio link, pushed through the circle and left the room.

Crouched down on her haunches, Karel gazed out at the lake through the narrow window set almost at floor level in the triangular wooden wall of the loft bedroom. Tom lay on the pine-framed single bed, fingers laced across his chest, eyes shut.

The room was filled with a mellow, golden light from the reddish-ochre orb of the sun sinking behind the trees, sending spiky shadows creeping out from the western shoreline.

From below came the dull murmur of voices, sometimes interrupted by an angry shout, a sharp exclamation; Karel had tried to overhear what was being said but the discordant babble defeated her.

'Who's going to win?' she asked Tom.

'Win what?'

'The argument – whatever it is they're fighting about.'

'Whoever's the strongest, I guess. The one with red hair – Morey? – I think he's willing to trust us. But that other little brat doesn't go for the idea. All he can think of is "Wipeout" – the answer to all problems. A perfect candidate for the A-Team.'

'I wish I knew which side Danny was on. She's changed so much. And she didn't say anything. What do you think?'

Tom shook his head, eyes closed. 'I don't know.'

'But she wanted you here – didn't she? I mean, it was she who sent for you. Isn't that right?'

'Yes.'

'Then she can't be like the others. She must want help.'

Tom laughed bitterly. 'I'm helping her now all right.'

'Maybe you are. If you've convinced them they can be cured –'

'There is no cure for old age. You just die.'

'Tom, these are *kids*. Nine, ten years old!'

'They were nine or ten years old a few months ago. Did you think I was just trying to scare them back there when I said they'd aged sixty years? For God's sake, you only have to look at them. They've acquired a heightened awareness, a vastly superior mental ability, but emotionally they've remained children. Their metabolism has gone haywire. They're young children with old bodies and old minds who haven't lived through the experiences to match them. They've never known adult sadness and regret, anger, joy, passion, all the emotions which mould you into a grown-up person. Their minds have been speeded up, they have intuitive mental powers a thousand times greater than ours, but emotionally they're stunted.'

'You were lying to them then.'

'Yes. No – I was trying to save them. And us.'

'They won't kill us,' Karel said, though she sounded far from certain.

'Why shouldn't they?' Tom said. 'I might if I was in their place.'

Karel grimaced as she stood up. She massaged blood back into her thighs, bending over so that her hair hung in fine silvery-blonde strands over her face. Tom had opened his eyes and was staring at the ceiling.

He sat up suddenly. Somebody was climbing the stairs.

The door opened and Danny came into the room. Tom's flesh crawled as she looked at them with her dead eyes, not seeing them but rather sensing their presence. Was she aware of how he felt? Could she sense his thoughts and emotions by the same mysterious process?

'They believe you're telling the truth, Tom. They're willing to trust you.' Danny stood in her soiled tee-shirt and jeans, hands limp and quiet by her sides.

'Good,' Tom said hollowly. He didn't look at Karel.

'I'm not so sure.'

'What do you mean?'

'Nobody can help us now. It's too late.'

Tom opened his mouth and Danny said, 'Don't lie to me, Tom. There's nothing they can do – anyone can do. I know you did it for the best of reasons.'

'I didn't promise anything,' Tom said wretchedly.

Karel said, 'But Danny, why bring Tom here if you knew that already? If you believe there's no cure?'

'Because we don't all agree. About the White Train. Most of them want to go ahead. But some of us . . .' Danny paused and her face clouded, as if she'd lost track of what she was saying. 'Some of us . . . have changed.'

Karel watched her intently with narrowed eyes.

'So what happens now?' Tom asked.

'I think,' Danny said slowly, 'they want you to help us.' Large drops of water had started to leak from her milky eyes. Tom stepped towards her and she flinched and went rigid. He gathered her in his arms and held the rigid, shuddering body close to him, her tousled matted hair against his chest. Her hands gingerly touched him and then gathered his shirt in handfuls. Tom rocked her tenderly in his arms.

Take me home, Tom.

'I will.'

You must stop them.

'I'll try.'

It isn't their fault. Not even Jimmy. He's scared like all the rest of us.

'I know.'

Tom went downstairs, leaving Karel and Danny in the loft. Danny stood in the middle of the tiny room, staring sightlessly towards the window. She touched herself with both hands and then slumped to the floor, head lolling on one side like a broken doll. Karel went down on her knees and lifted her bodily and carried her to the bed.

'Hurts,' Danny said muzzily. 'Hurting . . .'

'What? Where?'

'Here.' Danny moaned between her clenched teeth and touched her stomach. 'Pain here. Oh it hurts.'

Karel pulled Danny's hand away. Her stomach was hard and round and distended. Karel unfastened the tight brass button and unzipped the front of Danny's jeans. She lifted her hand and looked at the dark blood on her fingers.

Karel moved Danny's legs so that she could get at the sheet. She tore it into several long strips, formed them into a wadded bandage, and placed it in position.

'Is this your first period?'

Danny nodded without opening her eyes.

'Don't worry, the pain will soon go.'

'The same happened to Jodie.'

'And some of the other girls?'

Danny was breathing deeply, almost asleep.

'Don't know 'bout them. Thanks, Karel . . .'

Karel slipped off the bed and tucked the patchwork quilt round the sleeping child. In repose her face seemed to have shed some of its weary dragging age, assumed a pale, calm, peaceful expression of innocent slumber

At the sound of the latch Karel spun round. She stood without moving as a small hand with bitten nails gripped the edge of the door, and an impish leering face framed in long curly hair appeared.

Jimmy Yerke pointed his finger at her. 'I know who you are.'

Karel straightened up, standing in the confined space between the bed and the sloping wall, her back to the window, and faced him squarely in the fading golden light.

Jimmy Yerke sniggered. 'You're Karel . . . Lendrum.'

'So what, you little creep,' Karel said. She would have given anything for a gun, a knife, a weapon of any kind. She didn't even possess a nail file.

He came into the room, grinning at her.

'What's so funny?'

'That's too bad. Not even a nail file.'

Karel's stomach went cold. The backs of her legs felt as if the tendons had snapped. Icy sweat trickled down between her breasts. Certain thoughts, lewd and obscene and degrading, pawed through her mind like slimy fingers. Her chest heaved with sour repugnance. She felt his leering blind eyes probe into every secret, intimate place of her mind and body, defiling everything they touched.

'I want you,' Jimmy said.

'*What?*'

'Oh yeah,' Jimmy breathed shakily. 'You're built. I can just see us, you and me. Oh yeah. What couldn't I . . .' His face suddenly contorted, his red petulant lips drawn back against his teeth.

Karel gasped as the top button of her check blouse pinged open. Her blouse parted at the neck and billowed out like fluttering wings, freeing itself from the belt of her brown cords. The belt slid loose and her trousers unzipped themselves and slid to her ankles. Her bra slackened and fell away.

Cool air wafted over her as the heat of her body escaped.

Jimmy stood before her, grinning like a gargoyle, rubbing himself between the legs. Through his bitten fingers she could see the swollen hungry lump straining to break free.

Karel tried – fought – struggled to cover and protect herself but it was as if her arms no longer belonged to her. Empty, numb, lifeless.

She looked down at her nakedness and could see the flesh of her breast jumping from the beating of her heart.

Her briefs began to slide downwards.

The fine red line where they had clung to her appeared.

She watched a few fair springy hairs emerge and curl back on themselves.

From the depths of her stomach Karel summoned up a scream that surged up through her chest and pushed its way into her throat. It stuck there. Her locked throat strained, her mouth opened wide, but no sound except a faint despairing gurgle and dry exhalation of breath came out into the stillness and silence of the room's softly deepening shadows.

'How about this? Huh? How you like this, honey?'

Karel could feel the silky material of her briefs slithering over her thighs.

'Now look at this, honey. See what I got. For you –'

Jimmy Yerke stood holding an enormous erect penis with both hands. He sidled towards her round the foot of the bed, thrusting his groin at her. There was a wet sucking sound as he rubbed himself. Karel pressed back against the wall. He was almost touching her. She couldn't bear it. His thoughts were spilling into her head. He wanted her to say things, do things to him. Her arm raised itself from her body and her hand reached out.

Jimmy went stock still, holding himself. He turned his head jerkily to the left and then to the right, listening. There was no sound at all, not even a mild breeze rustling the leaves or bending the branches. But Jimmy was listening hard. Karel couldn't hear a sound but Jimmy could hear – or see, or sense – something.

His blank gaze travelled along the pine wall, past the window, then up to the apex of the roof.

And then Karel did hear something. The scything whoosh

and throb of helicopter blades, distant and very faint. In that same instant a babble of voices broke out in the room below. Karel grabbed her clothing, hardly aware that she had regained the power of movement. She dressed quickly, her weak fumbling fingers struggling to fasten the buttons on her blouse. By then Jimmy had gone, and in the room's deepening twilight Karel took hold of Danny's shoulders and shook her.

'What's going to happen to Tom – Danny, answer me!'

Danny opened her eyes.

'Stop them, for God's sake. Do something!'

Danny shook her head.

'You must!'

'I can't,' Danny said in a cracked, ragged voice. 'Not any more. Too late.'

28

Weiss blew out his cheeks and let the air go in a snort of disgust. He kept looking at Helen Murphy and then at Brinkmann, wagging his head and drawing in breath and snorting.

They were sitting in Dr Fabius's office. Helen Murphy had been crying, hard and frequently, and her face under the caked make-up was puffy and blotched. She was feeling better now, more in control, largely thanks to Brinkmann's firm yet sympathetic handling. Weiss had no sympathy to spare. He would gladly have strangled the woman.

'Didn't it occur to you to investigate when you noted this change in behaviour?' Brinkmann said. 'Surely it was a sign, an indication, of the breakthrough we were looking for? I do find that rather strange, Dr Murphy.'

'We didn't think – that is, Robert and I – that is, Dr Fabius and I didn't believe such a change was fundamentally important.' Helen Murphy's eyes brimmed with tears. She took a mighty gulp and went on in a quavering voice, 'You must remember we were under a lot of pressure. Dr Fabius in particular. Calls all the time – the State Department, the Department of Health and Human Services – every day, several times a day, it never stopped –'

Weiss uttered another snort of disgust and looked away.

'Did they become very calm?' Brinkmann asked quietly. 'Quite normal?'

'Yes. But we still didn't trust them.' Helen Murphy tightened her thin lips. She took a lace handkerchief and wiped the mascara from under her green spectacles. 'And we were right!' she broke out defiantly, spitefully. 'Look what they did to Robert, the vicious cold-blooded beasts! What they did to that poor, poor man!'

Weiss blew out his cheeks and after a stern look from over the top of Brinkmann's glasses released the breath in a despairing sigh.

'Just those two, you say? Clare Sachs and Craig Holley?'

Helen Murphy nodded and blew her nose.

'None of the others?'

'No.'

Brinkmann glanced inquiringly at Weiss, who shrugged his little round shoulders and spread his hands.

'Was either of those two put in the SD chamber?' Brinkmann asked, leafing through the medical files on Fabius's desk.

'No. Bromke underwent sensory deprivation and Dr Fabius was preparing Perera when – when he –' Her voice choked away into silence.

'It says nothing here about Clare and Craig receiving medication any different from the rest. They were treated just the same?'

Helen Murphy nodded and pushed her frizzy red hair back from her forehead.

'Then there can be no other reason for the change in their

behaviour,' Brinkmann stated. He flipped the files shut and used the arms of the chair to lever himself up. 'Other than puberty.'

Weiss stared at him for a full five seconds. 'You believe that? The hyperactive condition is stopped – is somehow cured – by something so simple?'

'There's no other explanation,' Brinkmann said. 'We know that Clare Sachs has started menstruating and that her behaviour has returned to normal. Craig Holley's behaviour has modified too, but with him we shall need to carry out blood tests and a hormone count to determine if there has been any pubertal development.'

Weiss had risen, eyes blinking rapidly. 'Can you be sure that's the reason? The *only* reason?'

'No, I can't,' Brinkmann said frankly. 'Not until we conduct tests on all the others. But you have to admit, Otto, it fits the facts pretty neatly. Every single recorded case has been prior to the onset of puberty.'

'It's a big assumption to make on the basis of a single case,' Weiss frowned. 'Pathologically it makes sense, yes – the production of hormones during puberty has major physiological effects on body chemistry and metabolism. It might even produce antibodies to combat the *T. gondii* parasite. But to be certain we need to carry out more tests.'

Brinkmann nodded. Something else crossed his mind, which had been nagging at him. Why no news from Krill these past couple of days? Had he managed to trace the source of the infection that Joe Stalito had been carrying? It was puzzling, and worrying. But there were more immediate matters to be dealt with.

He clapped his hands together and said briskly, 'Well, we have a candidate. Do you want to get started with Craig Holley?'

Weiss bustled forward. 'Yes, yes, of course.' He cast a withering glance down at Helen Murphy's bent head. 'Far better than wasting time with futile discussion.'

'Let me know the minute you have anything, Otto. If we're right I must inform Meg Willson immediately.'

Weiss stopped at the door. 'Of course – the other children! Perhaps they too have changed!'

'That would clinch it, wouldn't it?' Brinkmann said thoughtfully. 'If we knew that a post-pubescent change had had the same effect on them. Then we would know for sure.'

'But we don't know,' Weiss shrugged. 'Do we?'

Fred Holbeck stood with General 'Mike' Todd in the operations room of Command HQ listening to the field reports coming in over the shortwave link and watching as they were marked and cross-referenced on the map pinned to the blackboard. The classroom desks of Lebanon Junior High had been piled in a corner. The floor space was now taken up with communications equipment and a portable conference table which the General used for briefing sessions. In the school library next door he had installed his army cot, a Pavoni coffee-making machine, and his personal valet who was expert at making espresso.

'Come on, Holbeck. Now what d'you say?'

'You reckon that's conclusive, General?'

'Goddammit, man, how much more conclusive can you get?' General Todd jabbed the map with a blunt forefinger. 'See here? A dark-green Pontiac. Margison's vehicle. Parked on a dirt track not a half-mile from three habitable buildings. Double-tyred bus tracks – here, here and here.'

'So where's the bus?'

'How the hell should I know? In the lake maybe.' General Todd traced a small circle on the map. 'Three buildings in this area. That's all. In this one' – the finger stabbed – 'a family from Yonkers on vacation –'

He looked at the staff sergeant holding a clipboard, who said, 'Bellini. Married couple with child.'

'Right.' General Todd nodded approvingly. 'Good family name. We checked them out with the realtor. The chopper pilot spotted the wife and kid out front. So that leaves *two* buildings. Both lodges. One or the other. Has to be.' He craned back to look up at Fred Holbeck, who towered above the General's stocky, bull-necked five-feet-seven. 'Well?'

'We can't hit them both.'

'Why not?'

'Supposing there's a family in one of them?'

'Listen, Holbeck. You can't make an omelette without breaking a few eggs. Those kids are in one or other of those two lodges. D'you want us to get close enough to scare 'em so they set off that train? Will that be conclusive enough for you?'

General 'Mike' Todd stood impatiently with meaty red hands on hips, breathing audibly through his broad hairy nostrils.

'How near are your ground forces?' Holbeck asked, studying the map.

'Delta Force are within three miles.'

'So they could reach either of these lodges in – how long?'

'Ten minutes. Fifteen maximum.' General Todd's neck was bulging. The pressure was building up inside him like a volcano. He'd done everything that was asked of him and was now balked, stalled, waiting on these damn politicians.

'We've still got four hours plus to the deadline.'

'Yeah,' the General agreed sarcastically. 'What're you planning on doing, Holbeck? Waiting till twenty-three forty-five and rushing 'em?' He turned away, shaking his head. 'Listen, I don't know – do *you* know how fast these kids can act? The first whisper they get that we're anywhere near they might explode our nuke express just like that!' He snapped his thick fingers.

'Is there no other way?'

'Not unless you want a few hundred thousand lives on your conscience,' the General told him bluntly. 'And that's not counting a couple of million more in the radiation shadow. Long-term fallout. Panic. Mass hysteria. Stuff like that.' He waved his arm on his way to the library door. 'But you go ahead and take your time. I'm gonna take a little nap. See you around.'

Fred Holbeck kept staring at the map as if it might offer up an answer to his prayer. But of course it didn't. It couldn't. The Secretary of State had to decide, and decide soon. Holbeck glanced at his watch and turned grim faced to the operator at the communications desk.

Jimmy Yerke wanted him dead. There was no doubt about that. He belonged to an alien species – the hated and despised adult race, who were not to be trusted. It seemed to Tom that most of the other children felt the same. For a while it had been touch and go. The sound of the helicopter had thrown them into a frenzy, with Jimmy and Karen and Morey and even some of the younger ones working themselves up to the point where the room was filled with a seething, explosive hatred.

Their faces contained a febrile quality, as if some cruel and vindictive and revengeful rodent was gnawing at them deep inside. As if they had seen more, experienced more, lived through more than their frantically racing brains could hold, could keep pace with. The scales had been stripped from their eyes, the iron had entered their souls. Mentally they had covered vast distances while emotionally they yearned for bubble-gum and Cabbage Patch dolls and the sweet pain of growing up.

Hatred and anger were dangerous emotions – all powerful emotions were dangerous for them. Such powerful feelings could be focused and projected from their inner selves to the outside world, materialising as actual physical force, affecting people, events, even inanimate objects. But unless controlled, their anger and hatred and desire for revenge could spray out in all directions, like radiation from a leaking atomic core.

As they shouted and screamed, their shrill piping voices sounded to Tom like a bunch of kids squabbling over nuclear destruction as if it was a playground game.

'Why wait? What for? Do it now!'

'We said midnight. Let's stick to that.'

'We'll never see midnight. Why do you think they've sent the army in? I agree with Jimmy. Let's do it now, this minute.'

'Yeah, but what have we left to threaten them with? A threat isn't a threat once it's been carried out.'

'A threat isn't a threat unless you're prepared to use it.'

'Maybe – maybe they're prepared to take the risk and just write off the losses –'

'So what have we to lose?'

'They're gonna kill us anyway.'

'We don't know that. They want to stop us exploding the train – that's the only reason.'

'What are you saying, chickenshit, that we back down? Let them off the hook? After everything? After all this?'

'Nobody's backing down. We gave them a deadline, we all agreed to it. So all I'm saying is we wait till then.'

'See sense. They're getting ready to bust in here. They're not going to make any broadcast when they can terminate us with extreme prejudice. This is the U.S. Government we're dealing with, not the Salvation Army.'

'For fuck's sake, let's do it! Let's just do it and forget all this crap.'

'What about him?'

'Get rid of them both.'

'No.'

Everyone turned to where Danny was standing in the doorway. Her eyes were pale shining spheres. She touched the door with her outstretched hand and came into the room. Tom looked past her expecting to see Karel, but the stairway remained dark and empty.

'I don't care if he is your brother,' Karen said. 'He told them where to find us. He led them here.'

Danny shook her head. 'That isn't true. You know it.'

'But you know who that bitch is,' Jimmy said. 'Lendrum's daughter!'

'She had nothing to do with Biotech . . . she wasn't even aware of it.'

'So what?' Karen said. 'They're adults. They're the enemy. Let's kill them and get it over with.'

Jimmy Yerke stood up and stepped over the children sprawled on the floor. He stopped in front of Danny and said, 'Where is the bitch?'

When Danny didn't answer he struck her across the face, leaving the red imprint of his fingers.

'You fink!' he screamed at her.

Tom's hands twitched but stayed where they were, by his sides. He tried to flex the muscles in his legs and nothing happened. The thought in his mind was to leap across the room and throttle Jimmy Yerke with his bare hands. That's as far as it got. A thought in his mind.

'There isn't time for this,' Morey Lang said, grabbing Jimmy by the shoulder. 'We've got to decide what to do while we have the chance.'

'We have to concentrate on the train,' Karen said. 'If we don't do it now, we never will.'

'I say now,' Danny said. 'Let's do it now.'

Jimmy turned and looked at Tom, eyes wide and milkily opaque. 'I guess you would at that. If you got the chance,' he said aloud.

You bet I would, Tom thought, and saw Jimmy smile.

Karen grasped Morey's hand and pulled him into the centre of the room. Morey took Selwyn's hand. Selwyn took Jodie's hand, who was already clinging to her brother Paul. Danny and Jimmy joined the growing circle. It formed silently, hands linking hands, all joined together, until it was complete.

Tom watched as the children closed their eyes. Their limbs stiffened, their backbones went rigid, they raised their faces to the ceiling, and he felt a great column of power surge upwards and outwards straight through the red shingled roof of the lodge and into the sky.

29

An enormous cheese-yellow moon rose in state over the tops of the trees. By its light Karel was able to pick her way up the steep trail which traversed the western side of the valley. Below and to the left, Lake Dunmore had the appearance of a deep black hole in which the moon's yellow light was absorbed and quenched.

Karel stepped carefully over what she thought was a dead log and it turned out to be a shadow. The slither and crunch of her shoes on the pale sandy earth and loose stones sounded in her ears to be amplified through speakers. If there was anyone listening they might have thought a rhino was tip-toeing through the forest.

The crazy thing was, she hadn't the faintest idea where she was supposed to be going – or even why. Danny had pushed her through the narrow window of the loft on to the sloping roof of the boathouse. She had pointed to the trail and said in a mumbled whisper, 'Get out now – they won't know you've gone. Keep to that side of the lake.'

'What about Tom?'

'He'll be all right. Go. *Go!*'

'Danny, I can't just leave him –'

'You have to. It's the only way.'

And she had closed the window.

Night was coming on. The stars were steadily burning brighter, flung across the darkening sky from mountain-top to mountain-top. Behind her, the lodge was a darker pointed shadow against the dark mass of the forest, and as she started the trek above the western shore of the lake the same question kept nagging at her.

What did Danny mean: the only way?

The only way to what?

The vast moon now filled the bowl of the valley with mellow light. The trail ahead broadened into an oval flat area before splitting in two. One track bent at ninety degrees back down towards the lake, the other continued upwards less steeply now through the tall straight trunks of pines and firs, their overhanging branches forming a tunnel in which the trail was a faint pale blur.

Karel stepped cautiously into the dark tunnel of trees, placing each foot carefully and firmly on the ground. She was warm from the climb, and paused to unzip her nylon windcheater. Her breathing had steadied and didn't seem as raspingly loud in her ears. Her forehead was warm, yet the back of her neck was ice-cold.

She was about to move on when a chink of something metallic ahead and to her left had the impact of a pistol shot. Karel remained frozen in mid-stride, staring into the impenetrable wall of darkness, her senses taut and alert, nerve-endings tingling, straining for the slightest movement or sound.

There was nothing. Absolute stillness. Not even a whisper of wind to stir the trees.

Karel listened and then took a tentative step forward. At once she was gripped around the shoulders and arms and a large gloved hand wrapped itself across her mouth. She was bundled forward over rough sloping ground, stumbling and tripping but held upright and borne along, it seemed, effortlessly. She saw the hard gleam of moonlight reflected on curved metal, and was brought abruptly to a halt, the hands still holding her tightly, the gloved hand releasing her mouth to the cool air. A pencil-beam of light flicked on and shone in her eyes. A quiet calm voice said, 'Pleasant evening for a stroll, Miss Lendrum.'

Karel strained to see beyond the beam of light and could vaguely make out a helmet and a narrow face and a thick dark bar of a moustache.

She squinted and said, 'Do you mind?'

The pencil beam went off and Karel blinked to get her night vision back. The hands were still holding her, but less firmly, merely as a precaution. She now saw helmeted figures all around, masked from the moon's hard light by the canopy of branches. Some of them were standing, some squatting, others sitting in small groups with their backs to the slender trunks.

There was absolutely no conversation but occasionally the metallic clink of equipment, the creak of boot leather.

The lean-faced officer with the quiet calm voice and the moustache made a beckoning gesture with his hand and turned away. Karel was propelled into motion, made to follow him into the dimness between the knots of silent men.

She didn't see the dark-grey canvas tent at all, only realised it was there when a dull orange square of light showed under the raised flap. Behind the tent she got an impression of a solidly massive piece of oiled machinery supporting a cylindrical object which faintly gleamed. Then a hand tapped her shoulder and she was stooping to enter the large, square-framed tent. Three aluminium trestle-tables were set up in an H formation, at which were seated a worried-looking captain and two clerical non-coms. Maps in clear plastic slip-covers were lined up with military neatness next to a foot-high stack of ring-binders, each one bearing a title in raised characters on metal strips. A red clipboard holding a sheaf of documents also had a metal label which read METEOROLOGY REPORTS. Battery lanterns with red conelike shades hung from the support struts, throwing pools of light over the tables and casting the deeper recesses into terra-cotta gloom.

The worried-looking captain started to rise until the officer waved him down. The officer removed his helmet, tossed it on to a canvas-backed chair, and turned to face her. He worked his mouth beneath the thick moustache as though dislodging something stuck in a rear molar and nodded to the three-strong escort. 'Wait outside.'

He leaned back against the edge of a table, partly supporting himself with narrow, rather bony hands spreading out to long tapering fingers. The outer bones of his forehead were very near the surface, showing pale through his tan under the bright downward shaft of light.

He finished working his mouth and gave a sardonic lop-sided half-smile.

'I'm Lieutenant-Colonel Lennox. Assigned to this shitty mission because I'm somebody's favourite boy at Command.' His voice retained its quiet calm. 'That's the preliminaries over with, Miss Lendrum. Now I want you to tell me –'

'It's Ms Lendrum.'

'Okay, *Ms* Lendrum. Let's start again. You were down there in the lodge, is that right?'

'Yes. Lieutenant, I must ask –'

'It's Colonel.'

'All right. Colonel.' Karel spoke through clenched teeth. 'Are you in total command of this operation? I have to know now. If you're not I have to speak urgently to the person who is.'

'If it's that urgent, Ms Lendrum, I suggest you tell me,' he said lightly. There was a pause. 'You can start now.'

'But I have to know if you – you personally – can call this thing off. Do you have the power, the rank, whatever you call it, to do that?'

'That depends.'

'On what?'

'On what you have to tell me.' Lt.-Col. Lennox held his arm up and looked at the complicated device on his wrist, which had push-buttons on its square black face and a winking liquid crystal display behind smoked glass. 'Time's getting on, Ms Lendrum. We don't have much of it. Say what you have to and be quick.'

'The children know you're here. They know you've set up bases, command posts, whatever you call them, all around the valley.'

Lt.-Col. Lennox's narrow face had grown longer and stiffer. 'I find that hard to believe. We're at least three miles away from the lodge. Everything's secure and under cover.'

He shook his head slowly. 'I don't think so.'

'You're not a fool, Colonel, so don't behave like one,' Karel said wearily. 'These children possess some kind of collective sensory perception – you must have been briefed about it. Hiding away in the forest doesn't make a damn bit of difference.'

'Is that it? Your urgent message?'

'No.'

Lt.-Col. Lennox folded his arms.

Karel moistened her lips. 'There's no need for you to take action. The children won't carry out their threat. They won't detonate the White Train.'

'I'm supposed to take your word alone for this,' Lennox said, stroking his moustache. 'You walk in off the trail and say everything's fine, no sweat, panic over. And you expect me to believe you, just like that?'

'They won't do it, Colonel. They can't.'

'A minute ago you said they had this . . . collective sensory power. So what's going to prevent them?'

'They're changing,' Karel said. 'Two of them have already – maybe more. And they can't do it without each one of them, *all* of them, contributing their energy. The fewer there are, the weaker they are.'

'Changing?' Lennox was watching her closely. 'How?'

'Two of the girls have had their first period. Do you understand what that means? Once they've passed puberty they lose whatever power they had – I've seen it for myself, with Danny, Tom's sister. It just leaves them. They go back to being . . . normal.'

'You know this for a fact?'

'I've seen it happen!' Karel held out her hands, pleading with him. 'Why do you think I'm here? Danny made me leave, practically forced me. She realised what was happening to them. Don't you see? You can't wipe out a bunch of sick, defenceless, helpless kids.'

Karel pushed her hair back from her forehead with a

trembling hand. There was a moist shine in her blue-grey eyes.

'You've got to stop this. Call it off. Right now.' She took a breath and said in a small shaky voice, 'Please.'

Lt.-Col. Lennox eased himself off the table and stood up straight, tall and loose-limbed, well over six feet, and rubbed his bony knuckles in the palm of his hand. He spoke over his shoulder to the captain.

'What's our state of readiness?'

'Condition Purple and holding, sir. Waiting for the word.'

'Periods,' he mused quietly to himself. 'Puberty.'

He raised one eyebrow and gave his crooked half-smile.

'Somehow – just a hunch – I don't believe the U.S. Army "Rules of Engagement" manual has a section on menstruation. So how do you propose I explain this to General Todd? With diagrams? Pretty coloured pictures?'

Jodie fumbled for Danny's hand and clung to it fiercely. Danny could feel the little blonde girl shaking. It was too risky to say anything – even to think anything. All that Danny could do was to hold Jodie's hand in a firm, reassuring grip.

'I can't see,' Jodie said in a terrified whisper.

'Ssshhh,' Danny said. 'It'll be all right.'

'I can't see the pictures in my mind any more.'

Danny squeezed her hand, hoping it would comfort her and shut her up. She knew that Tom was nearby, simply because she had heard his voice, but that was all. No longer could she sense him, feel his presence. She felt drained of all energy, like a dead car battery: leaden, lumpen, inert.

'I don't know why any more than you do!'

That was Morey's voice, loud and angry. He'd been arguing with Jimmy and some of the others for the past fifteen minutes. They couldn't understand what had gone wrong, why it wasn't working. The circle had been formed, the hands clasped, the minds focused, and the power had surged forth, stiffening their limbs like divining rods and arching their bodies. Danny had felt a faint tingling in her fingertips, but no thrill of energy, none of that wonderful mind-expanding power radiating from her. Not even an image of the train in the bare red desert. Nothing.

It hadn't worked.

Danny listened to the ranting voices. She was afraid of them now, the kind of fear she imagined the adults must have felt. She was an outsider. Having seen inside Morey's mind she wondered if he would understand, but she was afraid to take the risk. Morey hated Jimmy too, but it didn't follow that he would show any sympathy for her and Jodie and anyone else who had become 'outsiders'.

How many of them were there? There was no real way of knowing unless, like Jodie, they admitted it out loud. And not being able to see their faces didn't help. Being blind hadn't bothered her until the pictures inside her mind had faded and she was left in total darkness.

Maybe Jodie's twin brother Paul had changed also. But – the thought petrified Danny into a heightened pitch of fear – if he hadn't he would surely know that Jodie had, because they were two halves of the same identity, shared a single whole consciousness. Nothing happened individually to either one of them without the other knowing about it.

There must be others who had changed, Danny decided. Enough of them to deaden the circle of power and interfere with the outward flow of energy. That's what Jimmy and Morey and the others couldn't understand: it had worked so easily and sweetly in the past, like a liberating sexual climax, and now the libido had failed, withered away, leaving them baffled and angry and impotent.

Jodie was shaking uncontrollably. She was stifling sobs under great long shuddering breaths.

Danny squeezed her hand cruelly, almost crushing the bones, to make her stop. None of the children ever cried. Not one had shed a tear all the time they had been together. That was kids' stuff. No call for it. No need of it. They had long since put away childish things.

'Jodie, don't, please don't,' Danny muttered, the words low and rasping in her throat.

A huge sob came up like a strangled hiccup.

'What's wrong with her?' somebody said.

There was a sudden terrible silence.

'Hey, look,' somebody else said in quiet astonishment. 'She's crying.'

Danny turned her blind face defiantly towards them.

'Leave her alone. She's sick, can't you see?'

'What do you mean – sick?' Karen said suspiciously.

Danny's scalp prickled as she felt their eyes and minds boring into her. There was a feeling in her head as of soft squirming fingers delving into her thoughts. She fought to resist this stealthy intrusion as their minds sent out feelers to probe into her innermost being.

'Leave 'em alone,' Morey said aloud. 'It's the virus.'

'I don't think so,' Jimmy said softly. Danny heard him moving, then became aware of his physical nearness. 'That's just what it isn't.' She felt his breath on her cheek as he peered into her face. 'You can't see me, can you?' He turned his head away and cackled at the others. 'Both of them are blind as fucking bats!'

'We know that already,' said Morey testily. 'Half of us here have got something wrong with our eyes. Even you.'

'Yeah, yeah – but we can *see* without our eyes. These two can't –'

Jimmy's voice changed. Everything about him changed. Danny could sense it even before he spoke.

'That's why it isn't working – they're not like us any more. That's what's wrong!'

Danny flinched and held on tight to Jodie's hand.

'The bitch knew all along it wouldn't work!'

'It's not their fault. They can't help what's happened to them,' Morey said.

'I'll fix her,' Jimmy said. 'I'll fucking fix them both.'

'Danny's blind but I'm not, you little shitface,' Tom said.

'I was waiting for you,' Jimmy sneered. 'Loving brother to the rescue. Ha! I'll fix you too –'

'Try it, mama's boy.'

'*Don't say that!*'

Jimmy Yerke screamed and swung round and turned the full force of his mindpower upon Tom. It was like being exposed to a searing white-hot furnace blast. It blazed through every fibre of his brain, illuminating every cell with a fierce searching light that shrivelled his mind to a dry grey husk. It was all Tom could manage, clamping his mouth tight, not to cry out in pain and terror.

'I told you!' Jimmy cried with an ugly, twisted note of triumph. 'I'll burn your fucking brain out!'

Danny couldn't tell what was happening. Jodie was whimpering and cowering against her. There were sounds of struggle and movements of feet and bodies. Somebody kicked her leg.

Locked inside her blind prison, Danny didn't know what was happening to Tom. She did know that she was helpless. The entire span of her life had been telescoped into a few speeded-up frenetic months and when it was done it had left behind a burnt-out body and an enfeebled mind, drained of the life-force.

She was old. She could do nothing to help him.

30

Karel hadn't been mistaken about the massive piece of equipment she had glimpsed behind the tent. As she followed the lieutenant-colonel's lanky striding figure through the darkness, she craned her neck to look up at the solid brute size of the mobile missile launcher, rearing up at an angle into the web of branches high above. The projectile itself was black and smooth and tapered, machine polished to a silken sheen. The caterpillar tracks on which it rested came up to her shoulder.

Lt.-Col. Lennox went up some steps and pushed open the door of a long, low trailer draped with camouflage netting. As she followed him inside, it reminded Karel of the interior of a nuclear sub – a dimly lit, cramped space with a constant electronic hum in the background. Operators and technicians wearing headsets sat hunched in front of hooded green VDU screens. An officer with lieutenant's bars on the collar of his tan shirt presided over an array of dials and gauges in stainless steel casings. On the curved bulkhead above his head a sign of large black letters engraved in white plastic read: MISSILE LAUNCH CONTROL.

On either side of this there was a clock. The one on the left showed the actual time – ten-thirty-four.

The clock on the right was marked off in one-second segments up to sixty, the red needle hand standing upright and motionless at zero. Underneath, a plastic sign said: TIME (SECS) TO TARGET.

What the target was Karel could see, quite plainly, on one of the displays, which showed a high-definition topographical view of the northern end of Lake Dunmore with the three lodges marked with red crosses. Overlaid on the screen a bullseye pattern of concentric circles centred on one red cross in particular.

The warhead of the missile would be non-nuke of course – though that hardly mattered; how many tons of high explosive did it take to obliterate a structure of cedar logs, wooden shingles, internal plasterboard partitions and every living thing it contained?

Karel realised that these boys weren't interested merely in killing, or even in overkill; they were deeply committed to total, unconditional, no-questions-asked, negative-margin-of-error destruction.

'Wipeout,' as Jimmy Yerke would say.

'Tell me something, Colonel. Who actually presses the button?'

'The Fire Control Officer,' Lennox said, indicating the lieutenant. 'But I give the order.'

'Do you think you can?'

'If I have to.'

'Do you have a family?'

'Yes, Ms Lendrum, I have a family.'

'That wouldn't – stop you?'

'No. Just the opposite. The White Train could be passing through my state – even through my town – any minute of the day or night. That personal consideration aside, we can't conceivably run the risk of a multi-megaton explosion anywhere in the United States. I'd give the order.'

'But there isn't going to be an explosion,' Karel said.

The tall gangling figure looked at her sideways out of the corner of his eye. He said, 'Lieutenant, raise the General for me, would you?' and unhooked a red phone from a recessed cradle in the bulkhead. When the connection was made he spoke for two or three minutes to General Todd at Command HQ in Lebanon.

General Todd's barked responses issued from the speaker grille. Lennox handed the instrument to Karel.

But before she could say anything General Todd said, 'It won't wash, young lady. Those kids have made a threat and given an ultimatum, and as far as we're concerned they mean to carry it through. That's the fact of the matter. You may or may not be right. But we can't gamble on your say-so. Not with the lives of thousands of American citizens at stake.'

Karel's throat was parched and aching. She fumbled for words and managed to say, 'Without even giving them a chance?'

'That's the way it is and has to be. You know damn well what they're capable of. If we tell them – make any kind of counter-threat – they could decide to go ahead there and then. I don't see an alternative.'

'But that's just what they *can't* do, General. Don't you understand that?' Her legs felt hollow, as if any moment they might collapse under her. 'Some of them have lost the power already –'

'Through puberty,' the General interrupted sceptically.

'Yes!'

'Uh-huh. That's a tough one to swallow, Miss Lendrum. Especially as your friend Margison is in the lodge with them. It's natural that you'd want to protect him.'

Karel raged inside, overcome by a kind of impotent fury. There had to be a way of breaking through the stone wall of implacable military logic. She had to find a way. She said bitterly, 'I get it. You give the command, eat your supper, and then retire for a sound night's sleep. I just hope you don't have any bad dreams.'

'None I can't handle,' replied General Todd imperturbably.

'You give the order but who gives the order to you?' Karel said desperately. 'The Pentagon? The White House?'

'The Secretary of State, Miss Lendrum.' The General sounded weary.

'Then I demand to speak to him. Get the son-of-a-bitch on the line.'

There was a pause, filled by a faint crackling buzz. Lt.-Col. Lennox, his jaw drooping, was gazing at Karel with a new expression of bemused, awed respect.

Another voice came on the line, a gentle Texan drawl.

'This is Fred Holbeck, State Department. I don't see what can be gained by letting you speak directly with the Secretary of State, Miss Lendrum. He's fully apprised of the situation. We're in constant touch with Golden Vale Clinic and there've been no fresh developments.' An apologetic note crept into his voice. 'We only have your word that these children have changed, and I'm afraid it isn't enough. I'm sorry.'

'You're sorry?' Karel said. She laughed. 'That's most touching. I think you'll be even sorrier when I let it be known that the cause of all this is a virus developed in the laboratories of Biotech by Dr Victor Lendrum on a contract for the U.S. Defence Department.'

'Miss Lendrum, that's a serious allegation –'

'It's not an allegation, you asshole, it's a fact. It's also a fact that the U.S. Government is spending a billion dollars a year on plagues that could affect future generations of children. Not Russian children, Mr Holbeck, or Chinese children, or Nicaraguan children – American children.'

Fred Holbeck tried to say something but Karel was in full spate.

'And furthermore, the children who contracted this virus, developed at the behest of the Defence Department and paid for out of public funds, were slaughtered by the United States Army acting on direct orders from the Secretary of State. Am I getting through to you, Mr Holbeck? Am I making myself clear?'

'Yes, Miss Lendrum. Perfectly clear. But I'm afraid it doesn't make any difference. The Secretary of State has made his decision. We go ahead as planned, to the minute.'

Karel found herself gazing at the screen in front of the Fire Control Officer. It was filled with blocks of indecipherable digital data, which until this moment she'd only given a passing glance to. She now noticed several words winking on and off:

MISSILE PRIMED
LOCKED ON TARGET
COUNTDOWN COMMENCES 38 MINUTES 42 SECONDS

She said hoarsely, 'When?'

Lt.-Col. Lennox's mouth twitched under his blond moustache.

'We launch at twenty-three thirty hours.'

Karel looked at the clock.

As she did so the black hand jerked up to ten-forty-seven.

* * *

The body lay on the floor. The face had the pallor of death, as if the brain had been squeezed dry. Jimmy Yerke stood over it, staring down with wide blank eyes, his red fleshy lips pulled back in a smile of triumph and revenge.

The others had fallen silent. Morey Lang saw the slight movement of Tom's chest, faltering and irregular, and a spasm of anger shot through him. 'Do you never stop to think? He was on our side. He wanted to help us, you dumb asshole!'

'Oh yeah – you really believe that?' Jimmy sneered. 'He brought them here, didn't he? Him and Lendrum's daughter. They led them to us.'

'Jimmy, you know that isn't true,' Karen said. 'You went into his mind – you know they didn't!'

'So what?' Jimmy whirled round on them, his face contorted. 'We're at war, aren't we? Kill or be killed. We got the power, we gotta use it. Like we did against Fabius and Werneth and all the rest. They're not on our side. *Nobody's* on our side except us.'

He looked at Danny and Jodie, sitting together in a corner of the room. Danny was cradling Jodie's head on her shoulder.

'And not all of us.'

'Leave them out of it,' Paul said sharply. 'You've done enough.'

'Enough?' Jimmy Yerke said incredulously. 'I ain't even started yet!'

'Well don't start on them.'

'They're not with us so they must be against us.'

'They're not with or against anybody,' Paul said, looking at his sister. Her mind was closed to him. A grey impenetrable void. It was as if his own mind had been cut in two. 'Leave them be.'

'What if I don't?'

'Try it and see.'

'Quit that, both of you,' Morey said. 'You're behaving like adults. We should be thinking about what to do next – they're not just going to leave us sitting here without trying something. Think. Concentrate. They're near, we can all feel them. What are they doing now, this minute?'

Hands reached out to form a human chain. Eyes closed. A vibrant surge of power hummed in the air . . .

. . . And from above, a long way above, it seemed to him, Tom observed them – and himself.

He could see his body stretched out on the carpet. His body was down there, dead and inert, while his mind was up here, alive and alert. It was disturbing and uncanny – a disembodied spirit hovering above them. And something else he had discovered. Like a mental x-ray, he could see the thoughts whirling like snowflakes inside their heads. He could see into Jimmy Yerke's mind, which was filled with images of violence and destruction. A truck-driver, coughing his lungs up, plunging his rig from a bridge. A signalman switching the points of a chemical train so that it veered off the tracks and crashed on its back in a tangle of sheared metal. An airline pilot pushing the column forward and diving into the side of a mountain. A doctor in a pitch-black room, beating soundlessly at the soft yielding walls, his screams deadened and absorbed.

A new image shimmered into life, seen as through the distorting prism of a score of different minds. The various fragments shifted, formed themselves into a coherent pattern, steadied and sharpened into focus.

An army lieutenant in a tan shirt sat before a green screen filled with digits and symbols. Words winked on and off. As the collective attention of the group zoomed in, Tom read:

MISSILE PRIMED
LOCKED ON TARGET
COUNTDOWN COMMENCES 22 MINUTES 35 SECONDS

The collective attention zoomed out and in again on two clocks. One was marked TIME (SECS) TO TARGET. The other showed the actual time of eleven-nine.

At once a blizzard of voices he felt rather than heard reverberated back and forth through Tom's head as a continuous stream of communication passed with lightning speed around and around the linked circle.

Close in tight . . . surround Fire Control Officer . . . shutdown outside environment . . . cancel target . . . prepare to detonate warhead . . . close in tight . . . read him . . . read him . . . tighter . . . homosexual . . . lover called Brent . . . they cook together . . . favourite dish cannelloni tomato sauce Parmesan cheese . . . smell of burning . . . turn down oven . . . black dial with white markings . . . target cancelled . . . open oven door . . . red stirrup lever . . . reach for it . . . mustn't spoil . . . prepare to detonate now . . . open door quick . . . grasp lever . . .

The Fire Control Officer's hand was on the lever. His fingers curled round it. Tom watched him. He saw the hand tighten. He directed his own thought.

. . . release lever . . . release it . . . release it . . .

The hand slackened convulsively and opened, fingers splayed.

A torrent of voices screamed in Tom's head.

. . . pull lever . . . open door . . . smell of burning . . . open door . . .

The hand wavered, half closed, touched the red stirrup lever.

Tom screwed his mind tight.

. . . look at screen . . . countdown commences in nineteen minutes nineteen seconds . . . release lever . . .

The Fire Control Officer shook himself out of his trance. Only a moment ago he had been making a meal for Brent. There was smoke coming out of the oven. He could smell burning. He blinked and the kitchen vanished. Instead he now saw the screen in front of him.

COUNTDOWN COMMENCES 18 MINUTES 53 SECONDS

He snatched his hand away from the red stirrup lever. *What the hell had come over him?*

Tom heard the thought in his own mind. He also heard a

confused and angry babble of voices cutting across each other. The circle of linked hands had been broken. Morey opened his eyes and looked at Karen, a deep frown on his freckled face. She stared back at him, shaking her head. Jimmy was frowning too, gazing down at Tom's body on the floor. He put his head on one side, as if listening, and slowly raised his blank sightless eyes – feeling, searching, probing.

Tom knew what Jimmy meant to do almost before Jimmy knew himself. A thought like black venom spurted in the boy's mind. His eyes ceased their wandering search and came down to rest on Danny. Jimmy Yerke's mind tensed and bunched itself in readiness. He grinned.

He grinned as he stood in front of her, looking down on Danny's dark curly head, now streaked with grey. She had stiffened, sensing his presence. She raised her face to stare blindly up at him.

'We've got to get out of here!' Karen hissed urgently. 'Please, Jimmy, let's go!'

'We can't stop the missile, Jimmy, and you're the only one who can help us,' Morey pleaded. 'We have to move now! Please!'

Jimmy ignored them. There was plenty of time. This wouldn't take more than a minute or two. He concentrated on a spot in the middle of Danny's forehead and the flesh sizzled and blackened and peeled away. Pale bone showed through. He summoned up all his reserves of mindpower and focused them in a single, laser-like beam of pure energy which pierced the skull and struck like a needle into the soft grey depths of the brain. The charred hole in the centre of Danny's forehead widened and split outwards into jagged fissures. The flesh fell away in strips to reveal a skeletal head and neck. Grey smoke puffed out of the gaping hole as the brain cooked inside. A worm crawled out of the empty eye-socket. Maggots forced themselves in a seething white mass through the head's clamped bony smile. Jimmy's leering grin went slack and sour. He tried to step back and found he couldn't. Now the skull was grinning at *him*. Skeletal hands reached out and bony clinking fingers unzipped his jeans, delved inside and pulled out his softly furled cock, caressing it so that it filled and hardened, engorged with blood. The head ducked forward, the mouth opened, and he felt himself being taken between the gaping jaws, the smiling teeth scraping over him until he was fully enclosed and locked inside the bony helmet of the skull.

The black eye-sockets stared up at him. In their empty depths he saw, or imagined he saw, an expression. He knew what it meant, he realised what was about to happen, but he was unable to move, held fast between those horrible grinning jaws. The teeth snapped together. Flesh and muscle parted cleanly. He was severed at the root. Jimmy screamed and gibbered.

The skeleton chewed and swallowed, digesting the morsel. It looked up at him and said with a grin: '*Wipeout!*'

'With respect, you can't do that,' said Jerry Derker flatly. 'Our stated policy is clear and categorical. We don't give in to terrorist demands, no matter what the circumstances.'

A faint scattering of stubble darkened his pale hollow cheeks. His eyes were hidden by the twin reflections of the desk-lamp in the rimless circles of his spectacles. Other dark-suited and uniformed shadows loomed like monoliths in the murky recesses of the room.

'I don't need reminding what our policy is, Mr Derker,' the Secretary of State told him icily. 'Neither do I consider these to be "terrorist demands". Not according to my definition of the term, by God.'

'No sir.' Derker folded his arms. 'We can argue about definitions some other time. The result, however we define the demand, will be the same. A thermonuclear detonation of a thirty-megaton yield, minimum. That's the bottom line.'

The brass-necked effrontery of the man was breathtaking.

At any other time the Secretary of State would have dismissed him from the room; he even toyed for a second with the idea, but it would have been melodramatic, and worse, a futile gesture. Worse still, of course, Derker was right. The exact nature of the demand was immaterial. A threat had been made. Moreover it was a threat (as had been only too graphically demonstrated) that could be carried out. There were no doubts about that. Everyone believed it.

The phone buzzed. In the silent, shadowy room it might have been a grenade going off. The Secretary of State reached into the lamplight, flicked the open-address tab, and leaned back out of the glare. He lit a cigarette. The amplified voice filtered quietly into the room.

For perhaps a minute he listened. He didn't say a word. The ember of his cigarette glowed and grey exhaled smoke billowed into the light and out again. When the voice eventually finished, with an anxious query, he said, 'Yes, I do understand, Meg. That's perfectly clear. Now let me ask a question. Is this another of Brinkmann's theories or are we talking facts here? Clinical evidence?'

'Dr Brinkmann has two cases – out of the five at Golden Vale – where this has actually, physically happened. It's a matter of medical record, Donald, observed and verified by at least four physicians. The children have definitely changed. Their hyperkinetic behaviour has modified with the onset of puberty. Dr Brinkmann believes it may have something to do with the secretion of hormones affecting the lymphatic gland –'

'Yes, yes, let's not get into that territory. There isn't time. So what precisely is Brinkmann saying? That the same thing's happened to these other kids – they've reached puberty and have lost whatever psychic ability, power, they had?'

'No, he isn't saying that. Dr Brinkmann hasn't made any claims whatsoever. He's simply reported his findings and conclusions, as we asked him to do. But two out of five *have* changed, Donald, that's the crucial thing. With the other children that must mean that ten of them, eleven – maybe more – have changed too. And we already know they have to join together collectively as a group to have any effect.' Meg Willson's voice sharpened, became more imperative. 'They can no longer do it – they can't. There's just no way.'

'That's one helluva big fat assumption,' the Secretary of State said testily. 'What's it based on? *Two* kids?'

'Goddammit, Donald, you asked for evidence. I'm giving it to you!'

'What you're giving me is hypothesis. Supposition. Let's face it, Meg, guesswork. Neither of us know if *any* of those kids have changed. Maybe they have. But if they haven't, and I take your word, we're in deep trouble. It's too big a gamble.'

'We're in deep trouble already.'

The Secretary of State stubbed out his cigarette and sighed. 'Yeah. But at least we have an option.'

'What option?' Meg Willson was mystified.

'Delta Force. They're in position. They're all set to launch in –' he looked at the quartz clock on his desk '– nine minutes from now.'

'Donald, I don't follow you. How on earth will that resolve the Biotech angle? For God's sake, Biotech produced the damn virus in the first place. It's going to create a bigger stink –'

'Hold your horses, Meg.' The Secretary of State leaned into the lamplight, head thrust forward, hands spread flat on the desktop. 'Biotech? Virus? What is all this? What are you talking about?'

Meg Willson told him. As he listened, the eyes of the Secretary of State roamed from face to face in the shadowy depths beyond the bright circle of light. They settled on Derker. He was standing with folded arms, absolutely still, his pale narrow face gleaming faintly in the reflected light. The guy was sweating. The Secretary of State said, 'How'd you come by this, Meg?'

'It's all contained in the documents Dr Krill sent to me

from Los Angeles. He found the donor of the contaminated blood and traced it back to its source. I'm expecting his full report in the morning. And the Centre for Disease Control at Atlanta have already identified the virus as a strain of the parasite *Toxoplasma gondii.* Naturally I assumed you knew about Biotech's involvement already.'

'Why? How should I know?'

'Well – they work to a technical brief from the Defence Department.'

'Sure. So what?'

'Developing a new generation of biological warfare media. The connection hit me straight away. We're poisoning our own kids, Donald – that's the deep trouble *I'm* talking about.'

Slowly, the Secretary of State leaned back in his chair. He sat stiffly upright, hands clasped to his chest, staring at the clock. Eleven-twenty-five. The countdown was due to start any second now. Maybe it had already started.

31

In the grey pre-dawn light the lake had the appearance of a sheet of lead, solid enough to walk on. With the sun still below the horizon the sky was blank and pale, without colour. There was silence in the forest. It was that dead interval of time marking the boundary of night and day. Even the birds were uncertain whether it was time to greet the new day; they were reserving judgement until the first real light gave a flush of life to the sealed drab dome of sky.

The lodge, less than a quarter-mile away, was indistinguishable against the rising perpendicular ranks of trees. There was no light showing. Karel feared the worst.

She looked at her watch. It was a few minutes after four. By now the military would have tightened their noose to within a fraction of strangulation. One final swift jerk and the neck would snap.

There were soft footfalls on the grass and Lt.-Col. Lennox knelt beside her. He murmured close to her ear, 'Ten minutes. We're all set. We just need a little more light. But not too much. And please remember what I said. You stay behind the advance party. Agreed?'

Karel nodded. 'As long as you remember you're not in Vietnam and these are children, not gooks.'

Lennox shot her a hard glance from under the rim of his helmet but said nothing. Oddly enough, Karel trusted him, despite the unkind jibe. Small comfort under the circumstances, trusting the man, but comfort nonetheless, Karel thought.

Karel sat huddled up, wrapped in an army blanket. There was dew on the grass and mist in the hollows.

She said, 'It's awfully quiet down there.'

'I expect they're asleep.'

Karel looked at him and said nothing.

He said, 'She'll be all okay, don't you worry. They'll find a cure.'

'Is there a cure for old age?'

'No, I meant –' He shrugged. 'It isn't permanent, you said so yourself. The virus is losing its effect you said. Maybe they're working on something right now.'

'Sure,' Karel said. 'Get the scientists on the job and they'll come up with an answer in no time at all. They have an answer for everything.'

The birds had decided it was dawn. An ear-splitting racket started up in the trees all around them. A few faint rays were streaking the sky pink. The leaden lake began to look like molten glass.

Karel shivered, though not from the cold. Her voice sounded muffled by the blanket. 'I still can't believe it. You really were going to fire that missile.'

Lennox looked away from her. 'In two minutes nineteen seconds if the order hadn't been countermanded.'

'Thank God it was.'

'I don't think God had much to do with it. Though I could be wrong.'

Lennox straightened up, tapped his wrist and pointed downwards through the trees. Already men were standing, stretching themselves, checking their equipment, getting ready to move.

The pointed roof of the lodge cut a sharp wedge into the brightening sky. There was still no sound, no movement, no activity at all. Karel waited under the last few straggling trees and bushes near the bottom of the slope.

A detachment of a dozen men, led by Lt.-Col. Lennox, ran swiftly and silently with lowered heads and tight elbows across the packed dirt perimeter on to the porch and flattened themselves against the rough log walls. They carried automatic rifles and machine-pistols. At a fanning gesture from the colonel, the men split into two groups. One group edged along to the rear of the house, the other peeled away and followed him along the opposite wall to the side door.

Karel saw Lennox reach out and touch the door handle.

He took a firm grip of it and the dial of his watch winked dully as his wrist turned. He leaned far back and pushed the door open with the toe of his boot. The scene froze for ten seconds. Then, so swiftly that Karel hardly saw it, he vanished inside, and at once five men went after him, leaving the sixth with his rifle held at the hip, aimed and ready.

Karel's ears ached with listening to the silence. She was waiting for a shot, a cry, a scream. But the silence dragged on, stretching her nerves to breaking point. A twig snapped nearby and she involuntarily stumbled forward a step or two. A captain wearing a forage cap with a fancy embroidered peak raised his rifle in a warning gesture.

* * *

The place was in shambles. Lennox had half expected this, his imagination running riot through a score of hellish scenarios; what he hadn't expected was the sweetish cloying smell of the geriatric ward.

He stood in the living-room feeling nauseous. He had taken off his helmet and his thinning fair hair was dark where it stuck in a straggling fringe to his bony forehead. His eyes had receded to needle points.

'We estimated about twenty-seven. Is that about right?'

Tom nodded woodenly. He looked past Lennox's shoulder. Blankets covered two small mounds in the middle of the living-room floor.

'Except for those two. A boy and a girl.'

Lennox stepped round Tom and knelt down. He pulled the covering back and gazed at the dead boy with tangled curly hair. His face was smooth and serene. There wasn't a mark on him. Lennox looked questioningly at Tom.

'That's Jimmy.'

'What happened to him?'

'He had a bad dream.'

Lennox stared at Tom but said nothing. He pulled the other blanket back. Underneath lay a shrivelled old woman with blonde hair that was almost pure white. 'Jodie,' Tom said. There was no need for Lennox to ask how she had died. She was ancient.

He covered her face and stood up.

'We've called in the medics. Are you okay?'

Tom pushed past him and went up the two small steps into the kitchen.

A ring of soldiers stood guard over a small pathetic huddle. The children had been split up into groups, here and in the two master bedrooms – 'Just in case,' the colonel had said. Tom's heart went hard and small. Just in case. The military mind. He stooped down.

* * *

Karel ran up the steps to the porch. 'Oh thank God –' She broke off as emotion choked her. Tom cradled his sister to his chest. Her eyes were shut, her small dark head resting limply in the crook of Tom's elbow. He hardly felt her weight: she seemed to float ethereally in his arms.

Needle-thin rays were filtering through the trees on top of the ridge. He stood holding Danny and looking at the flat dark expanse of water.

Karel leaned against the porch rail. She watched him looking at the lake and gripped the rail with both hands, the rough bark scraping the soft flesh of her palms.

'Is she going to be all right?'

'I don't see why not. She can always retire to Florida.'

'Tom, don't –' Karel's face collapsed and puckered up. With an effort she regained control, swallowed. 'She's passed through the worst time. She can only get better. The virus is out of her system now.'

'Faith,' Tom said dully. 'I wish I had some.'

Karel gripped the rail tightly. 'Tom –!'

Danny had opened her eyes. The milky orbs stared sightlessly up into Tom's face. 'It's me, shrimp. You're safe with me now.'

'Is it still night?'

'No,' Tom said. 'It's morning. The sun'll be on the lake in a few minutes.' The staccato beat of a helicopter sounded faintly, coming from behind the lodge. 'Hey. Remember when we went out in the boat at dawn one time and caught three bass?'

'We threw one back and kept the others.'

'Did we? Why'd we throw one back?'

'It was a baby. I'd like to go fishing again sometime.'

'Sure,' said Tom heartily. He had to speak louder as the helicopter thudded round above the trees in an arc. A large red cross in a white circle was painted underneath. 'We'll do some great things together. We'll have some swell times again.'

'All the family,' Danny said, frowning anxiously up at him.

'Right,' Tom reassured her.

Karel made a sound in her throat and hung on to the rail. Tom was staring tenderly down into Danny's face, cracked and crazed like old parched leather.

'We'll have some good times again.'

The helicopter ruffled the surface of the lake as it canted towards them, and settled slowly on to the patch of ground in front of the lodge. Soldiers with red crosses on their helmets jumped down and ran forward carrying stretchers. Tom stood holding the weightless burden in his arms and waited for them to come.

The sun was hot, the small hollow of the sandpit next to the climbing-frame at the end of the garden holding the breathless heat as in a warm cupped hand. Mary Ann pushed her red hair out of her eyes with the backs of her fingers. There was sand on her nose and cheeks and a few glistening grains caught in her fine eyebrows, faint as brushmarks. She smiled to herself as she patted the turreted castle with the little red spade. She was pleased. It looked great.

But it had been too good to last.

Caroline's afternoon nap was over, and with a high-pitched squeal her kid sister burst through the patio doors and raced towards her, the noisy ball of terror set free.

Caroline was five, while she was nearly eight and had graduated from taking naps in the afternoons. The past hour had been blissfully peaceful. Mary Ann had built the castle bucket by bucket, lost to the world in the absorbing task of construction, and she was quite determined. Caroline wasn't going to spoil *this*, as she tried to spoil everything else.

The ball of terror in the blue dungarees with the faded Donald Duck on the bib skidded to a stop at the very edge of the lawn. Her hair, a fiercer red than her sister's, was still frizzed-up from her slumber. Her eyes were round and huge and blue as forget-me-nots.

'That's far enough. Stay there.'

'What's-it, what's-it, what's-it?' chanted Caroline, bending forward, chubby dimpled hands on her worn blue knees. In one hand she clutched a small silver rocket, a free plastic toy from a cereal packet. 'Can I play, Annie?'

'No. This is mine. I made – *don't move!*'

Caroline had jumped down. For a second she teetered and nearly overbalanced, but Mary Ann's harsh command checked her rigid.

'You stay there, right *there.* Don't – touch – anything. Don't move and don't touch. Got it?'

Caroline blinked and nodded.

Mary Ann levelled off the tops of the turrets with the flat of the spade and rammed it into the sand. 'Need a flag,' she murmured to herself. 'Red and blue stripes.' While she pondered on this, and where to get one, Caroline squatted down. From the corner of her eye Mary Ann saw her sister lean forward, about to plant the rocket on the highest tower. Mary Ann made a grab, wrenched the rocket from her hand, giving her fingers a twist for good measure, and threw it away.

Caroline sat down with a bump and let out a wail. Mary Ann felt an inner glow of cruel satisfaction and smiled to herself. The ball of terror wouldn't be in any hurry to try that again.

Ignoring the sobs and snivels, she pushed her hair back from her damp forehead and bent forward to scoop sand away for the moat. She'd need a drawbridge too, just like the one the castle had she'd seen in the movie on TV. First she'd make a solid bit, like a wall, Mary Ann decided, and then tunnel through it. She began to hum under her breath.

Caroline had stopped crying but her lower lip still jutted and her eyes were brimming with moisture. She blinked it away with her fair, almost transparent eyelashes and stood up. Donald Duck trembled as she drew in a tiny shuddering gulp. She pulled the spade from where it was embedded in the sand and swung it down with both hands so that the red metal edge cut through the thin brown nape of the bent neck, slicing half of it away. She swung it high and brought the spade down again, neatly decapitating her sister. Mary Ann hadn't uttered a sound. Her head lay face down in the warm sand. With that job done, Caroline knelt in her faded blue dungarees and dug her tiny pudgy fingers deeply into the sand, scooping out a hole. She didn't like the castle, and she wasn't going to have it.

When the hole was deep enough, with smooth steep sides, she went and found the tiny silver rocket and stretched down to place it, upright, at the very bottom. It was well hidden there, but it still wasn't right. It needed a cover. Something to slide over it, and slide back again.

She squatted in the sand, listening with a preoccupied frown to the instructions in her head. 'Yes.' Caroline nodded impatiently. 'I *know*. I'll find one. And after that – what do we do after that?'

To the east of the Rocky Mountains, Montana, the two-man SAC crew in the reinforced concrete control chamber seventy-five feet underground went through the routine procedure of a practice red alert. They had honed the drill to a fine art. Always on standby, its guidance computer and gyro continually running inside a gold-plated package to control temperature and humidity, the missile in the hundred-and-fifty-foot silo could be primed and fired in under two minutes.

The missile contained seven nuclear warheads, each with an explosive energy a thousand times more powerful than the bomb that was dropped on Hiroshima.

Of course they never knew whether it was a dry run or the real thing until the very last second. Psychologically it would have been bad news for the Strategic Air Command crews, safe in their bunker from all but a direct nuke strike, to know that the rest of America, including their families, was about to be wiped from the face of the earth. Even at this moment the Russian rockets could be curving in over the Distant Early

Warning Line that stretched from Iceland to Alaska. The world as they knew it might cease to exist within the next fifteen minutes. So when they were told to fire their baby, they fired.

It was the guidance officer's job to set the target coordinates, working to longitude and latitude figures he now extracted in a sealed envelope from the time-locked safe next to his metal desk. He knew Moscow's figures by heart. 55.45N 37.42E. Today, however, Moscow wasn't on the menu – nor even the Soviet missile bases in the Khrebel Kolymskiy Mountains in Eastern Siberia.

Today it was 38.55N 77.00W. The guidance officer knew that one too. Washington DC. And he guessed why. Some five-star general at SAC headquarters in Omaha had conceived of a last-ditch fallback strategy in case the Reds infiltrated the Administration and took over the Pentagon. It was a feasible scenario – a sneak attack by conventional forces. Feasible enough, certainly, for them to have had seminars in training on such an eventuality and discussed the options left open to them.

Jesus H Christ, he thought with feeling, he wouldn't put anything past those sly underhand godless Commie bastards.

He fed the figures in and the coordinates popped up on the screen. He pressed a key to compute time and distance. The direct overland route from here to Washington DC was one thousand eight hundred miles, though the missile's curving arc through the stratosphere would nearly double that to over three thousand miles.

Time from launch to impact: nineteen minutes.

Wowee! Would they get a nasty surprise. Out of a clear blue sky. Wipeout! The red star wouldn't be flying over the White House for very long. Enjoy it while you can, suckers.

Still, it was only a practice drill, he reminded himself. Two hours from now he'd be back at the base with Jenny and the kids. He picked up the phone. 'Coordinates set. Primed and running. Open silo doors. Launch in one minute thirty seconds. Mark and counting.' He punched a button.

Above his head, like the rumble of an approaching apocalypse, the seven-hundred-ton steel and concrete doors started to slide open.

NORMAN MAILER

TOUGH GUYS DON'T DANCE

The brilliant new novel from America's greatest living writer – author of the classic bestsellers *An American Dream*, *The Naked And The Dead* and the Pulitzer Prizewinners *Armies Of The Night* and *The Executioner's Song*

Tim Madden is an unsuccessful writer addicted to bourbon, cigarettes and blondes with money. On the twenty-fifth morning after the departure of his wife, Patty Lareine, he wakes with a hangover and considerable sexual excitement.

He remembers nothing of the night before – but there's a fresh red tattoo on his arm bearing a name from the painful past, and the front passenger seat of his Porsche is drenched with blood . . .

So begins Madden's disquieting journey into the dark recesses of America's psyche.

'Hypnotic . . . thrilling, blood-spilling.' *Mail On Sunday*

General Fiction 0 7221 5768 1 £2.50

From the bestselling authors of
LUCIFER'S HAMMER and THE MOTE IN GOD'S EYE –
the ultimate novel of alien invasion!

FOOTFALL

NIVEN & POURNELLE

It was big all right, far bigger than any craft any human had seen. Now it was heading for Earth.

The best brains in the business reckoned that any spacecraft nearing the end of its journey would just *have* to be friendly.

But they were wrong! Catastrophically wrong!

The most successful collaborative team in the history of science fiction has combined again to produce a devastating and totally convincing novel of alien invasion.

FOOTFALL – the ultimate disaster

GENERAL FICTION 0 7221 6330 8 £3.95